The King

Dave Cash

Mandarin

A Mandarin Paperback
THE KING OF CLUBS

First published in Great Britain 1995
by Mandarin Paperbacks
an imprint of Reed Consumer Books Ltd
Michelin House, 81 Fulham Road, London SW3 6RB
and Auckland, Melbourne, Singapore and Toronto

A CIP catalogue record for this title
is available from the British Library
ISBN 0 7493 1564 4

Printed and bound in Great Britain
by Cox & Wyman Ltd, Reading, Berkshire

The King of Clubs

To Russell. Hey! It's a thriller.
Have a good read

[signature]

Also by Dave Cash
and available in Mandarin

All Night Long

We look from out the shadows
On through the future years,
For the soul would have no rainbow
Had the eyes no tears.

Thomas Hardy

My sincere thanks to:

Capital Radio for keeping Sunday
mornings alive.
Maria and Diki for insight into the
Romanian people and their traditions.
Dr Dellitant and the University of London
Slavonic Department
John, Louise, Beth and
the Mandarins
The Durrants Hotel
And in fond memory of Overtons.
Victoria will never be the same.

Prologue

The crew of *Elena* scrambled aboard the *Corova* and quickly disappeared into the welcoming warmth of the cabin.

'Have you opened all the sea-cocks?' asked the only man in uniform.

'Yes sir,' replied the last to cross the gunwales.

'Let's go!' yelled the uniform to the helmsman. 'Get back to Constanta before this weather sinks us all.'

TO: CEAUSESCU
FROM: SECURITATE HQ, BRASOV

6 March 1988

The problem with the mathematics professor and his wife has been resolved. I recommend a tactful approach towards the son as he is fast becoming a public figure and could cause trouble in the media unless advised of the consequences.

STENOZA

TO: CEAUSESCU
FROM: SECURITATE HQ, BUCHAREST

Saturday, 25 February 1989

Bellescu's performance on media training is class one. He could be a great asset to us as the new face of Romanian sport. He's beaten the Russians on everything except rings. He's a must for Gold next year on bars and floor.

I advise you work him hard in London (three or four interviews a day. See how he handles the pressure). Keep him well covered by Severin.

Also advise you attend airport to see him off. Full press coverage has been arranged.

STENOZA

One

Dominic woke suddenly, fully alert, five minutes before the alarm was due to ring. He carefully reached over Nadia's shoulder and depressed the clock button. She turned towards him, still asleep; her arm flopped into the space between them.

For two years Nadia Vasiliu had spied on Dominic for the Romanian Secret Police. They'd met at a sports council dinner when she'd been seated at his table. Her gypsy beauty and bright, intelligent eyes had immediately attracted him. She'd been delightful company and had charmed the entire table with her vivacious personality and witty conversation. When she'd accepted his offer of a lift home he'd felt elated. She had treated him to a night of extraordinary passion far beyond his previous experiences and within a month she was staying with him five nights a week.

Dominic loved the attention, the sex and the ego massaging, but as his knowledge of her grew so did his suspicions. She'd been too expert in the carnal arts to be the country girl from Transylvania that was stated in her passport, too knowledgeable of world affairs for a junior clerk at the Ministry of Transport, and her accent was wrong. She spoke with the flatness of a southerner, not the melodic metre of the mountain people. His suspicions were confirmed a year later when he'd overheard a tele-

4

phone call in which she'd quietly outlined his itinerary for the next three weeks to a silent caller she'd addressed as 'sir'.

As he'd listened to her clandestine conversation on that cold February evening Dominic thanked God for his early perceptiveness and the diligence with which he had avoided speaking loosely in front of her. His anger at the confirmation of her treachery swelled up in him to such a degree that he had wanted to hurt her; thrash out and explode with the total unfairness of it all.

He'd done what they'd asked of him. Since the age of seven he'd devoted at least four hours a day to gymnastics, had learned English, German and French to a flawless standard, and he'd won the Romanian gymnastic championship last year by six clear points.

That's when his life fell apart. A week after winning the championship his mother and father drowned in a boating accident on the Black Sea. A month later he'd been arrested by the Securitate and 'instructed on how to deal with media' – an intensive and vicious little programme spread over five days and consisting of no sleep, little food, verbal barracking and the constant threat of physical violence. Now, his worst nightmare: his lover was a traitor.

He had, however, been astute enough to play her at her own game. Always he'd shown outward signs of compliance, obedience and political correctness. His tactics had reaped handsome rewards. A bigger apartment, extra food and fuel allowance, a better public profile – all made possible by Nadia's positive reports on his behaviour patterns and attitudes towards the political establishment.

The more he found out about the methods employed by the Securitate the more he became convinced that his parents had not simply drowned in rough seas but had been murdered by Ceausescu's Secret Police. From a privileged academic platform his mother and father had spoken publicly about the austerity measures imposed in 1983 which were now proving unparalleled even in the bleak history of East European communist regimes. Bread, flour, sugar, milk, margarine, eggs and fuel were all rationed. Provision of hot water was limited to one day a week in state-owned flats, power cuts were commonplace in hospitals costing hundreds of lives as respirators and incubators were turned off and operations had to be stopped midstream. They had spoken the truth and they'd been killed for it: probably shot and buried in some remote woodland. As their bodies were never found, Dominic could only accept the official line publicly and privately guess at the truth.

His overwhelming drive for the last year had been to get out of Romania, out of gymnastics and out of Nadia's life. Information had to be the key. The more he knew, the better his chances of making a deal for his defection. As he'd set about collecting and compiling the information he'd become painfully aware of the extent to which atrocities were being perpetrated in the name of his country. Fuelled by greed and sadism and controlled by nepotism and fear, crimes of murder, rape, torture and extortion had become commonplace. As Dominic toured the country giving gymnastic displays in schools and village halls, several teachers, doctors and victims' relatives secretly told him their stories. Any one of his case histories would embarrass Ceausescu abroad, and he had six. All he needed now was the opportunity to flee the country.

In December 1988 his trainer in Bucharest, Petri Damchuk, told him the Russians had been invited by a British newspaper to send a gymnastic team to London in March 1989. It would be an exhibition, a celebration of the art form, free of the anxiety and strain of competition. The Russians saw it as a show of superiority before the world championships, something the propaganda machine couldn't turn down. Dominic saw his chance to escape. He pestered Nadia for weeks with stories of Russian achievement, stressing Romanian inferiority due to lack of international experience, and how, if he could go with them to London, even as an observer, he could spy on their latest methods and report back. Within two weeks he had been offered the position of special reporter for Romanian television on condition he passed a two-week study course on what to say and how to say it.

He completed his schooling with remarkable ease and found to his amazement that he enjoyed it. Camera technique came easily to him and, more importantly, the camera liked him. He looked his full six foot two in long shot, his square jawline was strong, his Mediterranean complexion the perfect camera tan and his Omar Sharif eyes and unruly black hair gave him sex appeal and personality. His tutors told him he had potential and could go far in Romanian Television if he had the right attitude. He locked their compliments away in his mind for encouragement and set his thoughts on escape.

It was 6.15; his flight left at nine o'clock. He felt sad at the thought of leaving his homeland, maybe for ever. But then maybe, just maybe, he could change things. From this positive point he gathered strength.

'Wake up Nadia.' He shook her gently. 'There'll be press to deal with at the airport and you'll want to look your best.'

Nadia's eyes snapped open like a camera lens and her face beamed a practised smile at him. 'It's your big day, darling. I just want you to be proud of me.' She placed a peck on his nose, swung away from him and slid out of bed. 'Are you wearing the nice blue double-breasted suit?' She eyed him coyly as she wriggled out of her pyjama bottoms. 'I quite fancy you in that.'

He studied the outline of her body and thought briefly of having sex with her one last time; of taking her roughly, the way they both liked. She was permanently available to him, always willing, teasing, provocative. Sex between them had always been wild, abandoned, passionate, lustful: it was all they really had in common. He fought the desire and lifted himself out of bed. 'Is my suit here or at your place?' he asked.

'Pressed and hanging in the wardrobe,' replied Nadia with uncharacteristic housewifely pride.

Two

Dominic had been in London for two of his permitted seven days when fate delivered a welcome and unexpected gift. He'd been assigned a minder, as was customary for any athlete spending time in the West, a Sergeant Ilyich Severin. Severin was a quiet man with the heart of a soldier and an eye on promotion to the officer class. He wore civilian clothes at all times and shadowed Dominic everywhere, fending off questions about involvement with the Russian team, making sure he ate properly and locking his bedroom door from the outside at night. At eight o'clock on Saturday morning he appeared in Dominic's room looking decidedly ill. A particularly evil strain of Siberian flu was doing the rounds and he'd succumbed suddenly and violently during the night.

'Go back to bed,' said Dominic hopefully. 'I can manage on my own today.'

'I have to be with you,' spluttered Severin, breaking into a rasping cough. 'Stenoza told me personally not to leave you.'

'Stenoza doesn't trust me.' Dominic handed his minder the box of tissues from the bedside table. 'I want to prove to him I'm trustworthy and I also want to prove I can do the job.' He smiled reassuringly. 'I want a career in media when I'm through with gymnastics and I'd be foolish to step out of line when things are starting to go right.

9

Besides, no one's going to thank you if you infect half the Russian team with flu.'

After considerable thought Severin reluctantly accepted Dominic's logic, kept the box of tissues and shuffled back to his room in a most unsoldierlike manner.

Dominic stood in front of the bathroom mirror finishing his shave and considering his options. Frustrating as it was, he had no definite plan of escape. Western media seemed to float behind the security screen accepting official quotes and never pushing for anything direct from the athletes. They held the reverse attitude toward their own stars; harassing, cajoling, even suggesting quotes derogatory to other performers in hopes of getting some juicy titbit to fill a back page. Dominic thought of copying Nureyev and going berserk at the airport on his way home. It was a last-resort plan: there was no guarantee that the British authorities would accept him. He wasn't a big star like Nureyev or Comaneci; no one knew of him outside Romania. He had his chronicle of government outrages that must have some value, but knew nothing of Western procedure in such matters. He clung to a blind belief that someone, somewhere, would help him once he'd managed to make contact.

The black embassy Volvo picked him up in front of the hotel and headed out on the Harrow Road towards Wembley. The driver was an unsociable man, about forty, with a bald patch and hardly any neck. He looked like an ex-bodyguard; probably awarded this cushy post as payment for some nefarious activity he'd performed for the regime. He said nothing during the journey, so Dominic could enjoy the springtime sights of London without the strain of politically correct conversation.

The morning passed uneventfully. Elena Chouchounova was superb on the beam, Sergei Sarotov majestic on rings. The Russian minders seemed to ignore Dominic as he set about lining up the afternoon interviews. Just before lunch one of them asked after Sergeant Severin. In his best pigeon-Russian Dominic told the story of Ilyich's sudden illness. The guard seemed to accept the explanation more out of difficulty in understanding Dominic's accent than in recognition of the truth.

Dominic slipped away from the main floor area without encountering further questions or challenges. Beside the dressing-room doors he looked back into the arena. All the minders seemed occupied elsewhere; if they were watching, they were well hidden. He hurried down the length of the corridor and up the concrete steps to the main concourse. As the show was not yet over the dressing-room area was deserted. He heard muffled conversations from behind closed doors, but nothing else. In the concourse, traders were preparing for the lunch rush, now only minutes away. The smell of hot dogs – another first for him.

A roar of applause signalled the start of the break. As waves of people flooded into the concourse Dominic joined the crowds and was invisibly swept along towards the exit stairs at the west end of the building. There he detached himself from the crowd and sprinted up the stairs to the first floor. Straight ahead of him, emblazoned on a white door in two-inch black lettering, were the words he'd been hoping to find: PRESS BAR. He'd been issued a press pass as his only form of Western authorisation; it had to be worth a try. He flashed the ID at the doorman with his broadest smile, keeping his hand across the lower part of the card and hiding the words 'restricted to floor area'. The man nodded and waved Dominic through.

As he entered the room he searched his mind for a collective noun that would best describe the sight before him. He'd often play mental games in times of stress; it helped him to concentrate, to focus on the task. There must have been a hundred people crammed on to twenty square feet of beer-soaked carpet: a collapsible porta-bar at the far end of the room dispensed pints of lager, glasses of wine and the odd large whisky and something to the anxious patrons desperate not to miss a second of free-drink time. An inebriation of journalists, he thought; yes, that would do.

Slowly he squeezed himself around the room, listening to conversations, hoping to glean something, anything that would relate to his predicament. Small talk and gymnastic talk was all he heard. As he pushed towards the bar in hopes of finding an orange juice he heard a snippet, just half a sentence, that focused his attention.

'... fucking commie bastards' pierced through the smoke and gossip. Dominic shuffled to the left and stood back to back with the speaker. 'I don't know how they've got the nerve to come over here,' continued the voice. Dominic's natural instinct was to be cautious. A favourite Securitate ploy was to trap you into confession by slagging off the government, and if you agreed with them, they'd arrest you. He looked around the room again in search of thugs in grey suits with bulges in their jackets but saw only people having a drink and a chat. This was England. This was the press bar at Wembley Arena. The realities he lived with were unthinkable here.

'Do you really mean that?' he said, silently praying for courage as he turned and took another step to the left to stand level with the speaker. 'If so, I have some information that might interest you.'

The man snapped his head round. 'I beg your pardon,' he pronounced, obviously annoyed by Dominic's intrusion. 'Do I know you?'

Their faces were no more than six inches apart. Dominic could smell stale whisky on the man's breath, and see broken veins on his cheeks, physical testimony to many years of travelling press coverage and stationary whisky bottles. He sported a bushy silver beard with matching handlebar moustache and at least a forty-five-inch girth. He was fat, but not jolly. Dominic tried to put strength and determination into his voice. 'My name is Dominic Bellescu. I'm a Romanian gymnast who's had enough of communism and I want to defect.'

The man's eyes glazed over and his shoulders slowly

dropped. Quickly Dominic glanced at the other members of the group. It was as if they hadn't heard. The two ladies had already started another conversation while a man on his right stood drinking beer, his eyes following a tall, busty woman in a long red dress who was squeezing between two shorter colleagues on her way to the ladies' room. The fat man inhaled deeply, holding his breath at its peak for a second before exhaling slowly through his nose. 'Are you serious?' he whispered, closing the gap between them to under an inch.

'I am,' replied Dominic, not daring to move.

He nodded at the press pass in Dominic's breast pocket. 'May I?'

Dominic removed the card and handed it to him quickly. The man's face remained expressionless as he studied it. His voice returned to normal. 'It says here you're a journalist.'

'I'm the Romanian gymnastic champion,' Dominic stated as firmly as he could without raising his voice. 'I've been sent here as a journalist to spy on the Russians.' He had to trust this man. In half an hour he was expected back in the arena to record an interview with Sarotov. To be late would mean missing the satellite link to Bucharest and that was sure to arouse suspicion. 'I've very little time, believe me. Will you help?' He blurted the question out, feeling helpless, like a small child in a room packed with adults.

'I think so,' the man replied, accentuating each word. A glint appeared in his eyes and a smile on his lips that made his cheeks stand out, red and rosy. He slipped his arm around Dominic's shoulder, shielding him with his bulk and guiding him towards the telephone booths that lined the east wall. 'Step into my office,' he smiled. 'We could do business.'

The cramped booth felt womb-safe to Dominic: private, cut off, secure. The man lifted the phone from its cradle and placed it on his shoulder as if waiting for a connection. 'My name's Harry Cassini,' he said. 'Tell me your story.'

'I have information to sell newspapers.' Dominic's English tended to let him down in moments of high tension. 'I have information to sell *to* the newspapers. I'm sorry, my English. . . .'

'Don't worry.' Harry patted him lightly on the shoulder. 'You were probably right the first time. Is this information backed up with any pictorial evidence?'

'I'm sorry, no.' Dominic's spirits fell. Only now did he realise the small value of his journal. Without photographs his stories were hearsay not fact. No paper would help him on the strength of unsubstantiated horror stories – no matter how gruesome.

'Are these political, business, or Securitate sticking pokers up backsides stories?'

'All three, but mainly the last one.' Dominic felt encouraged. Harry Cassini seemed to understand. 'I've got six cases of rape and murder in Brasov, Timisoara and Bucharest, all with victim names, dates, locations and details of witnesses.'

Harry replaced the phone and grabbed Dominic firmly by both shoulders. The smile was gone, but the sparkle in his eyes remained. 'This is not a fucking wind-up, is it? This is not one of Tony or Phil's little playettes? Tell me straight up you're for real, 'cause if you ain't I'm going to be well unhappy. D'you understand me?'

'I don't know any Tony or Phil,' said Dominic, failing to think of anything more convincing. 'I am who I say,' he continued in a stern voice. 'And if I fail to defect, or get caught in the attempt, I will be sent back to Romania and killed. That is the truth of the matter.'

Harry studied Dominic's face carefully, searching for the slightest sign of trickery or deception. He slowly loosened his grip. 'Where are you staying?'

'The Durrants Hotel.'

'Can you get out of the hotel tonight?' Dominic nodded. 'Good. Meet me at nine o'clock. Do you know where Piccadilly Circus is?' Dominic nodded again although he hadn't a clue. 'Meet me on the Shaftesbury Avenue corner.' Harry opened the glass, concertina door of the phone booth. 'Now get back to what you're supposed to be doing. I'll see you tonight.'

The black Volvo deposited Dominic outside Durrants Hotel just after six o'clock. He sat in reception for a few minutes and studied the hotel's *A to Z* of London. He had no English money for taxis or buses so he would have to walk. From the hotel he'd cut through Manchester Square to James Street, then Oxford Street, New Bond Street and left on to Piccadilly.

He phoned Sergeant Severin from his room and offered to deliver a stock of flu remedies from the chemist in Marylebone High Street. Severin refused the offer, saying sleep was more important and that he'd appreciate a call first thing tomorrow. Dominic told him how well the interview with Sarotov had gone, and the TV people in Bucharest were very pleased with the result. He wished him a peaceful night and replaced the handset slowly on to the cradle using great care to let it fall exactly in the centre. He reached into his pocket, pulled out his room key and placed it beside the phone. Tonight Severin would not be locking his door.

A loud knock heralded the arrival of room service and, he hoped, his last meal on the embassy expense account. To celebrate, he'd ordered the most expensive items on the menu, including a bottle of champagne. When the waiter placed the tray on the table next to the television and offered the bill for signature, Dominic added a five-pound tip, signed his name and added 'la revedere', Romanian for goodbye, at the bottom.

Pâté de foie gras on a bed of lettuce hearts, roast filet of venison served with redcurrant sauce, a platter of fresh vegetables, and a variety of soft French cheeses awaited Dominic's gastronomic pleasure. He ate the venison and vegetables while they were still piping hot and leisurely enjoyed the pâté and cheese while watching the seven o'oclock news on Channel 4. Since he didn't drink alcohol

15

he opened the champagne and left it undisturbed in the ice bucket.

By eight o'clock he was ready. A last thought of Nadia drifted across his mind. He would miss her. Despite her treachery there was a bond between them that transcended politics and police control. She had seemed genuinely saddened by the death of his parents and had been very supportive during that traumatic time. She'd taught him so much about sex but so little about love, and he felt sorry for both of them because of it.

He listened for noises in the hall. He thought of coach Damchuk and the gymnasium in Bucharest. Where coach Chienkov had fashioned his body with exercise and muscle building, Damchuk had focused his mind with positive thinking and martial arts. He'd execute short and long forms from Tai Chi before training sessions and discuss the basis for each discipline before a final run-through. Damchuk had taught Dominic to have confidence in himself, to believe in his ability. He'd also been a good friend over this last year; never pushy, but always there if Dominic felt like a chat. He remembered his coach's instructions. Blank out everything but the task at hand, feel the space around you, be aware of intrusion, seek the objective, move silently towards your goal.

Dominic stepped into the hall and closed the door firmly behind him. Turning smartly left he walked at a brisk but steady pace towards the stairway some fifty feet away. The corridor was deserted; he could hear no noise from the stairwell. On reaching the landing he looked over the railing and down three flights of carved oak stairs completely devoid of any living soul. Being a believer, but by no means devoutly religious, Dominic saved his spiritual connections for times of high anxiety, and right now his parents were coming through loud and clear. He could feel them, almost touch them, in the aura surrounding him. He descended two flights, jumping three steps at a time. Slowing to a walking pace on the mezzanine he started down the last flight, his senses razor sharp, his heart rate at competition level. The entrance hall looked empty. A low hubbub of conversation emanated from the restaurant to the left, a phone rang and was answered in the reception area to the right. He walked down the final flight, across the deserted entrance, passed the lone doorman and through the double glass doors into George Street. He quickened his pace slightly as he crossed the road and started down Spanish Street on his way to Manchester Square.

It had been so easy – maybe too easy – but there was no turning back now for Dominic Bellescu.

Three

General Roman Stenoza wiped the grease off his moustache with the sleeve of his tunic and threw the remnants of a leg of lamb over his shoulder. Three Dobermanns growled at each other as they tore at the remaining flesh with razor-sharp teeth. He slumped backwards into his chair where he farted, sniffed and burped in one continuous sequence. He looked like a walrus in uniform. A slovenly man lacking in both humanity and personal hygiene. An orphan of Romanian/Mexican parentage, he'd joined Securitate at fourteen and tortured and killed his way to the rank of Colonel by twenty. He was made a full General by a grateful dictator on his twenty-eighth birthday. He had no redeeming qualities save his love for the dogs to whom he showed continuous affection. They were the only living creatures he didn't physically beat on a regular basis. His mind was alert, astute, cunning; experienced and skilled in both political and military matters. He was Ceausescu's main adviser on security, and the most powerful man in the country outside the ruling family. He revelled in the distinction of being one of the most hated and feared men in Romania.

The red phone on his desk rang twice. He pressed the conference button. 'Has that whore arrived yet?' he belched at the machine.

'Severin's on the phone,' came the strident reply.

He picked up the handset. 'Put him through and watch your tongue, Private Olga Popescu, or I'll have to give you another lesson in discipline.' Stenoza laughed, a caustic, sadistic laugh, completely devoid of humour. 'Severin! How's London?'

'Bellescu's walked. Left the hotel ten minutes ago.'

Stenoza sat bolt upright in his chair. 'Are you sure?'

'He scribbled goodbye on the room service bill after ordering a £50 meal and champagne. He doesn't drink.'

'Fuck him!' Stenoza slammed his fist on the desk. 'Where's he gone?'

'I don't know. I didn't see him leave. I was in the bar.' Severin was lying. If he told the truth Stenoza would have him shot. Sergeant Severin was lying for his life. 'He said he'd join me for after-dinner coffee. When he didn't show I talked to the manager. He said he'd seen him leave a few minutes earlier.'

'I want that little fucker back in line by tomorrow morning or I want him dead! Is that clear?' Stenoza stood up. His belly came to rest on the table edge, the last of the lamb gravy dribbled from his mouth. 'Is that fucking clear?'

'I don't know where he's gone. . . .'

'Find him!!' Stenoza slammed the phone down. 'Po-pescu!' he screamed at the door. 'Get Nadia. I want that bitch here within the hour.'

Four

The lights of Piccadilly danced in the puddles left by a brief evening shower. The air smelled clean despite the traffic fumes: the smell of cleansing, the smell of freedom.

Dominic saw Harry standing outside a jewellery shop sucking vehemently on a large cigar. They were both ten minutes early. Harry was still wearing the ragged, grey tweed suit and the same loud, spotted tie; his shirt, however, was white, bright and clean, no more than two hours from the cleaners.

'Dominic! Wonderful!' His smile faded after the initial greeting. 'Did you get out clean?'

'As a whistle, I believe is your phrase.' Dominic offered his hand and Harry clasped it with both of his. A glow spread over his face and his smile returned. 'I knew you was no flim-flam,' he said, looking past Dominic up Shaftesbury Avenue. 'I know a pub with a quiet room. Let's have a pint and a talk.'

'What's a flim-flam?' asked Dominic as they jostled with the crowds hurrying to make the crosswalk light.

Harry stopped for a moment to let a woman with a loaded pram pass in front of him. His eyes searched Dominic's face then he nodded gently. He let out one short chuckle, patted Dominic on the back hard enough to start them in motion again, and ran his free hand over his beard. 'A flim-flam is a con-man, someone who winds you up. You're what I'd call a china plate, a good mate. China for short.' He hustled Dominic on his way. 'You'll get used to the language, don't worry.'

The small, Victorian pub was crowded and noisy. Harry barged his way to the bar; Dominic followed in his wake. 'Wotcha having?' he shouted back over his shoulder as his bulk came to rest on the oakwood slab.

'A mineral water, please. I don't drink alcohol or smoke cigarettes.' Dominic thought he'd better make that clear at the beginning.

'A pint of best and a Perrier!' shouted Harry at a passing barmaid. Then to Dominic: 'Not ever?'

'Not ever.'

'I can't imagine that.' Harry puffed on his cigar. 'I'm sure that's unhealthy, not having any vices.'

'I have vices, Harry. Just not those two.'

'Thank God for that.' Harry paid for the drinks and signalled for Dominic to follow him. They climbed a set of carpeted stairs to a small, deserted room on the right of the landing. A tiny bar occupied one corner and six small, round tables filled the postage-stamp area. They sat down to the left of the door.

'This is the form.' Harry placed his beer next to Dominic's mineral water, still not wishing to concede there were people who didn't drink. 'I'm a freelance reporter and I work mainly for the *Sun* newspaper, the biggest-selling tabloid in Britain. It's to the right of centre politically, prints sensationalist stories and usually has tits on page three. Its big rival is the *Mirror*, who put on the Wembley shindig. It's left of centre, prints sensationalist stories, and has bras on page three. I've worked for most of the other tabloids at one time or another so I'm well connected. If I help you defect I want exclusive rights on the story, and I want it in writing.' He produced a sheet of paper from his breast pocket. 'Have a read. Sign this and you'll be a star.' His arm found its way around Dominic's shoulder as he placed the paper in front of him and smiled like a plain-clothed Father Christmas.

The document, in letter form, was addressed to Harry Cassini c/o The News Group Newspapers Ltd., London. It started: 'Dear Sir, I, Dominic Bellescu, do hereby assign, for a period of six months, exclusive rights to any media story, print, sound or vision that . . .' Dominic looked across at Harry, who nodded at him to carry on. 'Six months, Harry. That seems a long time.'

'Jesus H. Christ!' Harry's response was surprise bordering on annoyance. 'You want to fucking negotiate?! Now? When I've set up the route out and the coverage?! Shit, son, you're not in any position to fucking negotiate!'

Although annoyance was clearly winning out, Dominic felt more the aggression of a sharp market trader than the bullying of a tyrant. He decided ignorance was not only close to the truth but also his best bargaining tool. 'Harry, Harry, calm down,' he said, shifting back into the chair and producing his best 'camera' smile. 'I can hardly read this, let alone understand it.'

Harry relaxed and, once again, nodded at Dominic to continue. Dominic drew a deep breath, slowly, as Harry had done at their first meeting in the press bar. 'I have a story I want to tell. It's not about being a good gymnast, a two-day media star, or beating the *Mirror* to a story. It's about people dying in a country three hours' flying time from here, it's about medical experiments that produce mutilated, unwanted offspring who exist in conditions pigs would refuse, it's about prisoners being used as live targets at the Securitate training range, it's about women being raped because there's nothing else for the bastards to do on a Saturday night and then killed to leave no witnesses. It's about being murdered for speaking the truth, and it's about a sadistic dictator who must be brought to book. That, Mister Cassini, is what I'm about, and if you can help me I will sign anything you want.'

They sat in silence. Dominic could almost touch Harry's thoughts as he cradled his pint in both hands and looked inquisitively into the Romanian's face. It was up to Harry now. Dominic had said his piece. Harry tipped forward in his chair, placed his beer on the table and picked up the paper. He folded it neatly and placed it back inside his coat pocket. Tilting forward he placed both hands on his knees as if about to get up. He rocked gently for a moment then pushed himself slowly to his feet and stood directly in front of Dominic. His bulk blotted out the bar light and cast a shadow over the corner. He offered his hand. 'It's not what I had in mind but you've got a point. I'll accept your handshake that you'll let me handle the story.'

Dominic was going to make it, he knew that now. 'You have my word, Harry.'

He walked at a sprightly pace for a large man. A group of young men in red shirts rushed by them as they turned left from Coventry Street towards Leicester Square. They stopped and chanted 'Liver . . . pool! Liver . . . pool', while waving green beer-cans above their heads. 'Fucking yobs,' muttered Harry, hurrying Dominic along towards the lights of the square.

'Are we in a desperate hurry, or can we stay here a while?' asked Dominic outside the Empire cinema as they passed a group of street performers juggling large red balls to the accompaniment of an out of tune penny whistle.

Harry pointed to the gate leading to the central garden. 'Let's sit down in there. I want to tell you about the geezer you're going to meet.'

'Geezer?' Dominic would have to start a mental dictionary if he was to learn the living language. Geezer would be his second word.

Harry laughed loudly. Dominic scanned the square quickly, first right, then left. Romanian paranoia was still his first reaction to anything sudden, He prayed for it to go away; he longed to feel secure in his own space.

'Still jumpy, lad,' said Harry, pointing an empty wooden bench. 'A geezer's a person in charge, a guvnor, the boss. Let's sit a bit.'

'I'm sorry, Harry. I. . . .'

'Don't apologise.' He sat down and gulped a lungful of air. 'You're going to meet a geezer called Malcolm Barrett. He's about thirty years old, owns one of the biggest computer companies in Britain and belongs to a club of businessmen who, shall we say, don't like communism. I think their long-term objective is to destabilise the economies of Eastern Europe and then buy in cheaply, but for now they busy themselves helping dissidents like you in exchange for anti-left propaganda.' He produced a hip flask from his coat pocket, flicked the hinged top off with his thumb and swigged a mouthful. 'He'll arrange a safe place for you to stay after we set the story.'

'It'll take days to verify my journal. We can't do all that tonight.' Logistics rather than mistrust prompted Dominic's reaction.

Harry produced his Father Christmas smile again. 'That's not today's story. We have to create media interest in you that will warrant front-page news when you blow the whistle, otherwise your story will be lost in two column inches on page seven. You, my good-looking gymnast, are to be photographed tonight with a beautiful girl having the time of your life at the best disco in town. Then you'll disappear from sight. First headline tomorrow reads: ROMANIAN ATHLETE MISSING, FAILS TO RETURN FROM WEST END PARTY. You sit in a nice cosy flat; we do a few 'Bellescu seen in Trafalgar Square, Manchester, Romford' pieces, add a little 'Body washed ashore near Dover, could be missing Romanian gymnast', with a pinch of 'My night of passion' by the girl in tonight's picture, and bingo – media stew. Everyone eats. When you tell your real story you'll have an audience of millions.'

'Is it really that simple?' asked Dominic, surprised by Harry's casual tone.

'That's not simple,' replied the reporter, knocking back another swig from his flask. 'That's fucking hard work. I hope you're up to it.'

Dominic stood up and clicked his heels together in best Bavarian fashion. 'Your challenge is accepted, sir. Show me this Western house of sin and tell me again about this night of passion.' They laughed openly as they walked from the square: to Dominic it felt wonderfully liberating.

A twenty-foot neon chariot marked the entrance to the Hippodrome Disco and lit the front of the whitestone building so brightly Dominic could see into the windows behind. Desks, computer terminals, phones and filing cabinets flashed into view in time with the lights. Harry spoke with two men dressed in oversized tuxedos who stood either side of matching chrome and glass doors. They waved Dominic and Harry through and immediately turned their attention to the couple behind who were somewhat the worse for wear and highly unlikely to see inside the chrome palace tonight.

The neon glitter of the atmosphere electrified Dominic. His first discotheque assaulted his ears, arrested his eyes and drove through his body. Black carpet, art-deco lamps, chrome-framed mirrors and photographs of rock and movie stars. His eyes flashed around the foyer, unable to take it all in.

Inside the club the music was overpowering. Dominic stood beside the main door and let the beat pulse through him. He loved the feeling. Gymnastics pulled at his muscles, trying to tear them from their anchoring, straining every sinew to breaking point. Music put him in charge. He controlled the extent to which his body stretched, determined the power exerted; the source came from inside him, not from an external set of bars or those murderous rings. Gymnastics was disciplined, confined by its rules to be tortuous; dance, driven by the soul, freed him from human regulation.

An endless procession of beauty and fashion filed past them. Women in miniskirts, maxi-skirts, shorts, see-through blouses, skintight Lycra, high heels, low heels, no shoes at all. Men wearing loose-fitting suits over tight-fitting singlets, blue jeans and studded leather jackets or shiny shellsuits emblazoned with colourful stripes. Every conceivable combination of the hip-human condition seemed to be represented in this glitzy beat brothel and Dominic was rapidly falling in love with the whole concept.

'Not bad, eh lad!' Harry shouted above the music. He pointed to the glass and chrome stairs that led to the first floor. 'Up there. He'll be up there.'

They approached a black leather banquette to the right of the upstairs bar. 'That's him,' said Harry, and Dominic saw a chubby, blond man dressed in an electric-blue jacket, bright yellow shirt and a black leather tie. He was sitting between two sensational looking women – a platinum blonde with massive blue eyes wearing a red low-cut silk dress, and an elegant brunette dressed in black, who blended so well with the furniture only her face was clearly visible.

'Malcolm, my friend!' exclaimed Harry, his voice ebullient. 'We've made it. This is Dominic Bellescu, gymnast supreme and defector *extraordinaire.*'

Malcolm leaned forward, his elbows sliding along the table top, his right hand extended towards Dominic. His face matched his body: chubby-cheeked with large, brown, deep-set eyes, a generous mouth and close-cropped hair. His handshake was firm. Dominic liked that.

'Dominic. I'm pleased to meet you. Harry. Please sit down. Let me introduce – ' he leaned backwards hooking his arm around the blonde's shoulder and waiting for the newcomers to sit down – 'the lovely and severely talented Miss Sara Owens, one of the country's most popular models, and – ' he turned his head towards the other woman but left his arm firmly around the country's most popular model – '*Ms.* Wilhelmina Howard, my public relations officer.'

Sara grinned sheepishly at Dominic and Harry and wriggled her body, adjusting to Malcolm's grip. Wilhelmina waited until Dominic looked in her direction before sliding from her camouflage. Her bright red lipstick and sky blue eyes looked surreal against her translucent complexion. A mane of shoulder-length black hair, parted in the middle, framed her sylphen face. A high-necked black velvet dress gave her the appearance of a precious porcelain doll; the determination in her eyes suggested she was unbreakable. She offered Dominic a perfectly manicured hand.

'Please call me Tilly, all my friends do,' she said, her eyes flicking momentarily in Malcolm's direction before locking disturbingly back on to Dominic. 'I gather we're to make you a star.'

'I look forward to it,' replied Dominic.

Her hand felt soft and warm; her nail colour matched her lipstick. She squeezed Dominic's hand lightly for a moment and he noticed that she was wearing a gold signet ring on the little finger of her right hand: it looked antique and bore the initial 'H', slightly raised in lighter gold. She wore no other jewellery.

'What must I do?' asked Dominic, returning the eye contact with equal intensity.

'You people sort that out,' interrupted Malcolm. He stood up and waved to the nearest tu-tued waitress. 'I'll get some more bubbly in and you can work it out with the girls. Harry and I need a slash. Don't we, Mister C?'

'I'm with you.' Harry was already on his feet. 'Order an orange juice for Dominic. He doesn't drink.'

'Brilliant,' enthused Malcolm. 'At last – a star who won't cripple the bank with his bar bill.'

Malcolm was renowned for his double-edged generosity. He'd quite happily spend £1,000 on a piece of jewellery for a casual date and bemoan a £100 drinks tab for close friends. It stemmed from his youth when he had been the school yid, the Fatty Arbuckle of the fifth form. So-called 'friends' teased him unmercifully, girls ignored him or laughed within earshot. When Malcolm first became successful he used his money to buy his pubescent friends, never trusting any of them and always making constant reminders of whose money was paying for the evening's entertainment. As the years progressed and the profits soared he'd shed the fifth-form failure for equally successful businessmen whose only size concern was contained on Ramco's balance sheets. He did, however, retain the habit of mentioning money every time a new person was introduced into his circle of aquaintances.

'Not ever?' asked Tilly once Malcolm and Harry had left.

'Excuse me,' said a slightly confused Dominic.

'Don't you *ever* drink?'

'Not if the date has a Y in it,' said Dominic in a frail attempt at humour.

'That's day! If the *day* has a Y in it.' Tilly burst into soft, cheeky laughter that made her eyes sparkle and her body shake.

Sara slid along the banquette to join them, filling the gap left by Malcolm. 'Are you really going to defect?' she asked, her voice flat. 'I think that's ever so exciting.'

'Yes I am.' Dominic couldn't believe she'd asked that. She hadn't a clue about the danger he faced, but, then again, why should she? Her life was probably lipstick, lovers and late-night dancing.

'And this is how we're going to do it,' said Tilly, composing herself and sitting upright at the table. 'The photographer from the *Sun* should be here any minute. When he arrives I want you two to spend about ten minutes on the dance floor. Just dance – he'll take some long shots from the balcony and I'll get the house bloke to run a video from the gantry. After that I want you at the bar, a few posed pictures, maybe in reception, then a couple of Dominic on his own in the street. I need some good lines from you, Sara: he's the best-looking fella I've ever dated, the ring I've got in mind isn't found in a gymnasium, that sort of thing.'

Dominic listened to Tilly expound her plan with growing interest. He'd never encountered such a woman. All the women he'd known had been products of a male-dominated feudal society where women knew their place and stayed in it. Any rebellion or attempt at advancement would have been met with suppression, usually involving physical violence. His parents had been regarded as avant-garde because his father had publicly invited his mother's opinion on political and social matters, a practice totally frowned upon by all sections of the ruling class. He'd done it out of love and respect for her, but it certainly made the Securitate aware of them and probably contributed to their eventual murder. Tilly was the first woman Dominic had met who looked as if she controlled her own destiny. Apart from her elegant appearance and stunning good looks, she carried a confidence about her that transcended her sex; she seemed confident and secure in her own self-esteem. Dominic found himself wishing he could dance with her instead of Sara.

'How old are you?' he blurted out.

Her piercing blue eyes seemed to read his thoughts, as if she knew his mind was wandering into personal areas. She was having none of it. 'Pay attention, Dominic.' She placed her hand reassuringly over his. 'This has to be handled correctly, your life depends on it.'

'I'm sorry,' said Dominic, pleased to be in such beautiful hands.

Malcolm and Harry returned to the table, photographer in tow. 'Look who we found in the bog,' said Malcolm proudly, as if the meeting had been divinely ordained. 'Now we're all here shall we get on with it, boys and girls?'

Malcolm had an arrogance born of success without the grace of humility. Sara cuddled up next to him, pleased to share his limelight. Her lips pouted provocatively and her half-exposed breasts rubbed gently against his arm.

Tilly ignored them all and continued to look directly at Dominic. 'Do you know what you've got to do?' she asked. Dominic nodded. 'I'm twenty-seven,' she went on, mouthing the words so only Dominic understood, then she stood and addressed everyone at the table. 'Ladies and gentlemen, let's go to work.'

Sara unwound herself from Malcolm, stood beside the table and straightened her dress with the subtlety of a sex

29

catalogue. Her big blue eyes, turned-up nose and voluptuous mouth had an endearing quality in a babydoll way but she was spoilt by layers of make-up. Her shoulder-length platinum blonde hair looked attractive at a distance, but closer inspection revealed an abundant use of hair lacquer preventing it from moving more than a centimetre in any direction. Sara's body was obviously her major asset and she knew how to show it off to its best advantage. The plunging neckline of her dress barely covered her nipples, her bra pushed everything up and centre to create a mountainous cleavage. A thick, black leather belt corseted her tiny waist and her dress covered her as if it were painted on. She wore black tights and black, patent leather stiletto shoes. It seemed to Dominic that self-preservation and advancement motivated her rather than the thirst for knowledge.

Sara took Dominic's hand as they squeezed their way to the dance floor. As they descended the stairs the music grew louder. The sounds of laughing, talking, drinking, clinking and kissing moved within the beat like percussion, filling Dominic with living music. As they reached the edge of the dance floor the music changed.

'*Fellas, I'm ready to get up and do my thing!*'

'You're at the Hippodrome ... drome ... drome!' shouted the DJ with extensive help from the echo machine.

'*Movin' it, you know, doin' it, like a, like a sex machine!*'

'Mister James Brown!'

'*Can I count it off. . . . 1 2 3 4!!!*'

Immediately the beat claimed Dominic's spirit and he submitted willingly to the feeling. Sara danced in a measured manner, concerned about how she looked rather than how she felt. Otis Redding followed James Brown, and then Wilson Pickett. By the end of 'Mustang Sally' Sara looked worn out and Dominic was warming up. He walked her to an empty table beside the dance floor.

30

'Stay here, Sara, and get your breath back. I'll return for you in a few minutes.' She smiled her agreement as the music changed tempo. *Pump up the volume, yeah, yeah.* Dominic loved this. Soul music was OK, in a ballroom kind of way, but modern music was his true freedom train.

A space began to clear for him in the middle of the floor as he executed flips, handsprings, leg splits and somersaults, all in perfect time to the music and with a great deal of style. The beat became part of him: his whole body danced, and danced, and danced. When the record ended the disco erupted in applause. Dominic bowed politely to the crowd, a broad smile shining through the sweat. Such an unexpected surprise has the sweetest flavour.

As the tempo and the lighting dropped, people moved together in couples, filling the space in which Dominic had performed. He looked around the room, searching for Sara. She'd left the dance area; he could just make out her sculptured backside at the top of the stairs as she headed back to the table. He followed as quickly as he could, stopping only once when a leather-clad black lady asked his name. Back at base he was greeted enthusiastically. Sara, no longer the centre of attention, looked slightly miffed. Dominic beamed her his best smile and slumped down beside Tilly.

'You're surprisingly good,' she said, handing him a large pink napkin to wipe the perspiration from his forehead. 'Don't get too comfortable, we're not finished yet. The photographer's waiting for you two at the bar.'

Pictures were taken at the bar, in reception with the manager, and finally outside the main entrance. Dominic kept a lookout for any sign of trouble in the form of police or plain-clothed military; he prided himself in spotting them at fifty paces. There was nothing. It felt like New Year's Eve: everyone, even the po-faced photographer, became positive and high-spirited.

A white Rolls-Royce limousine glided up Charing Cross

31

Road and stopped outside the club. Malcolm and Harry were suddenly at Dominic's side.

'Let's go,' said Harry, steering him toward the kerb. 'It's time for you to disappear.'

Five

Nadia picked herself off the floor and wiped the blood from her mouth.

'That'll teach you to be late,' snarled Stenoza. He slumped into his chair and looked across at the Dobermanns who sat salivating at the mouth and yelping as they strained against the chains that held them fast to the fireplace railing. 'I should let these bastards loose on you. Fuck up your looks, they would.'

Nadia stood upright, her face still stinging from his blow. 'I had no idea he was planning anything. You've read my reports. He's been class one all the way.'

Stenoza stood up and closed the gap between them in three strides. His right fist hit Nadia on the left cheekbone just below the eye. She tried to roll with the punch but only succeeded in glancing the blow on to her nose, which she heard snap from the impact. She fell backwards over a wooden chair and sprawled on the tiled floor, her hands protecting her face against further attack.

'You didn't look deep enough.' Stenoza stood over her and delivered a sharp kick into her ribs. 'He's going to be class one if he's planning something. He's not going to be a naughty boy here, is he? You should have realised he was up to something.' He grabbed her by the front of her shirt, pulling her up to him, at the same time driving his knee into her stomach. Nadia winced. Stenoza took

33

great pleasure from watching her pain. His eyes narrowed, he sneered his words into her face. 'I found you in a Brasov brothel. You were a cheap whore. You had fuck-all. I house you, feed you, educate you, teach you how to fuck properly and the first thing I ask you to do, you piss me off.' He dropped her back on to the floor and pulled his pistol from its holster. 'You've let that little shit get to you. You're in with him.' He brought the gun barrel down hard across her head, then cocked the hammer. 'Tell me where you're meeting him.'

'I'm not lying,' said Nadia, terrified of the situation and frustrated by her truth. Her mind raced to find the words that could save her. 'I've always been loyal to you. Everything I have is because of you. If I was part of whatever plan Dominic is hatching I'd be with him now, not here.' Nadia's voice petered out to a whisper as she repeated her last two words. 'Not here.'

Stenoza moved away from her and eased the hammer of his pistol. His voice softened, becoming almost paternal. Nadia knew this was the time to fear him most. 'Say you're right and he doesn't intend to run,' he said. 'Say he's just gone for a night on the town. In that case he'll try and sneak back into the hotel in the early hours and we'll nab him then. But if you're wrong . . .' his voice became menacing once more ' . . . it's you that hasn't done the job properly.'

'I'm sure he's just letting off steam at some night club,' said Nadia, knowing full well the consequence of failure.

'You'll stay here tonight,' Stenoza ordered, holstering his pistol and pressing the intercom. 'Popescu. Get me Severin and put Nadia in cell three.' He released the button before his secretary could answer and turned to face his prisoner. 'If I find out you are part of this I promise you a very painful time.' He spat at her. The phlegm landed on Nadia's shoulder. She was too hurt to do anything about it. Her face throbbed, her nose felt twice its size, her stomach and ribs shot arrows of pain through her body. Stenoza laughed raucously, pleased with his sadistic prowess. 'Get the fuck out!' he shouted, coughing another mouthful of phlegm and spitting in her direction.

Six

There had been so many 'firsts' for Dominic today: the smell of hot dogs, Harry's phone box, an English pub, the Hippodrome and now a Rolls-Royce. The smell of leather, the silence of the engine, the dark windows, the soft pile carpet, the rosewood panelling. He didn't ask where they were going, he didn't want the journey to end.

'You did well tonight,' said Malcolm, looking at Harry for confirmation.

'Yes. Real well,' injected Harry, more as punctuation than reply.

Harry displayed a subservience towards Malcolm bordering on the sycophantic. Malcolm accepted it as a matter of course, his arrogant logic perceiving it as normal. Dominic wanted to know more about this seemingly unstoppable businessman before he committed himself too far. He decided on something simple to break the ice.

'Is this yours or hired?'

'It's hired by a friend of mine. There's no way they can trace it.' Malcolm turned to face Harry. 'This boy of yours is well smart, susses all the angles.' He turned back to face Dominic. 'Relax. Everything is under control.'

Dominic would get no information this way; he did as requested.

The Rolls-Royce glided along for ten luxurious minutes, finally stopping outside a corner house with two street plaques attached to its wrought-iron fence. One said Chester Square, the other Lower Belgrave Street.

'Home sweet home,' exclaimed Malcolm, opening the car door before the driver had time to do his duty. 'Let's get you settled in, Dominic, while we wait for Tilly.'

The house had its main entrance in Chester Square, a solid-looking black wooden door at the top of seven concrete steps. All the windows on this side of the house had been bricked in leaving only an indentation as proof they ever existed. Malcolm unlocked three security bolts before signalling Dominic and Harry to stay put and rushing inside the house to eliminate the beeping that started the second he opened the door.

'Damn alarms are a bore, but you can't get insured without them these days,' he said, waving them inside.

The entrance hall was small, no more than two metres square, with a marble-tiled floor. The walls were dark red, almost purple; an ornately framed picture of Napoleon crossing the Alps covered most of one wall, a wooden-framed mirror and umbrella stand the other.

'Go on upstairs,' instructed Malcolm as he disappeared into the kitchen. 'I'll pour some coffee and be up in a minute.'

The first-floor drawing room conveyed an elegance of décor far beyond Malcolm's imagination. The carpet, walls, furniture, curtains and picture frames blended from gold to off-white in a pleasing and flowing spectrum. This was expensive interior design executed with taste and harmony.

'D'you like it?' Malcolm stood, tray in hand, framed in the doorway. 'A chap down the road did it; the whole house for under half a million.'

Dominic gladly accepted the mug of steaming hot coffee and three chocolate chip cookies. 'It's beautiful. How long have you been here?'

'About six months.' He set the tray down on the gold and glass coffee table in front of the double sofa on which Harry had spread his corporeal bulk. 'I've still got a place in Hampstead, that's my official address. Makes this hidey-hole perfect for keeping you out of sight. Any inquiries coming to me will go to Hampstead. It'll be weeks before the hounds sniff this gaff.'

'How big is it?' asked Dominic, still dazed.

'Three floors and a self-contained flat downstairs. That's where you'll stay.' Malcolm sipped his coffee loudly. 'What's your chest measurement in inches, Dominic?'

'Forty-two, forty-eight expanded,' he replied, somewhat baffled by the question and curious about which statistic Malcolm might ask for next.

'Waist?'

'Thirty-four. Why?'

Malcolm and Harry exchanged glances like friends sharing a secret. Harry reached into his pocket, produced his wallet and handed Malcolm a five-pound note. He flopped back further into the soft folds of the sofa cushions, a look of resignation shadowing his face. 'I bet him he couldn't guess your size from a photograph and the bastard was right on.'

Being saddled with two compulsive gamblers was not Dominic's idea of a stable relationship. 'Why did you bet on a thing like that?' he asked.

''Cause he took a fiver off me on the Arsenal game and I wanted my money back,' said Malcolm, walking back to the door. 'Come downstairs and see your new home. You coming, Harry?'

Compulsive, yes; serious, no. This was a game between them, no more.

Malcolm flipped a set of three keys off a cup hook on the wall just inside the kitchen door. The smallest Yale key fitted the lock on the last panel under the stairs. A door opened to reveal another set of stairs leading down.

Harry smiled. 'Go on down, Dominic, you'll like it.'

The stairs were carpeted in sage green and the walls were painted a lighter green with white gloss trim. Turning left at the bottom they entered an attractive room, as green as the upstairs was beige. A three-piece black

38

leather suite surrounded a gas log fireplace with black-grained marble slips, and behind the sofa was an antique pine unit of low-level cupboards and bookshelves. A large Sony television and video recorder stood to the right of the fireplace; full-length pelmeted curtains were drawn neatly across the front windows.

Dominic looked past the small kitchen and through the patio doors on to a floodlit garden of paving stones, shrubs and potted plants. In the far corner, against a trellised wooden fence, stood a statue of a naked woman. The jug she was holding emptied a constant stream of water over carefully placed rocks, channelling it into a small pond festooned with lilypads and bulrushes. Again the beauty of the place overwhelmed him. The sparse furnishings, bare floorboards and lack of heating in his Bucharest flat seemed a bad dream; as if someone else had lived his life, with him only observing the play.

'This way, Dominic,' Malcolm shouted from the outside.

The garden was bigger than it looked from inside the flat, and to the right a tall cement wall guaranteed privacy from all except the top-floor window of the house next door. Through a glass wall to the left Dominic saw a hallway and bathroom. Malcolm stepped through another set of glass doors at the end of the garden, and into the bedroom. Dominic paused to look at the waterfall before following. He inhaled the fragrance of the garden, the moisture of the night. He smelled jasmine but could see no plant. The gentle sound of the water eased his anxious mind.

The bedroom was autumnal, warm and inviting. A dark brown quilted bedspread decorated with embroidered leaves covered a large double bed, more antique pine furniture stood on rustic thick-pile carpet, and leaf-pattern wallpaper was complemented perfectly by a terracotta trim. Dominic bounced once on the bed trampoline style before following Malcolm into the hallway. Briefly he admired the blue and white tiled bathroom with its Jacuzzi bath and power-shower. He'd seen this bathroom before, he was sure of it, in a magazine at the hotel.

Turning right from the stairs led them to a utility room with washers, driers, freezers, central heating boiler and two sinks. A full-sized pool table stood in the middle on a wooden parquet floor. Dominic could say, unreservedly, this was the nicest private dwelling place he'd ever seen. He was about to compliment Malcolm when what seemed like a fire alarm went off beside his head. Everyone ducked. Malcolm grabbed an old newspaper from the pile beside the door and jammed it between the bell and the wall, muffling the sound.

'I'm sorry about that,' he said. 'I had it undampened so I could hear it on the top floor. Big mistake. It's only the front door, probably Tilly with the closing prices.' He skipped up the stairs three at a time, followed by Harry and Dominic at a much more leisurely pace. They could hear Tilly and Malcolm's conversation on the stairs above them.

'Do you know how good this is?' from her.

'Good smood! What do I know about dancing?' from him.

'Look at this tape, please.'

Harry listened intently and quickened his pace. 'It's the gantry VHS,' he said, slapping Dominic's back. 'It's showtime!!'

Tilly loaded the video as Harry and Dominic reclined on the sofa; Malcolm stood at the wall unit pouring large amounts of whisky into small crystal tumblers.

Tilly turned to face them, smiling broadly, her expression bright and eager. 'Gentlemen,' she said confidently, her eyes touching each of them in turn. 'What we have here is nothing short of sensational. In the last hour I've spoken to the BBC and LWT. They called me, which means they had people there tonight who were mightily impressed. I've fended off all deals until after this morning's papers because my guess is the Purley train crash will still be on the front pages and we might want to hold back a few more days on the main story. All we have now is a diary piece, or at best a glamour pic and three lines of text.' Malcolm was about to interrupt but she raised her right hand. 'Let me finish. I want Harry to go back to Wembley and snoop around, see if anyone's talking about Dominic, ask for him, find out what excuse they give. Then I want you to go to the Romanian Embassy and say you've heard a rumour that Dominic's defected and could they confirm or deny. If they deny, ask to see him. Let's shake the can and see how many worms drop out.' She turned her attention to Malcolm. 'I want you to say nothing at all to the press. You thought he was a good dancer, you had a great night and you dropped him off at his hotel before midnight. I want Dominic to go missing, I want the country asking where he is, and I can do it – with your help, gentlemen, and this tape.' She pushed the play button.

Dominic enjoyed the first few minutes as he sharpened the memories of his first taste of freedom. Sara looked much better on video; in fact she looked sensational. He lost interest during the last soul number, closed his eyes and listened to the music. He thought of how Tilly had controlled Malcolm just now. He couldn't imagine anyone speaking to Malcolm in that way, and yet she'd done it without a moment's hesitation. Outer beauty and inner strength: a remarkable woman.

Harry nudged his arm. 'Wake up, son! You're the star here!'

'And as such should be allowed to rest,' replied Dominic, keeping his eyes firmly shut.

'Dominic, I need your input,' said Tilly, not abrasively but nevertheless commanding.

Dominic opened his eyes. 'I'm sorry, Tilly. How can I help?'

She switched off the machine, accepted a drink from Malcolm, and sat in the chair opposite Dominic, placing her untouched drink on the coffee table between them. 'The reason television people are interested is not the fact that you're a defecting communist or that you've got a horror story to tell. They want you because you dance like Michael Jackson with the class of Fred Astaire. You're a natural, Dominic, and you do something different. You bring a very high level of gymnastics into modern dance. You are "Son of Breakdancing". They want you in light entertainment, guesting with Des, Wogan, Ross; that sort of thing.'

None of this made sense to Dominic. 'Who's Des Wogan Ross?'

It's extremely offputting when people are laughing and you haven't the faintest idea why. Being naïve and therefore blessed with a natural excuse, Dominic's embarrassment was limited. He knew they'd correct his mistake as soon as the amusement had run its course. Tilly was the first to regain her composure. 'It's Des O'Connor, Terry Wogan and Jonathan Ross. They have TV shows that book guests.' She glanced at her watch. 'The morning editions will be on the street in four hours and I need some sleep.' She stood up slowly. 'Goodnight, Dominic. I'll see you first thing in the morning, and don't worry – everything will work out fine.'

As he watched Malcolm escort Tilly from the room, the sparkle of determination still evident in her eyes, he had a warm, comforting feeling that she could be right.

Seven

A gentle knocking sound penetrated Dominic's slumber. He opened his eyes on his first full day of freedom to see Tilly framed in the doorway looking like a page out of *Vogue*. Her bright yellow suit, white shirt and spotted navy-blue tie introduced a breath of spring into the autumnal room.

'Good morning, young man.' She didn't enter the room, remaining instead in the doorway, her smile the only traveller. 'I'm sorry to disturb you but it's nearly ten o'clock, you're in the morning papers and we have work to do. Malcolm and I are in his office on the top floor.' She placed an envelope on top of the tallboy by the door. 'He asked me to give you this. Why don't you have a shower, get yourself together and join us upstairs? There's food in the kitchen. You can grab some breakfast on the way up.'

Dominic pushed himself up in the bed and felt a slight tinge of embarrassment as he exposed his torso.

'See you later, then.' She beamed a shy smile in his direction before averting her eyes and closing the door quietly behind her.

He slid out of bed and stood naked in front of the glass patio doors, looking at the garden in the morning light. Swaths of ivy trailed upwards through the trellising on the wall, from wrought-iron corner brackets pampas grass

43

cascaded down from moss-lined hanging baskets. Terra-cotta pots overflowing with primula, crocuses and wild violet ringed the pond. A small shaft of sunlight danced on the water, casting diamond shadows on the wall behind. A lilypad moved, a flash of white and gold broke the surface of the water, then was gone. There were fish in the pond. Splendid, thought Dominic, absolutely splendid.

He opened Malcolm's letter on his way to the bathroom. It read:

Good morning Mister Dancer, There's a second dividend on my bet with Harry in that the clothes in your wardrobe should fit. Just a few items to get you started: socks and underwear in the tallboy, shaving and dental equipment in the mirror cabinet over the sink and a bathrobe behind the door. Be careful of the shower – the heat control is very sensitive. See you upstairs when you're ready. Welcome to England, M.B.

The dark blue towelling robe removed his body chill immediately. He walked back into the bedroom and opened the wardrobe. A blue suit, a brown suit, a tweed sport jacket, and a double-breasted blue blazer hung side by side. Beside them were black, beige, blue and grey slacks clipped smartly into trouser hangers next to four silk shirts in matching colours. He looked at the label inside the blazer: *Yves Saint Laurent*. The suits were the same. The tallboy contained six pairs of white boxer shorts, a half-dozen pairs of black cotton socks, four plain white T-shirts and two pairs of Levi 501's. The decision on what to wear would be a pleasure taken during his shower, assuming he could get the temperature correct.

The luxury of unlimited hot water was another welcome first for Dominic. The trauma of panic soaping in cold water was replaced by a tranquillity bordering on laziness. He stood for at least five minutes letting the water wash not only the dirt but years of frustration down the drain. As the water ran down his back he revelled in its soothing heat. He soaped himself three times just for the hell of it and decided on the third rinse he'd wear a pair of Levis, a yellow silk shirt and the blue Saint Laurent blazer.

Breakfast proved another treat. Along a marble worktop in the opulent kitchen stood bowls of apricots, grapefruit, oranges, prunes and pineapple. Cornflakes, branflakes and muesli awaited him to the right; large jugs of orange, apple and tomato juice vied for his attention to the left. The spread was more comprehensive than at the hotel, without the annoyance of jostling guests. He half filled one of the floral bowls with cornflakes, added slices of apricots and ice-cold milk from the fridge. With a full measure of orange juice in a large crystal tumbler he made his way up the two flights of stairs towards the frantic conversation emanating from the top floor.

'First things first,' he heard Tilly say as he approached. 'I've got to start with basics or I'll never get organised. Suggestions are always welcome but the method we use is mine. If you want to run this show, do it yourself.'

'I don't want fingers pointing at me,' replied Malcolm, his anger clearly audible. 'Dominic is special. I don't want a fuck-up.'

'I don't "fuck up", as you so delicately suggest. I must spend time with him, explain what's going to happen. The man is an innocent: I will not have him blow this story through ignorance.'

Being described as innocent made Dominic feel falsely virginal. He was uneducated in the ways of the Western media but hardly innocent. He felt it was they who didn't understand the consequence of failure: they could carry on with their lives regardless of the outcome of this little drama. As he entered the room they stopped talking. A flicker of embarrassment flashed briefly across Tilly's face as she realised Dominic had overheard at least part of the conversation. Without the slightest hint of discomfort Malcolm opened both arms. 'Good morning, my friend,' he said. 'That jacket looks great on you. Don't you think, Tilly?'

'We must talk,' said Dominic before Tilly could answer.

He dumped the breakfast tray on Malcolm's desk, startling them both. 'This is not a game to me. I am here to avenge the death of my parents, expose a corrupt and sadistic regime and get a new life – in that order. Discovery or capture at any time will mean death for me. And, believe me, when they know for sure I'm missing they'll come looking for me with all the weapons in their arsenal, and that includes snipers, bombs and poison-tipped umbrellas.'

'A bit James Bond,' said Malcolm dismissively.

Dominic sat down opposite him and folded his arms on the desk top. 'Let me tell you a story, Malcolm. Less than three months ago on the weekend before Christmas, General Stenoza and four of his henchmen found themselves stranded in Andreisu, a small, mountain village west of Focsani. They called a meeting at the village hall and announced they were looking for someone to represent the region at a Christmas festival the following week in Bucharest. The person had to be young, presentable and should be able to folk dance. All expenses would be paid and the person would receive a fee of fifty US dollars. Mr and Mrs Caprianu proudly put forward their daughter, fifteen-year-old Svetlana, who met all the requirements. Stenoza and his men went to the Caprianus' house to audition the girl. Once inside, they tied the parents to the kitchen table and made them watch as they all raped Svetlana in turn before mutilating her body with a hot fire-poker. They then shot all three and left. Now tell me those men won't go for me when I talk publicly.'

Tilly's face turned pale. Malcolm sat back from the desk, clasped his hands together and rotated his thumbs around each other nervously. 'You've got all this documented?' he asked.

'And more. Some I can prove, some are hearsay, but it's all happened in the past year and it's going on right now.'

'Then they'll come after you,' he said with a sigh.

'Exactly. Now can you see why this is not a game to me?'

'I can,' said Tilly in a manner that made Dominic believe she'd understood completely. 'But we still need to get you known before you tell your story, and that requires the basics to be done. Now, if you'll excuse us Malcolm, the sooner we start the sooner – '

' . . . you finish. I know.' Malcolm stood up and walked out of the room, slapping Dominic briskly on the back as he passed and pausing at the door to issue one last order to Tilly. 'I want him finished by lunch, I've another job for you this afternoon.'

'You'll get used to him. I did,' said Tilly when she knew he was out of earshot.

'You cope with him very well. I think I'd lose my temper after a while. He's a bit of a bully.'

'A lot of that is shyness.' She smiled warmly and ran her hands through her hair, twisting the ends around her fingers. 'But then a lot is due to the fact he's a male chauvinist pig with an obscene amount of money.' She delivered the line with just the right amount of sarcasm to make it funny.

Dominic chuckled. 'I admire what he's done in business terms,' Tilly continued. It's not easy to be that successful without the advantage of a privileged education. He's a tough street boy who's made good and that's to be applauded.' She placed a blank sheet of paper on the desk top and produced a pen. 'Enough of him. How do you spell your last name?'

'B. E. double L. E. S. C. U.'

'Age?'

'Twenty-four.'

'Married?'

'No.'

'Children?'

'Not that I'm aware of.'

She looked quizzically at him. 'All single men say that. It must be programmed in at birth.' She studied his face

47

carefully. 'Eyes – brown. Hair – black and curly, no, wavy. Complexion – I'll put Mediterranean. Height?'

'Six foot two.'

'Weight?'

'Eighty kilos, about 175 pounds.'

'Brothers and sisters?'

Dominic shook his head.

'Education? No, that doesn't matter.' Tilly put her pen down and stared at him across the desk. She had a penetrating look of honesty that unnerved Dominic. She looked back at her notes, her eyes releasing him, leaving only the memory of their lapis-lazuli colour. 'How many horror stories have you got in that little black book?' she asked without moving her eyes from the paper.

'Six,' replied Dominic, offering no further embellishment.

'Are they all as bad?'

'The ones about the children's orphanage are worse. There's a place near – '

'Please don't,' she interrupted, her eyes meeting his again. 'I'll deal with it when I have to, but not today. Today is about you, what we're going to do with you. The gore can wait.' For the first time Dominic saw frailty in her, a chink in the armour, and it pleased him. Tilly Howard was human after all.

'What else do you want to know?' he asked.

She stood up, walked slowly across the room and quietly closed the door. Gathering the tabloid papers from the desk she settled on the sofa. 'Come, have a look at these. Some of the pictures are very good.'

Some invitations should be accepted without a moment's hesitation and this was one of them. Tilly had a correctness about her that Dominic found intriguing. He had wanted to be close to her since their first meeting at the Hippodrome but she had always kept a distance between them at all times.

'This one in the *News of the World* is remarkable,' she said, sliding pages five and six towards him across the

48

leather cushion that divided them. 'You photograph very well.'

Dominic was drawn to the headline first: SARA SNARES SOVIET SWEETHEART. This was indeed remarkable. For a moment he thought he was reading the wrong story. It continued:

Page three lovely, Sara Owens (18) fell head over heels for a communist gymnast with the Russian team currently touring Britain. Dominic Bellescu (24) flipped over Sara's 38, 26, 36 curves and decided a night of partying at the Hippodrome with Sara was much more fun than an early night at the team hotel. The couple left the trendy London disco shortly after midnight and haven't been seen since. Sara's agent and former boyfriend, Peter Langford (28), said 'Sara's a big girl. I'm sure she knows what she's doing. I expect I'll hear from her when they surface.' Dominic is the Romanian gymnastic champion and is in England as a reporter for Romanian Television. The Romanian Embassy would not comment on his night of passion with our sexy Sara, only that he was due at Wembley today to continue his series of interviews with Russian gymnasts.

The main picture showed them dancing; the smaller shot that appeared at the end of the text was taken in the bar: Sara in front and up front, Dominic with his arm around her waist, his head resting on her shoulder. He thanked God his eyes were looking straight ahead.

'Where *did* Sara spend the night?' he asked, his mind moving a few stories down the line. 'If she turns up somewhere today and gets photographed it'll disprove the story.'

'She stayed at my place,' said Tilly. 'Malcolm's paying her by the day. She'll stay put till she hears from me.' She looked inquisitively at Dominic. Her eyes scanned his face, searching for a sign or a truth she could relate to; a starting point. 'I've tried to imagine what it's like living in your country under such a evil man and all I come up with is my worst nightmare. I can't imagine trying to live with the knowledge you possess, or having my parents

49

killed by the same people responsible for my career and livelihood, or what it must be like to suddenly find yourself surrounded by all this.'

She paused for a second, allowing Dominic time to reply. But he had nothing to say; he wanted to listen to this woman. It was the first time anyone had even begun to scratch the surface, to become aware of reality in Romania. Sensing his feeling, her eyes dropped slightly, a cherub smile curled the corners of her mouth. 'The first change you'll notice is that we are, on the whole, a peaceful society. We still argue, disagree and get quite nasty at times, but we don't go around killing each other.' Her right hand came up a millisecond before Dominic thought of interrupting. 'I'm not talking Ireland, gangland or psychopaths, I'm talking about our circle of life – Malcolm, Harry, Sara, other people you haven't met yet. I mean us, Dominic, the people you'll be involved with.' Her smile broadened. 'At least, we haven't killed anyone so far.'

Happiness and joy are such rare commodities they should be eternally remembered. Dominic felt both, and returned her smile slowly and deliberately. 'Thank you, Tilly. I was beginning to think I'd gone from circus to circus.'

Tilly knew what he was trying to say. 'You mean out of the frying pan into the fire.'

'Thank you again,' said Dominic brightly. 'I think I could eat breakfast now.'

'It'll be all soggy. Let's get a fresh one. I think I'll join you. How about some eggs?' She stood up and offered her hand. 'Please don't tell me about waste and starving babies; I already know.'

Dominic knew she was going to speak again and wanted to hear what she had to say.

'Over breakfast I want you to tell me stories, Dominic. Nice stories, about the good side of your life.'

He opened the door and bowed, gesturing for her to walk through. She glided by him, her scent lingering as she walked to the top of the stairs, where she turned around and smiled. 'Manners are most important to me, Dominic, I'm glad you have a full complement.'

She was serving the scrambled eggs before he'd finished his first story about a holiday with his parents on the Black Sea coast when he was seven. The sandcastles they'd built had been trampled by army horsemen and his father had said they should build sand horsemen and maybe they'd be trampled by a herd of sandcastles. They laughed together and Dominic felt at ease and safe.

They ate toast and thick-cut marmalade as he told her how his good friend Ali would make snow sleds out of old packing crates and metal tubing and whiz past the checkpoint at the entrance to the village, scaring the guards by whistling as loud as he could. He missed out the part where Ali had been thrown off the Buzau rail bridge for sticking his tongue out at a Securitate officer: he was eleven when he died. Tilly listened intently, drinking in his stories with her coffee and feeding off the knowledge contained within them.

'It sounds like a beautiful country,' she said, holding his gaze once again. He felt she knew he was holding back, knew he had secrets and was determined to uncover them. 'What about you?' he asked, the embarrassment of discovery creeping into his voice. 'Tell me some of your stories.'

She relaxed and her face became radiant, almost joyous, as she remembered her childhood. 'I've been sledging lots of times,' she said, 'with my younger sister Charlotte. I had to look out for her as she was five and I was eleven. We lived in the country then, near Bristol, and one winter it snowed for three days. My father took our tractor across the sloping field, drag-chained the last twenty feet so we couldn't slide off into the road, and gave us two large tin trays. They were terrific! We could steer them anywhere and if you went too fast you fell over laughing.'

'How did you get from the country to Chester Square?'

'The country to Fitzroy Mews,' she replied pertly. 'I live in Fitzroy Mews.'

'Same question, different address.' She laughed at that, so did Dominic: friendly comfortable laughter.

'Country is for weekends, walks and big log fires. The city is for business.'

'That's not what I asked,' he said, testing her honesty.

Her head perched to one side, she clasped her earlobe and rubbed it gently. Her face took on an impish look as she sat up straight, again assuming the pose of correctness: hands folded on her lap, hemline on the knee, shoulders back but not too far. 'I had what the English call a minor public school education and read psychology at Bristol University. Four years ago I joined a London PR firm, two years ago I set out on my own, and last year I gained Ramco as a client. Ramco is Malcolm's company.' The impish look returned. 'Satisfied?'

'For now,' he replied, not wanting to relinquish all the advantage.

'I've asked a photographer friend to come over and take some portrait shots for the file,' she said, obviously wanting to change the subject. 'It's a bore and you'll only have to do it once, but I must have a good mug shot. From the Saturday fans to the *Sunday Times*, everyone requires an eight-by-ten black and white sooner or later.'

'Tell me about Ramco.' Dominic couldn't miss this opportunity.

'Not here,' she replied quickly, giving him a visual once-over. 'I think a white shirt. Yellow looks grubby in black and white. If you go downstairs and change, I'll follow with some fresh coffee and the answer to your question.'

Dominic was halfway through deciphering the ridiculous combination of plastic, cardboard, pins, clips and cellophane that holds a Western shirt in its display state when 'not here' came back to him. They had been alone: the room must be bugged. He'd expected it, he was used to it, but what a shame. He struggled with the piece of plastic held on by a pin and attached to a piece of cardboard that went all around the collar. Any race of people that will go to such lengths to display an item of clothing has got to be in more trouble than Romania, he thought, naming the garment the shirt from hell. Finally he got it on but not before a last concealed pin hidden in the arm gouged a sizeable chunk from his wrist. After weeks of shelf life at Monsieur Laurent's boutique, the shirt showed three deep creases across the front: it would have to be ironed. Walking into the army stores in Bucharest and being handed a 'size large' on a plastic hanger in return for a signed clothes coupon had its advantages.

'Are you in there?' filtered through the bedroom door. Tilly's voice soothed his annoyance. 'Yes.'

'I'll wait for you in the lounge.'

He heard her footsteps fading down the hall. Lounge, drawing room, living room were all the same place. It was like moving from Emily Brontë to Hemingway in one sentence. He was grateful for the time he'd had in Romania to read English books: it had helped him grasp the living language. Although some of his English was awkward he was having no real trouble either communicating or understanding, and that had always been his biggest worry. Gingerly removing the shirt, he put on the blue robe and, taking the shirt firmly in hand, walked smartly through the garden to the kitchen. 'Do you know where the iron is?' he shouted through to Tilly in the lounge/drawing room/living room.

'Give it to me,' she said, walking into the kitchen. 'Martha will do it.' Tilly took the shirt. 'She's just arrived with Samuel the cook. That's why I didn't want to talk upstairs.' She smiled and was gone, leaving Dominic restored and a little ashamed of his suspicions.

He stood in the garden watching the morning light that reflected off the pond in such a way as to reveal the fish. He counted three, all gold and silver.

'You're a bit of a thinker, aren't you?' Tilly's voice drifted into him then out; a fish broke the surface and gulped the sentence from the air. Again the scent of jasmine. 'Do you smell that?' she said, stepping into the garden. 'It smells like . . .' she paused.

'Jasmine,' he said, turning to face her.

'You're right, jasmine, but it's the wrong time of the year.'

'And I don't see a plant.'

She looked around the garden, her eyes searching for the elusive flower. 'Right again, it's not here. We must have a magic flower.'

'Tell me about Ramco,' Dominic persisted, eager to solve the puzzle.

Tilly looked pensively into the pond as she spoke. 'Malcolm comes from a professional family. His father is an accountant and his mother was a nurse but doesn't work any more. About ten years ago, just before home computers started to make an impact, he borrowed £10,000 from his father, went to Taiwan and made a deal to import a component into Europe called a RAM, random access memory. It's small, but apparently it makes everything work inside a computer. The key to his success was his landed price in this country which was 21 per cent lower than his closest competitor. Within four years he was turning over £200 million, and with Europe opening up this year he's looking at doubling the present figure of £350 million. That's Ramco – and Malcolm and his parents own the lot.'

'What about the club he belongs to? Harry told me he was part of an anti-communist group.'

'I don't know much about that. He runs it from the Hampstead house. He's got a special computer room where they all talk to each other through a coded modem.'

'A what?'

'It's a private network that links them together. They can pass messages, text, data, and hold conference meetings without anyone knowing the others' identities. A bit spooky if you ask me, but it seems to get things done, it's a great red-tape slicer.'

Although Malcolm had dampened the doorbell last

night, the sound still made them jump. 'That'll be Julian,' she said. 'I'll bring him downstairs. I don't want Martha and Samuel to get a look at you because they're both *News of the World* readers.'

'What about the shirt?'

'I told her it belonged to my lover who'd stayed here overnight.' There wasn't a trace of embarrassment on Tilly's face. She'd told a professional lie in the interest of her client, and that was that. The bell sounded again. 'Stay in the garden,' she said, disappearing into the house. 'He might prefer natural light.'

Julian, or Jewel as he liked to be called, turned the photo session into a five-act play. He kept calling them Sweetie and Ducky, couldn't make his mind up about the lighting, and made sexually explicit references to everything from his camera to Dominic's freshly ironed shirt. It came as a great relief to both of them when he left an hour later trailing his tripod behind him and promising to have proofs on Tilly's desk in four hours.

'He's outrageous but he's discreet.' Tilly flopped on to the sofa. 'Fancy lunch? Samuel's cooking a mild fish curry and there's cold king prawns with garlic mayonnaise to start.'

'Any news from Harry?' asked Dominic.

Tilly looked at her watch. 'Give him an hour, maybe two.'

Eight

The sound of a pneumatic drill thundered through the bars of Nadia's cell and woke her from a spasmodic sleep. Her nose and the left side of her face were swollen; the purple black of bruising coloured her cheek and eye. As she tried to move from the bed a shaft of pain cut across her ribcage and forced her back. Her eyes scanned the room for the first time in daylight.

Like most of Bucharest's buildings, the predominant colour was grey. Nadia looked despairingly at the four grey, empty walls, the grey steel door with peep-hole but no handle, the concrete floor that sloped to a small steel drain in the far corner. Next to the drain a half-used roll of green toilet paper added the only colour to the cheerless room. She looked through the small, glassless window to the grey sky beyond and felt resigned to her helplessness. What Stenoza had said last night was true. Since she'd run away from the orphanage at the age of fourteen she had made her living from prostitution. She'd been an exceptionally bright child in an institution of subnormals; a bizarre legacy of Ceausescu's insane belief that the bigger the population the more important he would become. Contraception and abortion had been illegal in Romania for twenty years. Stenoza, a non-paying client of hers, had spotted her potential and taken her under his wing. That was how the Securitate worked: they'd recruit hit men, controllers and spies from the unfortunates of society – bright, desperate people with nowhere to go.

Her time with Dominic had been the best years of her life. They'd had real fun together despite her spying activities and she was genuinely fond of him. If he had planned an escape without her knowing he had done it very well. She allowed herself a mental smile in recognition of his stealth.

She heard footsteps in the corridor, then a key in the lock. Her muscles tightened. Frightened and apprehensive, she was unable to move. The door clanked open. Nadia saw a brown uniform, black jackboots and a mop of shoulder-length blonde hair.

'I'm Private Popescu. He wants to see you.' Her voice was calm, almost sympathetic.

Nadia tried to sit again, this time holding her side to ease the pain. Popescu clopped across the floor, her steel heels echoing around the empty cell.

'Let me help,' she said, slipping her arm around Nadia's waist and assisting her to her feet. 'Take these. They might help.'

Nadia stared at the four brown pills in Popescu's hand. 'Poison?' she asked hopefully.

'Only opium, I'm afraid, but it will dull the pain considerably.' The young soldier smiled at Nadia. Another ex-orphan girl; they recognised each other's origin immediately.

'Thank you.' Nadia took the pills and popped them into her mouth. 'Mustn't keep the fat shit waiting, must we?' She returned Popescu's smile.

'How the fuck can this happen?!' yelled Stenoza at the two soldiers standing rigidly to attention in front of him. 'I've just got a fax from London. Bellescu is in four papers this morning having a good time with some whore and then he doesn't show up at the hotel.' He walked around behind them. 'This is a set-up. A pre-planned, more to come, fucking set-up!' He picked up a riding crop from his desk and smacked one of the soldiers across the face. The man flinched then remained motionless. 'What's the fucking point of having people watching people if they don't keep their fucking eyes open.' He dealt the same punishment to the other soldier. 'Bellescu's got something, otherwise the West wouldn't be interested. I want you two to join Depescu in London by tonight: he's already tracking down the main players. I want whatever it is Bellescu's got, then I want him dead. Is that clear?'

Both soldiers stiffened. '*Sir*!'

Stenoza threw the crop back on to the desk and clapped his hands three times. 'Then what's keeping you?'

'*Sir*!' The soldiers turned smartly left and marched from the room.

Nadia passed them in the doorway.

'Ah! My little whore with big tits and no savvy,' sneered Stenoza, pointing at a wooden chair in the centre of the room. 'Have a seat. I'll be back in a minute.'

Nadia did as instructed and prayed the opium would soon take effect. Stenoza walked into the small office bathroom and urinated in the sink while snorting a large line of high-grade Colombian cocaine from the dirty glass shelf above.

'Now, young lady,' he said, zipping up his fly as he re-entered the room. 'We've got a serious problem with your Mister Bellescu.'

The opium started to work. Nadia felt a numbness flow through her body; her mind became detached, unfocused. She felt the weight of his blow to the right side of her face but no real pain. The sound of her hitting the floor seemed magnified and in echo.

'That should do it,' said Stenoza, propping himself backwards against the desk. 'Come on girl, sit up. What's wrong with you?'

Nadia clawed her way back on to the chair, trying desperately to focus her mind. 'You're a lucky little hooker,' she heard him say. 'We need you alive for the moment.'

She concentrated all her remaining power into her speech. 'I know nothing of what Dominic's up to. That's the truth.'

'I'm sure it is. It's lucky *I* know what the fuck is happening.' He belched, farted and smiled to himself, enjoying the timing and effect of his bodily functions. 'Your boyfriend has done a bunk. He's all over the British press, arm in arm with some bitch with tits the size of Timisoara.' He grabbed her blouse and ripped it. 'Nice touch,' he smirked, stepping back and admiring his handiwork. 'I've prepared a press release for you to sign saying that Dominic beat you up on a regular basis and forced you to have perverted sex. Popescu will take your picture.' He laughed raucously, pleased with his creativity. 'I'm going to beat that asshole at his own game and *then* I'm going to kill him.'

Nine

Chester Square. Sunday noon

Before removing his coat Harry set about beheading and shelling the nearest crustacean. He scooped a huge dollop of mayonnaise on to the naked morsel and deposited the lot into his mouth in one flowing movement. 'God I'm hungry,' he said, attacking prawn number two and turning to face Dominic. 'Are you big news at Wembley or what? Christ, I got offered a fortune to give you up.' He wagged the headless prawn at both of them before continuing: 'They're really upset. Severin was there; he looked like shit. He said if I saw you to tell you to come back now before this all gets out of hand.'

'What did you say?' asked Tilly.

'I told him I met Dominic at the disco. That he spent the evening with his hands around Sara's bazoomers.' He saw Dominic's puzzled expression. 'Tits,' he said, holding both hands up to his chest. A plop of mayonnaise landed on his lapel. He scooped it off and almost made his mouth. 'Shit!' he said, using the prawn to wipe the mayonnaise from his beard before shoving it unceremoniously into his mouth. 'Tits!' he repeated, masticating loudly. 'Boobs, jugs, bazoomers, mammaries!'

Dominic found Harry's manner somewhat offensive in front of Tilly but it didn't seemed to faze her at all. She looked indifferently at him: she'd heard it so many times from Harry it didn't seem to matter any more.

'Were you followed here?' asked Dominic.

'I'm not stupid.' Harry's attitude changed in a second, becoming hard, professional, correct. 'I changed transport three times and walked the last half-mile. I had someone on me from Wembley, I lost him at Baker Street.'

'Well done, Harry.' Dominic's relief at knowing he was being taken seriously showed in his voice. Harry's Father Christmas grin made another fleeting appearance.

'Listen, my son, I know how fucking dodgy this can get. Before I left the arena I caught a whisper that Ceausescu already knows and is well pissed with you. He wants you dead, and now.'

'How did you hear?'

'A mate of mine works for the *Telegraph*, knows a bit of Russki. He overheard a couple of minders. It's only a rumour, but that coupled with Mister Tailpiece I thought: hang on, the odds are shortening.'

'Just a minute, gentlemen.' Tilly fidgeted on the sofa. 'Are you telling me that there could be a contract out right now on Dominic?'

'If not now, in the next few days. Hey, baby, this is a hot one!' Harry attacked another prawn.

Macho posturing was the last thing Tilly wanted. Dominic watched her lean forward, her hands clasped on her lap. 'This is ridiculous,' she said, fright and anger equal partners in her voice. 'This is London 1989 not Chicago 1925. Are you telling me if they knew where you were at this moment, they would come into this house and kill you?'

'If they knew I was here they'd blow this house up and kill everyone in it to get at me.' Dominic couldn't put it clearer than that. Tilly had to be scared to be careful and she was getting the message, but Dominic thought he should lighten it a little in case panic set in. 'The thing is, Tilly, they don't know I'm here and they're not liable to find out unless we place an advert in the paper.'

'That's not the point.' There's a thin line between command and anger and Tilly was about to cross it. 'If I line up TV shows and press interviews with the threat of assassination over our heads nobody will be safe. Innocent people could be killed, I can't be responsible for that.'

'Then we'll find someone who can,' interjected Harry. 'This could be the biggest story of the decade. You've got yer handsome defector who's a talented dancer, yer list of atrocities, and blood on the streets. It could run till next year.'

'We could all be dead next week.' Tilly was challenging Harry's remark, but there was more fear in her voice with every sentence.

'The point is – ' Dominic paused to ensure their complete attention – 'the dice have been thrown, we can't stop it. If I give up now I'd be dead before the plane landed back home, so I've no choice in the matter. Harry's in it for the story: his choice. Tilly, you can still walk away and I wouldn't blame you if you did. This is slightly different from organising a press lunch for a computer company.'

Tilly looked at the two of them, first at Dominic, then at Harry, then back to Dominic again. Her face showed confusion, anxiety, uncertainty. Harry winked at Dominic and stayed silent. 'How much of this does Malcolm know?' she asked flatly.

'He'll know it all once I tell him,' offered Harry.

She looked only at Dominic now, searching for an answer he didn't have, pleading with her eyes for him to tell her this was all a joke, one of Malcolm's irritating little wind-ups. He had to say something, give her some support.

'We can still do the television and radio, we just don't announce it beforehand. It's all the rage now. Salman Rushdie and the Ayatollah were just the start.'

She wasn't convinced. The realisation that men with real guns could attack them at any time from any direction seemed to mesmerise her, blocking communication. She stood up and walked away from them towards the small writing desk at the far end of the room. She stood with her back to them, her head lowered, her hands on the desk top.

'You're right about one thing, Dominic,' she said clearly, with the slightest hint of a chuckle. 'This is certainly not press lunches for computer companies.' She turned back to face them, the brightness, if not the confidence, returning to her face. 'Malcolm's due back any minute. Let's see what he has to say.'

'Bloody Ada shitting bricks!!' was Malcolm's reaction as Harry relayed the morning's events. 'And you're sure you were followed?'

'Positive.'

'In that case we'd better make arrangements.' Malcolm picked up the phone.

'Before you do,' Dominic interrupted, 'I think you should hear how Tilly feels about all this. It's not in her job description to be shot at.' He knew it was presumptuous of him to speak for her, and was prepared to be severely reprimanded, but he felt she'd find it awkward approaching the subject and time was at a premium.

Tilly grabbed the opportunity gladly. 'I feel I'm getting involved with something beyond my scope of knowledge. I don't know how to arrange security at this level and I would hate to make a mistake that cost someone's life. I couldn't live with that.'

Dominic expected Malcolm to dismiss her there and then. He half hoped he would, so she'd be out of danger. Malcolm stared at her for a moment, sipping at his scalding hot coffee. 'Trouble is, my dear Miss Howard, you're already in the plot. You know about this place, the journal, our plans. What I'm saying is if they get hold of you – they can easily check today's story and find the PR – then you know enough to get us all killed.' He grinned at her, shrugging his shoulders in a gesture of inevitability. 'You can quit but you can't leave, so why not join us and let me handle security at home? You find out how Rushdie organises himself publicly and work Dominic the same way.'

'That's my point,' said Tilly. 'Rushdie is news clips and *The Late Show*, which are relatively easy to deal with. They want Dominic on light entertainment shows where there's no security and a live audience.'

'Find a way around it,' returned Malcolm.

Tilly, sitting next to Dominic on the sofa, looked pensive, unsure. Dominic watched her closely as her tenacity and self-confidence slowly resurfaced and restored her command. 'As I can't leave, I may as well work,' she said, with a slight chuckle in her voice, but the attempt at trivial humour was unconvincing.

'First of all I'll have four mobile phones sent over from Hampstead,' said Malcolm imperiously. 'I want everyone contactable all the time.' His expression softened as he looked at Tilly. 'Is Sara still at your place?' he asked.

'Yes,' replied Tilly, relaxing into the sofa.

'Send her and the dozy boyfriend, Peter Smallbrain.'

'Langford,' corrected Harry.

'Yes, him. Send them both to Spain for a couple of weeks. They can stay in the villa at Lloret. Where's the plane, Tilly?'

'Lydd Airport, Kent.'

'Perfect. I want them out privately and I want them out tonight. I think you should move in here, Tilly. They can find your address with a phone call. Pack a case when you pick up Sara. You can have the master bedroom, I'll stay in Hampstead. Harry, I want you to babysit. Use the PC upstairs to write your stories and use the modem to a mailbox; that way it's untraceable. Dominic, get to work on your information. I want it in English and easy to read. The sooner I know what I'm dealing with the faster I can get it placed.'

Malcolm walked over to the sideboard and opened the lower left door, behind which stood a green Chubb safe. Producing a plastic card from his wallet he inserted it in the slot above the matrix combination. He tapped six numbers and moved the safe handle sharply clockwise. From the safe he removed a nickel-plated revolver, a black automatic pistol and two boxes of shells. 'Smith & Wesson .38,' he said, waving the nickel-plated gun in front of him. 'Stop anything with two shots. Beretta 9mm.' He placed the black gun on the sideboard. 'Twelve-round fast-change magazine, fully automatic.' He tossed the silver gun to Harry, who caught it with one hand.

Dominic could feel Tilly's tension as she sat beside him, her shoulders tightening, her eyes darting from weapon to weapon. He placed his hand momentarily over hers. 'We must take precautions,' he said, hoping to relieve at least part of her anxiety. He could see a shiver go through her. She clasped her hands tightly together until her knuckles turned white. She was afraid.

'Dominic's right,' said Harry slipping the gun into his jacket pocket out of sight.

'For God's sake, woman, it's only an empty handgun,' scorned Malcolm, picking up the Beretta and waving it in the air. He pulled the trigger, the gun clicked. Tilly's whole body tensed.

'Guns scare her, Malcolm,' said Dominic with a tinge of anger. 'Please, put it away.'

'All right, all right.' Malcolm replaced the pistol on the sideboard. He walked to Tilly and placed his hands lightly on her shoulder. 'I'm sorry, Ms. Howard. I didn't mean to scare you.'

For the first time Dominic heard a touch of compassion in Malcolm's voice. Not enough to suggest he was a caring human being, but enough to hold out hope that one day he might be.

'Unless there are any questions, I think we can get started.' Malcolm offered his hands to Tilly. 'Off you go. Take the Rolls and use the carphone to call Lydd Airport. You'd also better stop at the *Sun* and pick up Harry's messages as he's playing dodge the editor at the moment.'

Dominic stood up with her. She turned towards him, courage and determination once again evident on her face.

He wanted to hold her, reassure her, calm her. 'Thank you,' she said, looking directly into his eyes. 'And don't get shot till I get back.'

'I worry about her,' said Harry, watching from the window as the white limousine turned into Lower Belgrave Street and out of sight. 'This is not her kind of job. You saw how she reacted to the guns.'

'Don't underestimate Tilly,' Malcolm said, pouring two large whiskies. He was visibly happier now there were only men in the room. 'She'll come to terms with it. She's strong, she likes success and money. This story could make her career and she knows it. Don't let shy Miss Primrose fool you; that's an act, she's tough as nails underneath.'

'She seemed genuinely afraid of the weapons,' said Dominic. 'And earlier she recoiled when I told her about the children's story. I agree with you, Malcolm. She's tough and all you say, but violence on the scale the Securitate can deal out is foreign to her.'

'Then she's in for a quick education,' retorted Malcolm, opening a full-length door at the end of the wall unit and lifting out a double-barrelled shotgun. 'Remington 11–87. Set to scatter, it'll take three people at a time,' he said proudly.

'I thought guns were illegal in this country,' said Dominic, inwardly relieved they could now defend themselves adequately.

'It's all legal. I belong to a gun club. Besides, who's going to ask for a licence if and when those commie pricks show up at the front door?'

'I'd keep the shotgun where it is, put the automatic in Dominic's bedroom and I'll carry the thirty-eight,' said Harry assuming a sergeant's role. 'I also think we should keep the curtains closed at all times.'

'Agreed,' said Malcolm. 'Dominic, start to work right away. Harry, tomorrow's story. I'll make a few calls and gather provisions.'

*

Two hours later Dominic handed Malcolm three sheets of typewritten paper. He'd finally shared his dangerous knowledge. Now if he died there would be others to complete the job. Malcolm read each page carefully; expressions of disgust and disbelief crossed his countenance at regular intervals as he digested the horrors depicted graphically before him. 'Jesus H.,' he whispered to himself as he reread the rape of Svetlana and the murder of the Caprianu family. He photocopied each page three times and handed the originals back to Dominic. 'Come on,' he said.

Dominic followed him downstairs and watched closely as he folded the copies and deposited them in the Chubb safe, in the section previously occupied by the handguns.

Ten

Having left Malcolm's Rolls-Royce parked on a meter in Warren Street, Tilly walked at a steady pace through the pedestrianised square, stopping once to admire the saffron yellow crocus that peppered the grass in random clumps. She breathed in the fragrance of the daffodils that stood to attention around the base of the old sycamore and thought about her new client. She'd known Dominic less than twenty-four hours and already she found herself thinking about him in more than a professional light. Tilly was used to gorgeous-looking men paying attention to her; she had a diary full of disappointing dates whose characters and sense of humour fell far short of their physical attributes. Something about Dominic's presence made her feel uneasy, anticipatory; he gave her butterflies in her stomach, although she was loath to admit it, especially to herself.

The square looked lovely in the spring. Often Tilly would sit on one of the wooden benches and sort out her professional and personal life to the sounds of young boys on BMX bikes and pigeons pecking at morsels of bread. Especially she thought of her oldest sister, Gwen, when she looked at the spring flowers. The carefree days of childhood in the Mendip Hills, the walks to Five Counties Point, the summer picnics on the heathered slopes of Burrington Coombe. And then the awesome pain when

68

Gwen had been killed in a car crash while celebrating her twenty-third birthday. The shock turned her mother into a timid, mouse-like creature who feared the outside world, and her father into an alcoholic with a foul temper. Tilly had left her home a year, to the day, after her sister's death.

Today her thoughts were on much happier things: positive things, challenges, excitement, adventure . . . Dominic Bellescu. It was Dominic who caused her lightness of step as she walked from the square, past the Italian restaurant on the corner of Cleveland Street and right into Fitzroy Mews. She lived in a two-bedroomed penthouse at number 15, a modern block built in the sixties on a site destroyed by one of Hitler's V2 rockets. It didn't have the class of the John Adams architecture that adorned the square, in fact it looked quite ugly by comparison, but it had all mod-cons and as the windows were double glazed the flat was draught-free.

The front door to the building was held open by a large red fire extinguisher. People moving in or out, she thought as she pressed the lift button and waited patiently for the cage to descend.

She emerged from the lift on the third floor still thinking of Dominic and his unruly hair. She must get him to a good hairstylist in the near future: trim him up a bit, a clip around the edges. Taking the key from her purse she moved towards her front door. She noticed it was ajar and froze in her tracks. Someone was in her flat.

Her first thought was to call Mr Anderson, the caretaker; her second to run from the building and ring the police from the public phone across the street. But natural curiosity made her do neither. Gingerly she pushed the door open with her left hand, holding her handbag tightly in her right ready to swing it at the intruder. The hallway was empty and undisturbed except for the half-moon wall table that was now tipped on its side and moved a little further down the hall. The hat-rack, telephone table and plant stand were exactly as she'd left them this morning.

69

'Is anyone there?' she called into the flat in the most commanding voice she could muster. There was no answer. She walked slowly down the corridor, past the guest bathroom and the kitchen. She looked into her office: nothing there was disturbed. At the end of the hall the double doors that led to the living room were ajar. Tilly pushed them fully open and stepped aggressively into the room. Immediately she could see that something had happened here. China ornaments from the fireplace surround lay broken on the floor, her oil portrait of Red Rum hung skew-whiff on the wall. Dark red stains discoloured the bright yellow wall paint. The large, comfortable armchair she sat in to watch television had been tipped over on to its back, taking the side table and lamp with it. A naked foot was protruding from behind the sofa.

'Sara?' she whispered as she moved closer.

As Tilly rounded the sofa she saw Sara's naked body bleeding on the floor. Her large, perfect breasts were peppered with cigarette burns, long, deep cuts ran the full length of her stomach and blood oozed from between her legs. In the centre of her forehead a single, seeping hole marked where a bullet had ended her life.

The nausea Tilly felt was instantaneous. She put her hand to her mouth, her stomach heaved, she vomited through her fingers on to the carpet. Her eyes were mesmerised by the sight before her; she didn't want to look but couldn't look away. Such cruelty, torture, sadism, perpetrated in *her* home, a place, until now, packed with only good memories of loving times. And in that instant she knew it could easily have been her lying in Sara's place. She turned and ran from the room, down the hall and into the bathroom. She knelt in front of the toilet and vomited again. Frightened, sick, and desperately alone, she sobbed uncontrollably for several minutes until she heard the voice of survival scream a primary command from deep within her.

Her brain started to focus on the reality of the situation. She filled the sink with cold water, immersed her face in it and splashed handfuls of water on the back of her neck. She felt for the small guest towel hanging neatly beside the sink and covered her face, taking deep breaths in a valiant attempt to regain her composure. In the mirror she could see no detail, just a white, ashen outline. 'Get yourself together,' she snapped at the mirror. 'You are alive!'

She walked quickly from the bathroom and into her office, picked up the mobile phone and called Chester Square.

Malcolm answered on the third ring. He listened intently as Tilly explained as best she could the events at Fitzroy Mews. He pulled a mobile phone from his jacket pocket, placed it on the table and punched in a number. 'I'll deal with this,' he said, his voice calm, his tone firm.

The mobile emitted a ringing tone that was answered immediately. Malcolm picked it up. 'This is King's Knight, put me through.' He could hear Tilly shouting on the other phone. 'I'm back with you, Tilly. I'll have you out in a few minutes. Tilly! Tilly! . . . I know. Stay calm. You're phoning on the mobile, right? . . . Good. Don't use the phone in the flat, don't even pick it up. Go into the bedroom, pack some clothes. Wear a track suit or something you can move in, bring your passport, chequebook, and plastic. Has the place been trashed? . . . What's missing? . . . OK. And the portable? . . . Thank God. Tilly, listen to me. Move nothing you're not taking with you, just get your things together and wait by the front door. . . . Tilly! You must trust me, just stay calm and be ready in ten minutes, I must go.' He replaced the phone. A muted voice blurbed from the portable. 'You heard? She's at 15 Fitzroy Mews, top flat. Her name's Tilly Howard. When she's gone I want everything cleaned up. . . . Fine, thank you.' He switched off the portable and turned towards Dominic. 'You'd better sit down.'

'What's happened?' Dominic stayed on his feet.

'Sara's dead, shot in the head at Tilly's flat.'

Dominic knew he should feel remorse and sorrow but

his first instinct was for his own survival. 'Did she know we came here last night?'

'No. She didn't know this place existed. I was going to bring her here for a shaft last week. Lucky I didn't.'

'Shaft?' inquired Dominic.

'Sex,' he replied, sparing no further time for explanations. 'They took Tilly's diary, phone book and diskettes. Thank God all her Ramco files are on hard disk. They left the mainframe and didn't find the portable. Fucking Ada, these blokes are quick.'

'And still watching Tilly's place, I'd guess,' offered Dominic immediately.

'Good point.' Malcolm pressed the redial on the portable. Again the call was answered immediately. 'King's Knight. . . . Thank you.' He raised his eyebrows at Dominic as he waited to be connected. 'I need a covered escape for Tilly right away,' he said in a clipped manner. 'I think she's being watched. . . . Ambulance would be fine. . . . Thank you, Goodbye.'

'That's one hell of a service you're with,' said Dominic, hoping for at least a snippet of information.

'It *is* rather handy at times like this,' answered Malcolm, giving absolutely nothing away.

Dominic, Malcolm and Harry waited impatiently for Tilly's arrival. Malcolm explained to Dominic that she would be smuggled out of the building on a stretcher and into a waiting ambulance. He assured Dominic she'd be treated sensitively: the crew were specially trained to cope with this type of emergency. Harry paced nervously around the room sipping from his second glass of whisky.

The men jumped as the clatter of the doorbell resounded through the house. Harry picked up the Smith & Wesson from the coffee table and hurried down the stairs. Moments later he returned, a red-eyed Tilly following closely behind. She sat down on the sofa, her eyes once again filling with tears. 'She'd been burnt with

72

cigarettes all over her breasts,' she spluttered between sobs. 'And there was blood down below, I couldn't look.'

Securitate, thought Dominic; no doubt about it. Their method of interrogation was unique in its cruelty. 'There's nothing you can do now,' he said, trying to reassure her. He felt that words of comfort, no matter how well intentioned, were totally inadequate when a human being was falling apart, especially such a Junoesque creature whose only crime had been her choice of employer. 'Malcolm will take care of everything.'

'How can he?' She was almost shouting, anger driving away her insecurity. 'There's a dead woman in my home.'

As if on cue, Malcolm marched noisily across the room. 'I need your flat keys, Tilly.' His voice sounded cold, devoid of feeling. 'I'm having Sara put on ice until we can work this out.'

'You can't do that!' sobbed Tilly, turning to face him. 'You've got to phone the police. Sara's been murdered, for God's sake!'

Harry headed straight to the wall unit where he poured out a stiff measure of brandy. He handed it to Tilly, his eyes locking on to her as he'd done to Dominic at Wembley and in the pub. 'This is not very pleasant but we have to safeguard our position,' he said. 'If you'll just calm down I have a plan that could get us out of this mess.' Tilly took the glass and the handkerchief Harry offered. His voice became calm and soothing. 'Have a sip or two of the brandy. We all need to have our wits about us now and I value your input, Tilly – and yours, Dominic.'

'Harry wants to make a deal,' said Malcolm, spoiling Harry's timing, punchline and mood.

'Thanks a bundle.' Harry spat the words out, his eyes hard, narrowed. 'Do you want to do this?'

Malcolm flopped into the lounge chair opposite, his expression complacent, his attitude mollified. 'No, Harry. Please.'

Harry refocused on Dominic and Tilly. 'I think we have

enough to do a deal with Ceausescu and stop this nonsense.'

'You can't deal with him, he won't honour it no matter what he says.' Dominic was totally confident.

'No, Dominic. *You* can't deal with him: but *I* can.' Harry sounded smug, self-assured.

'Can you do a deal to get Sara back?' asked Tilly bitterly.

'What I can do is make sure it doesn't happen again.' Harry was about to talk detail. It showed on his face as his eyes sparkled and danced from Tilly to Dominic and back again. 'We have Dominic's list of atrocities that could keep the media fuelled for a month and we have one dead body. Ceausescu has visited the UK, he's done deals here and in the States. He might keep a slavehold on his people, but out in the big bad world he's just another tin-pot dictator with a reputation. State publicly he's a mass murderer, back it up with Dominic's dossier, and all the foreign aid goes away, all his deals are cancelled. He calls off his hounds and we keep the goods in the safe. Dominic gets to stay and, more importantly, work in England free from threats and therefore free from security.' Harry opened his arms; a broad smile lit his face. 'And we all make lots of money and retire to the South of France.'

'What about Sara?' Tilly was unimpressed with Harry's attempt at humour. 'Are we supposed to forget they've killed a woman in cold blood?'

'There's nothing we can do for Sara now except use her death to ensure our safety. I know it's not legally, ethically or morally right, but if we don't stop this now we'll all be looking behind us for the rest of our shortened lives. Those hoods won't stop till they get us all. No, we have to deal or run – and I'm too old and too fat to run.'

'I compiled that list to expose Ceausescu, not to bargain our lives with,' said Dominic flatly. 'If we deal, my whole defection has been in vain.' He understood their reasoning but couldn't agree. If his list stayed in a wall safe his

74

parents would have died for nothing and Ceausescu would remain untouched.

'Is it important to you that Ceausescu is exposed or that it's *you* who exposes him?' asked Harry.

'That he's exposed,' answered Dominic immediately. 'It doesn't matter who does it.'

'Correct!' Harry continued with contagious excitement. 'The Romanians will think this whole thing is put to bed, but that's far from it. From tomorrow morning I'll have five top investigators checking your list. Within a month, maybe two, we'll have our own confirmations and we'll go with the stories independently. Ceausescu's hurt and none of it is your fault.' He beamed his broadest smile at Dominic. 'Now, do you have a number for Stenoza or must I use Directory Enquiries?'

On the surface it made sense, but Dominic was reluctant to agree without more proof that Harry's plan was viable. 'How can you investigate what's been expertly covered up?'

'Tourism,' replied Harry confidently. 'We sent four reporters in that way before Ceausescu's visit here; they didn't find anything because they didn't know where to look. With the agents we now have and your record of place, time and detail, we're bound to get a result.'

'If you make a deal he'll be suspicious of anything like that for months if not years. Your team will end up as dead as Sara.' Dominic felt Tilly recoil.

'O ye of little faith.' Harry turned his bulk half left. 'Tell him, Malcolm.'

'We have a network inside Eastern Europe bigger than British Intelligence and the CIA combined.' Malcolm took a sip of whisky to allow time for the statement to register. 'I can get any information I need as long as I know where to look. Your list is as accurate as an Ordnance Survey map, so we'll have no trouble verifying the stories. I probably would have checked them before going to print anyway. Harry needs as much protection as you.' He smiled at his friend. 'I agree with Harry. Let's make the peace, make Dominic a star, make a lot of money and make Ceausescu pay properly a few months down the line.' He sat back into the chair thoroughly pleased with his use of the English language.

Tilly patted her eyes gently with Harry's handkerchief. 'I thought I was working for a computer company,' she said, taking her first drink of the brandy and slowly standing up. 'My first reaction to all of this, gentlemen, is disgust. I seem to be the only one surprised by these events.' She looked straight at Malcolm. 'You said you wanted a few glamour shots for the Sunday papers. A night's work, you said. Now I find you've got a network of spies, can pervert the course of justice at will, and most likely have a hand in several covert operations which I would be expected to explain away through ignorance. You've compromised me professionally and if I could walk away from you this instant, I would. But as I seem to have a dead body in my flat, and nowhere to go, I'll go along with making a deal. But when this is over, Malcolm, you can find yourself another press officer.'

'Fair enough,' said Malcolm, not fazed in the slightest by Tilly's outburst. 'But it ain't over yet. In fact, it's just beginning. So if you'd be kind enough to give me your flat keys I'll sort that mess out first.' Tilly produced three keys on a Garfield key-ring from her track-suit pocket and threw them across the room at Malcolm, who caught them easily.

'Thank you. Come on, Harry, we have work to do.' He stopped in the doorway, turned around and locked his gaze on to Dominic. 'I don't have to tell you to stay put, do I?' Dominic shook his head. 'Have you given Harry your Bucharest numbers?'

'No.'

'Then please do so right away.' He left the room, continuing to shout from the hall, 'You stay put too, Tilly. I don't want either of you outside till we get back.'

Dominic took a small brown address book from his jacket pocket. It contained all his personal information as well as private phone numbers, and he was reluctant to give it up, even to Harry; it was like giving away his security blanket.

Harry took the book gently from Dominic's hand. 'Gawd bless you, son,' he said knowingly, then turned and followed Malcolm.

'Where are they going?' Dominic asked Tilly as he heard the front door slam.

'To Hampstead. He can talk to the world from his computer room.'

'Couldn't they do that from here?'

'They could, although I suspect everything's traceable through this set-up. Anyway, I think I prefer them to play their games elsewhere.' She smiled bravely. 'Besides, I'm in great need of a cup of tea.'

Tilly looked pensively at Dominic as she placed two tea-bags in the brown china pot. 'Do you think I was foolish to tell Malcolm I'm leaving?'

That was the last question Dominic had expected. Tilly struck him as a person who didn't seek career advice, who knew what she was doing a hundred per cent of the time. Either the shock of the day's events had prompted the need to communicate or she'd blasted away at Malcolm without thinking and now wanted confirmation.

'I think you were brave and honest with him. He has compromised you – but I'll bet he thinks twice before holding back the truth in future.'

'I won't be here in the future. I'm worried about him giving me up as part of some wacky deal with your friend Ceausescu.'

Dominic swivelled on the kitchen stool and faced her. 'Firstly, Ceausescu is not my friend. Secondly, for all Malcolm's faults I don't believe he's the kind of man who would sell his colleagues. Thirdly, there's no logical reason, and fourthly, if he did I'd kill him.'

'I believe you would,' she said, pouring the boiling water with great care. 'I fancy tea in the Jacuzzi. I need to relax.'

She scanned his face looking for something only she

would recognise. Her stare unnerved Dominic as it had at the club. He felt awkward, unsure of himself.

'Did you bring much with you?' he asked, hoping to open a new subject of conversation.

'Two suitcases. They're in the entrance hall,' she replied. 'I'd appreciate it if you'd carry them up to the bedroom.'

As he deposited the smallest case on the blue-quilted double bed he inspected the room with great interest. The designer from down the road had taste. Royal blue, thick-pile carpet covered the room. The walls were expertly stubble-painted in two shades of blue, and the mustard curtains had a gold-trim pelmet and sash. Two dark oak wardrobes covered most of the wall opposite the windows, with a matching tallboy and dresser under an ornately framed mirror to the left of the door.

Dominic walked through to the *ensuite* bathroom which was covered floor to ceiling with slabs of beige-grained marble. Twin sinks, a toilet, a bidet and a bath/shower unit, all in gleaming white enamel with gold fittings were spaced graciously across two walls. Full-length, mirrored, sliding doors occupied half of the remaining two walls, and in the last corner, circled by three marble steps, stood a wooden-sided Jacuzzi, six feet in diameter and filled with heated, pine-scented water. Dominic undressed to his shorts, climbed in and sat on the wooden seat that circled the inside of the tub; the water came to armpit level.

'I could get used to this,' said a small voice behind him. 'That tub looks heavenly.'

He turned to see Tilly unzip her track-suit top. As she bent down to remove her trainers the fullness of her breasts became apparent to him for the first time. She wore a black, one-piece bathing suit that focused Dominic's attention as she slipped into the water with ease. This was no time to think of sex. Dominic closed his eyes and thought of Mrs Ceausescu as a last resort. It worked.

Tilly sat directly opposite him, her arms stretched along

the edge of the tub. 'Turn on the bubbles,' she said, pointing to a chrome button near his right hand.

A gurgling sound emanated from under the seat for about two seconds before the jets started to blow. 'This is great,' he shouted, more from excitement than the need to be heard. 'How long can we stay in?'

'About twenty minutes maximum. Is this your first time?'

'I'm a Jacuzzi virgin,' he said, moving so that the jet hit the centre of his back. 'I'm having my full twenty minutes, not a second less.'

Tilly smiled. 'And so you shall, dear boy.' She glanced at the ceiling in a gesture of mock disgust. 'I'm sorry, that's the best Noël Coward impression I can do.'

'As in *Private Lives*?'

'You've seen it?' It was Tilly's turn to be surprised.

'No, but I've read it,' answered Dominic proudly.

She looked at him quizzically, her head to one side. 'How did you get a copy of *Private Lives*?'

'An old Muslim merchant named Taric gave it to me the month after I'd won the championship. He visited the gymnasium one morning, introduced himself, handed me a neat brown paper parcel and left. Inside was a paperback copy of the play and a letter saying he'd seen my interview on television where I'd said my hobby was English fiction and he felt I should have this, as his time was now spent reading the 114 suras of the Koran.'

'Did you get most of your books that way?'

'That was the only one. Most of them came from other students of English who'd pass them on or as payment for pictures. My people have a craving for photographs, especially in junior echelons of government. They want a picture of themselves with someone even remotely famous to stand framed on their two square feet of desk, and they were willing to barter. One clerk from the Ministry of the Interior offered a Tolkien Bestiary, *Led Zeppelin: A Visual Documentary*, Thomas Harris's *Red Dragon* and Ira

Levin's *Boys from Brazil* all in exchange for a picture with him and his family.'

'Incredible. Which book did you like best?'

'All of them, for different reasons.'

Tilly smiled and let her legs drift upwards with the bubbles. She kicked Dominic playfully on the chest. 'Tell me.'

'The Tolkien book was more useful than interesting – a dictionary of Middle Earth with pictures. The Led Zeppelin I loved: it was a twelve-year diary of a rock band. Dominic stood up and placed his feet either side of the large well-jet. 'D'you know, I've never heard their music.'

Tilly's expression changed; the horror of the afternoon was flashing across her memory again. She launched herself gently from the side of the tub and drifted slowly across the few feet that separated them. 'Any chance of a hug?' she asked, as if they'd been lovers for years.

'Every chance,' he replied, happily accepting her in his arms. Her head rested on his shoulder and he inhaled the almond fragrance of her hair. Her body fitted perfectly; her wet shoulders glistened almost olive in the light reflected from the water. He moved his hands slowly up and down her spine, massaging each vertebra in turn. She folded into him, her breasts flattening against his chest, and he placed a hand on each shoulder blade. As he pressed them down, then away from the spine, her body went limp. He felt a clunk as her back slotted into place.

'Oh thank you,' she whispered in his ear. 'That's been out for days.'

She slid her hands around his waist and locked them together behind him. They both knew they would kiss. Their faces drifted slightly apart, both seeing the other in close-up for the first time. Dominic cupped her face in his hands and pressed his lips gently against hers; then pulled away, as did she, just a fraction. They folded into each other, their bodies moulded by the Jacuzzi jets, their kiss strong, soft, blending their senses, filling their need in one simple act of physical contact.

They heard the front door slam, and separated immediately. Tilly put her hand to her mouth, cutting her laugh to a chuckle. 'This is silly,' she said. 'We're adults.'

'Probably better,' he replied. 'They'd tease us unmercifully.'

'Agreed.' Her impish smile returned. Dominic hoped she'd never find out what that smile did to him, for there she'd find his Achilles' heel. Her voice dispersed his mini-daydream: 'I wonder if there's a bathrobe in here.'

Dominic stepped from the tub, down the marble steps and walked across the floor. He'd always thought of marble as cold and unfriendly, so expected cold slabs; the underfloor heating fooled him completely. He slid open the glass-panelled door. Six white towelling robes hung in a row above a dozen fluffy white bath towels. He took the first robe and held it open for Tilly. She glided down the three steps, her wet bathing suit clinging to her skin like oil paint in the rain.

She slipped both arms into the warm towelling then turned to face him, placing the lightest of kisses just below his right ear. 'Have you any idea how much I adore good manners?' she whispered.

'Anybody up there!' came the shout from two floors down.

Dominic fastened a towel around his waist and slipped on a robe before walking through the bedroom to the hall. 'We're up here. In the jacuzzi!' he shouted, hoping not too much of the disappointment he felt was evident in his voice.

'Come down when you're dressed.' It was Harry's voice. 'No hurry, but hurry up, if you know what I mean.'

'Five minutes.' Dominic stepped back into the bedroom and shut the door. Tilly was digging in a suitcase pulling out belts, make-up bags, hair brushes and finally a small laptop computer which she placed next to the phone on the dressing table. 'Before you go, Dominic, could you be Mr Wonderful one more time and put my other suitcase in the wardrobe.' He did as requested. 'Bless you,' she said. 'I've put your clothes on the bed. See you downstairs in five minutes.'

'I think I'll wear something else,' he said smugly, enjoying the luxury of domestic staff for the first time in his life.

'It won't take you long to get the hang of this,' she teased as he left the room and the clothes.

Half of Dominic wanted to confront Malcolm and Harry, to demand the truth, there and then. The other half didn't want to know, in case the answer shattered his dreams of freedom, hot tubs and Tilly. He walked slowly up to the main floor, hoping the news would be good but fearing the worst. He heard Tilly descending the stairs above him and waited for her in the hallway. She looked so tough and businesslike in her black Chanel wool suit, white shirt and black tie. A matching Chanel clasp held a thick, black leather belt around her waist. She squeezed his arm as she passed in brief acknowledgement of their new relationship. 'Let's do it,' she said, a professional coolness returning to her voice.

Harry greeted them warmly, placing a rare kiss on Tilly's cheek and shaking Dominic firmly by the hand. 'Right, you two, we have good news.'

Dominic looked at Tilly, then Harry. 'Tell us, please.'

'Stenoza's a real toerag,' said Malcolm disgustedly. 'That bastard deserves to be boiled in oil.'

Dominic knew Malcolm had spoken to the right man. The General created the same impression on everyone. Obnoxious, rude, satanic, cruel, wicked, diabolical: he'd heard all those descriptions before. Toerag was new, but it fitted perfectly.

'I set the deal as we discussed,' continued Malcolm. 'I don't trust the son of a bitch but he knows he has no choice. As long as we hold the Dominic file he's got to play our game.'

'What about Sara?' asked Tilly.

'We need to change our story on that one,' answered

Harry, his voice ebullient with victory. 'We've moved her to her flat in Islington. Robbery and rape will be the motive, her boyfriend will find her in a few hours and report it to the police, hopefully in time for the early editions. I've already written the story.'

'What about my connection?' asked Dominic.

'There isn't one,' chipped in Malcolm. 'You left her at midnight Saturday and came here with us.' He looked briefly at Tilly. 'I think the quote should be something like: "I'm shocked at such horrible news. I can only hope the police catch this maniac before he strikes again" – that sort of thing.' Tilly nodded in agreement. 'We tell the truth about Dominic,' said Malcolm with a smirk. 'Makes a change in this little scenario.'

'You'd better be sure Stenoza's called off his hounds before you give this location away,' said Dominic, watching concern return to Tilly's face.

Malcolm stood up, almost to attention. 'Stenoza knows if anything happens to you, whether it's his fault or not, the papers get published. If you see any of his goons it'll be to protect you, not to do you in.'

The sound of the doorbell clattered through the house again. 'I'll go,' said Harry, touching his jacket pocket where he'd concealed the Smith & Wesson.

Tenseness filled the room as they waited for Harry's return. Tilly tugged at her earlobe, Malcolm lit a large Cuban cigar and Dominic listened for any sign of trouble. He heard the door open, muffled conversation and then the door slam shut. Harry shuffled back up the stairs and into the room. He handed Tilly a large brown envelope before flopping lackadaisically on to the sofa. 'Your poof photographer said to give you this.'

'Tolerance,' scolded Tilly. 'You seem to have a distinct lack where homosexuals are concerned.'

'Nonsense!' Harry looked at Malcolm for support but found none. 'It's just that Ginger gets right up my hooter. Always "Ducky" and "Sweetheart" – drives me up the wall.'

'Are those Dominic?' asked Malcolm, not wishing to spend another second badmouthing someone he considered a freak of nature and a waste of space.

Tilly emptied five eight-by-ten black and white photos and two sheets of proofs on to the coffee table. Malcolm picked up the proof sheet.

'You'll need a couple of these for the passport,' he said, studying them carefully. 'You take a good picture, Dominic,' he conceded. 'Can you get your television people on line for next week?' he asked Tilly.

'Trying to keep them away will be a problem after tomorrow's papers.' Tilly turned to Harry: 'Have you a transcript of your story?'

'It's on the machine upstairs. I'll print you a copy.'

Tilly chose a photograph and placed it to one side. 'Just tell me how Dominic features.'

'I've headlined with PAGE THREE BEAUTY BRUTALLY BATTERED IN BOYFRIEND'S BEDROOM. I've said her last public appearance was at the Hippodrome on Saturday night where she'd danced with Romanian gymnast Dominic Bellescu. That's all I've said. The rest is her personal details and a "find the Islington rapist before he strikes again" ending. I can add a quote from Dominic, if you like. I've not sent it yet.'

Tilly showed Dominic the photograph. 'I think this one. You have a nice smile and your hair looks right.' She stood in front of him, turning her back on Harry and Malcolm. For an instant her eyes softened as she looked into his face. 'I'll make a few phone calls and see who wants you first.' She turned to Harry. 'I think – "I only danced with her for a few minutes. She seemed a lovely person. I'm horrified at what's happened. I came to England to escape this sort of thing." She thought for a second. 'That should do it.'

'I don't think Dominic should comment on Ceausescu; not yet, anyway,' said Malcolm, scooping his whisky glass from the table.

'Point taken,' said Tilly, walking towards the door. 'Cut

the last piece, Harry. End on "horrified at what's happened." ' She beamed a smile at everyone. 'I'll be in the office if anyone's making coffee.'

'Some woman,' sighed Harry as the door of the upstairs office closed quietly. 'If I were your age, Dominic, I'd be there like a bullet.'

'I have a girlfriend in Romania,' said Dominic as convincingly as he could.

'You said she was a spy,' said Harry, picking through the remaining photos and selecting the only full-length picture. 'Make up your mind, my son.' He held the photograph so they could both see it. 'I'll use this for my piece. Nice movement – doesn't looked posed.'

'Don't send the boy goose-chasing,' interjected Malcolm. 'Tilly's an ice maiden. Nobody's popped her cork in all the time I've known her. She's into designer clothes and US dollars. I bet she's got a Gucci vibrator.' Both men laughed raucously; Dominic pretended not to understand. Malcolm seemed more at ease in the company of men, or at least with Harry. There was a tenseness about him when Tilly was around. He'd been fine in Sara's company, perhaps because she'd posed no threat to his authority, but Tilly was a different matter. She could, and did, stand up to him. Dominic suspected that Malcolm had tried hard to suppress and perhaps even seduce her when they'd first met and, having no joy, decided she was a professional virgin and therefore unworthy of inclusion in his inner circle, except on matters of public relations in which she excelled beyond his wildest dreams.

'Nadia helped me get to England,' Dominic continued, not wanting to drop the subject until he'd made his point. 'I think I could persuade her to leave Romania once I'm established here. She could bring many more stories with her.'

'That'll be months from now,' said Malcolm dismissively. 'Right, now I've a game plan to run by you. See what you think of this.' He took a long drag on his cigar, letting the smoke escape and pollute the air around his head.

'Depending on what Tilly lines up, we should start a media awareness job on you tomorrow. I could get you a British passport through my contacts at the Foreign Office but I think you should go to Petty France and apply in the normal way. It's a great photo opportunity and I'll grease the cogs so there'll be no hold-ups. I'll also arrange for you to have some credit cards and a bank account.'

'I have no money,' laughed Dominic, slightly embarrassed.

Malcolm took a wodge of £20 notes from his wallet and placed them on the table. 'You have now,' he said.

Dominic was about to protest vehemently at his polemical gesture but Malcolm sensed rejection and continued unabated.

'You'll earn five times that amount each day by the time we're finished with you. Look at it as an advance. I'll keep a record if you wish and you can pay me back.' He counted the notes in front of him. 'Three hundred and forty pounds,' he said arrogantly. 'Now, long term, I've got a plan that could make us all an indecent amount of dosh.' He stood up, cigar in one hand, glass of whisky in the other. Dominic could tell from his flurried expression that whatever was coming next would be important. 'There's a building in the Strand that's up for sale. It's called the Lyceum and it would make the best club in the Western hemisphere. Buying and conversion will cost about three million. You're a natural dancer, Dominic. You're also good-looking and about to become a media favourite. With you dancing twice a night the people, especially women, will flock in; we'll make our money back within a year. What do you say, Dominic? Your own club, a thousand a week and 20 per cent of the profit.'

The suddenness of his offer triggered Dominic's caution; the amount triggered his greed. To earn £1,000 a week for doing what he loved seemed absurd. To receive 20 per cent of the profit without investing a penny seemed foolish on Malcolm's part and therefore totally out of character. 'Are you sure you want to pay me that much? I might be a flop, a two-week wonder.'

Malcolm sat down and looked at Harry, who lounged quietly next to him sipping his whisky. Harry took over the conversation once it was clear that Malcolm had finished. 'Dominic,' he began in a tone of voice fit for an errant child, 'You've got to look at the wider spectrum. Malcolm's too modest to say, but three million is a drop in the bucket compared to Ramco's profitability. It's a tax deduction, a dabble into show business, it's less than he invested in the British film industry last year.'

Dominic knew he should be impressed but he felt only worry. The phone on the writing desk chirped into action. Malcolm answered it and listened intently for at least half a minute before speaking. 'Fine,' he said. 'Very good indeed. Is Tilly's flat cleaned up? . . . Good.' He hung up without saying goodbye or exchanging any sort of pleasantry, and his face was imperious. 'We have a result, gentlemen. The police have found Sara and are convinced she died in her flat. Harry, you can file your story now.'

'They might convince forensic on the scene but when they get her body to the lab they'll know she was killed elsewhere,' announced Dominic with conviction.

'I have one of my doctors working on it,' replied Malcolm, his arrogance again manifest in a dismissive wave of his hand. 'The mutilation is not being reported, out of respect for the family and to give the police a filter for the prank calls they're bound to get. My doctor will record death from a single bullet to the head following a sexual assault; nothing else. The CID are saying robbery was the prime motive, probably drug related. Sara disturbed him, or them, resulting in her murder. A clean, tight story we can all live with.'

Dominic was tempted to point out that the notable exception to the 'story we could all live with' was the unfortunate Sara, but it seemed futile to say so to someone who seemed devoid of sympathy. A change of subject was the only way to keep his temper. 'What's the plan for the rest of today?' he asked, directing his question at Harry.

'I'm going upstairs to fax my story in, then I'm going to the Dog & Duck and get seriously pissed.' He lifted his half-empty glass in salute and looked at Malcolm with bacchanalian eyes. 'Are you joining me, Mr Barrett?'

'Not tonight, me old mucker. Tonight I'm taking the old girl for a Chinese at Mister Kai's, she loves all that Peking rubbish. I'd just as soon have fish and chips from Lisson Grove, but your mum's your mum and you gotta make 'em happy otherwise they give you more rabbit than Sainsbury.'

There was a fleeting tone of compassion in Malcolm's voice that even his offhand delivery couldn't disguise. 'Anyway, I've got to get her to sign the annual report and if she's eating her favourite nosh she's unlikely to ask too many questions,' he said, his familiar arrogance returning.

'Why don't you take Tilly out to dinner?' inquired Harry. 'Go spend some money. Enjoy yourself.'

The thought of escape, even from such luxurious surroundings, filled Dominic with anticipation. He wanted to walk the streets of London and drink in the atmosphere of the great city. To be with Tilly would ice the cake. Although he was sure Malcolm remained unaware of the chemistry between himself and Tilly, he was equally sure Harry had noticed at the Hippodrome and had been keeping score from that moment. His suggestion, made in friendship, was very much appreciated. Dominic still felt awkward about making his own plans in the middle of Malcolm's military manoeuvres. 'What do you think, Captain?' he asked, looking squarely into Malcolm's face. 'Is it safe to go out?'

Malcolm surveyed both men, trying to evaluate any covert plan in operation between them. 'I suppose it's safe if you stay local,' he said. 'Just stay away from the West End and the trendy gaffs where the paparazzi hang out. I don't want some greasy git with a long lens dictating our story.' He pulled a small black phone from his jacket pocket and placed it on the table. 'Take this with you everywhere – and I mean everywhere. Me and Harry's numbers are in memory one and two. If anything happens, anything at all, you press "memory number one" followed by "send" and I'll sort you out. Got that?'

'Perfectly.'

Harry winked at Dominic over the half-moon spectacles which he wore to study the proof sheet. 'I've got to go,' he said, pushing himself to his feet and returning his glasses to their case. 'Time and *Sun* editors wait for no man.' He offered Dominic his hand. 'It's been quite a day, Dominic. Have a pleasant evening. I'll see you tomorrow.' He turned to Malcolm. 'I'll call you around midnight with the first editions.'

Malcolm gathered a few sheets of graph paper from the desk and placed them in his briefcase. 'I'm going too; I'm late as it is.' As he passed Dominic he stopped and placed his hand on the Romanian's shoulder. 'Think about what I offered. You could be a very rich man if you play your cards right.'

Dominic left the smoke-filled drawing room for the fresh air of the downstairs garden. He carried one of the kitchen chairs outside and sat with his back to the patio door watching the pond carefully for signs of fish. The tranquillity allowed him to think clearly, to start deciphering the real reasons behind Malcolm's apparent generosity. Maybe it was the years of mistrust and betrayal he'd endured in Romania that wouldn't allow him to accept the offer at face value. To be philanthropic towards your fellow man is to be admired, but somehow, although Malcolm's motive of the advancement of capitalism was always in plain view, Dominic had a nagging feeling there was a hidden agenda just inches under the surface. Why would he not want his mother to ask questions about Ramco? Were millions of pounds whizzing around the world financing arms, drugs, governments? Was his father in with him? Ceausescu, Saddam Hussein, in fact most dictators used nepotism as a means of staying in power.

How many more Barretts were seeded in positions of influence? A visit to Hampstead was a priority. He must see this room that could talk to the world and find out more about King's Knight and the rest of the human chess set.

On second thoughts, the money seemed more reasonable. Maybe it would cost that amount to maintain this lifestyle. He'd know more tonight when he paid for dinner.

Two fish broke the surface of the water; the ripples they left expanded then disappeared at the pond's edge. Dominic thought of Nadia lounging in a hayloft near the airforce base at Timisoara. After he'd given an exhibition at the base in the afternoon they'd sneaked off to a nearby farm around four o'clock for a couple of hours' rest and relaxation. They'd walked about half a mile when the heavens opened. The hayloft was a hundred yards away; by the time they got inside they were soaked. Dominic remembered lying naked in that warm, enveloping hay, the rain cascading like a waterfall off the circular roof, Nadia rubbing his bruised arm with arnica oil: it was a prime moment in his life. At this moment he missed her very much. He hoped she was coping and had not been made the scapegoat for his defection by those bastards in Bucharest.

'Is this a private party?' Tilly rested her hand lightly on his shoulder.

Dominic had decided to tell this lady the truth at all times. It was a spontaneous thought, a caveat of reality. After years of subtle whoring he wanted truth or nothing. 'I was thinking of Nadia. I hope she's all right.'

'Do you love her very much?' There was no jealousy in her voice, just concern.

'I never loved her,' he said, not at all sure his honesty could withstand her probing. 'I was very fond of her and I'd hate to see her hurt, but she's a government spy first and my lover second. Falling in love with your enemy is a biblical aspiration not a modern-day reality.'

She stood behind him gently massaging his shoulders,

as Nadia had done so many times in Bucharest. 'Do you want to contact her? If you have a number I'm sure we could get through.'

'I'd rather take you to dinner,' he answered quickly, swinging his hand around and touching her behind the knee. He wanted to talk to Nadia and make sure she was safe: he just didn't have the courage to do it in front of Tilly. Total honesty would have to wait. 'We're allowed out as long as we don't get photographed.'

'I know, and I'm starving.' She moved around in front of him and cupped his face gently in her hands. 'I'm going to shower and change. Do you like fish?'

'I love it.'

'There's a fabulous restaurant ten minutes away that serves the best scollops in the universe. Let's meet in the drawing room in half an hour and we'll go from there.' Her hands slid off his face and came together, her fingertips touching her mouth, as if in prayer. 'If you decide to phone Romania the code for Bucharest from here is 010 40 – .' She stepped back into the house immediately, saving Dominic the embarrassment of answering.

He didn't phone. Instead he showered, all the time thinking of Tilly standing naked in her shower three floors above. He fantasised about making love to her, entering her while the soothing water lubricated their bodies, holding her tightly against the hard tiles as they reached climax, and rubbing away her daily stress as they drifted soporifically in the afterglow.

He should have phoned Nadia. He was ashamed of himself for not doing so, but *this* was his new life and he didn't want anything to spoil his chances – no past loves, no old memories, no Romanians, period. Tilly was brand new and the excitement of infatuation ruled his thoughts. Whether or not they consummated their relationship seemed irrelevant; if they never saw each other again, the memories of his first two days in the West would be inexorably linked to Ms Wilhelmina Howard.

Eleven

Stenoza's Town House, Bucharest

General Stenoza lived in opulent style. His newly decorated and lavishly furnished six-bedroom house in the centre of Bucharest boasted several major works of art pilfered from deceased political opponents, classic French furniture bought with stolen money from the world's leading auction houses, and the latest video and television equipment donated by hopeful American companies in search of lucrative defence contracts.

He sat on a red and gold chair as a young blonde girl dressed only in black stockings knelt in front of him, her mouth hesitantly caressing his vast stomach, her nervous hands slowly masturbating him.

'Suck it,' he said loudly, pushing her head between his legs. 'If I'd wanted my belly licked I'd get the fucking dogs to do it.' He grunted; his lips curled back, his teeth gnashed together. He grabbed his pistol grip but kept the gun holstered. The red phone beside him rang twice. 'Stenoza!' he yelled into the mouthpiece.

'Severin here, sir. We've eliminated the girl.'

'Tell me about it, you dumb asshole!' Stenoza pulled harshly at the girl's hair, twisting her off his phallus and depositing her on the floor beside him. 'I've had to make a fucking deal to keep them from dumping it on our doorstep because you didn't have the common sense to dump the bitch in the river instead of leaving her in Barrett's secretary's home.'

'Are we dealing with Malcolm Barrett?' Severin sounded genuinely surprised.

'We are.' Stenoza slapped the girl sharply across the face and pointed to the door. She sprang to her feet and ran across the room, pleased to be free from his clutches, free to seek the sanctuary of the toilet where she could take the numbing cocaine Stenoza had given her earlier. 'And what's more,' he continued when she had left, 'Belle-scu's got documentation on some of our party nights and they're threatening to go public unless we leave them alone.'

There was a moment's silence from Severin, then he said, 'We must find out what and where and steal it back.'

'Not we. You, son of a bitch.' Stenoza slapped his hand on the chair arm. 'You! *You* get it back! And quickly! I want that Brasov bouncer dead within the week and I want his stories fucking shredded. Is that crystal fucking clear?!'

'Yes sir.'

'Then do it!' Stenoza slammed the phone down and collapsed into the chair, angry, frustrated, bordering on fury. 'Popescu!' he yelled. 'Get the fuck in here!' His hands gripped the chair arm, his knuckles white.

Twelve

Tilly looked stunning as she joined Dominic in the drawing room exactly half an hour after leaving him in the perfumed garden. She wore a red, high-necked dress with narrow pleats from waist to knee-length hem, black tights and plain black, low-heeled shoes.

'Can you make a dry Martini?' she asked, placing a kiss lightly on his cheek. 'I would really like a good dry Martini tonight.' She held on to him as he tried to leave her embrace. 'Why don't you drink alcohol?'

'I've never really thought about it,' he replied with guiltless honesty. 'All my coaches said not to touch it and the price in Romania of anything decent was far beyond my means.'

'I shall take it upon myself to educate you in the finer points of social drinking, starting now.'

'Does that mean I'm getting drunk tonight?'

'Not at all!' Her voice mocked him, daring him to cross the line. 'Tonight you learn how to make a dry Martini and pay the restaurant bill.' She hooked his arm and steered him towards the wall unit. 'First you get a glass and add three ice cubes.' He did as he was told. 'Secondly you ask the lady what type of Martini she'd like.'

Dominic bowed before her. 'What type of Martini would Madam like?'

'Gin please, very dry.' She curtsied.

'What does that mean, dry? All I see is wet.'

Her eyes stayed firmly fixed on Dominic as she removed the glass from his grip and placed it on the sideboard. 'Pour in enough gin to cover the ice cubes,' she said. Her eyes widened and narrowed in the space of the sentence. 'Remove the top of the Martini bottle and fill the cap. Tip capful into drink and – presto, very dry Martini.' She lifted the drink and sipped. 'Excellent!' She threw back her head and laughed. 'I think you should try some. A chef should sample his food.'

Dominic took the glass from her hand and took his first sip of alcohol. It tasted juniper sweet with a touch of almond. 'Not for me,' he said, handing back the glass. 'Maybe I'll try some food with wine.'

'Try some wine with the food,' corrected Tilly. They smiled knowingly at each other.

He helped her on with her coat, opened the front door and set the alarm as per Malcolm's instructions. Tilly tucked her arm in his as they turned left out of the square into Lower Belgrave Street.

As they walked in the brisk evening air Dominic felt the warmth of his parents. He had always thought of them as a single spirit. Maybe because they'd died together and in grieving for them both he'd found a oneness, or maybe because they *were* together spiritually. Whatever, the feeling he received from them was unmistakable: a warm glow inside that radiated contentment, a belief in love, a captured moment. He thought of them swinging him between them on the beach at Constanta. He was four years old and wanted to swing, climb, jump, run: anything except walk in a straight line.

'Tell me about your mother and father,' said Tilly, squeezing his arm gently.

Some of the astonishment he felt filtered through to his face. Tilly smiled.

'Sometimes I seem to know what you're thinking. Does that frighten you?' she asked.

'You're damn right it does!' Honesty through shock:

there was nothing he could do to stop it. 'Can you do this with everyone?' he blurted out, wanting her to say yes, if only for his own protection.

'Very few, and then only after knowing them a long time. With you, since the Hippodrome, from the first moment. It scares me a little too.'

They stopped, for the red light at Buckingham Palace Road. She looked straight ahead, her eyes fixed on the pedestrian sign across the road. Finally she turned to face him, her eyes reflecting diamonds through a tiny tear. She hugged him around the waist, closed her eyes and pecked his chin with her lips. 'I sometimes cry when I'm happy. Can you live with that?'

'Do I have a choice?'

'Not really.' She looked across the road again. 'Light's green.'

Walking with her gave Dominic a feeling of belonging, the safeness he needed. Outwardly he gave the impression of harmony and control but inwardly he was desperate for a sympathetic soul. Coach Damchuk had come closer than anyone to filling that void over the last few years. Dominic missed his counsel and his humour and thought how good he and Harry Cassini would be for each other. Harry would knock the communist stuffing out of the coach and Damchuk would curb Harry's drinking.

Tilly stopped outside a glass-panelled wooden door. 'Here we are. Overtons. The home of the grilled scollop.'

The building looked like a house. They climbed floral-carpeted stairs and were greeted at the top by a man speaking French.

'*Bonjour* Madam, Monsieur. *Pour deux? S'il vous plaît.*'

'*Merci*,' replied Tilly quickly, in professional style.

This *was* a house, converted many years ago. In a narrow hallway two tables were set in window alcoves, three small rooms led off to the left and at the end what had been the living room accommodated seven tables and a wall-sized, ornately framed mirror.

'*Vos pardessus, s'il vous plaît.*' The little balding man

took their coats. '*S'il vous plaît*,' he said again, gesturing for them to sit.

'*Merci*,' Dominic replied before Tilly could react. She smiled at him. He raised his eyebrows in sweet victory. Manners were the game; one-nil to the new boy. Dominic spoke perfect French but he chose to hide it from Tilly for a few more moments: not to gain some sort of advantage, but as a lover's ploy. He would admit it when her laughter was guaranteed, laughter she would never forget.

'May I order for us?' she asked, rendering Dominic helpless with her smile.

'Of course,' he replied. 'I'm in your hands.'

'Excuse me,' she said. 'Could we order right away, please?'

'Immediately,' said the parting *maître d'* without the slightest trace of a French accent.

'He's from north London,' Tilly whispered across the table. 'I'll bet that opening gambit is the only French he knows.'

Dominic smiled. '*Certainement, ma chérie. Probablement, il n'est jamais allé plus au sud d' Dover*,' he said in a faultless accent.

There was a second of silence before Tilly's laughter filled the room. Wonderful, spacious laughter that made Dominic feel proud of his timing and happy for her joy.

Je t'aime, she thought fleetingly, not daring to translate her feelings.

A tall, gangly man with a tie that stopped six inches from his belt crossed the room in four giant strides. Tilly looked serenely at him, disarming his sombre expression with a halcyon smile. 'We'd like to have Gravadlax to start and grilled scallops to follow with broccoli and new potatoes. Bring us a bottle of Chablis right away, please, and a bottle of mineral water.' The waiter scribbled on his pad and shuffled from the room.

'There's a potential problem in our relationship I'd like to clear up before it rears its head,' she said, directing her attention back to Dominic, a serious expression clouding her face. 'Sex,' she concluded.

Dominic had no way of telling if this devastating honesty was indicative of Western women in general or confined to Tilly and her peers, but either way he had to adjust to it. Outside academic circles in Romania it would be highly unusual for women to even contribute to such conversations, let alone make the running; and to do so in such a public place would be considered outrageous. Dominic thought only another question would avoid embarrassment. 'To what particular aspect of sex are you referring?'

'Safe sex,' she replied directly. 'Whatever I might feel for you I will not have unprotected sex. Contraception is banned in your country, so I don't expect you to know much detail but I'm sure you've heard of condoms. If not, I'd be happy to show you.'

'Show me!?' This was too much. She could have suggested he talk to Harry or Malcolm, recommended a book or video – but show him! She was going to walk into one of these sex shops he'd seen dotted around town and calmly ask for a packet of condoms and a demonstration. 'Just like that?' he ventured, dreading her reply.

She looked around to see if they were still alone. At last, a moderate show of modesty. 'If you go to the Gents,' she said, 'you'll probably see a machine on the wall. Put in a pound coin and pull the knob. Simple.'

They both laughed; easy laughter, pure and liberating.

'And when do you see us getting around to this sex?' questioned Dominic with a slight touch of comical sarcasm.

'When the time is right,' she replied, cupping his hands. 'We've only known each other a couple of days. We both know there's something special between us but I want to be sure. We're attracted to each other physically but you come from a place with an AIDS epidemic. I wouldn't feel relaxed even with a condom, Dominic.'

She'd spoken her basic truth and he understood her

perfectly. Thoughts of making love to her tonight reluctantly evaporated. Thoughts of never making love to her hammered at his imagination. He felt terribly saddened. 'Is there an answer?' he asked.

Tilly placed her chin on her hands and studied his face for a few moments, her eyes gliding over the surface as if seeking an aura or vibration. 'We could be tested, both of us together.'

'How long before we get the results?'

'A couple of days. We could go tomorrow morning and we'd know before you do *Wogan* on Wednesday night.'

'You never told me about *Wogan*.' Dominic felt elated; gold-medal time. 'Why didn't you tell me?'

'They called when I was getting ready. I wanted to surprise you.'

The lanky waiter reappeared carrying two plates of Gravadlax and a bottle of cold white wine. He poured a small amount of wine into Dominic's glass. Tilly picked up the glass, took a sip, held it in her mouth for a few seconds and swallowed.

'Lovely, Thank you.' She replaced the glass on Dominic's side of the table.

The waiter filled both glasses and retreated from the room. A third, Arian-looking man delivered the mineral water and two ice-filled tumblers with slices of lemon attached to the rim.

'Try the wine,' she said, lifting her glass.

'Tell me about *Wogan*.' Dominic's gaze remained fixed on Tilly.

'You're first on the Wednesday show. You'll be great.'

Dominic raised his glass. 'What do you say? Cheers?'

Once again her smile captivated him. 'That's right. Cheers.'

The wine tasted much better to Dominic than the gin Martini. A dry, tangy, refreshing taste and no burning sensation. 'It's very nice.'

'It's such a shame,' mused Tilly as she studied her glass, turning the stem between her slender fingers. 'The

99

beautiful little town of Chablis was destroyed in a World War II tank battle. It's all concrete and corrugated iron now. Thank God the hills around the town were spared so the wine is still as good as ever.'

France was one place Dominic dearly wanted to visit and he was sure Tilly would make an excellent guide. 'I'd like to see it one day.'

'I'm sure you will.' Inadvertently, Tilly's foot touched his leg under the table. She looked coy, almost embarrassed. 'I want us to go shopping tomorrow. I think you'll suit Armani better than Saint Laurent. You'll need to look right for *Wogan*.'

'Whatever you say, Tilly.' If her fashion sense was half as good as her choice of food Dominic knew he had no worries.

The salmon and the grilled scallops were superb. They managed a *crême brûlée* with fresh fruit *compote* for dessert, then two cups of steaming hot, black coffee. They talked of the future, of success, the possibility of a club where they could dance every night, of spending a weekend in Paris. Dominic drank over two glasses of wine during the meal and was beginning to feel slightly light-headed as the bill arrived.

'Let's go back to Chester Square,' said Tilly. 'I feel another Jacuzzi coming on.'

As they left the restaurant Dominic saw a black Volvo parked outside the Burger King opposite. Although he couldn't see through the blacked-out windows he felt sure he recognised the short man with no neck before his window slid shut.

'What's that?' he said, pointing to some steps across the street.

'The Underground,' replied Tilly with surprise.

'Come on.' Dominic grabbed her arm and pulled her unceremoniously towards the red circle sign.

'What's the matter?' Tilly stopped at the top of the steps. 'What's the hurry?'

'I think we're being watched. Don't look now,' he said

as Tilly started to glance around. 'They're in the black Volvo over the road. Is there another way out of the Underground?'

'There must be four or five exits; Victoria's one of London's main stations.'

'Let's go down.' Dominic leapt down the stairs three at a time and waited at the bottom for Tilly. 'We can come up inside the station, then keep hidden and see if they follow.'

Tilly was not really sure what she was looking for. Spies, assassins, covert operations – these scenarios had never entered her life until three days ago. She held on to Dominic's arm, her eyes flitting from one group of travellers to the next. 'What do they look like?'

'Like nobody here. They've gone home. They knew I saw them.' Dominic watched the hustle of late evening commuters and backpacking tourists as they jostled around the concourse of Victoria station and felt an overwhelming surge of freedom. A transport policeman smiled as they stopped beside the Gatwick Express platform and gave each other a spontaneous hug. Sex became inessential; he wanted Tilly in a way that transcended the physical act. Just to be with her tonight, to share her space, to wake up next to her, that was Dominic's dream. A dream that was about to come true.

Thirteen

Monday morning began at seven o' clock with the beeping sound of Tilly's small portable alarm. She leaned over Dominic and switched on the bedside radio. The announcer's voice stirred him to complete consciousness.

'BBC Radio 4. The news at seven o' clock read by Alistair Green.'

'The death toll in Saturday's train crash at Purley has risen to five. A British Rail spokesman said . . .'

'There goes our front page,' said Tilly, retuning the radio to 95.8 FM. 'We'll be lucky to make page five.'

'Is that so important?' Dominic pushed himself into a sitting position.

'It would have been nice,' she said, smiling. Even first thing in the morning Tilly had an unmistakable freshness about her. Nadia was the only other woman Dominic had woken up with and she'd usually start the day with a session of frantic sex that left them both dishevelled and exhausted. Tilly had fallen asleep with their first cuddle last night, and now waking up with her produced a feeling of gladness and joy within Dominic. He'd never experienced such a soothing emotion and it came as a welcome replacement for unbridled lust.

'What's our agenda?' he asked, watching her disappear into the bathroom.

'After I'm dressed I'll go out and get the papers,' she

shouted. 'Why don't you make us an omelette and we'll read all about you over breakfast.'

'Sounds good to me,' he shouted back before sliding back under the duvet where Tilly's sweet scent lingered like the jasmine in his secret garden.

All the tabloids headlined the Purley train crash and continued the story with endless comparisons and comments for at least three pages. The *Sun* ran Sara's murder on page five, just as Tilly had forecast. There was a small picture of Sara and Dominic dancing at the Hippodrome in the bottom right corner of the article with a caption that read: *The last person to see Sara alive was Romanian gymnast Dominic Bellescu who is also reported as missing. The police say there is no immediate connection between Dominic's disappearance and Sara's brutal murder but they want to interview him in order to eliminate him from their inquiries.*

The main picture was of Sara topless, wearing white stockings and holding a bunch of daffodils. The *Mirror* devoted half of page six to the story calling for tougher sentences in cases of rape and used a head and shoulders picture that must have been taken when Sara was still at school. The *Star*, *Express* and *Mail* also reported the story, but with no picture and no mention of Dominic's involvement.

'What do you think?' Dominic offered her the last piece of hot, buttered toast.

'It's a disaster from our point of view.' She accepted the toast, broke it in two and placed half back on his plate. 'I want a front page to kick us off. Maybe Wednesday if I can raise a good story by then. That would work out good for the *Wogan Show* that night and I'll try for Carole Malone in Thursday's *Star*. She can get quite acid over injustice.'

'Is she a journalist?'

'One of the best.'

'There could be a problem there. I promised Harry exclusive rights.'

Dominic's concerned manner crystallised Tilly's attention. She studied him over the rim of her cup. 'When?'

'On Saturday night before the Hippodrome.'

'Did you sign anything?'

'No.'

Her expression softened. 'That's all right, then. We can do what we want.'

Dominic's mind flashed back to the pub in Shaftesbury Avenue, and his immense relief when Harry accepted his handshake. 'I gave my word,' he said stoically.

Tilly poured herself another cup of coffee. Dominic could almost see the scenarios whizzing around her quick-silver mind as she tried to find an acceptable solution. 'Harry is a news journalist; Carole writes a weekly column. There's no competition between them. If it makes you happy we'll ask Harry first, but I'm sure he won't mind. I've got to talk to him this morning about Wednesday's story; I'll mention it then.' She sipped her coffee, collected the empty plates and loaded them into the dishwasher. 'Time to get moving. The doctor's first, then Armani in Covent Garden followed by lunch at the Hard Rock Café, you'll like that. I'll set up a meeting this afternoon with Malcolm and Harry to cement our plans for the rest of the week. Tonight I thought a quiet dinner here, unless you want to go out again.'

'Sounds heavenly.' A wry smile escaped his lips.

'Mind out of gutter,' she quipped, again reading his thoughts with pinpoint accuracy.

Fourteen

Durrants Hotel, Room 302

Sergeant Ilyich Severin sat in his room watching the evening news on television and contemplating his future prospects. There was no doubt in his mind that Dominic had betrayed him by escaping in such a manner. He now looked a fool in the eyes of his superiors, notably Stenoza, and the only road to redemption lay in capturing the evidence and eliminating Dominic. Anything else would be regarded by Stenoza as failure and would mean death for the sergeant.

Severin was convinced Dominic was being kept at the Hampstead house. Romanian intelligence had known of Malcolm Barrett and his organisation for some time. They considered them subversive and mildly dangerous to the state, but as yet no real threat to the stability of the country. If Severin could resolve the Dominic affair and damage Hampstead into the bargain his credibility would be fully restored in the eyes of his mentors and he'd be back on track for the promotion he so desperately craved.

His main problem was infiltrating the Hampstead security system. He knew Barrett employed ex-SAS and Paras to guard the building and had installed the most up-to-date electronic surveillance to back them up. If he were to stand any chance of success he would need men of a much higher calibre than he'd used on the Sara fiasco. To this end he had arranged a meeting with Boris Procarnov, an ex-KGB hard man currently cooling his heels in London following a rather arduous sortie in America that had left five dead and a huge hole in Nevada where a biological research station had previously stood.

The meeting was professionally cordial, morally sparse and financially rewarding to the Russian. Twenty thousand pounds changed hands in Procarnov's favour; he, in turn, promised to deliver the papers. Bellescu's elimination would cost extra.

Fifteen

'Wake up sleepyhead!' Tilly stood beside the bed, excitement glowing from her face. 'We've made front page.'

Above one of Julian's portrait pictures the headline read: ROMANIAN DEFECTOR TO FACE POLICE PROBE OVER MODEL'S MURDER. Dominic sat bolt upright in bed. This wasn't part of the plan. Malcolm had promised he wouldn't face questioning. Malcolm had said he'd square it with the police and for Dominic to worry about nothing apart from getting the dancing right on *Wogan*.

'Don't worry,' Tilly assured him. 'It's only one of Harry's specials. Read on; it's a great piece.'

Dominic Bellescu (24), the missing Romanian gymnast, is coming out of hiding to face police questions over the death on Saturday of page three model Sara Owens. Dominic has asked for political asylum in England but is unlikely to be accepted until this matter is resolved. A police spokesman said Dominic is not a suspect in the brutal rape and murder case that shocked the country last weekend but his presence is required in order to eliminate him from police inquiries. Bellescu, who is also a talented dancer, will appear on *The Wogan Show* tonight where he will face further questions about his involvement with the murdered model. A spokeswoman for the Romanian star said he desperately wants to clear his name so he can start a new life in the West and is very excited about being able to dance on television for the first time tonight. Dominic's exceptional talent was spotted by the show's producer as he danced with Sara at a London disco on Saturday night, just hours before she met her death at a house she'd rented in Islington.

'This is fabrication,' said Dominic, astounded by what he'd read.

'This is the front page of the *Sun*,' replied Tilly, her tone judgmental, her voice abrupt. 'Please allow me to inform you of reality. If you can retain tabloid coverage at this level, you'll be a millionaire within a year. They're that important.' She threw the *Star* in front of him: it featured the story on a banner flash down the side of the front page, with a reference to page two. 'We have to pick up your suit from Armani and be at Shepherd's Bush studio by noon for the *Wogan* rehearsal.'

Tilly walked to the bedroom door, her black pleated skirt swaying provocatively with each step. She turned to face him, her eyes locking on to his. 'You may end up a misogynist if the test proves positive.'

Another new word for Dominic to learn. 'What's a misogynist?'

'Someone who hates women.' Her smile broadened. 'Somehow I can't imagine it, though.'

She closed the door quietly behind her. Dominic slid reluctantly from bed and shuffled into the bathroom where the shower quickly restored his body heat to duvet temperature. Today he would find out if Romania had left a fatal virus in his body and tonight he would dance professionally for the first time. He felt confident he'd be HIV negative, but then, there was no guarantee after indulging in unprotected sex for over three years. He felt less confident about putting on a good show for the television. AIDS was out of his hands. He'd live or die by the result: *fait accompli*. Mr Terry Wogan was another matter. What he did in his allotted time on television would determine his commercial viability in the eyes of Malcolm Barrett, and that thought scared Dominic rigid.

Sixteen

At one o'clock precisely the black London cab deposited Dominic and Tilly outside the BBC studios at Shepherd's Bush. The edginess Dominic felt during the morning evaporated when the doctor delivered a negative test result. The fitting at Armani had taken longer than expected but the outcome had been worth the wait. Dominic was now the proud owner of blue wool, single-breasted suit with wide lapels and baggy trousers. It felt comfortable and was loose enough to ensure that nothing would rip when he performed the more acrobatic movements of his dance. Tilly led the way to the stage door and gave their names to the commissionaire, who ticked them off his list and pointed down a long corridor to his left.

'Go to the end and turn right,' he said, touching the peak of his cap and smiling broadly at Tilly. 'Room 106, ask for Marion. She'll show you to your dressing room.' The security lock on the first door buzzed and they walked down the hospital-green corridor and turned right.

A short, plump, red-headed lady appeared from the door marked 102. 'Tilly Howard!' she exclaimed, nearly dropping her armful of papers in excitement.

'Claire Rosen!' replied Tilly with equal enthusiasm. The two women embraced, genuinely glad to see each other. 'God, it's been years. Claire, this is Dominic Bellescu, my new client. We're here to do *Wogan*. Dominic – Claire Rosen, the hottest vision mixer in town.'

Claire offered her left hand, her right clutching the papers. 'Pleased to meet you.' She viewed Dominic up and down slowly, deliberately. 'No lighting problem with this one,' she said to Tilly. 'I'll bet he'd look great with no light at all.' She squeezed between them, giving Dominic the full benefit of her ample cleavage. 'Must dash, darlings. Camera line-up in five minutes.' She disappeared through a door marked 'Gallery'.

'She's a bit bold.' Dominic thought it rude not to comment after such an obvious flirtation.

'The woman's sex mad,' said Tilly in a matter-of-fact voice. 'Been that way since school. I've known her fifteen years and I can't remember her holding a relationship together for more than a week. A shame really, a lovely lady with a libido like Lolita; a lethal combination. Still, she fancies you, which means you'll get all the good camera angles. Just remember who you're taking home.'

Dominic heard the slightest tinge of jealousy in Tilly's voice. It made him pleased. 'When do I meet Terry Wogan?' he asked in a quick move to change the subject.

'Not until six o'clock or thereabouts. This afternoon is camera line-up and musical rehearsal. Most of the time you'll be sitting around waiting to get on.' Her expression turned haughty, correctness once again taking control. 'I'm sure Claire could amuse you if you get bored,' she said, opening the door marked 106.

Malcolm and Harry arrived at half-past six. They all sat in what was called 'the green room', Harry and Malcolm drinking lager from pint mugs. Tilly and Dominic sipping mineral water from long-stem wine glasses. Why it was called the green room was beyond Dominic's comprehension. The banquettes around the walls were covered in red velvet, the carpets were black, and the flock wallpaper dark maroon. Harry said it was because it was the last stop before going on: green for go.

111

Tilly introduced Dominic to Terry Wogan, who proved to be charm personified. He had a relaxed manner that put the nervous gymnast at ease. His accent, which Harry said later was typically Irish, sounded almost musical. Dominic liked him instantly and for the first time since the booking was confirmed started to enjoy himself. He was to be first on. A short interview and a three-minute dance routine to 'Pump up the volume' by Marrs.

Dominic waited nervously in the wings as Terry delivered his opening monologue to a packed and partisan studio audience. They all loved Terry Wogan, that was plain to see; Dominic hoped they would feel the same warmth for him.

'My first guest has just escaped from communist Romania to start a new life in Britain. He's Romania's top male gymnast and if he's anything like that little fireball, Nadia Comaneci, he'll have a great future ahead of him.' He lowered his voice making his delivery intimate, as if about to give away a closely guarded secret. 'A little bird tells me he's also a terrific dancer.' Back to normal level: 'Ladies and gentlemen, please welcome for the first – but I'm sure not the last – time on British television, Dominic Bellescu!'

The applause faded as Dominic settled down to Terry's right. Being on an open living-room set was much more relaxing than the 'behind a desk two shot' he'd been subjected to back home.

'First of all, welcome to England.' Terry's smile was reassuring.

'Thank you for having me.' Dominic returned his smile.

'Now, Dominic, trouble seems to follow you like night follows day. You've escaped from what we all know is a very oppressive regime. You're in this country less than a day and your first dancing partner is brutally murdered. I'm your first interviewer, so does that mean I'm next?'

'I certainly hope not.' Dominic drew in a lungful of courage. He'd rehearsed his replies several times with Tilly during the afternoon, and hoped he could remember them now when it counted. 'What happened to Sara was tragic. I met her at the Hippodrome on Saturday night and most of our time together was spent dancing. She seemed a lovely young lady. I was hoping to see her again. Unfortunately, I had to leave in a hurry. If I could've stayed for a couple more hours maybe this awful tragedy would have been avoided.'

'Had you met Sara before last Saturday?'

'No. As you can imagine, defecting from a communist country has to be a well-planned operation. We'd spent months working out every detail. Sara was invited to partner me so I wouldn't look conspicuous on my own. The police told me her death was probably drug related. They think she came home early and surprised a thief.' Dominic looked directly at Terry and forced out his best camera smile. 'Can we move on to more pleasant things?' He could feel the tension in the studio ease. A small ripple of applause told him he'd said the right thing.

'Tell me about the friends you've left behind. Can we expect a wave of Romanians following your lead?'

For a split-second Dominic felt like telling the truth and blowing Ceausescu and his thugs out of the water in front of six million viewers. He wanted to tell about the Caprianu family, the orphanages where twisted, AIDS-ridden children grovel on the kitchen floor eating potato peelings to stay alive, while their minders dine on roast beef and champagne. He glanced off stage-right. Tilly stood shaking her head.

'I don't think so,' he said, snapping back to their rehearsed responses. 'A good many people are happy in Romania and wouldn't want to leave. Others can't afford to or don't have the contacts. Our country is 80 per cent rural. Life outside the cities hasn't changed much in hundreds of years. The only reason I wanted to get out is because there's no Western music back home. No modern dancing. I want to dance and I could never make a living doing that in Romania.'

'We're going to see you dance in a couple of minutes,

113

but first tell me about your long-term plans. You'll not be making a good living appearing on shows like this.' Terry turned briefly to the audience, who offered polite laughter as punctuation. 'Will you be looking for work in the West End in a show like *Cats* or even *Starlight Express*, given your athletic ability?'

Dominic had heard of West End musicals but had never seen one. This question required a generic answer. 'My dancing is not choreographed: I freeform. I don't know whether I'd be able to learn set pieces. My main plan is to build a club in London where I could dance every night. I'd be the permanent cabaret.'

'We're all dying to see this freeform dancing so why don't you head over to the stage and get yourself ready.' Terry offered his hand, Dominic shook it firmly. 'Ladies and gentlemen – Dominic Bellescu!'

The studio audience applauded long enough for Dominic to cross the studio to the stage area. Terry looked straight into camera one. 'For the first time on television Dominic Bellescu is Pumping Up The Volume!'

Having listened to the track several times during the afternoon's rehearsal Dominic was now used to the music and could anticipate the breaks faster than he had at the Hippodrome. He was marginally aware of the studio audience as he executed the first series of back-flips ending in a full leg-split. After that he was lost in the dance. The feeling elated him: it was better than escaping, better than sex. Physical and spiritual freedom, becoming one with the music, each nuance triggering spontaneous movement with real control only peripheral, just enough to contain him within the parameters of the dance floor. He finished with a four-turn shoulder spin and handspring to a standing position. The applause was overwhelming. He drank it in, confident he'd done enough to achieve his main objective: impress Malcolm.

'Ladies and gentlemen,' said an excited Terry Wogan. 'Dominic Dance!'

Dominic caught Tilly's eye as she stood clapping loudly

in the wings. He winked at her and took a final bow as the cameras moved to their next positions and the floor manager signalled he was clear. He ran to her immediately, gathering her in his arms and holding her tightly.

'Dominic Dance. I like it,' she whispered in his ear.

'So do I,' he whispered back.

Terry Wogan may have made an error, but he'd given Dominic his professional name. Bellescu was such a mouthful. Dominic Dance would work perfectly.

Malcolm shook Dominic's hand ferociously as he entered the green room. Harry was slumped on a banquette, unable or unwilling to move, four empty glasses on the table in front of him.

'Bloody brilliant!' enthused Malcolm. 'I loved it when Wogan called you Dominic Dance.'

'That seals it,' said Tilly with excited authority. 'From now on he's billed as Dominic Dance.'

The post-show gathering broke up shortly after Terry left at eight o'clock. Tilly had introduced Dominic to numerous people who all commented favourably on his performance. He smiled constantly and shook a lot of hands. Harry had miraculously sobered up and was taking great delight in telling everyone that it was he who had first spotted Dominic and organised his defection. Malcolm spent his time in clandestine conversation with Claire Rosen, who was getting steadily drunker with each whisky Malcolm poured.

'I've a great idea!' exclaimed Malcolm to the seven who remained. 'Let's all go to dinner. Somewhere nice. Tilly, you choose.'

Tilly summed up the room with one sweeping glance, looked at her watch and then at Malcolm. 'Chinese would be nice. Let's go to Leicester Square. We could go on to the Hippodrome afterwards.'

'That's my girl,' said Malcolm, directing his remark at Claire, whose left hand was beginning to encroach slowly but steadily on the inside of his thigh. 'This could be one hell of a night!' he leered, covering Claire's hand with his own and moving it sharply upwards. Claire leaned against him, slipped her free arm around his waist and ran her tongue along the outside edge of his ear.

'I'll just visit the ladies' room before we go,' said Tilly, showing a glimpse of the embarrassment of which Claire seemed incapable.

'Is it close to the Gents?' asked Dominic, hoping for an early escape.

'I'll show you.' Tilly took Dominic's arm and ushered him from the room. His dressing room was closest, just three doors down on the left. Tilly locked the door behind them and slid into his arms. 'Please don't ever do that to me in public. I'd die if you did.'

Her correctness was so endearing. She was continuously physical with the people around her, touching arms, hands and faces: she treated all her friends in a tactile manner. But sexually explicit behaviour in public struck against everything she stood for. The more Dominic knew about Tilly Howard the more captivated he became. She was right about so many things. The thought of living his new life without her, regardless of the amount of fame or wealth he might achieve, filled him with sadness. He wanted Tilly in his life permanently.

'Not in public or when there's a time limit,' he replied, kissing her gently on the lips.

Four of them made it to Leicester Square. Harry begged off, pleading an early start in the morning. He'd been assigned the British Rail inquiry into the Purley disaster and was none too pleased. He grumbled on about bloody Oxbridge editors and left the party at Shepherd's Bush Underground. The other two late stayers, a cameraman and the continuity lady, were seriously engrossed in each other and slipped away quietly to exorcise their passion. That left Malcolm, Claire, Tilly and Dominic.

The happy quartet sat around a table for six, Malcolm and Claire playing footsie, kneesie, handsie and anything elsey under the table, Tilly sipping her mineral water and shouldering the embarrassment of her unsubtle school-friend. Dominic sampled each morsel of food with pruri-ent curiosity. The combination of the negative AIDS test, success on *Wogan* and the possibility of making love to Tilly turned everything he ate into a sensual delight. As the waitresses offered delicacies from their glass and chrome trolleys, he played a game of 'spot the phallic food' much to the chagrin of Ms. Howard, who kept mouthing 'behave' at him and digging him playfully in the ribs.

'I've got some great news,' said Malcolm, wincing slightly as Claire touched something tender under the table. 'In fact I've got two chunks of great news. Firstly, I've put an offer in for the Lyceum which I'm sure they'll accept, and secondly Claire and I are going back to Chester Square tonight.' He raised his eyebrows a couple of times, stuck a chopstick in his mouth and started puffing on it like a cigar. 'I'm a very busy man.'

Tilly burst out laughing, then turned to face Dominic. 'He's supposed to be Groucho Marx,' she explained, trying hard to contain herself. 'That's the worst impression I've ever heard, Malcolm.'

'What bothers me,' answered Malcolm, placing his chopstick back on the table and patting his mouth with a napkin, 'is you giving up your bed tonight, Tilly. We intend to christen the upstairs bedroom. Do you think you could sleep back at Fitzroy Mews? If not, I'll pay for a hotel.'

'That's very generous of you, but there'll be no need.' Tilly reached under the table, took Dominic's hand and placed it, locked into hers, on the table top. 'I'll sleep downstairs with Dominic.'

Claire sat rigid in her seat, her eyes fixed on Tilly in a blank stare. Malcolm's jaw dropped and stayed open for at least five seconds. 'How long's this been going on?' he said finally, almost spitting the question across the table.

'Only a few days,' answered Dominic, hoping Malcolm would see the humour in his statement. He didn't.

'Can you possibly be serious? You've known this guy

five minutes.' There was now open hostility in Malcom's voice. Jealousy, pure and up front.

'I've known him five thousand years,' answered Tilly in a voice so soft and warm it completely disarmed her boss. She squeezed Dominic's hand. 'Just like you two, we're first-timers tonight.' She directed her gaze at Claire. 'I thought you'd be happy for me.'

'I'm deliriously happy for you,' said Claire, reaching out for Tilly's free hand. 'It's wonderful you've found each other. I wish you both every luck.' She looked at Dominic with a cold, measured stare. 'This woman has waited so long for the right man. If you hurt her I'll personally cut your balls off.'

'*Claire*! Please!' Tilly squeezed both their hands then centred her attention on Malcolm. 'I didn't mean to upset you. If you rather I didn't represent Dominic I'll quite understand, but I won't give him up.'

Her words flowed through Dominic like spiritual electricity. He couldn't have hoped for anything better. Malcolm's expression softened as he tried to compose himself. Dominic wondered if he'd been in love with her from the start – or maybe he'd tried and she'd rejected him, as he'd thought earlier. It made no difference to Dominic now. 'Won't give him up' was good enough.

'Please forgive me,' said Malcolm humbly. 'I didn't mean to sound judgmental. It's just that it's so sudden.'

'I'm full of surprises. You should know that by now.' Tilly's voice carried the tone of the victor. Dominic was now convinced that Malcolm had made an unsuccessful pass at her. Embarrassment was clearly visible on Malcolm's face. She'd slashed the Gordian knot of his masculinity. She'd exposed a rare sign of weakness in his otherwise flawless defences. Dominic was proud of her: not only for her courage in admitting their involvement, but also for the way she'd stood up to Malcolm in such an exemplary fashion.

'I think this is wonderful,' said Malcolm, trying hard

118

to regain the conversational high ground. 'This calls for champagne.'

'Not here,' argued Tilly. 'Tea is the only beverage suitable for Chinese food. Let's celebrate at Chester Square. Let's skip the Hip and go straight home.' She looked sympathetically at Claire, who had already resumed her under-table caressing. 'I'm sure we could all use an early night.'

'I'm so excited!' squealed Claire. 'Do you know, Dominic, I've known Tilly since the masturbatory days of the fifth form and I've never seen her look more radiant than she does tonight. You must be one hell of a lover.' She flashed a glance at Malcolm. 'I hope your friend has equal prowess.'

'You've not been listening,' said Tilly, stopping mid-sentence to give Dominic a light kiss on the cheek. 'This will be our first night together. He may be a total washout.'

'And Arnold Schwarzenegger's a scrawny weakling.' Claire's sarcastic delivery defused any remaining awkwardness.

'Eat up, everyone. It's party time at Chester Square!' Malcolm set the seal on the discussion and returned them to the culinary delights of Wong Fu's dim sum.

As the Rolls-Royce glided to a stop outside Chester Square Dominic could see lights in the living room and the corporeal bulk of Harry Cassini silhouetted against the net curtains. He feared this idyllic evening was about to be shattered by another crisis. Malcolm and Claire sat locked together on the back seat and were far too busy to notice the intruder at home base. Dominic nudged Tilly and pointed at the window. 'Oh damn,' she sighed, more in resignation than anger. 'What the hell does he want?'

'Does who want?' questioned Malcolm.

'Harry,' Tilly replied. 'He's in the house.'

'Probably couldn't sleep. The bastard never sleeps, he just passes out twice a week.' Malcolm disengaged himself and leapt instantly from the car. He ran up the front steps and into the hallway, leaving Dominic to escort the ladies into the house. By the time the three of them had reached the first-floor living room Harry and Malcolm were huddled over the writing desk in deep conversation. He could make out muffled references to agents, riots and guns, but nothing definite. Malcolm broke off the conversation and walked across the room, a saccharine smile his face.

'I'm sorry,' he said. 'There's been some trouble in Yugoslavia, a region called Kosovo. I've got people there I've got to get out.' His concern seemed genuine. So did Claire's anger. Instantly she changed from party girl to pissed-off parrot as if a switch had been thrown inside her, marked 'No sex for Claire tonight'.

'I tell you one thing,' continued Malcolm. 'If someone doesn't stop those assholes the whole area will go up in smoke, then we'll see a mighty ding-dong. Serbs, Croats, Muslims, Albanians, Jews – they'll be kicking the crap out of each other for years.' He turned his attention to Claire whose expression was fluctuating from anger to disappointment. 'I'm so sorry, baby, I've got to go and sort out the world. Can we continue tomorrow?' His voice sounded patronising and dismissive.

'Continue what tomorrow?!' Anger won the day. She looked at him sourly. 'Screw you, Mister Big-shot Barrett! You could've had the world tonight without leaving home.' She turned on her heel and stomped from the room.

'Silly bitch!' Malcolm shouted after her as the front door slammed. He turned towards Tilly and Dominic. 'I would've sent her home in a cab if she'd not been so tetchy. Why *are* women so damn tetchy?'

'Because they have to put up with moronic men,' answered Tilly, defending her friend ferociously. 'How can you sweet-talk somebody all night then tell them to bugger off like that? If nothing else, it's rude and bad-mannered.'

'I wasn't rude to her. I have a crisis here. I've no time

for tetchy moods.' Malcolm studied them both for a few seconds. 'I don't understand women.'

'Precisely my point!'

If time had permitted, this could have been the argument of the century. Malcolm and Tilly were squaring up for round one; only Harry's intervention prevented the bell.

'We must get to Hampstead,' he said, tugging at Malcolm's arm. 'Greg and Rafael could be at risk.' He patted Dominic's shoulder as he passed. 'You two can have a day off tomorrow. I doubt you'll see us this side of Friday.' He dragged Malcolm unceremoniously from the room, allowing no further communication.

'Damn! You make me so angry!' shouted Tilly after them as the two men scurried down the stairs towards the front door.

'Dominic, sort her out!' It was Harry's voice that shouted the last command as the black oak door slammed behind them.

Dominic didn't want to fight. Besides, he agreed with her: Malcolm had been as sensitive as an eviction order.

Tilly fought hard to control her temper. She sat, teeth clenched, lips drawn tight, eyes narrowed and piercing, watching the gas flames lap around the fireproof logs in the artificial grate. 'That man has an uncanny knack of bringing out the worst in me,' she confessed. 'Claire may have a slight hormonal imbalance but she's an extremely intelligent lady, and he treated her abominably.'

A bit strong, thought Dominic, but along the right lines. He had to talk this out with her or jeopardise the evening. He'd try diplomacy first: maybe he could slide out of the conversation sideways and change the subject in the same move. 'It's a problem between Claire and Malcolm. I think you should let them sort it out. We've just been given a day off and it starts now.'

Her eyes flashed at him from the fireplace, the anger still very much within her. 'You're a fence-sitter, Dominic. The man is a disgrace to your gender. His attitude to

121

women is chauvinistic and degrading; he's living fifty years ago. Either you support him, in which case I eagerly await your argument, or you deny him and agree with me. You can't try and change the subject to get an easy ride. That makes you as bad as him.'

Dominic discarded diplomacy. 'The way he handled Claire was insensitive, I agree with you on that point. But the man is responsible for my freedom and I won't condemn him out of hand just for having bad manners. There is obviously a major problem in Kosovo, and after all it was Harry who insisted they go to Hampstead immediately. Malcolm was simply complying with his wishes. They could be saving lives within the next few hours. I would say that's more important than offending a woman who's only annoyed because she's missing out on a night of sexual gratification.'

Tilly's eyes softened, the sparkle reappearing as her anger started to subside. Dominic didn't want to waste another second arguing. They should be grateful. Whatever havoc Kosovo might unleash, at least it had emptied the house and he was determined not to waste the opportunity. 'If we must continue cutting chunks off Malcolm's credibility can we at least do it in the Jacuzzi?'

She moved towards him, her smile broadening with each step. She slipped her arms under his and placed her hands either side of his spine pressing him to her. Her lips were close to his mouth as she murmured, 'If I promise not to mention his name again, will you promise not to go to sleep until sunrise?'

Dominic held her around the shoulders and placed a feather-light kiss on her lips. 'Of which day?'

'I've got a surprise for you,' she said, taking a step backwards. 'Follow me.' She took his hand and led him to the kitchen. Opening the fridge she reached in and lifted out a cold bottle of Dom Perignon. 'Glasses top left cupboard.' She pointed with her free hand. 'Last one in's a rotten apple.'

She laughed as she skipped across the kitchen and into

the hall. Dominic collected two crystal glasses and followed as quickly as he could. He almost caught her near
the top of the second flight of stairs when he managed to
grab her left foot, but she slipped away with a feline twist
of her leg, leaving him on one knee holding a slightly
scuffed shoe. She leaned over the railings, smiled down at
him, and removed her other shoe. She dropped it over
the banister, it bounced and hit him lightly in the chest.
'You'll have to be faster than that,' she quipped, vanishing
into the bedroom and slamming the door.

Dominic gave up the chase, collected both shoes in one
hand and crawled up to the landing. Gingerly he opened
the bedroom door, half expecting her to be hidden behind
it. The door opened flat against the wall. He could hear
her shuffling about in the bathroom, then the splashing
of water and the gurgling of bubbles as the jets were
turned on. Placing the shoes and the glasses on the bed,
he undressed as quickly and quietly as he could. Then,
with a glass inside each shoe, he lay down beside the
bathroom door. He pried it open, hoping the jets would
cover the noise, and started to crawl along the marble
floor towards the Jacuzzi.

'Dominic! Where are you?' Tilly's voice was directly
above him. He snaked his way up the first two steps,
pushing the shoe-covered glasses ahead of him. 'Dominic!'
she called again. He eased his head over the rim of the
Jacuzzi. 'You called, madam?'

'Oh my God!!' Her whole body reacted in surprise, her
shoulders clearing the water, as her eyes opened wide.
'You beast!' She slapped her hand on the surface sending
a plume of water in his direction. He ducked his head and
felt the wet warmth splash his back.

'Pax!' he shouted, depositing the shoes on the rim.
'I come bearing drinking utensils.' Her musical laughter
echoed around the marble room and warmed him inside.
His body was lying flat on the last step. One good side-
vault and he could be in the tub. He placed his hands on
the rim and pushed his knees up under his chest. Springing

123

with both feet together, his legs straightened before continuing the ark over the shoes and twisting in mid-air so he landed facing her in the centre of the Jacuzzi, his arms raised: mandatory when finishing any gymnastic movement. 'Jacuzzi Delivery Ltd. at your service,' he said to an astonished lady with carefree, laughing eyes.

'5.9, 5.9, 5.9, 5.9, and a 6 from the judge with the bottle,' she said, waving the champagne in the air.

He took her in his arms for a long, gentle, timeless embrace, their bodies relaxing, blending, caressing, healing each other. Her touch washed away everything but the moment. Dominic felt her fold into him as he moved his hands over the small of her back, rubbing little circles around the indentations on either side of her spine. She inhaled sharply through her mouth, then exhaled slowly, her face nuzzling into his neck. Her lips closed softly on his earlobe; gently she sucked it into her mouth and sent a shiver of ecstasy through his body. Slowly turning her head she released his ear, puckered her lips and slid them along the edge of his jaw. As she reached his chin he moved his face down to meet her lips. They gave freely to each other for the first time.

'I love you too,' she whispered, a second ahead of him, as usual.

'Shall we open the champagne and celebrate?' he inquired, feeling totally smug and elated.

She floated away and hooked her arms over the rim. 'Either that or smash it on the wall like they do at ship launchings.' Dominic picked up the bottle and drew his arm back. 'Don't you dare!'

She lunged at him, grabbing his wrist and sending a wave splashing over the edge. Dominic lost his footing and sat down in the centre well, the water covering him completely but with his bottle hand up and the champagne out of the water. She took the bottle but made no move to help him, so he climbed her body like a ladder until finally he stood upright in front of her.

'Thanks for the help,' he said, a pretend snarl curling on his mouth.

'I saved what's important,' she teased, waving the bottle in front of him. 'Be a gent and open it. That wire thingy tends to break my nails.'

He took the bottle, slowly removed the green plastic covering from the neck, twisted the wire off the cork and threw it over his shoulder. It clattered into the sink on the far side of the room. 'Shot!' she said, with a nod of approval. He started to ease the cork from the neck with his thumbs.

'Not like that, Dominic!' She winced, anticipating the pop. 'Twist it off. The only people who pop champagne corks are Grand Prix winners.'

He eased the cork away from the bottleneck with the merest fizz of escaping air. Tilly held out a glasses as Dominic stood mesmerised by the sudden flow of bubbles ejaculating from the dark green bottle. 'Come on, silly. Pour it,' she said, trying unsuccessfully to catch the bubbles in her glass. 'I hate to waste a drop.'

He poured; they drank, sipping the sparkling liquid, toasting each other with every mouthful. He watched Tilly's expression mellow. Her eyes seemed distant as if lost in a thought beyond this moment. As he was unable to read her thoughts, he resorted to spotting mood change. She felt distant, disconnected; he thought he'd lost her to some greater influence. 'Hello,' he ventured softly, almost in a whisper.

She smiled, snapping out of her mood and offering him her glass. 'Fill, if you please. You must never let a lady's glass stay empty for more than a second.'

Dominic complied. 'You seem miles away. Is anything wrong?'

She floated across the tub, entwining her arms around his neck and planting a delectable butterfly kiss on his cheek. 'Nothing. I was thinking of involvement, surrender, support, encouragement, loyalty, understanding: all the

125

things a woman must cope with when she says "I love you".'

He returned her kiss, his mouth sliding on to her neck. He took a gentle nip of her flesh, his hands sliding under the water, caressing her and hooking her thigh so her leg curled around his waist. 'Do you have a problem with that?'

'Only if it's a one-way street.' She hooked her other leg around him, her arms now tight around his neck. The water made her weightless. 'Are you a no-entry sign, Mister Bellescu?'

'I don't know what I am. This is new territory for me.'

Tilly seemed touched by his admission. She slid her legs slowly down his body, the swirling currents filling the gaps between them as they twisted together, blissfully suspended by the water. 'Please take me to bed,' she whispered. 'Take me to bed now.'

He lifted her from the tub and carried her through to the bedroom. On the satin bedspread they rolled the full width of the king-size bed and back again, laughing, kissing, feeling each other uninhibitedly for the first time. Finally they came to rest in the centre of the bed and slid together perfectly, their bodies merging, their hearts combining. The joy of the world passed through them and left a love they would both share.

Of all the alarms in the world, nothing works better than a woman who has been to the bathroom and crawled back into bed with cold hands and feet. Dominic vacated his warm patch to escape her wintry extremities only to be jolted by the cold sheets. Now fully awake, he looked at his morning love curled beside him and thanked God for his blessing. To feel so happy first thing in the morning was indeed a rarity. He thought of his mother and father. He was sure they would have approved of Tilly.

'Why d ... and fe ... pers,' came the muffled voice through the pillow.

He slid back on to the warm patch, cupping Tilly's head

126

in his hands and turning her face out of the pillow. 'What did you say?'

Her eyes snapped open, fully awake and alert. 'Why don't you get dressed and fetch the papers. Good morning. I love you.' She beamed her first smile of the day, heating the parts of Dominic the warm patch couldn't reach.

'I love you too,' he said, kissing her forehead. 'I'll go if you cook breakfast.'

'Deal,' she said, turning her head back into the pillow and pretending to sleep.

A plateful of Spanish omelette greeted Dominic on his return from the newsagent. He'd bought every paper on the rack, fourteen in all, and now busied himself laying them front page up in a neat line across the breakfast bar.

'How many are you in?' came the lilting question from the sink area.

'I haven't looked,' he replied, tenaciously tucking into the food. 'That's your job. You're the press officer.'

'Has the star forgotten how to read?' she scorned, removing her rubber gloves.

'The star hasn't had time,' he mimicked, shovelling a forkful of egg and green peppers into his mouth.

Tilly picked up the *Sun* and scanned through to the television page. 'Here we are. Oh, this is good. Listen.' She sat down opposite him and poured herself a coffee. 'Terry Wogan may be the inspiration for a thousand media jokes but he still has an eye for spotting new talent. Last night Romanian defector Dominic Bellescu showed his unique abilities to a mesmerised television audience for the first time. The grace and timing of his freeform dance routine combined with his athletic body and rugged good looks prompted over five thousand calls to the BBC switchboard, mainly from women wanting more information. Dominic, who's financially backed by Malcolm Barrett, one of Britain's leading computer manufacturers, stated his intention to open his own club in London. Michael Jackson move over.'

She picked up the *Star*, relegating the *Sun* to the floor.

'Oh goody,' she giggled, pushing page five across the bar. 'A quarter-page picture of you outside the green room. Remember?'

'I do. That photographer took twenty rolls of film. It took for ever.'

'Worth every second,' she countered. 'I love the headline – MURDERED MODEL'S LAST PARTNER GOES SOLO – that's so *Daily Star*. Brilliant!' She thumbed through to page twelve. 'Carole Malone has done a piece on the orphanages. Good, good, good. What a good morning.' She looked so pleased with herself, so victorious. 'Today, my love, we will do nothing but good things. Good walks in the park, good food in nice restaurants and good lovemaking all night long. How does that sound?'

'Like heaven,' he replied, his mind lingering on the lovemaking. 'Any chance of going back to bed and starting again?'

'Not till I've finished reading the papers,' she announced. She scooped the news-sheets into her arms, deposited them on top of the *Sun* then folded her arms on the bartop, her mouth forming an impish, wicked grin. 'Finished,' she said, raising her right eyebrow ever so slightly.

TO: CEAUSESCU
FROM: SECURITATE, BUCHAREST

9 April 1989

Have been advised by Severin that Bellescu is definitely not at the Hampstead house. I therefore doubt the documents are there either. Advise we hold off elimination until the papers can be found and secured.

I am going to allow Severin time to locate. If he fails, I will release pictures and a statement from Nadia Vasiliu to discredit Bellescu with the British press. They seem to have taken to him. He is in at least one daily paper every week and has several columnists reporting his progress in glowing terms. This is mainly due to an excellent public relations campaign run by a Mrs Howard. I am checking to see if pressure can be put on her. I'll keep you informed of progress.

If the smear tactics work we can blame his death on a revengeful Englishman, thereby avoiding any connection.

STENOZA

Seventeen

Malcolm and Claire had patched up their differences and were now enjoying a somewhat casual affair driven mainly by hormones and lust. There had been another slight hiccup last week when Claire remarked how Englishmen counted their stamina in minutes instead of hours and that if it hadn't been for her vibrator she'd still be unsatisfied. Malcolm took serious offence at the remark and called her a silly bitch, an oversexed prick teaser and a gold-digging shag-bag all in the space of two sentences. She retaliated by kicking him firmly in the testicles. The ensuing row ended with both of them fully clothed in the Jacuzzi splashing gallons of water at each other. They then entered into a mammoth, noisy sex session that could be heard not only by Dominic and Tilly downstairs but also by half the population of Chester Square.

It reminded Dominic of Nadia during their last year together. A bit, rather than a part of his life, lived with intensity and passion in the time it consumed. However, they both seemed happy: Malcolm always looked wasted in the mornings and Claire never again mentioned her vibrator.

Malcolm sat at the breakfast bar sipping his coffee and reading *The Times*. 'The Stealth Bomber's up and running,' he gleefully announced to an empty kitchen. 'Fan-fuckin'-tastic!'

'What is?' questioned Claire, shuffling through the door, her rubber-soled slippers squeaking on the tiled floor.

'The Yanks have got the B2 off the ground in California. That plane will make radar obsolete and we have it.'

'Deep joy,' said Claire sarcastically. 'For a split-second I thought you'd invited Arnie to dinner. He makes other men obsolete.'

He turned to face her. 'Can you think of nothing else?'

She pushed her way between his legs, opened his bath-robe and took his limp penis in both hands. 'No,' she said, rubbing him expertly and slowly producing an erection. 'Ah, breakfast,' she whispered, dropping to her knees.

Malcolm held her head securely. 'I have work to do. We close the deal on the Lyceum this morning. I'm due at the Strand in forty minutes.'

'Then you'll be a little late, won't you?' She pressed her breasts either side of his manhood. 'I want you inside me. On the floor. Now.'

Malcolm's Rolls-Royce pulled up to the kerb outside the Lyceum a full twenty minutes late. He made no excuses to the five men who waited impatiently on the entrance steps. 'Good morning, gentlemen,' he said in a manner that implied they were early and he was, in fact, on time. 'Shall we go inside for a look-see?'

'I have another appointment in fifteen minutes,' muttered a grey man in a blue suit.

'We'll excuse you,' quipped Malcolm, smiling insincerely at him. 'I'm sure it's more important to you than the fifty-grand commission on this relic of Victoriana.'

Malcolm had a very direct way of dealing with people who didn't fit into his timetable. He'd once sacked a stock manager who didn't wait past six o'clock to attend a five o'clock meeting. 'I pay. You wait,' he'd said. And he'd meant it.

'I expect you've all seen the proposals drawn up by my solicitor.' He looked around the gathering. They all nodded. 'Good. The survey pointed to some problems regarding fire regulations. I think we should see for ourselves and then discuss possible solutions. Other than that, if there's no further details that need ironing I think we can sign today.'

Malcolm understood, above all, the power of money. The sight of a purple Coutts chequebook open in front of him, requiring only his signature to turn a worthless piece of paper into maybe millions of pounds was the most powerful weapon, leadership tool, controller and aphrodisiac in the world. Today he would sign a cheque for £500,000 and he would make these five men sweat for every penny.

Dominic stretched out the unmade bed and split his concentration between the *Sun*, *Star*, *Mirror* and the shafts of morning sunlight bouncing around his garden. He felt quietly annoyed at Harry's lack of progress in confirming his Romanian stories despite assurances that things were proceeding as quickly as humanly possible. It had been four months since his defection and although his life both publicly and privately reached new heights with each passing day, he felt frustrated that nothing was being done about the appalling events back home.

During the last month security on him had dropped to a minimum. He'd been issued with a British passport and a National Insurance number. There had been no attempt by the Securitate to eliminate him, although he always had the feeling they were watching, keeping a tab on him, ensuring he was in easy range. Last week, the Romanian ambassador had invited him to a cultural evening at the Embassy. He'd refused, of course, but it did show a certain willingness on their part to forgive and forget. Not so with Dominic. He wanted Ceausescu discredited, and soon.

'Last one in owes a fiver!' shouted Tilly from the bathroom just as the phone rang,

'Be right there,' answered Dominic, reaching across the bed and flicking the phone from its cradle. 'Hello.'

'Stay where you are. Don't go outside. I'll be there in ten minutes.' Harry's voice sounded urgent, worried.

'What's wrong?'

'Can't talk. Stay put. Wait for me.' The phone went dead.

'Who was that?' asked Tilly as Dominic shuffled into the bathroom.

'Harry. Something's wrong. He's coming over.'

She popped her head round the shower curtain, her face tight, concerned. 'What?'

'I don't know. He didn't say.'

A smile crept back on Tilly's face. 'Probably wants more of Malcolm's champagne,' she said coyly, determined not to let anything spoil what she called her lubricated morning massage. 'Come and do my shoulders. My right blade's as stiff as a board.'

Dominic slipped off his bathrobe and stepped in beside her. She turned her back to him and he rubbed her shoulder gently in small circles, taking care not to apply too much pressure. The soothing water cascaded over them, washing Harry's words of warning temporarily from their minds.

'My editor's just given me this lot,' said Harry, throwing a large brown envelope on to the table between them.

Dominic grabbed it fractionally before Tilly. He slowly pulled out two black and white pictures and a typewritten sheet of paper. The first picture was of him and Nadia at last year's gymnastic championships. He was dressed in his national strip, she in a full-length peasant skirt and white blouse. He felt sick as he looked at the second picture. Nadia's face was cut and bruised, her left eye puffed and closed, her nose swollen and broken. 'Oh my God,' he said softly, handing Tilly the photographs.

'This is Nadia, isn't it?' Tilly was equally appalled.

'Yes,' said Dominic, unable to offer more.

'According to the statement you did this to her on a regular basis,' said Harry, picking up the typewritten sheet.

'It says you beat her and forced her to have sex with another woman while you watched. It also says you tied her up, had anal sex with her and forced her to copulate with your friends.'

'This is rubbish!' Dominic's face turned grey with anger and loathing for what Stenoza had done to her. It was his handiwork, of that Dominic had no doubt. 'None of this is real except for the first picture.'

'As I thought,' said Harry, taking the photos back from Tilly and placing them upside down on the table. 'Just when we thought you were safe.' He smiled briefly at Dominic, pulled a portable phone from his coat pocket and punched in a number. 'The problem is, the other papers will have it too. We've got to squash this before it undoes all the good we've done. Hello. Gerald Brooke, please. This is Harry Cassini.' He looked at Tilly and Dominic as he waited to be connected; his expression seemed sad, resigned, disappointed.

'Hello, Gerald. . . . Fine, thank you. Gerald. Have you received a spoiler on Dominic Dance within the last few hours? . . . Well you will soon, I'm sure of it. Gerald, none of it is true. It's a Romanian government fabrication. I'm with Dominic now and he assures me there's no truth in it. . . . Fine, thank you. You can reach me any time on the mobile. . . . I appreciate it. Goodbye Gerald.'

He pressed 'clear' and slumped into the sofa. 'I think you should get on the case here, Tilly. We've no way of knowing how many of these are being circulated. I'll do the *Mirror* and *Express* Groups, you do the broadsheets, just in case.'

Dominic picked up the second picture of Nadia and studied the background closely. 'This is Stenoza's office. No, part of the corridor outside. Look, there. You can see the picture of Ceausescu next to the window. I've been there enough times. It's Securitate headquarters in Bucharest. No doubt about it.'

'Brilliant!' shouted Harry, snatching the picture and studying it closely. 'If you're right I can blow the whole story out of the water. Where exactly in the building is this?'

'Third floor. Turn right at the top of the stairs; it's at the end of that corridor. There's a red door to the fire escape just out of shot on the right.'

'Excellent! I should be able to get a picture from our lads over there and have it here tomorrow. We might yet win this hand if Uri can deliver up an ace.'

'Who's Uri?' asked Tilly before Dominic could speak.

'A gentleman of the night is the polite description.' Harry placed his finger beside his nose. 'Best first-floor man in Romania.'

Eighteen

Brasov, Romania, just before dawn

Uri Scentalin walked quickly round the corner and flattened himself against the brick wall. The wail of sirens grew louder, searching lights pierced the morning gloom around him, then continued, growing dimmer as the sirens faded. He waited for a minute before walking cautiously into the street, his senses alert, his eyes scanning for any sign of movement. He ran across the road, jumped athletically over the open sewerage ditch and scampered into a grey, ten-storey apartment block. He ran up the stairs three at a time to the fourth floor, where he slowed to a silent walk down the concrete corridor and stopped in front of door 411. He produced a silver key from his pocket and slipped it into the door lock. The door opened silently on well-oiled hinges.

'I knew that was you,' came a female voice from the darkness. 'One of these days they'll catch you.'

'Thanks for the vote of confidence,' he replied. 'Any light?'

'Power's cut. Has been all night.'

'Candles?'

'One left.'

'Light it then. I've got something to show you.'

A sound of scuffling, the striking of a match, then dim light in the room. Uri moved towards it. 'I've got the plans for the Timisoara prison,' he said, placing a miniature camera on the upturned wine crate that served as a table. 'And look what else I found.' He placed a gold necklace studded with diamonds and emeralds in front of the woman. The light from the candle bounced off the gems reflecting shards of light around the room. 'Isn't that the most beautiful thing, Shanah?' The woman picked it up and placed it around her neck. 'Second most beautiful thing,' corrected Uri.

Shanah smiled at him. 'I worry so about you. You mustn't take these things. It's bad enough you steal things for the English, but someone is going to miss this and they'll know you've been in their office.'

Uri reached over and gently ruffled her hair. 'They don't know it's me. Besides, it's probably stolen in the first place.' He took the necklace from her and stuffed it back into his pocket. 'Any news from Harry?'

'He wants you to take a picture of the Securitate Headquarters in Bucharest. The third floor, west side. The window and the picture of Ceausescu. God knows why.'

'When does he want it?' The softness had gone from Uri's voice. It sounded professional and focused.

'Now. Today.'

'There goes sleep. Why do the British always want everything yesterday? What's wrong with tomorrow?' He thought for a moment. 'You must come with me. We'll do the tourist looking for the toilet routine.'

Shanah stood up, her ample figure silhouetted against the grey concrete wall. 'I'll pack some clothes,' she said, resigned, but not happy with her task. 'Can we go on to Zarnesti afterwards? I want to check on the cottage.'

'An excellent idea. The further away from Brasov the better, after last night. I'll hide the necklace in the woods.'

Nineteen

'What bothers me is why they chose to do this now,' said Harry as he attacked his first beer of the day.

'Because Ceausescu and his cronies are losing their grip.' Dominic walked to the desk and produced a small bundle of press clippings from the left hand drawer. 'I kept these from *The Times*, the *Independent* and the *Guardian*. They're dated ten days ago, 8 July. Listen to this. "The Warsaw Pact summit started this week in Bucharest under allegations of 'unprecedented disunity' between all participating states. *Pravda* marked the opening yesterday with a scathing attack on the domestic policies of the Romanian leadership. The meeting between Ceausescu and Reszo Myers, Chairman of the Hungarian Socialist Workers' Party, ended in deadlock. Observers say the discussions were 'very heated' and 'totally unsuccessful'." – And that's in the *Guardian*. *The Times* says the summit is a disaster plain and simple, and forecasts the break-up of the communist bloc. Any one of my stories fully substantiated by your people could bring them down. He has to discredit me now or run the risk of exposure, deal or no deal.' Dominic handed Harry the clippings. 'Why is it taking so long?'

'Because hearsay is not proof, because people are scared to talk, because like it or not Ceausescu still controls and Stenoza still covers up. I'll get what I need but

138

it'll take more time.' Harry put an arm around Dominic and led him towards the wall unit. 'Remember Bianu, the witness in the live target story?' Dominic nodded. 'He's in Timisoara prison. One of my men is getting the plans for the place as we speak. We'll break your witness out within the next month, if he's still alive. I want to bring him to England and let him testify in person. You see, I *am* working on it. Now have a mineral water and relax.'

'I don't doubt you, Harry. I'm just impatient.'

Twenty

Uri parked his battered Land Cruiser in a disused barn near the main road into town.

'Take the big handbag,' he said to Shanah, 'and lots of papers to spill out of it. I want that guard totally confused.'

'I know what to do,' answered Shanah, a slight irritation shadowing her voice.

'Just as well, dearest,' he mocked, chucking her under the chin. 'No mistakes means we live to eat dinner.'

Uri was an orphan who lived outside the system: the son of first-generation urban peasants who had obeyed Ceausescu's call to leave the countryside and move into prefabricated tower blocks, only to find slave labour and unbearable living conditions. His father was shot while protesting their case in Bucharest. His mother died a year later from what the death certificate called pneumonia and Uri knew to be lack of heat and medicine combined with foul sanitation and her general lack of the will to live. He was eleven when she died.

He was a bright child who'd learned patchy English and French from the tourists he hustled and for nine years he had survived on the streets of Brasov and Bucharest by stealing food, or the money to buy it, and sleeping rough, with the occasional respite at Shanah's place where he could clean himself and beg the odd night in a soft bed. Shanah was a late child whose parents were also forcibly
140

moved from the country into Brasov. They lived in the same block as Uri's family and after his mother died they tried to keep an eye on the scrawny orphan.

Shanah was twenty-four, three years older than Uri. She'd seen him through grief, puberty, injury and drunkenness; she was his sister, friend, mother and, since last month, his lover. It had happened suddenly and naturally as they mourned the death of Shanah's mother from a similar combination of pneumonia, pollution and dejection. They were the last two, the tragic legacy, the new family. Shanah dreamed of marriage, a real family; of rebuilding the cottage at Zarnesti and of returning to work the land, but survival and intrigue ruled by day and night for Shanah Kratanu. Uri was not only a thief by trade but was also working for the British. To be caught on either count would mean execution for them both.

Shanah, a large, robust woman, was strong in arm, mind and spirit. Uri looked spidery. Nearly six feet tall he had thin, sinewy legs, a tight, strong, if somewhat small torso and a waif-like face that could charm with a smile or fill with anger until he looked like a snappish ferret. He had a remarkable and agile talent for climbing anything. Buildings, trees, mountains: Uri could climb them all, and with the minimum use of tools or safety aids.

He'd been recruited by Malcolm's organisation six months earlier as he tried to sell a gold watch to a Western tourist. The tourist asked him if he was a good thief, and, if so, would he like to make some American dollars? Within a month Uri was given a camera and $100 to photograph the inside of a government villa on the Black Sea coast. He completed his mission, undetected, within a week. The British were very pleased, and offered more assignments. He worked strictly freelance; this jaunt was worth $500.

They boarded the bus into Bucharest, sat near the back and remained silent during the trip. The bus was crowded with farmers, factory workers, mothers with children and at least one plain-clothed Securitate officer. As there was no way of telling who he was, silence was the best policy. They disembarked a block away from Central Building and walked briskly towards their objective.

'Feeling sick, must go to the toilet, guard stops you, drop bag over desk, you move left, I palm passes, say sorry, bag search, off we go,' muttered Uri as he linked her arm and guided her into the square.

'Got it,' she replied clearly. Her concentration was totally on the task.

They walked up the twenty-seven worn stone steps, each one deliberately, using the climb as a metronome to syncopate their timing. Shanah started to wobble as they passed under the entrance archway with its two ornate steel doors pinned back into recesses in the arch and secured open. Uri put his arm round her and ushered her across the marble floor towards the lone guard standing behind a small desk in the centre of the room.

'My wife is sick. I need the toilet,' said Uri, taking most of her weight as she seemed to faint. 'I need water for her.' His voice sounded urgent, with the touch of madness that life and death situations generate. The young guard's first reaction was to help, a point quickly developed by Uri. 'Can you lend a hand? I think she's fainted.'

As the guard reached over the desk Shanah fell on to it, her handbag opened and spilled all before her. Uri let her go, the guard tried to catch her and both ended up on the floor. Before the guard's eye level could return above the desk Uri had taken several white security tags and slipped them into his jacket pocket.

'Sweetheart, are you all right?' Uri slid his arms under hers and lifted. Shanah stumbled to her feet. 'I need to attend to my wife. Please, we're only just married. She may be pregnant. Please, let me attend to my wife.' All malice and annoyance had left his voice; only compassion remained. It was a masterly performance. 'Please. She is sick. You can see.'

The guard straightened his uniform and looked nervously around the resounding marble hall for any sign of

142

his superiors. 'Go on then. Quickly. Get away from this desk.'

Uri gathered the contents of Shanah's handbag from the desk and floor and stuffed them back into the bag. He led her away at once. They crossed the remaining floor space trying not to walk too fast. This was the worst moment: if they could reach the toilet they'd be safe. An army officer in a brown and red dress uniform arrived at the exit door a second before Uri and Shanah. He grabbed the brass door handle with a stiff right arm, snapped his head around and looked menacingly in the couple's direction.

'She's pregnant,' Uri said again, nodding towards the door. 'Can you help?'

The soldier snapped to attention and opened the door in military fashion: the edge of the door, fully open, tucking neatly against his side. 'To the greater glory of Romania,' he trumpeted. 'May you have many more.'

Uri smiled his thanks and helped Shanah down the hall and into the white-tiled toilet. As he locked the door Shanah stood to her full five-foot ten inches. 'Arrogant asshole.'

'*Stupid* arrogant asshole,' corrected Uri, pulling an ink pad, rubber stamp and an implement for sealing plastic from his inside jacket pocket. 'We've got only a minute.'

From his top pocket he extracted two passport photos of himself and Shanah, from his outside pocket the stolen passes. He placed everything on the toilet seat and set about his work. The Securitate changed the colour and type of paper on security passes on a random, daily basis so although a good deal of Uri's camouflage could be prepared earlier, it still required 'live action' on the day. He revelled in the challenge – not only to put the wool over their eyes but to knit the jersey. He loved fooling the foolish, especially Securitate fools, the ones responsible for so much pain and suffering.

He printed Ceausescu beside the name on each pass. If they were close enough to read the name, their surprise would give Uri the edge. That's all he needed on his own; it was more difficult with Shanah along. He slipped the photos into place, rubberstamped both and sealed the plastic. 'Ready. Forty-five seconds. Good.'

Sternly he looked at Shanah, his face fox alert, eagle eyed. 'Tidy your coat. You're an official, not a pregnant woman.'

Shanah obeyed, grateful for such expert coaching. She tidied her hair and applied a small amount of lipstick. It didn't look right. She was a peasant girl: no change of clothes or make-up would alter that. Uri looked believable. The smart, dark blue suit hidden under his ragged overcoat transformed him from beggar to bureaucrat. He unstrapped a thin, black leather briefcase from his back. It contained a 35mm camera and a 9mm Beretta. 'Best I walk you to the stairs. You wait for me, I'll go alone.'

Shanah felt torn from him. She could endanger him, but she wanted to be with him, to share the danger. But she saw no room for dissent in his eyes. 'If you think it best.'

Uri crammed his overcoat into the waste bin, scooped the pass paraphernalia into the briefcase and adopted a superior posture. 'If my lady will please go before, I will escort you to a seat where you can wait peacefully for my return.'

They walked back down the corridor and across the main hall. Uri talked constantly of farming quotas, livestock allocations and crop rotations: all drivel, but it stopped anyone interrupting them.

'You sit there,' said Uri, pointing at the line of plastic chairs along the far wall that belittled the grandeur of the hall. 'I'll see if there's anything I've left upstairs, I won't be long.'

He strode purposefully up the central marble stairs, looking neither back nor to the side, nodding the occasional greeting to other men in suits, but never to those in working clothes. On the third floor he turned right, and looked down sixty feet of pillar-lined corridor.

Five desks, three right, two left, lined the hallway. Four were empty. At the fifth, nearest the window, sat a young woman in an army uniform. Uri walked up to her, clicked his heels politely and looked at her name plate.

'Private Popescu. Will you please direct me to the Land Allocation Office.'

'Sixth and seventh floors.' The soldier redirected her eyes to her paperwork. Uri looked at the office door: General Roman Stenoza. He walked back down the hall as quietly as possible.

Uri sat down at the last empty desk before the stairwell, opened the internal directory and scanned the pages until he found the name Popescu. He dialled 3009. 'Main desk here, Private Popescu. The General's next appointment is here. . . . I wouldn't know, Private, I only know there's a five-star General standing in front of me with an appointment card. I suggest you get down here and sort it out.'

Uri hung up and walked quickly to the stairs, climbing up half a flight and hiding behind the lift shaft. He kept a sharp lookout above him and a sharp ear below. He heard Private Popescu clunk her way along the corridor and start down the steps. He set his camera to flash automatic and held it in his right hand under his jacket. The briefcase in his left hand stiffly by his side, he moved silently down the stairs and along to Popescu's desk. He framed the picture as instructed; the camera flashed. He wound the film forward and waited for the flash to recharge. Orange light, up and focus, flash. He wound on again and waited.

'Tomorrow at ten, then.'

Someone was leaving from the third office along. Uri dared not risk another picture. He placed the camera in his briefcase. Now he could hear speech and footsteps from inside Stenoza's office. He hurried away from Stenoza's door, slowing only when he heard it click open. Again he looked straight ahead, briefcase still clutched tightly by his side. He passed Popescu on the second floor and smiled at her. She ignored him.

Shanah saw him at the top of the stairs. She looked nervously around the hall trying to identify any Securitate thugboys, the venomous grey-suited, short-haired bullies with two-way radios who would appear from nowhere and single out a target to arrest, brutalise and cart away, all by remote control. If Uri had been suspected, now was the time they'd strike. Uri appeared through the crowd at the bottom of the stairs, walked directly to Shanah, took her by the hand and walked undisturbed from the building.

'Gotcha!' he said, slipping the films into his pocket and steering the Land Cruiser on to the Zarnesti road. 'The British have promised me a transmitting video camera,' he said proudly.

'I'm sure you'll find good use for it,' replied Shanah, not knowing what he was talking about but feeling another crystal-sharp pain of pending danger.

Twenty-one

Tilly hadn't slept in her flat since Sara's murder. She preferred to stay with Dominic at Chester Square, as if not going to Fitzroy Mews would somehow erase the memory of that horrific March morning. Like today, she'd go once a week to pick up mail, but she'd only stay a short time and she always felt a shiver run through her body as she unlocked the front door.

The sun's heat was magnified through the patio doors, raising the living-room temperature into the mid-nineties. Tilly unlocked the four security bolts in the aluminium frames, slid open the double doors and stepped on to the tiled patio. Watering can in hand, she set about tending and talking to the three small fir trees, two pots of ivy and the indoor rubber plant she was keeping outside for the summer.

She had loved this flat. It had been in bad repair when she'd bought it. She'd spent six months and a good deal of money decorating it just as she wanted. It had been finished in time for last Christmas and she'd held open house over the entire holiday period. A constant stream of friends flowed through her new home, bringing gifts, wine and good wishes. She'd been so happy. Now she felt only sorrow and fear.

Her watering can empty, she stood against the balcony railing looking across Cleveland Street at the block of flats opposite. Her terrace stood level with the fifth floor of the six-storey building. She looked at each window, searching for a half-hidden face or camera lens and felt uneasy, apprehensive. Dominic seemed to take all the uncertainty and danger in his stride, living for the moment, filling each minute with sixty seconds of time fulfilled. She envied his ability to drain the day of everything it offered and to fill the nights with future dreams. She loved him for the same reasons but she never took him for granted, even for a second. Dominic was a special man starting a wild and wonderful journey on the rollercoaster of show business. The press loved him, the public adored him, and Malcolm was backing him. There would be so many temptations, so many women, so many better offers. Tilly loved him day by day with no definite plan for the future. She had only one priority – to sell Fitzroy Mews.

She stepped back inside the rapidly cooling room, locking the patio doors behind her and drawing the curtains. Her portable phone chirped inside her handbag.

'Hello. Tilly Howard.'

'Tilly. Harry. I've got the pictures from Romania. Dominic was right, they're a perfect match. Where are you?'

'At Fitzroy Mews. I was just leaving for Chester Square.'

'Any of your broadsheets running the story?'

Tilly's looked into the mirror and smiled. 'My broadsheets knew it was fake from the start. Their only interest is whether Malcolm makes or loses money because of it.'

'Easy for some,' said Harry, reflecting on the unpaid man-hours this episode was costing. 'I've got to stop the *Screws* from front-paging it on Sunday, and the *Mirror*, and the *People*.'

'A reporter's work is never done,' mocked Tilly, walking through to the kitchen and depositing a dirty vase in the dishwasher. 'I've got Malcolm and the *FT* this afternoon to discuss his expansion into Europe, otherwise I'd give you a hand.'

'Never mind,' consoled Harry. 'I'll call you before close of play with the result.'

'I'd appreciate that. Thank you, Harry. Goodbye.' She slipped the phone back into her bag and checked all the rooms one last time before leaving the flat and bolting the front door securely using both new deadlocks.

30 July 1989

> We now know Bellescu is living in Chester Square
> with the press officer, Howard. Malcolm Barrett and
> Claire Rosen, a television technician, are cohabit-
> ing. Since the failure of our spoiler, I think it prudent
> to put the house under surveillance and see if we
> can piece together a story on the four of them.
> There is no sign they intend to use their information
> at present so I advise we observe and wait. My
> men are close enough to strike quickly if needed.
>
> I have dealt with Severin as per your instructions.
> Korescu now in charge of London operation.
>
> Stenoza

Twenty-two

Chester Square.
20 December 1989

Reluctantly, Dominic turned off the hot water and stepped out of the shower. A warm white towel wrapped itself around his neck; two slender hands rubbed and wiped his shoulders in the same riverine movement.

'To say this is your big day would make me guilty of understatement.' Tilly laid her face on his right shoulder-blade, slid her arms around his wet waist and squeezed him tightly. 'I'm so proud of you,' she said, squeezing him again. 'You've been wonderful to work with and wonderful to live with. And I love you. Good morning.'

'Good morning,' he replied. 'What do you mean "you've *been* wonderful"? Are you leaving and it just slipped your mind to tell me?' He said it jokingly, although he feared her reply.

She slipped away from him, walked across and collected her bathrobe from behind the door. 'As soon as the club's up and running I'm quitting Malcolm,' she said, her voice determined. 'I said I would in March and I meant it. I want to get away from him. I long for the peace and quiet of corporate presentations.'

Dominic had suspected it for weeks. Small things, like the lack of a 1990 business diary; only her small, personal Filofax carried on beyond February. The increase in trade papers from different spheres of business – insurance, travel, banking. Last week he'd seen a transcript from the

151

European Parliament on food subsidy. When he'd asked her about it Tilly had said she was 'keeping abreast of affairs'. It was a bad time to ask, as 'abreast' and 'affairs' led to other words that made a serious answer impossible. He felt a tiny tremor of shock run through him at the prospect of change. They were a team 'on and off the field', as Harry had said.

'Are you taking another job?' he asked as nonchalantly as possible.

'Another client, Dominic. I have clients.' Her correctness underlined her determination. 'And also I need to have my own place again. Chester Square is lovely but it's Malcolm's house. I want to have my things around me. My life is in storage at the moment.' She fastened her robe and tucked herself under his arm. 'Do you know?'

He hugged her shoulder. 'Yes, I know.'

'I want to go back to the work I'm familiar with and you need a real agent. They're all after you. Noel Gay, London Management – you can have your pick. And believe me you'll need a proper agent when the club's a success.'

'I'm happy with you looking after me. We've done well to date.'

'We've done *very* well to date. All the more reason to find a good professional. I'm a corporate press officer with a few show-business contacts. Without Harry's help I'd be lost. You'll need a specialist like Yvonne De Valera to maximise your potential.' She patted his stomach playfully and looked up at him, her eyes sparkling, happy, excited. 'Next year is the operative phase. This year we have a club to open and Christmas to survive. Speaking of survival, any news from Romania?'

'Harry's due about now with the latest news.'

Tilly's interest in that part of his life remained semi-detached; it was as if it didn't really exist or was all part of someone else's war on another planet where it couldn't reach her. He didn't blame her: she had every right to distance herself from such violence. She was also right

152

about having her own place. On several occasions over the past few months Dominic had felt like the guest who's outstayed his welcome. It was never spoken, Malcolm's manners on the subject were impeccable, but he had hinted that he'd like to move his communication centre out of Hampstead, and Dominic knew the downstairs flat at Chester Square would be a perfect place to relocate.

His main concern was Tilly's singular phrasing: *her* place, not *ours*. They'd been working, living and sleeping together for the past nine months. His dependency on her both privately and professionally was reaching saturation point. In a selfish way he welcomed that, as it made his life simpler and he loved and trusted her completely. He could see in her, however, a need to find space of her own, to retrieve the personality that was slowly being smothered by the closeness of their relationship. He'd fallen in love with her strength of character as well as her physical beauty and if living separately meant preserving that strength, then so be it. She was also right about it being next year's problem. The next two weeks could change everything.

He scooped her into his arms, arched his back and spun her around. Her feet left the ground. He leaned forward, flicking her over his back, her legs narrowly missing the sink, and deposited her feet first in front of him.

'Very Torvill and Dean,' she said excitedly. 'Now can I have my stomach back?'

Happiness was his again. Her impish smile repaired the cracks in his confidence and he was ready to face this landmark day.

Tilly was right about them doing well. In August Dominic had added fifteen numbers to his repertoire and two female dancers to the troupe. The girls were loosely choreographed, which proved an excellent move: it focused Dominic's mind on the disciplines of dance and added style and glamour to the routine.

They'd guested on shows in Blackpool, Brighton and Margate, and appeared on virtually every local radio station in the land. Dominic had survived countless interviews without once finding a satisfactory answer to their favourite question: 'How do you dance like that?'

Tilly and Harry were becoming a formidable team in the arena of high-profile public relations. Tilly's professionalism, creative thinking and commercial connections combined with Harry's experience, savvy and tabloid knowledge had secured Dominic two lucrative contracts with leading public companies to endorse products, twelve national television shows including another *Wogan*, and at least one picture story in the daily tabloids each week. Everyone agreed the zenith had been reached on the second weekend in October when Dominic danced at the Palladium in a charity show for UNICEF and achieved a clean sweep of the Sundays, including the front page of the *News of the World* with Linda Lusardi and the *Sunday Express* with Lusinda Green. Also published that weekend was a cover story for *The Sunday Times* on Romanian orphanages and an article for 'Heroes and Villains' in the *Independent* on J.R.R. Tolkien, which Dominic had written a month previously.

Harry's team of investigators had visited all the locations in the dossier and had compiled enough hard evidence to seriously embarrass Ceausescu in the eyes of the international community. Harry said he wanted to publish in January 1990, after the silly season, as he called Christmas, when tabloid front pages weren't obsessed with missing children and the sex life of soap stars. He also referred to the investigation as 'something of substance to start the decade before replunging into the depths of mediocrity and mammaries'.

Malcolm had been a pillar of support throughout the autumn months. He'd spent over £2 million rebuilding the Lyceum, not only restoring it to its former Victorian glory but also installing an unrivalled stage and light show. As the expense rocketed past the original £1 million budget Dominic kept apologising, as if the extra materials and underquoted estimates were somehow his fault. Malcolm always laughed, patted his shoulder and said, 'Dance how you dance, Mr Dance, and I'll recoup within a year.'

They'd find out if he was right soon enough. Tonight the 'Dance Emporium' would open its doors to the public for the first time.

Despite several appeals Dominic still hadn't seen inside the Hampstead house. The reports he'd received from Harry, some only hours old, were always accurate and he grew increasingly impatient to see for himself how they were gathered.

Over the last few days word had reached them that people in the west of Romania were starting a revolution. On 15 December Father Laszlo Tokes, a Protestant pastor who had persistently criticised the government's treatment of his fellow ethnic Hungarians, received a deportation order from Ceausescu. On the 16th several hundred people surrounded Father Tokes's home in Timisoara in an attempt to prevent the police putting the order into effect. The crowd became enraged when Tokes appeared at a window bearing the marks of a severe beating. They marched through the centre of town chanting 'Down with Ceausescu!' and 'Give us bread!' By the next day, 17 December, the crowd had swollen to several thousand. From inside tanks and helicopter gunships the Securitate opened fire indiscriminately on the crowd. By yesterday the death toll had risen to nearly a thousand. On the 18th demonstrations were reported in the towns of Arad and Brasov where workers at the Red Star vehicle factory staged a strike in protest at having to work in sub-zero temperatures. Yesterday British television reported that the US and Soviet governments were expressing grave concern over the Timisoara killings; East Germany and Czechoslovakia withdrew their ambassadors. Ceausescu was coming unstuck – Dominic's evidence could be the final nail in his coffin. He eagerly awaited Harry's arrival with the latest news of overnight events.

Dominic's excitement about the club opening and the

events in Romania was reaching fever pitch. Both filled him with anticipation and hope. First-night tickets to the club had sold out within six hours of going on sale. Thames Television had been filming a documentary for the last four months on the rebuilding of the Lyceum and would be there tonight, as would the BBC, ABC America, and a freelance outfit called Nufilms who were recording all the dance sequences over the Christmas and New Year period for a video to be released in January. Back home, Ceausescu was due back in Bucharest after a three-day visit to Iran. Tonight he would address the nation on television. Harry had promised that a tape of the speech would immediately be biked to the club; Dominic was determined not to miss a single punch in the fight for his country.

Malcolm went on record in the *Express* saying that Ceausescu and the Ayatollah were a 'Satanic alliance', a quote Tilly quickly modified to 'disturbing alliance' for the second editions, fearing another Rushdie controversy could result in high security for the opening, something she wanted to avoid at all costs.

Harry arrived within the hour bearing good news from the home front. Despite the killings, the demonstrations had grown in magnitude overnight. Workers had occupied the petrochemical plant at Timisoara and threatened to blow it up unless the troops returned to their barracks. Harry had just received confirmation that the army had left the streets two hours ago.

'This is so frustrating!' said Dominic, refilling Harry's coffee cup. 'I want to be at Hampstead. Why won't you take me there? I know all about it. Why this secrecy?'

'Malcolm doesn't want you involved. He thinks you should concentrate on the club. He doesn't want to burden you.'

'I *am* involved. It's my bloody country!' Dominic was getting uncharacteristically angry and he didn't care. 'You treat me like a freak to be kept in the dark and let out to perform tricks for money. I'm a Romanian who loves his country and a good many of the people who live in it. I can't stay at arm's length from this fight because of Malcolm's paranoia. I also know the lay of the land better than anyone you have in the field so I could help in deciphering the material. I want to see Hampstead, and I want to see it now.'

Harry leaned back in his chair, as he always did when requiring thinking time, and looked at the ceiling for a moment before answering. 'All right, me old son,' he sighed before tipping forward and locking his gaze on to Dominic with almost sinister intensity. 'On your head, Sunshine. If Malcolm gets iffy you deal with him. All right?'

Harry remained silent as he drove his scarred Volvo out of Belgravia, along Park Lane and up the Edgware Road. Dominic sensed not annoyance but concern. Harry's mind was covering every possible consequence of his decision. 'I'm not sure of this, not sure at all,' he said as he turned right into St John's Wood Road.

'I don't see the problem,' offered Dominic. 'I get all the information second-hand anyway. What's so different about watching it come in?'

'The difference is,' Harry replied, leaving a long enough pause to ensure Dominic's complete attention, 'you get screened Romanian information. At Hampstead you'll see the whole operation and therefore be able to talk about it. Malcolm is security conscious to a fault. He will not take kindly to a security breach, and make no mistake, Dominic, by bringing you here unannounced I am seriously undermining that security.' He flashed his Father Christmas grin. 'We could both be looking for work before this day's through.'

He said nothing more until he pulled the car into a circular driveway on Christchurch Hill and parked in front of an imposing three-storey Edwardian house with double-fronted bay windows, bright white double doors and two-foot-high turrets along the top of the walls obscuring the slope of the roof. No outward signs suggested that this was anything more than another family home in a middle-class area. No guards, cameras, electric fencing, dogs; nothing. The only clue was the size and disposition of the butler who answered the door. To call him ugly would be kind. He had a face that was obviously attracted to flying chairs and other mobile instruments of damage. His attitude was openly hostile until Harry calmed him down by explaining that Dominic was Malcolm's new protégé and that security clearance had been obtained. Only now did Dominic realise the weight of Harry's decision. What he'd laughingly called Malcolm's executive toy could prove much more serious.

They walked the length of a wood-panelled hallway and into a lift at the rear of the building. Harry produced his tethered key-ring and inserted the smallest key into the slot beside the number 3. A small panel opened to the right of the key, revealing a rectangular screen. Harry placed his right hand on the screen and said, 'King's Bishop.' The lift door shut silently and the upward journey began.

They walked out on to a small landing and a steep set of wooden stairs. As they climbed, Dominic heard the sound of generator hum. Another narrow landing led back the length of the stairs, on the left two steel doors housed the hum, straight ahead a wooden door with no handle barred their progress. Again Harry gave up his right hand for inspection and stated his code. The door clicked open. Dominic stepped across the threshold into an electronic palace.

A T-shaped room set in the roof rafters stretched right, left and away from the door. Three unoccupied desks stood to the right, a lounge area with two leather sofas, a glass coffee table and a kitchen unit to the left. Down the middle a custom-built unit some twenty feet long housed banks of computer terminals, telephones, cassette machines and printers. Seven high-backed chairs stood along one side of the unit. Rows of television monitors

158

angled down from the roof-ceiling opposite. Only one person, a woman in black overalls, was visible. She sat at the far station talking in French into a headset connected to the table.

Harry extracted a beer from the kitchen fridge and slumped on to the nearest sofa. 'Help yourself. Coke, 7Up, water.'

'What the hell is this, Harry?' Dominic had expected a computer or two and the odd telephone, but this amount of equipment coupled with the intensity of security suggested something much more complex.

'Malcolm's executive toy. You said so yourself.'

Dominic chose a small bottle of Evian from the fridge and drank half, alleviating the dryness that was quickly forming in his mouth.

Harry smiled and swigged his beer. 'You want to know what we do? OK, I'll tell you.' He settled himself into the sofa and lit a large Cuban cigar. 'This operation is called K7. The K stands for Knowledge.' He took a long drag on the cigar. 'Over the next few years we reckon the public will have access to both military and government information. In America the Freedom of Information Act has screwed a lot of people. If and when similar laws are passed over here our aim will be to stay out of the reach of such legislation so we can continue our work without fear of exposure. We can't call ourselves Military Intelligence, as in MI5 and MI6, it's too well known: hence the name K7. The references to chess squares as code names makes lineage of command easy to decipher.'

His obvious pride in the operation manifested itself in more vehement sucking on his cigar. 'This is just a start. Within a few years we'll be office-block size. We're independent of the government and the military so we can't be made to talk.' He looked at Dominic and grinned, amused by his astonishment. 'It's one of the advantages of privatisation.'

'Are you telling me this is government backed?'

'Contracted is the word we use. We have contracts to

159

supply information. We receive information through agents using electronic-gathering machines and satellites.' Harry let out a raucous belly laugh. 'Malcolm wants to be an underground CNN and, knowing him, he'll do it.'

'Where's the connection? What has Malcolm to do with the military?' Dominic thought Malcolm had neither the background nor the finesse to oversee such a sophisticated operation. As in rebuilding the club, Malcolm contributed money, and lots of it, but Dominic had severe doubts that his imagination could grasp the next phase of British espionage without massive prompting from a well-informed source. He looked Harry square in the eyes, searching for the real truth. For nine months he'd heard snippets, shards of information with no real substance. Now this. A professional, secure, state-of-the-art operation, with the man who planned his defection very much in command.

'It's you, isn't it? You're in charge,' said Dominic, more questioning the theory than stating a conviction.

Harry studied his protégé with paternal pride. 'I'm afraid so.' Harry's face turned serious but remained friendly. 'As a nipper I was part of Special Services. On my first and only mission I got smacked in the leg by a .44 high velocity. The leg healed, but not enough to let me back in.' Dominic now realised why Harry rocked back and forth before standing up, and why he would sometimes stumble on a seemingly even surface. 'The Brits aren't a people who waste that amount of training on one mission,' continued Harry. 'So they made me a reporter and put me undercover.'

Dominic noticed a poster sealed inside the glass table top. It was printed with white lettering on black paper and read: We have not learned anything, we don't know anything, we don't have anything, we don't understand anything, we don't sell anything, we don't help, we don't betray, and we will not forget.' On the white border at the bottom left-hand corner, were the handwritten words: Czech Freedom Poster.

'Dubcek wrote those words in case I ever lost the faith.' Harry rocked twice and stood up. He put his arm around Dominic's shoulders as he had that first day at Wembley, only this time he squeezed considerably harder. He was a cumbersome, middle-aged man, but Dominic didn't fancy having to square up to him for real. 'You wanted to know and now you do. There is one thing.' Harry tightened his grip to near hurting point. 'I'd appreciate your help with Romania, but as we can't invoke the Official Secrets Act, being a private company and all, if you open your mouth to the press I'll have to get handsome Charlie downstairs to shut it. Get my drift?'

The threat was real enough and duly noted. 'Perfectly,' replied Dominic.

'Good!' Harry moved towards the centre console, his mood once again ebullient, his manner friendly, as if the act had been duly signed. 'Drag over that chair and sit beside me.' He plugged two headsets into the table sockets and handed one set to Dominic. 'Put them on and let's see what going on in Bucharest.'

Dominic did as instructed, listening with great interest to the sounds of electronic tracking. He was fascinated by Harry's prowess. He entered codes, called up satellite transponders and checked ground stations with the ease of a seasoned professional, his work instantly traced on a world map flashing from a television monitor in the slanted ceiling opposite. Turning his attention to the phone he punched a thirteen-digit number into the matrix. Dominic heard beeps and echoes through the headset as a bright red line zigzagged across the screen, plotting the connecting path as it hopped satellites and grounded in Bucharest.

One double ring then a click: Harry keyed control/F8 into the computer. There were two beeps then a disconnect tone. The bright red line disappeared instantly from the monitor.

'He'll get back to me in a minute,' said Harry, keying

in £&* and the word OPEN. He glanced at his watch. 'Almost noon. Want to see what the world thinks?'

Dominic was desperate to learn more. 'Yes please!'

Harry entered another code. Six ceiling monitors came to life, each showing a programme from a different country – Russia, China, America, Iran, Romania and the BBC. 'We tailor-make our monitoring to fit the story. We'll show Russia, China and America, RCA as we call them, on all stories. I've called up Iran because Ceausescu's there at the moment.'

A red light flashed in the centre of the console. Harry typed RECORD ALL and pressed return. The screens went black. 'We'll look at that later. Right now it's showtime!' He keyed control/insert and typed ALL. The six screens brightened back to life. All showed the same picture: the town centre at Timisoara.

Dominic had been there many times, but the pictures before him bore no relation to the town he knew. Half the smaller buildings had been reduced to rubble, the larger constructions stood pitted with rocket and mortar holes against a grey, wintry sky. Dark shapes patterned the snow that covered the main square, patterns the cherry-red colour of blood. Dominic sat mesmerized by the sight, the horrors of the atrocity coming to life in his mind.

Harry's voice cut through the headset. 'K7 Control to Bishop's Pawn. We have a down link completion. You're live.'

'This is Timisoara town centre. Not a lot left now.' The voice spoke English with an accent. Not Romanian; possibly German, Austrian or even Russian. 'I've got some footage an hour ago from Communist headquarters. You'll love this.' The screens went black. Through the headset came the sound of changing cartridges in the camera.

Harry looked over at Dominic. 'He can use the camera as a playback facility as well as live broadcast. Well useful.'

'Here it comes.'

The screens brightened again, revealing the Communist Party Headquarters and the police offices. Not hundreds, not thousands, but tens of thousands of people were storming the building. Wrecking, smashing, shouting, looting; with the army off the streets there was nothing to stop them.

'Latest word is fifty thousand stormed the building. They've destroyed everything in their path – furniture, police records, land deeds. It's impossible for the government here to continue. I heard ten minutes ago that the Mayor has invited the people to elect a committee to voice their grievances and the Prime Minister is on his way here from Bucharest to meet them.'

'Are you getting any hassle?' asked Harry.

'Nobody cares what I do. Securitate would cut off my balls but they're scattered in the countryside or have returned to their bases. The people control the entire area and since they stormed the police station they've got guns. I heard ten minutes ago they caught two Securitate on the edge of town.'

'Did they detain them?' asked Harry, hoping for prisoners from whom he could extract vital up-to-date information.

'They killed them. These people have had enough. I can't see Ceausescu and his thugs holding on to power for more than a week.' A Romanian voice became clearly audible through the system, saying 'Come, come, I've got picture for you, come, come.' 'Stay with me, Control!'

Further clunking crackled down the line as the cameraman reloaded his tape, then a close-up of the road as he ran along beside the mystery voice, going west out of the main square into the Hungarian sector. About two hundred yards along Oradia Street he stopped and entered a building through a green door. The cameraman switched on his lighting and scanned across the small, square room.

At first it looked as if someone had dug up the floor, then, as the camera focused, it became apparent they were

163

bodies piled three deep. Mutilated and decaying bodies, some without heads, limbs, breasts; some with burn and acid marks covering most of their skin.

'The stench is appalling in here and my batteries are almost dead!' shouted the cameraman. 'Ten more seconds and I'm out of here!' His voice carried the horror of what he was seeing. The camera shook as he scanned the room one more time. 'Are you getting this?'

'Every foot!' shouted Harry into the headset.

The camera finally backed out of the room and was laid on the pavement outside the building, still filming the melting snow as it trickled away into the gutter.

The link map superimposed itself on the middle screen, a yellow light appearing on the travel line between Romania and the first up-link. 'We have a tracer, Bishop's Pawn. Am disconnecting now!'

Harry keyed CONTROL/f8. All screens went to black. 'They're still there, but they'll have to be faster than that!' he exclaimed with more than a touch of self-satisfaction.

'Have you ever been traced?' Dominic asked, removing his headset and placed it on the console.

'Nope. We have a tracking device called "satlock" that links the betacam direct with the nearest satellite within seconds. It also enables us to change routes instantly, so by the time they've locked on to us we're somewhere else.' Harry was enjoying the game, if not the content. He reran the footage taken inside the room. 'How many bodies do you think? Two hundred?'

Dominic couldn't bring himself to look at the screen. Harry cut off the sound, which somehow made it more bearable. Hesitantly, he looked at the silent, invidious tomb. This was genocide on a Nazi scale. These had been people tortured by the Securitate and dumped back in their own area to teach the rest a lesson. These were Hungarians whose only crime had been to speak their own language, for which they'd paid the martyr's price.

'Close to that, I'd say.' Dominic averted his eyes, unable to study the carnage any more.

164

A laser printer to Harry's right clicked into action. He keyed CONTROL/P. The right-hand screen lit up and copied the printer's output verbatim. The message read:

'CEAUSESCU BACK FROM IRAN. MUCH RANTING AND GNASHING OF TEETH. MRS C IS FURIOUS. TELEVISION SLOT BOOKED FOR 17.45. SUGGEST USE INTELSAT FOR BEST RECEPTION. WILL CONFIRM PREFERRED ROUTE BY 17.00.'

There was no heading or signature on the message.

'Game on!' shouted Harry, his voice sanguine, excited, betraying his innermost thoughts. Harry Cassini loved his work.

'What can I do to help?' asked Dominic.

'Nothing for the moment, thank you.' He studied Dominic's face carefully as if looking for disapproval or self-reproach. 'I took the biggest chance of my life bringing you here, Dominic. I still might regret it.' His expression softened, his smile returned. 'Too late to worry now, eh my old son? Anything bothering you? If so, get it off your chest now.'

Dominic had so many questions he hardly knew where to start. 'What's Malcolm's real role in all this?'

'In it for the money at first. This is a *very* profitable business. Last year the government spent over £750 *million* on MI5 and MI6. The more he saw of the crap that was going on out East, however, the more involved he became.' He emitted one of his gravelly chuckles. 'He's more bloody political than me these days. He gets so pissed off when things go wrong I sometimes think he's going to grab an AK47 and shoot all the commies in the world single-handed. He also knows how lucky he's been with Ramco and he wants to put something back.'

'How many people work here?'

'Eighteen in all, excluding me. We work flexible shifts, depending on the situation.'

Harry waved at the woman at the far end of the room, who smiled and returned his greeting. 'That's Yvette. She's monitoring the French farmers' row over lamb imports.

Not everything we do is war based. Except for your country's problems and the Panama thing with Noriega there's no real action going on at the moment.'

He swigged the last of his beer and propelled the empty bottle into the waste bin with Exocet accuracy. 'The lull before the storm, I reckon.'

Dominic felt he was being recruited: Harry was inviting him to join the team. 'To which particular storm are you referring?'

'Yugoslavia. I feel it in my water. That whole place could go bang at any moment and we're very thin on the ground over there.' He stood up and beckoned Dominic to follow him. 'Come on, I'll take you for lunch in the village and then, my friend, you have to be a star. Tilly will have my balls for bookends if you're late for the press call.'

'Do you want me to be a field agent?' asked Dominic hopefully.

'Diplomat or go-between are the words I'd use,' said Harry, having anticipated Dominic's question by at least two weeks. 'I want you to be famous, be up front where everyone can see you. I want you to be the King of Clubs. When you've achieved that high a profile every non-Ceausescu Romanian will flock to you. We'll be standing behind you to sift the information.' He rocked in preparation for standing up.

'The downside is that if Ceausescu goes after the Timisoara massacre you've got about two weeks to get seriously famous.'

Twenty-three

Harry parked the Volvo outside the Lyceum stage door in Burleigh Street at five minutes to four. 'There you go, young man,' he said calmly, his earlier frustration with London traffic placated now he'd delivered his passenger on time. 'I'll see you later with the Ceausescu tape.'

A mountain named Tor opened the stage door at the second ring. The new club security boss could best be described as a not-so-gentle giant. He stood six foot six in his Doc Martens with a chest the size of an average wine keg and an attitude just to the right of Genghis Khan. Of Nordic stock, he'd come to England to compete in a strong-man competition last summer and decided to stay. Malcolm had pulled his usual strings in order to obtain a work permit. 'Miss Tilly wait for you in dressing room. You go now,' he said in his best English.

'Thank you, Tor. Is Malcolm here?'

'Boss come five o'clock. Best you go Miss Tilly now.'

'I'm on my way.' Dominic slipped past him and hurried off in the direction of the backstage area.

The Lyceum's interior design was now totally different. The stage area had been extended to incorporate a double bank of footlights and the ground floor seating had been replaced by a polished wooden dance space. Above that, a massive aluminium gantry supported every conceivable lighting effect modern technology had to offer. Travel

167

spots, strobes, colour banks, revolving whites, fluorescent tubes, laser guns and starbursts packed every inch of the twenty-square-foot scaffolding which was anchored to the restored ornate by steel chains.

The balconies contained seating for 200 around plexiglass tables for six, all emblazoned with a double 'D' motif. Individual boxes to both sides of the stage had also been fully restored and were available for private parties at a premium of £50. Oakwood bars across the back of each floor were serviced by six dumb-waiter lifts connected to the kitchen in the basement. Apart from the dance area and stage, the entire floor was covered by deep red carpeting and the walls and balcony fronts were painted matching red with white trim. The original Victorian motifs had been restored by thankful craftsmen glad to find traditional work in these modern, simplistic times.

The backstage area contained four guest dressing rooms, each with *ensuite* bathroom and wall-size lighted mirrors; a main office area, and Dominic's suite of lounge, double bedroom, shower, dressing area and walk-in wardrobe. As it was below ground level and without windows, he'd had it painted bright white and installed two banks of variable spots in each room. All food could be ordered directly from the main kitchen, so the only culinary appliance was a large Westinghouse frost-free fridge to keep the champagne, beer, fruit juice and mineral water at drinkable temperatures.

He heard the sound of running water as he entered the room and guessed that Tilly was showering in preparation for the onslaught of the next few, crucial hours. He tiptoed into the bedroom and saw her exquisite form silhouetted behind the shower curtain. Steam formed droplets on the plastic, distorting her image like an Impressionist painting. Silently he locked the bedroom door, undressed in less than ten seconds and slid open the curtain with one quick flick. It was a playful, juvenile attempt to scare her and it failed miserably. Tilly stood under the shower, her arms crossed in front of her, and grinned at him as if humouring a spoiled child.

'I heard you come in,' she said, dropping her arms and standing vulnerably in front of him. 'If you want a shower together you only have to ask.'

The tower of business and personal strength gave way to the defenceless woman in love. The unbreakable china doll transformed into a delicate gossamer butterfly, fragile and susceptible to control. In the past Dominic would have used such vulnerability to gain advantage; now his only thought was to protect and comfort the one person on earth who held his love in her heart. He gathered her into his arms, the warm, soothing water lubricating their bodies. 'I love you,' he whispered, running his hands slowly down.

'I know,' she whispered back, burying her head in the curve of his neck and inhaling his scent as she gripped him tightly around his waist. 'Can you do it in three minutes?' she teased, moving her right hand between them and holding his expanding manhood with measured firmness. 'If not, tell me about Hampstead.'

'I can do both,' he replied, lifting her leg around his waist and allowing her to guide his penis into her. She swung her other leg round his waist and placed both her arms around his neck, drawing him inside her. He pushed her against the hard, wet tiles. The water poured over them like a shield against all intrusion. It lasted but a minute, both of them shuddering towards climax with frenzied urgency.

'I love you so very much, Dominic, I feel I'm going to burst,' she said, still gripping him firmly inside her. 'Sometimes it scares me, I love you so much. No man has ever done what you do to me.' She kissed him full on the mouth, her tongue exploring, her arms tightening around his neck: timelessly, tenderly. '*And* you still have a minute left to tell me about Hampstead,' she said with a cheeky smile as they stood face to face in the warm rain.

'I don't know how much I can tell you. How much do you know?'

'I know it's a mini-listening post and is connected with the government in some way.'

'Then you know as much as me,' he lied, feeling guilt at his dishonesty. 'Harry was very economical with information. He showed me some pictures from Romania and asked me to detail streets and locations.'

Dominic felt he had to tell her more. He wanted to tell her everything – the massacre at Timisoara, the agents with cameras, the roomful of bodies, the extent of Harry's involvement, everything. He also knew that to arm her with such knowledge would put her in danger.

'What did you think of the equipment up there?' she asked, grabbing a towel.

'State of the art, definitely. They have ground-to-satellite communications that are years ahead. I thought I was on the *Starship Enterprise*.'

Tilly wrapped the towel round her shoulders, squeezed passed him and gracefully stepped into the carpeted bedroom.

'I didn't understand most of it but it looked very impressive,' Dominic went on.

She looked back over her shoulder, her lips pouting, her eyes teasing, daring him to chase after her. As she had the only towel, the decision was easy. He turned off the water, jumped from the shower and tackled her rugby fashion around the waist. His momentum carried them both across the room and on to the bed.

'Dominic! We have a press call in five minutes! One quickie per day is all you get. Further lovemaking carries a minimum time of one hour.' She wriggled out of his grasp and stood up beside the bed leaving him a coital memory and a soaking wet towel.

'I thought I'd wear the electric-blue blazer and black trousers,' he said, forcing himself to stop thinking of her breasts.

170

'Very good choice,' she replied. 'Your fashion sense has come on in leaps and bounds.'

'One tries.' He lowered his eyes in mock embarrassment, so didn't see the playful left hook until it was too late.

'Pay attention,' she commanded. 'I want you to talk to Thames Television first, then spend five minutes with the BBC so we'll all know what we're doing. I've moved the photocall back to half-past five.' She kissed his cheek at the spot where she'd hit him. 'Hurry up and get dressed, and let's set this town on fire!'

Dominic dried, dressed and was ready in five minutes, as was Tilly. They inspected each other for fluff and flaws. 'You look smashing,' she said, her voice brimming with pride.

'And you look very beautiful,' he replied, placing a silent kiss on her forehead.

They walked hand in hand down the corridor and arm in arm on to the stage. Three camera crews busied themselves on the empty dance area taking cutaways and detail shots for editing into their final programmes at a later date.

A large, effeminate man dressed in a silver-grey suit and a shocking-pink tie shouted orders at one of the crews from the second-floor balcony. 'Over there, darlings. I want a shot of the empty table, then lock it off and we'll put the lovely Brian in the picture for the opening speech.' His voice was clipped and full of sibilants. He spotted Tilly and Dominic and waved frantically at them. 'Darlings!! You both look marvellous!' Then to the crew: 'Forget that. Get me a two shot of the lovebirds.'

Instinctively Dominic and Tilly moved apart as they did every time cameras pointed in their direction. It was silly, really, as everyone knew they were a couple, but so far they'd avoided the media stare with some considerable skill and they wanted to keep it that way. Ninety per cent of Dominic's fans were female and Tilly thought it foolish to break the eligible bachelor image. She also wished to

171

keep out of the limelight herself, preferring to stay in the background and work stories from the position of anonymity; a method that had proved both successful and conducive to a reasonably quiet private life.

'Come on, Dar . . . lings!' he shouted again, accentuating the last word like a cry for help. 'It's opening night. Let's open with a picture of you two. I'll still-frame it. It'll make *all* the papers!'

They looked at each other like Bonnie and Clyde just before the federal guns opened fire. The producer was right. It was the story that would guarantee them good coverage in the tabloids, and with General Noriega nicking the headlines for the past three days, they could use all the help they could get. It would also mean the end of their private affair. The second they admitted their love they would become public property.

'You're an absolute sweetheart, Adrian, but no thanks!' shouted Tilly as she walked down the stage steps and on to the dance floor. 'Save your tape for Dominic when he dances. That's front-page news!'

They all knew it wasn't, but Dominic had learned not to argue with Tilly's decisions on press coverage. She was master of the hidden agenda, cajoling one journalist to take an angle on a story he didn't fancy while quietly feeding another the real thing in exchange for better coverage. They often had lively discussions about the ethics of her methods; she calling it diplomacy, he suggesting it was good old-fashioned lies. Whatever plan was now forming in her deliciously devilish mind would be all right by Dominic Dance.

. He stood centre stage and surveyed the panorama in front of him. The trellis of lights, the polished dance floor, the painted balconies, the lush red carpets – he took everything in, sound, smell and vision. The months of preparation and millions of Malcolm's money would tonight pay a dividend and it was down to Dominic to deliver. He inhaled a long, deep breath of electrified air: he was ready.

'Dominic!' Tilly's voice cut through his thoughts. He looked in her direction. She was pointing to the right side of the stage, the only part of the room free of camera crews and workmen. He walked over there and waited as Tilly finished her conversation with the director from Thames Television. She glided towards him, her slim, black Dior dress accentuating the curves of her body. A follow-spot picked her out from the top balcony. She turned round, shielded her eyes from the glare with her right hand and signalled a thumbs down with her left. The light was switched off.

'Adrian's got a point,' she said, looking around to make sure they weren't overheard. 'If we face the press together there's a good chance we'd double tomorrow's coverage.'

'You're the boss,' replied Dominic, hoping to divert the responsibility.

'And you're no help at all.' Her voice was clipped but not angry. 'If we go public there's always a chance my ex's could come out of the woodwork and sell their stories. Could you handle that?'

He tried putting mock horror into his reply in order to keep the conversation light. 'What *were* you up to before we met?'

'Not as much as I get up to with you,' she said with a chuckle. 'But you know the tabloids. Admit to wearing stockings in bed and they'll call you Miss Whiplash.'

'Do they have any pictures, and if so can I have a copy?' This time he saw the left hook coming and grabbed her wrist. 'Did you ever beat any of your lovers?'

'Only verbally.' She raised her eyebrows, retrieved her arm and straightened her dress. 'I'm trying to ask you a serious question and I haven't much time. Now, tell me what you think.'

He wanted to take her in his arms and kiss her in front of Adrian, the workmen, the camera crews, everyone. Success tonight would be totally hollow without her and he could keep his love hidden no longer. 'I think we should tell Adrian to take his pictures and tell the press

173

how we feel about each other.' He raised his voice above the noise around them. 'I love you, Tilly Howard!'

'Shhhh.' Tilly placed her hand over his mouth and planted a kiss on his cheek. Her eyes sparkled with happiness. 'Forget Adrian,' she said. 'We'll do this properly. Go to the dressing room and call Harry on his mobile. I'll call Dempster, Pollard, Morgan and Malone.' She glanced at her watch. 'It's too late for the *Standard* but I can still catch the rest if we hurry.' She took two paces towards the door, stopped, turned round, and produced a smile bright enough to replace the entire lighting gantry. 'I love you too, Dominic.'

Harry was overjoyed. He offered his congratulations and promised at least a page three in tomorrow's *Sun*. 'Have you told her about Hampstead?' he asked just as Dominic was about to hang up the phone.

'Not in any detail.'

'Good boy.' He disconnected without further conversation.

Dominic took a fresh bottle of Perrier from the fridge, wandered into the bedroom and flopped lazily on to the bed. He felt relatively calm despite his anticipation of the night ahead. He drifted into a soporific state, sweet daydreams of Tilly in her little black dress dancing languidly through his mind.

'Hey!' Malcolm's voice returned Dominic to reality. 'How can you sleep at a time like this?'

Slowly Dominic opened his eyes. 'I always sleep before a big event so I wake up relaxed. Except, that is, when somebody breaks into my mood.'

Malcolm's reaction was almost apologetic but with a slight edge of self-importance. 'Heaven forbid I should spoil your karma. We do, however, have a club to open and the press and your beloved Tilly are waiting in the foyer.'

Dominic looked at his watch: 5.45. He'd been asleep for an hour! He arched his back and handsprung off the bed, impressing the hell out of Malcolm and surprising
174

the hell out of himself. 'On the case, boss, and at your service.'

To Dominic's utter astonishment Malcolm put his arms around him and hugged him tightly. He'd never shown that type of affection before and it caught Dominic totally off guard. He'd thought Malcolm far too macho to indulge in physical contact with the same sex. Dominic returned his embrace with guarded enthusiasm. Malcolm's next remark left Dominic even more flabbergasted. 'I'm so proud of you, Dominic,' he said. 'You've fought the lot of them and won.'

Dominic had always thought of himself as someone who ran away, escaped a prison maybe, but basically a runner. He hadn't really stood and fought anyone. He hadn't had the courage to avenge the death of his parents or to try and stop Ceausescu's evil regime from within the country. He'd got the hell out at the earliest available opportunity and now this normally untactile man was embracing him and saying he'd fought and won. It didn't make sense.

'Harry's told me you've joined us in K7,' he continued, releasing his grip and looking at Dominic with pride shining from his eyes. 'Ceausescu will fall within the week and you will have played a major part.'

'By doing what?'

Malcolm's face turned placid. The information trail stopped here. 'Another time, Dominic, another time. Right now you've got to rock 'n' roll!'

The foyer was packed with journalists and photographers. Malcolm had spared no expense in bringing this part of the building back to its former glory. The six oak and glass entrance doors, the raised cornice motifs around the top of the walls, the ornately carved reception desk were all fully restored with tender loving care. The craftsmen had done a magnificent job. By way of a bonus Malcolm had rewarded them with life membership of the club. Many would be here tonight.

Dominic walked straight over to Tilly, put his arm round her waist and smiled as the cameras flashed out of sync.

'Ladies and gentlemen,' said Tilly, raising her hand in an unsuccessful attempt to silence the room. 'Dominic and I have a personal announcement to make.' That did it. The room fell silent within a second. 'First, let me thank you all for coming here tonight. The Dance Emporium will soon be open for business. The first five nights have already sold out due mainly to the exceptional talent of our resident host and co-owner of the club, Dominic Dance!' Muffled applause emanated from those not holding cameras.

'As we're also all aware of the tragic events going on in Dominic's country at the moment,' she continued, 'you will appreciate his concern for family and friends, and must ask you not to ask any questions about these events as he has been instructed to reply "no comment" in order to protect relatives still living in Romania.' Dominic had no relations left in Romania and Tilly knew it, but her announcement ensured even more sympathy from an already partisan press.

'What about you two?!' shouted a disembodied voice.

'I think Dominic should answer that,' she said, throwing him straight in at the deep end.

'Ladies and gentlemen of the great British press,' he started, knowing it was a bit strong but not caring. 'It took me six months to plan my escape from Romania and it took me six seconds to fall in love with Tilly Howard.' To his amazement even those with cameras applauded. 'I'm proud to announce that as soon as the club is up and running I intend to make Miss Howard my wife.'

He couldn't believe he'd said that; it had just popped out spontaneously. They hadn't discussed marriage or even engagement. The remark was at best presumptuous, at worst insulting. Dominic felt his face turn red. He also felt Tilly's hands cupping his cheek and her lips pressing firmly against his. The flashes from fifty cameras lit the room.

'Yes I will,' she whispered, as the reporters, photographers, camera crews and club staff vanished completely from their world.

'I'll drink to that!' Malcolm's voice boomed out across the foyer. Tilly and Dominic turned towards him and into the brightness of another barrage of camera flashes. 'We have crates of champagne that must be finished tonight,' he continued. 'So please, ladies and gentlemen, drink your fill and help us celebrate two great events – the opening of the first of several Dance Emporiums and the forthcoming marriage of the best press officer a company could ask for to the best freeform dancer in the world.'

Dominic could now touch Tilly openly for the first time in public. They held hands, linked arms, cuddled, kissed, completely free of the constraints of what had been a clandestine affair. Dominic longed to dance, to manifest his feelings in the art of movement. Tilly read him perfectly.

'Do you want to put on a show for the press before the punters arrive?' she asked, patting him playfully on the bottom.

Dominic returned her playful gesture, much to the delight of the photographer from the *News of the World*, whose camera clicked three times before Dominic could remove his hand. Tilly announced that Dominic would dance. A general hubbub of approval floated around the room as the crowd began to funnel through the doors on each side of the reception desk and into the club.

'Give me five minutes to tip off the television people,' said Tilly, handing Dominic her full glass of champagne. 'What music do you want?'

'I think Technotronic, "Pump up the Jam".'

'I'll tell the DJ.' She was gone in an instant, lost in the gaggle of journalists and photographers jostling each other for the best vantage point on the dance floor.

The joy Dominic felt from his love and the freedom he felt from sharing the news made his jumps six inches higher, his airborne time a second longer and his interpretation of the music immeasurably better. For those magic minutes he forgot about Timisoara, Ceausescu, Securitate and the suffering of his people. For that moment his heart was light and his soul was free.

After a quick shower and change of clothes Dominic rejoined the foyer festivities. Only the hard-core heavy drinkers from the press were left, the rest having moved on to the next photocall or back to their offices to fill up their column inches. As he entered the area Malcolm was about to address the staff who had gathered by the entrance. Dominic hadn't been sure about the staff uniforms at first, but now he saw them all together he was prepared to admit Tilly had been right. The men's outfit started with the basic formal suit. Those working the foyer wore jackets; those inside the club had brightly coloured waistcoats instead. The women could choose between knee-length black skirts and tailored trousers with white shirts, waistcoats and matching bow-ties.

'You all know what we expect,' Malcolm was saying in his most executive voice. 'Be welcoming, polite and helpful to every customer, and above all have fun. People come here to enjoy themselves and they can't do that if they see the staff with long faces.' He held up a photograph of himself holding a pot of white paint. 'I've decided to start a caption competition and this is the first one. I'll pay £25 for the best caption if you have the guts to sign your contribution.' Laughter all round. 'That's good. Let's keep that attitude and good luck to everyone. We open in fifteen minutes.'

Dominic felt Tilly's hand on his shoulder. 'I need you to do BBC Television before we open,' she said, steering him back into the club. 'And don't forget to mention you got your first break on *Wogan*.'

The lovely Brian was installed behind a table on the first-floor balcony. He offered Dominic a limp handshake as the sound engineer clipped a tiny microphone on to the lapel of his jacket. Dominic didn't share Harry and

Malcolm's intolerance of homosexuals. The ones he'd met, mainly through Tilly's connections, had been witty, amusing, and in the case of Anthony the designer, extremely talented. In Romania it was not an issue. Homosexuality was totally underground and seldom referred to by either the media or the government. A very unhealthy attitude, given the AIDS problem, but understandable from the gay point of view: being open meant being dead if the Securitate caught up with you.

Following a five-second countdown and a blown kiss from Adrian, Brian spoke straight to camera. 'Tonight sees the opening of a new club in London. A club with a difference. The Dance Emporium boasts room for two thousand people, restaurant seating for two hundred, and its own star cabaret in the form of a man who captured the country's imagination when he first appeared on *Terry Wogan* last spring and thrilled us all by dancing with the grace of Nureyev and the funk of Michael Jackson. He's a Romanian refugee who defected to Britain with only the clothes on his back and his remarkable talent. Now he's set to become a millionaire within a year, thanks to the backing of Malcolm Barrett, one of England's brightest young businessmen. Dominic Dance will be the first major star of the nineties.' He turned to face Dominic.

'Dominic, how do you feel about your future in the light of the terrible things currently happening in Romania?'

Dominic's reaction was cobra-quick. 'Like you, Brian, I've only read the stories in today's newspapers. The *Express* says the death toll could be over two thousand. If that's true it's a disaster.'

Brian smiled, but not with his eyes. 'Do you have friends or family who've been killed?' He wanted sensationalism not fact and there was no way Dominic was playing that game.

'I'm sorry,' he said, standing up and moving out of shot. 'I'm not prepared to answer questions like that. If I name people they'll be in great danger. This is supposed to be an opening of a club piece, not the nine o'clock news.'

'Cut!' shouted Adrian, walking from behind the camera to join them. 'Listen, darling, this is the big story. We'll mention the club, honest. You want the publicity, don't you? I can't guarantee it gets to air unless we have a hard news angle.'

Neither the director nor the presenter had any idea what harm a careless name dropped in England could do back in Romania. Dominic's anger swelled inside him; he looked straight into the director's eyes.

'First of all, Adrian, I'm not your *darling*. Secondly, I will not risk anyone's life for a few seconds' worth of publicity on the television, so I suggest you take your camera and the *lovely* Brian and piss off out of my club!'

'Well!' he responded, placing both hands on his hips. 'If that's your mood. . . .'

'That *is* my mood,' Dominic said, removing the microphone from his jacket. It was then he noticed the Thames crew, who had been filming the whole incident from the far side of the balcony.

'What's the matter here?' Tilly was suddenly beside him, her voice strident.

'Your prima donna's throwing a wobbly,' stated Adrian, flicking his hair in a defiant gesture. 'He won't answer Brian's questions.'

'About what?'

'Well . . . Romania.' His hesitancy proved his treachery.

'And I should think not!' Tilly scolded him like a teacher telling off a naughty little boy. 'I asked you to stay off that subject and you said you would. You're chancing your arm, Adrian Parfit, and I'll not have it!' She turned to Dominic, her eyes flashing with anger. 'Capital Radio are in your room. They want a live piece for *The Way It Is*. Go to them. I'll sort this.'

As Dominic walked down the stairs to the ground floor he could hear Tilly delivering a stern lecture to Adrian and Brian and his smile returned. Tonight was going to be A.OK.

And so it proved. The Emporium was packed, the music

180

mix brilliant, the food delicious, the champagne cold. Dominic danced three sets, two with the girls and one alone. Between shows he and Tilly wandered through the club signing autographs, chatting to the customers, posing for pictures and taking requests for the DJ. Everyone seemed to be relaxed and having fun. The dance floor was continuously full during the fast numbers, and much to the delight of everyone Tilly and Dominic took full advantage of the spare space during the slow sections and danced together publicly for the first time.

Just before midnight a bike arrived from Hampstead with the Ceausescu tape. Tilly and Dominic watched it together in his dressing room. Ceausescu declared a state of emergency in Timisoara and blamed terrorists, fascists, imperialists, hooligans and foreign espionage services for the disturbances. Seeing that man's face again sent a shiver down Dominic's spine. He translated the speech for Tilly, who sat rigidly beside him unable to believe what she was hearing.

'Can't the people see through the lies? Don't they know he's conning them?' Her voice was angry, yet filled with concern.

'Of course they see through him but until now they've been powerless to do anything about it. It still might end up as a local rebellion. The Securitate are seriously evil. They've killed two thousand already, another three or four thousand won't bother them. The only real hope we have is if the army turns against them.'

'I thought the Securitate *was* the army.'

'Not at all.' Dominic turned off the video machine. 'Ceausescu formed Securitate on the same lines as Hitler's SS and Haiti's Tontons Macoutes. Most of his top men were recruited from orphanages as teenagers so they have no family ties. He gives them money, power and position within the community and in return they do his bidding, no matter how diabolical. They like the power they wield so the reign of terror gets worse each year until stories like the Caprianu family become commonplace and the

181

people's attitudes revert to the three monkeys: hear nothing, see nothing, say nothing.'

Tilly placed her arm around his shoulder and nuzzled close. 'It seems so inadequate to say it'll be all right, but I'm sure it will.'

Twenty-four

Dominic slept until noon the next day. Any movement from Tilly would usually wake him immediately, but this morning she'd slid out of bed very quietly. Dominic was aware of nothing until she perched noisily beside him, morning papers in one hand, a steaming hot cup of coffee in the other.

'Come on, sleepy, wake up. You're a star in every paper.'

His first reaction was to bundle her back into bed but he thought of the hot coffee and changed his mind.

'Good morning, queen of the press. How many front pages?'

'None, I'm afraid. The Americans have put up a million-dollar reward for General Noriega and that's captured the headlines. Romania has been relegated to page five.' She opened the *Sun* to page three. 'You and I, on the other hand, share page three with Marie Whittaker.'

DOMINIC DANCE TO WED WOMAN WHO MADE HIM A STAR bannered the top of the page in one-inch type. With the exception of the topless model, the rest of the page was devoted to the story. It carried two pictures, a head and shoulders of them kissing in the foyer and a great interior shot of the club. Dominic read the copy out loud.

'Romanian defector and dancing star Dominic Dance (24), took time out from opening his new London club to ask Tilly Howard, the woman responsible for his meteoric rise to fame, to marry him. Her skilful handling of his short but brilliant career has made him a household name in Britain in under a year.

'Last night he repaid her confidence and hard work by popping the question at a star-studded reception held at the old Lyceum Ballroom in the Strand which has just undergone a £2 million facelift and been renamed the Dance Emporium. As we sipped champagne and toasted the success of Dominic's first business venture he told me it had taken a year to plan his escape from Romania and a minute to fall in love with his beautiful and elegant press officer.

'The only black spot on the glitzy and celebrity-filled evening was the news that two thousand people had been killed by security forces near Dominic's home town of Timisoara. "I'm very concerned," he told me privately, "but I believe the people will win in the end and this evil dictator will soon be overthrown." Dominic will dance three times a night at the Emporium. Tickets to the club have already sold out until mid-January 1990.'

Timisoara wasn't Dominic's home town, he hadn't given Harry any quotes, and the time it took to plan Dominic's escape seemed to grow longer with each article. Apart from those slight factual deviations it was splendid.

'I gave him the quote,' said Tilly, her thought-reading antennae as sharp as ever. 'Have a look at the *Express* and *Daily Star*. Great picture in the *Express*.'

Half of page five in the *Express* carried a picture of them in the foyer looking extremely pleased with life. They didn't mention Romania in the caption, preferring instead to concentrate on 'The Happy Couple'. The *Star*, whose front page was exclusively devoted to 'Rat on the Run' Noriega, gave them a quarter of page four. They led with LUCKY TO BE ALIVE DANCER TO MARRY WOMAN WHO SAVED HIM FROM EVIL DICTATOR. Another slight bending of the truth, but a good piece. Carole Malone also footnoted them in her column, wishing the best of luck to the 'nicest people in show business'. The *Mirror* and the *Mail* ran smaller articles.

'Not bad for a night's work,' said Dominic, closing the *Mail* and dropping it on the bed beside Tilly.

'This is my favourite,' she said, opening the pink pages of the *Financial Times*. ' "Ramco's managing director Malcolm Barrett set to cash in on latest entertainment craze." He'll love this!' Pride bristled in her voice. 'It means so much to him to be written up positively in the *FT*.'

'Why?'

'Because his only school tie belongs to Edgware Comprehensive.' She sipped delicately from her coffee cup. 'To make it in this country without the benefit of an Eton/Harrow and Oxbridge education is hard enough. To be recognised by those who did is even harder.'

Dominic plumped his pillows up against the headboard, flopped back and admired the wintry beauty of the garden through the patio doors. The dark green ivy sparkled with the remnants of last night's frost, while slivers of ice around the perimeter of the pond bore witness to the severity of the overnight temperature. He studied the water and pondered the differences between their two cultures.

At home, propaganda relating to factory output and false productivity figures led people to believe manual work represented the highest level of achievement. Education was secondary and limited to the chosen few, or gifted people with the tenacity to push themselves forward. In England the *type* of education was the most important factor. Whether you were clever, gifted or shrewd came second to the importance of attending the right school. Stupid really, and in its own way more hypocritical than the repressive Romanian system. Dominic had read in the *Guardian* last week that 90 per cent of the Tory Party graduated from the same ten schools. It seemed that every form of government had its own way of maintaining the status quo.

'Penny for them.' Tilly leaned across the bed and put her head into his lap.

'I thought you could read them.' He gently stroked her hair.

'Not at the moment.'

'I was thinking how a so-called "right" education is a separatist, elitist and morally corrupt way of going about things. I was thinking that in a country as prosperous as England all its citizens should have an equal chance regardless of their ability to pay.'

'Nothing heavy then.' She nuzzled into his stomach, digging her arms under the bedclothes and around his waist.

'You did ask.' Dominic let her put her hands anywhere she wished.

'And I'm glad you told me the truth.' Her voice turned serious as her embrace tightened. 'I hate it when you try and fob me off with a sexist remark or a funny line.' She shimmied up the length of his body until they were face to face. 'I'm going to enjoy being married to you.'

'I should hope so.' He kissed her lightly on the forehead. 'Do you think I'm right?'

'Spot on. But that's the system we live under and though it's not perfect it's better than most others.'

'Agreed.'

'People who support it will tell you it guarantees the continuation of the higher genetic lines, although I think that's a load of crap. Also, since the war, thousands of lower-class people have risen through the ranks by means of the grant system.'

'Which war was that?'

'The sec——' She dug him sharply in the ribs. 'You're off again, you creep.' She tucked her legs up and scrambled inside the bed. 'How about a ten-minute cuddle before breakfast, I'm sorry, lunch?'

'How about an hour's cuddle *instead* of lunch?' The phone chirped its interruption from the bedside table. 'Is the answerphone switched on?'

'Damn! I turned it off when I got up.' She rolled away from him and picked up the handset. 'Hello . . . Yes, he's here. Hang on.' She handed him the instrument of frustration. 'It's Harry. Sounds urgent.'

Dominic sat bolt upright in bed. 'Harry, good morning.'

'I think you should come to Hampstead.' His voice sounded uncompromising and businesslike.

'What's happened?'

'I'll tell you when you get here. I need your help.'

'I'm still in bed. Can you give me an hour?'

'As soon as you can, my ol' son.' The phone clicked dead.

Dominic handed it back to Tilly. 'Sounds serious,' she said, sliding back down into bed. Her voice had a pleading quality and they both felt the frustration. She wanted talking time; Dominic craved Harry's information.

'He didn't say. He wants me at Hampstead. Something must have happened.'

'I can use the time for some Christmas shopping. I've got this fiancé I need to buy a present for. How about an early dinner before the club?' She was making the best of it. They both wanted to spend the day together to talk plans, to phone friends, to enjoy being in love. 'Please be careful,' she said softly. 'Don't expose yourself to danger.'

'There's no danger in Hampstead apart from the dog muck on the pavement. Harry needs my knowledge of the country to verify his information, that's all.'

She kissed his chest, her mouth lingering. 'I love you, Dominic,' she said softly as she broke her embrace and slid out of bed. 'I'll run the bath. At least we can have a bath together before you desert me.'

Dominic wanted a quick shower and a fast cab but the word 'desert' made him think again. Romania could wait another half-hour. He smiled as Tilly glided from the room leaving behind her Gucci fragrance to remind him of his real priority.

Dominic allowed himself two minutes of quiet reflection before struggling reluctantly out of bed and going through to the bathroom. 'You hop in the bath, I'll be back in a minute,' said Tilly, giving his bottom a playful slap. He stepped into the warm, pine-scented water and submerged his head below the bubbles for a few seconds.

Tilly stepped into the bath as he emerged. She slid up close, put her arms around his neck and hugged him tightly. Not the demonstrative hug of sexual foreplay but the clinging grasp of impending loss.

'You'll go back to Romania, I know you will,' she said.

'I'm not going anywhere,' he reassured her. 'If and when I go back you'll be coming with me as my wife and then only if Ceausescu and his cronies are long gone. Whatever help I can give from here will be my contribution. I'm no use to anyone as a footsoldier and Harry has no intention of risking his best human database for the sake of a few dead Securitate.'

'Harry?!' She pulled away. 'What's Harry got to do with it?'

Dominic had always prided himself in putting his brain into gear before putting his mouth in motion. This time he'd voiced a sworn secret without the slightest thought. There was no point trying to cover up his *faux pas*, Tilly was far too intelligent. He had to tell her.

'I'm waiting,' she said, as he tried to gain thinking time by fumbling in the water for an imaginary bar of soap.

'How much do you know about the Hampstead operation, I mean *really* know?'

'Mainly what Malcolm told us when Sara was killed. He runs a network of corporate spies in Eastern Europe in an attempt to destabilise their economies. Hampstead is the control centre and can also be used for getting political information about situations like Romania.'

He took hold of her hands and clasped them under the water. 'You must promise me that what I'm about to tell you never – and I mean *never* – leaves this room.'

The tiniest of smiles curled the corner of her mouth. Her eyes remained serious and gazing into his. 'I promise,' she said.

'The fact is, the reverse is true. It's a political operation which is sometimes used for business. Malcolm is only the financier. Harry's the boss. He used to work for Military Intelligence, now he's a privateer. The government contract him to gather information. He's got agents all over Eastern Europe and Russia who are connected to Hampstead via Betacam and satellite.' She let out a long, slow sigh, her eyes slowly closing. 'By telling you I've broken my promise to him. So you see why you must never breathe a word.'

'It all starts to make sense now,' she said, her eyes opening, an expression of concern replacing mistrust. 'I'll never mention it again. Oh, Dominic.' She leaned forward and kissed him. 'Thank you for not lying.'

'Had you suspected Harry was more than a journalist?' he asked, looking for justification.

'I knew he was capable of more. I thought his boozing probably impaired his promotion chances. I can see now it's all part of the act.'

'The boozing's real enough. He seems to be able to work despite it. His prowess on the computers is astonishing.'

A flash of worry crossed her face. 'Do you think this flat is bugged?'

'I'll find out when I get to Hampstead,' said Dominic, releasing her hands and standing up. 'I must go.'

'May God go with you, my love.'

Her blessing cleansed his conscience. If he fell foul of Harry for betraying his confidence they would face the consequences together – as they would all things in the future, good or bad.

Handsome Charlie greeted Dominic at the front door of the Hampstead house in a much more pleasant mood this time. He escorted Dominic up in the lift and into the top-floor room. Dominic noted his password was King's Castle: very appropriate, considering his size. Today the room was a hive of activity. Four stations along the central console were manned and busy sending and receiving information in French, Russian, Hungarian and English. Behind a desk to the right, two women in black overalls spoke German and French respectively into lightweight plastic headsets. Harry was in front of the station nearest the door, rewinding and playing back a videotape of crowd scenes outside the main square in Bucharest.

'Dominic! Come 'ave a look at this!' he shouted above the noise.

Dominic stood beside him and studied the pictures on the ceiling screen. Thousands of people waved their arms in clenched salute and chanted 'Death to Ceausescu! Freedom for the people!' drowning out the speech the dictator was trying to delivery from a first floor balcony. Bursts of warning gunfire from the Securitate stationed on the steps of the building quietened the crowd momentarily, then they would start up again louder than before.

'He's offered them all a pay rise of a hundred lei a month and they've told him to piss off.' Harry smiled victoriously. 'Great stuff! I got this footage an hour ago from our man in Bucharest. He's had to pack up filming because the Securitate were getting too close. I'm just trying to re-establish contact.' He pointed to the chair next to him. 'Grab a pew. Big show on today.'

Dominic pulled the seat over to Harry and shook his hand. 'What's happened so far?'

'Apart from this little party the army seems to be taking the people's side more and more in the country areas. Timisoara, Brasov, Cluj, and even Sibiu where Nicu Ceausescu is party leader, have all reported huge demonstrations and the army's doing nothing to stop it. Here, look at this. Is this man regular army?'

He keyed an instruction into the computer: it produced a split picture over four screens. The pictures were very wobbly as the cameraman dodged around the crowd trying to focus on a tank while staying out of sight and range of its machine-gun, which was spraying intermittently into the crowd. From the right of picture a man in uniform ran alongside the tank and placed a grenade in the track. As he tried to escape the tank's gun opened fire and he dropped to the ground. Two seconds later the grenade exploded, blowing off the tank-track and stopping the death machine.

Another man, also in uniform, jumped on top of the tank and threw a grenade into the slit window to the left of the main gun. It exploded almost immediately. This man made his getaway unchallenged. Twenty or more people then swarmed over the tank. Dominic could just make out a body being hauled out through the hatch when the picture went dead.

Harry keyed in F9/RETURN and the sequence started again. He freeze-framed as the first man turned away, having planted the grenade.

'There! On his shoulder! Is that a regimental flash?!' His excitement was contagious.

Dominic felt elated as he watched history unfold. 'I think so!' He desperately wanted it to be true. If the army was really turning against the Securitate they had every chance of winning. Dominic studied the rest of the uniform. 'Can you zoom in on his feet?'

'No problem.' Harry keyed in F9 and typed ZOOM. Using the joystick he manoeuvred the picture until the man's feet filled the screen. 'How's that?'

'Perfect. They're army issue. That man's a soldier.' Harry looked puzzled. 'You can get anything from the surplus stores except boots,' Dominic explained. 'The army never sell their boots.' Dominic was pleased he had useful knowledge to contribute to this seemingly flawless information unit.

'Have you got anything from my home town of Brasov?' he asked.

'As a matter of fact I have.' Harry keyed another code.

Pictures of the town centre ringed with tanks flashed on to screen one. The cameraman was on the roof overlooking the main square so the pictures were much clearer than the Bucharest footage. People ran for cover as flashes of fire spat from heavy machine-guns indiscriminately claiming several helpless victims. Dominic watched in horror as at least a dozen people fell before the relentless onslaught of Ceausescu's Secret Police. As the camera scanned the frightened faces around edge of the square he felt a sudden shock of recognition.

'Rewind, Harry! Please rewind!'

Harry turned towards him and placed his hand firmly on Dominic's shoulder. 'Take it easy, my son. Calm down. What do you want to see? You direct me, I'll find it.'

'Back along the square! Slowly!' He backtracked frame by frame. 'There! Right there. Zoom in now!' Harry complied, tapping instructions that enhanced the image as the picture narrowed. He finally stopped full frame on the face Dominic knew.

Nadia Vasiliu was alive.

'A relative?' asked Harry, his voice calm, reassuring, helping Dominic to compose himself.

'An old enemy,' he replied, thinking of Tilly's earlier bathside prediction. Seeing Nadia as a frightened, helpless girl on the war-torn streets of Brasov after remembering her as cunning and resourceful filled Dominic with remorse. He wanted to bring her to the safety of London. His stomach churned with anxiety. Not the feeling of a lover but a deep brotherly love, as if Nadia was the last remaining member of his devastated family and he had to rescue her before she perished like the rest.

'That's Nadia, the woman I lived with in Bucharest,' he explained.

'The government spy?'

'The same.'

Harry studied the screen, his eyes straining to clarify detail in the enlarged, still-frame picture. 'She's a beautiful woman, Dominic. You certainly know how to pick them.'

'She picked me,' he said, remembering the first time they'd met.

'You're not going to Romania,' said Harry, anticipating

his next question perfectly. 'Malcolm wouldn't allow it, for a start.'

'I thought you were the boss,' countered Dominic, unwilling to capitulate.

'Of this operation, yes, but Malcolm owns the club and he's invested too much money to let his star run off to a war zone and play rescue the maiden.'

He keyed another command into the console; the printer to his left started the buzz-clack of ink-jet reproduction.

'Three things, Dominic. One: I need you here. Two: you can't let Malcolm down. Three: we can find her faster than you.'

He stood up, walked to the lounge area and took a beer and a small bottle of water from the fridge. He opened the beer and took a long swallow as he walked back to the console. Handing Dominic the water he sat down and pulled the finished item from the now silent printer: a black and white copy of Nadia's face from the still-frame on the screen. 'We have a name and a face. We've found people with far less.'

What he said made sense; Dominic knew that. The Romanian borders were closed so he would have to be smuggled in as well as trying to smuggle Nadia out. The club was sold out on the strength of his appearances, which left no room for manoeuvre on that front, and he was sure Harry's people on the ground in Brasov could track her down in less time. 'It's important to me she gets out safely,' he said, resigning himself to an observer's role.

Harry smiled and finished his beer in one mighty mouthful. 'Nothing's guaranteed but we'll do our best.' He turned back to the keyboard and changed the picture on the screen. 'Now, this is Sibiu two hours ago. I've got a face in a car I think is Nicu Ceausescu. If you can confirm it would be very helpful.'

Dominic arrived back to an empty Chester Square just before five o'clock. Tilly had left a note saying her shopping excursion would last until at least six and that he shouldn't eat too much as she intended to take him out to dinner for a pre-Christmas treat. An hour alone was a welcome break for Dominic. He made himself a pot of fresh Colombian coffee and ran a brimming Badedas bath.

Pictures of the revolution haunted his mind as he relaxed in the chestnut-oil bath. The sight of the young soldier laying down his life to demobilise a tank filled him not only with sadness for the soldier's death, but with hatred of the people who were committing this genocide. The Russian media had reported 50,000 killed since 15 December and although Harry's sources estimated the lower figure of 20,000 it was still a horrifying statistic.

The peace and luxury of his surroundings served a double blow to his conscience. He thought of Nadia trapped in Brasov, Coach Damchuk, who he was sure would be ferociously fighting his corner in the Bucharest gymnasium, and the kind-faced Mrs Antonescu with her armfuls of other people's laundry. He prayed they'd be safe and at least physically untouched by this obscene reign of tyranny.

Dominic needed music; he needed to dance. He emptied the bath, dried himself, walked naked into the bedroom, clamped on the music centre headphones and let Tina Turner gradually repair his soul.

Tilly found him just before seven o'clock, face down on the bed, headphones up full blast, singing 'simply the best' into the pillow at shouting volume and completely out of tune.

'I can't take you out like this,' she said to herself as she rolled him over, removed the headphones and applied her tickling torture to ensure that he offered no resistance.

He squirmed away and stood upright beside the bed. He could feel her eyes drink him in, a lustful look masking her sylphen face. 'See anything you fancy?' he asked, slightly embarrassed.

'Yes. Desert. And if you'd be so kind as to put a cover-

194

ing on it I'll take you out for the starter and main course.'
Tilly tipped her head to one side. 'Are you happy?'

'Deliriously.' By the way she'd asked the question Dominic knew there would be more. Tilly sometimes hedged around things. The more hedging, the more important the real question. 'Are you happy' was a seven out of ten hedge. Dominic decided on the direct approach.

'You're holding something back. What is it?'

'I think I've found us a place to live,' she said, almost apologetically.

'That's wonderful! Great news!' There was still more to come. 'Go on.'

'It's a lovely flat at number 40 Chester Square. I looked at it this afternoon.'

Still she hadn't delivered the key remark. This was turning out to be a major hedge. 'What's wrong with it?' asked Dominic.

'Absolutely nothing. It's got three bedrooms, a wonderful kitchen and a delightful breakfast room. I fell in love with it the moment I walked in.' She smiled impishly at him and hedged from major to mega.

'Tilly, will you please tell me what on earth is wrong with this perfect flat!' Dominic's voice carried the smallest touch of irritation.

'The price. It's £200,000.' Tilly said the figure very rapidly as if that would somehow make it less expensive. 'I've got £90,000 from Fitzroy Mews. We could mortgage the rest.' She spoke that phrase rapidly too, for reasons Dominic couldn't fathom.

Having spent most of his life believing that $10 was a lot of money and then watch Malcolm pay £2 million to refit the club, Dominic's sense of values had been turned upside down in the last few months. The interior of Malcolm's house cost twice as much as the flat Tilly had her heart set on. Dominic could feel her anxiety.

'Sounds reasonable to me,' he said as nonchalantly as possible. 'Do you think anyone will give me a mortgage?'

'Oh yes, yes, yes, I'm sure of it. I have a friend at the

Halifax. We'll work something out.' She was still talking at speed. Hurried, excited, energetic, happy talk that told Dominic they would soon be moving out of number 82A Chester Square.

The audience at the Dance Emporium was sensational; even better than the first-night party. Dominic had worked out a routine to 'Swing the Mood' by Jive Bunny that, although far removed from his usual choice of music, was extremely well received by the pre-Christmas revellers. Of all his routines, the swing beat allowed more gymnastic movement and it felt good to return to the basics of his craft after months of complying with the British press's obsession that he should dance like Michael Jackson. Tilly had said she didn't care if they compared him with Postman Pat as long as they spelt the name correctly.

Malcolm and Claire were in exceptionally high spirits due mainly to their liberal consumption of Bollinger. Dominic was constantly surprised at the way the relationship between them kept improving. On the surface Malcolm's chauvinistic attitude and Claire's openly feminist views should clash like Margaret Thatcher and Mao Zedong. Instead, tolerance seemed more and more to win the day, producing a feeling of mutual well-being even without the help of stimulants. They kissed and cuddled openly and called each other by pet names. She called him Cum-cum, he called her Zag. Tilly thought the whole thing sex based and that once the passion had subsided they'd both move on to the next challenge. Dominic hoped she was wrong and felt they went well together in an oil and water kind of way.

After the third show, a requested encore of the Jive Bunny routine, they retired to the dressing room where Malcolm entertained them with a series of unrepeatable Joan Collins jokes. Dominic prompted him by saying how much he'd enjoyed her sister Jackie's book *The World Is Full of Married Men*. The word 'married', when spoken in front of Claire, always produced a change of subject from Malcolm within two sentences.

They drove home in the unashamed luxury of Malcolm's new Bentley Mulsanne Turbo. He was understandably proud of his new toy and drove it with great care along the wet, slippery Strand, round Trafalgar Square and down the Mall towards Belgravia.

He'd given up his chauffeur last month when he'd discovered a discrepancy in his service and petrol bills to the tune of £1,500. Most people would have had the man arrested and charged with theft, but that was not Malcolm's style. First he proved the crime by checking with the service department at Rolls-Royce, and only then did he challenge the man who, after much prompting, admitted to the error of his ways. Malcolm grabbed the hapless reprobate by the scruff of the neck, called him a useless dago wanker and ejected him from Chester Square, planting a firm boot in his testicles on the way out.

Dominic switched on the car radio as Lynn Parsons was introducing the two o'clock news on Capital FM. The Americans' hunt for General Noriega dominated the bulletin, with Romania relegated to a ten-second piece near the end.

Fighting was still going on and the death toll was rising. There was no mention of towns affected or numbers of casualties. For Dominic, the sparseness of the British media's information highlighted the importance of the Hampstead operation. The Americans had broadcast live action on TV and radio since the Vietnam war; they still did today, as the detail on the Panamanian story proved. The British government must know about Timisoara, Brasov and Sibiu but chose not to release the information to the media.

Their reasons were beyond Dominic's comprehension. Surely showing the pictures of Ceausescu's brutality, especially the young soldier attacking the tank, would galvanise the British people into at least verbal condemnation, which would put more pressure on the Romanian

197

army to overthrow the tyrant. Maybe he overestimated the British sense of fair play; maybe the Whitehall wizards were cooking up another more sinister plan. He couldn't believe the great British leaders would sit back and do nothing while thousands of people were being butchered, but he knew he could be wrong about that.

'Why such a serious look, Dominic?' said Malcolm as they turned into Chester Square. 'It's Christmas time! It's party time! It's boogie time! Enjoy yourself – you deserve it and, besides, it's good for the soul.'

Tilly laid her arm alongside Dominic's on the leather armrest. She knew where his mind was travelling; she felt his unrest. 'He *is* enjoying himself,' she volunteered. 'He's just a master of disguise.'

Malcolm laughed, Claire laughed; Tilly squeezed Dominic's hand.

Dominic declined Malcolm's invitation to share a Jacuzzi in favour of another hot bath downstairs, his third of the day. They seemed to do their best talking in the bath. The intimacy of being naked, warm and wet worked wonders. They'd talk about their day, their hopes, their problems and they'd laugh: magical moments that would stay in their memories for ever. Usually they sat at each end of the tub as the designers had thoughtfully placed the taps in the middle, but tonight Tilly sat facing forward, her back resting on his stomach, her feet barely reaching the far end of the tub.

'You've heard from Nadia, haven't you?' Her face was hidden, her voice expressionless.

'I saw a video of her at Hampstead. She's in Brasov. Harry's trying to find her and get her out.' Tilly was listening to the tone of Dominic's voice, searching for the truth in the inflections, listening for the nervousness of lies. 'How did you know?'

'Are you going in to get her?' She'd ignored his deflective question. This time there was no hint of the mocking tone she usually employed when she'd instinctively read his thoughts.

198

'Harry won't let me.' There was no point in hiding his feelings about Nadia despite the wave of embarrassment he felt at the mention of her name. It was like being caught in some clandestine affair, as if he was somehow cheating on Tilly just by admitting he was concerned. 'When I saw her in such danger I wanted to risk everything to save her. I don't love her, Tilly, not the way I love you, but she was a big part of my life in Romania and I would hate to see her hurt.'

Tilly slid away, turned in the bath and shimmied back towards him. She placed her hands either side of his face. The look in her eyes allayed all his fears. Saying nothing, she drew his face to hers and placed a lingering, gentle kiss on his lips. 'Let Harry deal with it,' she whispered. 'Take me to bed.'

They made timeless love. Touching, holding, kissing, she massaging away the tiredness of aching muscles, Dominic stroking her velvet skin until she purred with contentment. For nearly an hour they lay in each other's arms, their eyes exploring the hills and valleys of their bodies, exchanging love vows and secret desires.

'I want you to taste me,' she confessed as her hand softly caressed the inside of his thigh. 'I want you to taste all of me.'

His mouth slowly traced the outlines of her slender neck, across the satin slopes of her breasts and down the softness of her quivering stomach, his head finally coming to rest on the welcoming cushions of her silken thighs. He was lost in her, overwhelmed completely by her intoxicating beauty and burning with the white heat of passion. Her hands held his head firmly, guiding him to where she wanted his mouth to explore, moving her hips in tiny circles and offering her sex with studied hesitation. Dominic felt his desire flame like a furnace with sensual, creative power. All-consuming. Unstoppable. Coital thoughts beat the air around him with steel wings. She applied pressure to his head, commanding him to rise. He slid his tongue back up her body, across the outside of her womb, through the cleavage of her breasts and locked on to her mouth with urgent ferocity. All sense of time and space was lost in symmetric bliss as they made love until finally they lay exhausted in each other's arms, and together watched the first rays of morning sun reflect off the tranquil pond in their magic garden.

Twenty-five

Harry woke them up shortly after three o'clock in the afternoon. Tilly kissed Dominic and let the phone ring seven times before reaching over and clawing it into bed. 'Hello,' she said, resting the phone on the pillow between them.

'Good is the operative word. Afternoon is the right time zone.' Harry's voice was ebullient. 'Ceausescu's on the run. I need Dominic's ass up here. I've sent a car, it should be there in five minutes.' The phone went dead.

Tilly swung her legs out of bed as Dominic tried to focus on what he'd half heard. She replaced the phone and stood up. 'This is the day you've been waiting for,' she said, her voice resigned rather than happy. 'I'll get some cereal and coffee together while you take a shower.'

'What's happened?' Dominic was now fully awake.

'Harry wants you at Hampstead. Ceausescu is apparently on the run.'

Dominic felt stunned as twenty-four years of frustration started to flow from his mind and body. His jubilation was followed by foreboding as he thought of the thousands who would die in what was bound to be a bloody battle.

'I must go right away,' he said, his face turning stormy, his eyes unfocused and anxious.

Tilly sat back on the bed beside him, took his hand and looked straight into his eyes. 'Calm, Dominic, stay calm.

Don't let your emotions get on top. If you're to do any good you must be calm. Dominic, are you listening?'

'Yes, I hear you.' He focused on her eyes and returned her good-morning smile. 'Thank you, Tilly.'

'It's what I'm here for,' she replied, slipping off the bed and standing naked before him. 'I'll get you something to eat before you go.' She wagged her finger. 'No argument. The car will be here any moment.' She picked up her bathrobe and walked out.

Dominic ate the cereal, sipped at the hot coffee then added more milk to cool it down. The doorbell rang. Tilly had chosen his clothes to save time: a pair of jeans, a white shirt, a bright red tie and black leather brogues. 'Formal but funky,' she said, helping him into a royal blue Armani jacket. 'You look great.' She kissed him on the cheek. 'Claire and I are going to look over the new flat. Leave a message on the machine if you're missing supper, otherwise I'll see you at eight. You're not on at the club till midnight tonight cause the first set's a personal appearance by D. Mob.' Dominic was a lucky man to be so well organised. He returned her kiss and slipped out, looking back once for a final wave and a blown kiss goodbye.

Dominic sat in the back of the Ford Scorpio as the silent driver concentrated on picking and weaving his way through the traffic at considerable speed. He'd obviously been told to deliver Dominic post-haste and was willing to risk a ticket in order to fulfil his mission.

The car screeched into the driveway and skidded to a halt three feet from the door. Dominic thanked the driver, jumped from the car, nodded as he passed Handsome Charlie in the doorway and ran down the corridor and into the lift. But he had to wait for Charlie as he had neither key nor password. As the doors closed Charlie looked over at Dominic and, for the first time, gave a broad, welcoming smile but remained silent.

The operations room buzzed with activity. All seven stations were tuned in to some part of the Romanian saga.

Harry sat at station one shouting orders to everyone and monitoring six different pictures on his overhead screens.

'Dominic! Thank God!' He nudged the lady beside him. 'Take over, Sylvia. I'm having a break.'

He extracted a can of Fosters from the fridge and plonked his bulk on to the sofa, the broadest of grins beaming from his face. 'We've cracked it!' he exclaimed.

'Tell me.' Dominic sat down beside him and shook his hand.

'We got a radio report first thing this morning that the Defence Minister had committed suicide. Ceausescu denounced him as a traitor. Our man thinks he was shot because he wouldn't order the army to disperse the crowds by force and, apparently, so do the citizens of Bucharest. Come look at this.'

Harry rocked forward and made it to his feet on the first attempt. He ushered Dominic to station one and keyed instructions into the computer. A picture of the Communist Party central committee building flashed up on screen one. About a thousand people were gathered outside shouting 'Death! Death!' The army, not the Securitate, were guarding the entrance but were not threatening the crowd.

'Now watch this,' said Harry, taking a large swig of beer. 'First-floor balcony. Ceausescu walks out and tries to address the crowd.'

Dominic watched intently as the most hated man in Europe tried desperately to hold on to power. Every time he started to speak the crowd would shout him down with more chants of 'Death! Death!' He looked scared and lost: it was the last throw of the dice from a man already beaten. Finally he turned and disappeared back inside the building. The second he was inside the crowd rushed forward and the troops guarding the door stepped aside and let them pass. Suddenly the camera panned up to the roof.

'Look! Look at this!' Harry was bursting with excitement. A surge of adrenalin rushed through Dominic as he watched Nicolae and Elena Ceausescu and their five bodyguards run across the roof and board a waiting helicopter. Two of the bodyguards carried large suitcases as well as automatic pistols. They took off seconds before the first demonstrators arrived on the roof.

'That was twenty minutes ago,' said Harry. 'We know they headed out of the city going north-west, but then they dipped below radar so they could be heading anywhere. We know they didn't head south because we've got the Bulgarian border covered. I wouldn't think the chopper's got the fuel to make Ukraine or the open sea so they'll need a jet to get out of the country. Where do you think they're heading?'

'A private airstrip is my first guess. He's had several built over the years.'

'But not that way.' Harry finished his lager and threw the empty can into the waste bin. 'He's got three between Bucharest and the Soviet border and one south-east near the Black Sea, all of which are being watched. He's got nothing north-west. And where's he heading? He won't go to Hungary, they hate him; so if he hasn't changed direction he must be trying for Yugoslavia. I'll bet he's done a deal with the Serbs.'

'There's a small airforce field at Boteni, near Tirgoviste. They could have a jet there. But I can't see the airforce helping him.'

'Neither can I – but where else?'

Dominic knew Ceausescu was too smart not to have an escape plan and too cunning to do the obvious. 'I think you're right, Harry. I think the Serbs would take him in, especially if he was bringing several million dollars with him.'

The brightness in his eyes gave away Harry's real feeling for the events that were unfolding. His years of planning, placing agents, learning technology, building Hampstead, all culminated in this moment. An East European tyrant was running for his life and Harry's handiwork allowed at least part of the Western world to watch it live on television.

'He's off to Iran!!' Harry's rough, whisky voice crackled through the room, securing everyone's attention. 'Belgrade's a station stop!' His exacting gaze settled on a young Slavic lad who looked no more than twenty years old and sat uprightly at station four. 'See if you can raise your brother.'

The lad nodded obediently and returned to the console before him. Harry lowered his voice as he directed his attention back to Dominic.

'He's only come back to Bucharest for the money. Do you see? He had to come back from Iran to get the money, and now he's going to Belgrade to finish the deal before going on to live happily ever after in a nice hot climate.' He face saddened slightly. 'If he gets into a plane, Dominic, it's going to be hard to stop him. Forty minutes, an hour top weight. Any ideas you have regarding possible routes that little bastard's likely to take could be the difference between catching him or running a repeat of the Idi Amin story.'

'I'd guess he'd cross as close to the Bulgarian border as possible to keep the maximum distance between himself and the main airforce base at Timisoara. It's rough country but he could slip through easily if he had. . . .'

Some ideas are heaven sent to those with righteous causes. In a flash Dominic knew what Ceausescu had planned.

'Go on,' said Harry.

'He's not flying out. He's going by road. Can you put up a map of the south-west region?'

'South?' Harry seemed surprised by Dominic's request but could see the expression on his face was steadfast and concentrated. 'South-west it is, Dominic.' He typed DATABASE SW ROM VIEW ALL. Within a second the map filled six screens.

Dominic looked at the map for a few seconds. 'He's going to dump the helicopter somewhere near Boteni airbase and he'll try and make either Kladovo or Brza Palanka on the Yugoslav tongue in a four-wheel-drive civilian motor.' He pointed to the spot a few miles north of the Yugoslav/Bulgarian border. 'See, there. The Yugoslavian border cuts twenty-five miles into Romania like a tongue as it follows the River Danube. There are not many major roads in the area and a lot of heavily wooded country. Any four-wheel-drive would have no trouble in that terrain and would be totally anonymous. At a good speed he could make the border by nightfall, a perfect time to cross. He'll change cars at least once in case anyone sees the helicopter land. All that remains now is to work out where he's got the transport hidden. Can you zoom in on the area between Tirgoviste and Boteni?'

Harry zoomed in with speed. Dominic studied the map closely, trying to relate his knowledge of the area to the various symbols. Many of the smaller hamlets were known to him and could be eliminated – they were too small to hide a vehicle for long without arousing local suspicion. Ceausescu needed a place that only he and the inner circle of Securitate knew about; a place a four-wheel-drive vehicle would look inconspicuous.

'What's that?' Dominic pointed to three squares with the initials AC below them.

'An agricultural centre, a collection and distribution point for the local farmers,' replied Harry.

'That's it!!' shouted Dominic with total conviction. 'He's heading there. I'm sure of it!'

For a few seconds Harry studied the Romanian without moving, reluctant to commit agents on the strength of a hunch.

'He's there,' said Dominic softly. 'Or if he's not, he soon will be. That's where he's got the transport hidden. If he gets into open country in a vehicle we don't know about he'll be clean away.'

Harry tapped more instructions slowly into his computer as if he were thinking as he worked. The red lines tracing satellite link-ups were superimposed on the map.

He looked Dominic straight in the eye as he waited for the link to complete. Dominic smiled sheepishly, suddenly unsure. The beeps of connection made Harry turn back to the screen. Hurriedly he put on the headset.

'Bishop's Pawn, this is control.'

This time the agent's urgency cut through the rather crackly connection. 'Control, this is Bishop's Pawn. Ten minutes ago revolutionaries took control of both state radio and television. They have broadcast the news of Ceausescu's flight to the entire nation, branding him a tyrant who should be arrested on sight. They have also appealed to the people not to kill him but to hand him over to the army.'

'Wonderful news!' exclaimed Harry, giving the thumbs-up. 'We are sure Ceausescu will ditch the helicopter and switch to land transport stored at map reference C 37/18. I repeat, C 37/18. Please inform local army commander immediately. Do not, I repeat, do not reveal source of information. Re-establish audio only contact with us as soon as this is complete. Do you copy?'

'Message understood. C for Charlie 37/18.'

'Control out.' Harry pressed CONTROL/F8 and as the screens went black he leaned back in his chair and let out a long, resigned sigh. 'I do hope you're right, my o' son,' he said, tapping Dominic lightly on the shoulder. 'A good chunk of the money he's ripping off is British aid.'

Twenty-six

Bucharest

Uri scrambled on to the roof of the six-storey office building opposite the Central Hall and propped his shiny new camera against the air duct beside him. The square below was reasonably quiet compared with the riotous assembly that had taken place a few hours earlier. A few hundred people were left chanting slogans more in celebration than in anger, but there was no visible army presence, no Securitate and no Ceausescu.

Uri had relayed his last instructions from London on to the army commander at Timisoara and now he wanted time to regroup his thoughts and reload his camera. He chose the highest accessible spot in the square, where he felt safe and secure. He'd left a remote-control grenade at the top of the fire escape in case a rogue Securitate should have the same idea.

His orders from Harry had been precise: observe Central Hall and report every hour or as developments warranted. The high-powered field glasses he'd liberated from the airforce base at Timisoara allowed him not only to look inside the building opposite but also to read the memos on the walls. He focused on an excited youth on the second floor who kept stabbing a poster of Ceausescu repeatedly with a letter opener; vicious, tormented, psychotic strokes that gouged out the dictator's eyes and mouth. Other men and women in the crowded room ignored the boy as they looted anything of value and destroyed the rest. Uri felt pride in their courage and sorrow for the young boy's rage. He was probably a recent orphan who was confronting the man responsible; he saw no joy in what was happening here today.

A sound from behind him crystallised Uri's attention. He slid the Beretta from its shoulder holster and silently eased off the safety. Hearing footsteps, he pulled the remote from his jacket pocket, expanded the aerial with his teeth and placed his thumb under the red switch. A round, unshaven face appeared at the top of the fire escape.

'Oh no. Grenades,' grumbled the face. 'Is this Uri or am I a dead man?'

Uri clicked the safety back on and removed his thumb from the button. 'Your lucky day, Titus.'

Titus Roman was also a thief. He'd been saddled with his name by a drunken father who thought because Roman was as common as Smith, Chang or Patel, he'd name his son after the ancient Romans, hence Titus. The father didn't stay around long enough to witness the effect on his offspring. Titus learned to fight at a very early age, a talent that had kept him king of the street for the past two years.

'Nice camera,' he said, sliding across beside Uri. 'English?'

'Japanese, supplied by the English.' Uri greeted him warmly.

'You've got a nice situation there.' Titus pulled a full bottle of vodka from his coat and offered it to Uri. 'Warm up? Want to sell the camera?'

Uri gladly accepted the drink, took a mouthful, swilled it round, gargled and swallowed. 'Doctor, doctor,' he said, handing back the bottle. 'I can't sell. I need it. I'm in the market to buy guns if you're holding.'

Titus took a large drink from the bottle. Bypassing the mouthwash stage he swallowed it noisily at once. 'Both our lucky days. I've got an AK47 with 500 rounds, a lovely

209

sawn-off twelve-bore with a hundred shells and a couple of .38 handguns but, unfortunately, only a dozen shells.' His mouth flashed a gappy grin. 'By the time I killed him he'd fired most of his ammo belt.'

'How much?'

'Four hundred dollars for the AK, $300 for the shotgun and $50 each for the handguns.' Titus took another swig.

'I'll pay you $500 for both long-barrels, I don't want the handguns. Cash on delivery, here, as soon as you can.'

'How does five minutes sound?' Titus gave Uri the full benefit of his few remaining teeth.

'Off you go,' said Uri, turning from him and looking out over the square. 'Mind the grenade wire.'

He listened to the footsteps clunking back down the fire escape. Titus had dealt too quickly and settled too low. He hadn't heard him come up the fire escape until the last few feet. Why did he make so much noise on the way down if not as a signal to someone below? And a full bottle of vodka was very un-Titus.

Uri hurriedly connected the small silver dish aerial to his Betacam and pressed the autolink button. He inserted his earpiece, clipped on the lapel microphone, plugged into the small phono-jack at the front of the camera and waited impatiently for the connection. A small red light beside the aerial flashed twice then remained constant.

'Control. This is Bishop's Pawn,' said Uri softly.

'This is Control,' crackled through his earpiece.

'I have to relocate. Will call when secure. Out.'

There was no answer from Control, as was the routine when an agent ended a sentence with the word out. Uri dismantled the aerial and packed the camera into its padded black plastic case and strapped it to his back, pulling the sling across his chest as tightly as he could. He ran across the flat tar roof in a stooped position until he reached the fire escape side of the building. He was thirty feet from the ladder.

He looked over the edge and saw four men climbing

past the second floor. Beyond them, on the ground below, he could just make out the still body of Titus Roman lying face down in the road.

Uri unstrapped the camera and placed it on the roof beside him. He attached the silencer to his Beretta and looked cautiously over the side. As the men reached the halfway point on the third floor Uri aimed at the top man and squeezed off two shots, then one each at the men below. Immediately Uri ducked back and ran across the roof and again looked over the edge. Two men had joined Titus on the ground, the third clung desperately to the ladder while the fourth scanned the roof holding his automatic pistol upwards in front of his head. Uri had a full second to aim and send two more silent killers on their way. The man was thrown from the ladder by the impact of the bullets and noiselessly joined his colleagues on the street below. The remaining man stayed motionless.

Uri walked back to the ladder and detached the grenade from the railing. He looked over again, jerking his head back quickly when he saw movement, just in time to feel the warmth of a bullet fly past his face. He pulled the grenade pin. 'Thousand and one, thousand and two, thousand and three.' He lobbed it gently over the edge. 'Thousand and four, thousand and fi——' The explosion silenced his count. He looked over the edge, his Beretta pointing downwards at the full extension of his arm. The man was embedded in the ladder like a squashed fly.

Uri ran back to where he'd left the camera. He reloaded the Beretta, hung the field glasses around his neck and strapped the camera once more to his back. He scampered down the fire escape kicking the blood-soaked corpse before him. The grenade had blown a five-foot gap in the ladder just below where the man had been, but Uri traversed it with ease. He made a mental note not to come up that way again.

Briefly he stopped in the centre of the five dead men. He took their rings, watches, wallets, ammunition belts and guns; among them an AK47 and a shotgun.

'You should never have been in such a hurry,' Uri said sadly over the body of Titus Roman. 'Me you could have trusted.'

Twenty-seven

Hampstead Control

Time dragged. Dominic drank three cups of coffee, which was most unusual for him; Harry paced up and down between the computer stations and polished off four cans of ice-cold beer, about average for him. Bishop's Pawn confirmed within twenty minutes that he'd passed the information on to the army commander. All they could do was wait.

Dominic tried phoning Tilly but only managed to raise the answer machine; Malcolm's mobile was constantly engaged. Dominic felt in his heart this would be the end for Ceausescu but there still remained a small, niggly corner of his mind that said the despot would get out of the country and bribe his way into a comfortable safe haven, as Idi Amin had done ten years previously, and escape prosecution or accountability to live his declining years in unashamed luxury paid for by the blood of thousands of his countrymen. Dominic clenched his hands so hard his knuckles turned white and prayed with all his might that this would not happen here today.

'Waiting's the worst part,' said Harry, opening can number five. 'I never get used to it. Last year during – ' The flashing red light on the number one console interrupted the entire room and focused everyone's attention. Harry typed *print/view*. The message started to reveal itself on screen number one. It was on headed paper. It read:

ROMANIAN TELEVISION, BUCHAREST.

22 December 1989.

15:00HRS. NICOLAE AND ELENA CEAUSESCU HAVE BEEN ARRESTED BY AN ARMY UNIT ON PATROL NEAR THE AIRFORCE BASE AT BOTENI. THE CEAUSESCUS HAD ABANDONED THEIR HELICOPTER AND WERE TRYING TO FLEE OVERLAND INTO YUGOSLAVIA. THEIR FIRST CAR BROKE DOWN AND THEY WERE FORCED TO COMMANDEER ANOTHER VEHICLE FROM A LOCAL FARMER WHO RAISED THE ALARM. THEY WERE CAPTURED WHEN THEY STOPPED AT A NEARBY AGRICULTURAL STATION TO OBTAIN FUEL AND AT PRESENT ARE BEING HELD UNDER CLOSE GUARD IN AN ARMOURED CAR. THEY ARE BEING TAKEN TO THE ARMY BASE NEAR TIRGOVISTE. MESSAGE ENDS.

Dominic excused himself and sat alone on the black leather sofa. He buried his face in his hands and quietly cried cleansing tears for himself, and hopeful tears for his country and for a justice so long overdue.

Harry pressed a mobile phone into his hand and ruffled his hair as if he were a young boy receiving praise or encouragement. 'It's Tilly,' he said, his eyes sparkling even brighter. 'She was worried about you.' He walked back to his console.

Dominic cradled the phone to his ear and tried to regain his composure. 'Tilly, hello. Ceausescu's been arrested.'

'I know. Harry told me. It's wonderful news. I'm so pleased.' Her voice sounded concerned, sympathetic; more than that, it sounded relieved and happy. 'I'd love you to see the flat before Christmas. Is there any chance you can come home now?'

Dominic instinctively looked across the room at Harry who sat at number one console beaming back at him. He nodded his head and broadened his smile for a second before breaking off to answer another call on his headset. 'I'll be home in half an hour,' Dominic said softly.

But there were still things to be done before he could

relax and enjoy his first free Christmas. He stood behind Harry waiting for him to finish the string of commands he was issuing over the lines to Bucharest. He was directing position changes and report timings to at least six operatives with coolness and unhurried authority. Keeping calm under stress was a quality Dominic admired; interrupting Harry would be unthinkable.

'What a bloody marvellous day,' said Harry, knocking off his headset and placing both hands on his knees in anticipation of standing up. 'And you, my son, have played a major part.' He tipped precariously to his feet, wobbling for a second before gaining a firm stand. 'Without your hunch we'd still be chasing the little runt or, worse still, he might've scarpered.'

'I only pointed in the right direction,' replied Dominic with some pride, suppressing his real feelings lest he be thought boastful. 'It was the car breaking down that was his downfall.'

'That's not what happened!' Harry's voice sounded genuinely surprised at Dominic's naïvety. 'It went down just as you predicted. The agricultural station was where they had the second car waiting. The army found it ten minutes before the Ceausescus arrived. The military can't admit to outside help and we don't want them to, so the second car story was made up to keep the arrest internal.' Harry tugged at his beard with his right hand. 'Do you think if Ceausescu had taken a car he would leave the owner alive to raise the alarm?'

'I guess not.' The mention of killing changed Dominic's train of thought. 'Any news on Nadia?'

'We've found nothing.' Harry's face turned slightly sullen. 'We've hunted everywhere. If she's in Brasov she's well hidden. Do you have an address for her in Bucharest?'

'She had keys to my old place, but I should imagine someone else is living there now.'

Harry clasped his arm around Dominic's shoulder and ushered him towards the door. 'I'll check it out. If she's

215

in the country we'll find her, I promise you that.' They stopped at the steel-plated door with no handles and stood facing each other.

'You might like to know that Stenoza is also on the missing list. We know two truckfuls of small-arms ammunition were delivered to his barracks a week ago, but since then nobody's seen or heard from him. Do you think Nadia would team up with him?'

The thought was totally repugnant to Dominic but he still found himself weighing up the possibilities. Survival makes strange bedfellows, and faced with a death or join choice it was conceivable she'd be with him. 'I don't know,' was all he could offer.

Harry pressed his hand against the security screen and the door clicked open. He embraced Dominic; the first time he had done so. It was a strong embrace, transferring the energy of his emotions. Dominic couldn't reach around his girth so he patted his sides in recognition. 'There's no more you can do here,' said Harry, standing back and swinging open the door. 'Go and look at your new flat, be with the woman you love, and enjoy a wonderful Christmas. I'll keep you informed of any developments and I'll let you know the moment we have any word on Nadia.' He almost pushed Dominic through the door, allowing no argument whatsoever. 'And send Handsome Charlie up with some more beer!' he shouted after him.

Dominic did as requested then left the house and walked across East Heath Road and out into the crisp, clean air of a winter's afternoon on Hampstead Heath. The giant oak trees stood bare like veins across a darkening sky, the smaller shrubs and evergreens, showing a fraction of their summer beauty, circled a rough-edged pond where the last few wing-clipped ducks and moorhens huddled in the shelter of the bulrushes searching for warmth and the very occasional morsel of food. A family of four walked linked arm in arm: father, son, daughter and mother sharing their time and laughing together.

'Would you be so kind?' asked the mother, holding out

216

a small black camera as they passed close to him. 'It's our first Christmas together.'

'My pleasure,' answered Dominic, hoping it was an automatic that would not tax his limited knowledge of photography.

'Just press the red button,' she said reassuringly. As Dominic took the camera the woman studied his face. 'You're Dominic Dance, aren't you?'

'Yes I am. Have you been to my club yet?'

'We couldn't get tickets,' said the father. 'We tried, didn't we Rosie? They were all sold out.'

He held out his hand. 'I'm Terry Driver, this is my wife Rosie, my son Peter, and my daughter Rebecca.'

'I've seen you dance on television,' said Rosie in a voice Tilly called 'pre-grab' – the tone a fan uses before they jump in for a stolen kiss, hug or, even worse, a piece of clothing or a tuft of hair.

Dominic reached quickly into his pocket and produced one of the new cards Tilly had had printed with the Emporium logo. 'Come and see me perform live,' he said, handing her the card. 'Call that number any evening and ask for me or Tilly Howard. Be my guest for the night.'

Rosie had to hug someone and Dominic was thankful she chose Terry. 'You've made our Christmas,' he said. His voice became apologetic. 'I don't want to hold you up, but could I take a picture of you and Rosie? She's such a fan.'

Dominic felt like Father Christmas, Peter Pan and good King Wenceslas rolled into one. 'Let's use up the film,' he said.

When Dominic arrived at Chester Square Tilly was wearing her waterproof Barbour jacket over blue jeans and the bulky, blue woollen sweater Dominic had given her as a Saturday present. As they were both inclined to spoil each other with gifts Tilly thought a Saturday present would limit their extravagances to once a week and hopefully save money. A good idea, but unworkable, as they'd spend more on the single present than the other six combined.

'No messages, no things to do, and the agent's waiting for us at number 40,' she said, guiding him back up the stone stairs to street level. 'I want you to see the flat now so we can talk about it over Christmas.'

As they walked arm in arm across the square, Dominic told her about the Driver family and sketchy details of the Romanian operation; she told him nothing of her day on the grounds that it would spoil his Christmas surprise. She did, however, remind him he had to do all his shopping by tomorrow night as Christmas Eve was a Sunday and the shops would be closed. She urged him to use his newly acquired American Express Gold Card as the bills would then be paid by the company. Dominic made a mental note to spend an obscene amount of money.

A smallish man dressed in a blue three-piece, pinstriped suit and garish red tie met them at the entrance to number 40. 'Hello. Yes. So glad you could come, Mr Dance. Right this way. Yes.' His manner was ingratiating. Dominic didn't fancy him following along like a lost puppy yelping on about central heating and integral parking.

'Could you just let us look over the place by ourselves? I assure you we won't steal anything,' said Dominic, nudging the salesman's arm.

'I usually have to ah . . . I suppose it's all right, being it's you, Mr Dance.' He hunched his shoulders and looked at the floor, diminishing to a blue-suited dormouse.

'You're a good man,' said Dominic confidently, taking the keys and ushering Tilly inside. 'If you wait here, we'll be as quick as we can.'

The apartment block looked fairly new, definitely post-war. They climbed the wide wooden stairs to the second floor. Tilly unlocked the two Chubb deadlocks, turned the Yale lock twice, opened the large, oak door and hurried inside to cancel the alarm. Dominic strolled in and let his mind settle on to first impressions. Even when the two elaborate Victorian lights were switched on, the hallway

218

still seemed dark. Maroon carpet continued halfway up the wall where it gave way to maroon and white striped wallpaper.

'Forget the hall,' said Tilly, hurrying him on. 'I see black and white floor tiles and plain white walls.' She opened a pine door to her right. 'Little loo,' she said, closing the door before Dominic could look inside. 'Another dark room that'll have to go.'

'I trust this does get better.' Dominic opened the door again and saw more red carpet used as wallpaper, a Victorian-style toilet with dark wooden seat, and a matching sink boasting gold taps with porcelain handles.

'Come on, sweetheart,' called Tilly from the end of the hall.

Dominic strolled up beside her and realised why she'd fallen in love with the place. The hall ended at three sets of double oak doors. The left set opened on to a magnificent drawing room at least twenty feet square with two double, floor-length windows overlooking the Chester Square gardens. Although the same carpet covered the floor it looked much lighter in this airy room and didn't double as wallpaper. The light walls were peach trimmed with brilliant white gloss. To the right an identical set of doors led to an equally airy but slightly smaller dining room. The carpet here was royal blue, the bottom half of the walls were a painted marble design in yellow and blue, the top half above the white, gloss-painted divider rail was a light canary yellow. Through the dining room more double doors opened on to a large kitchen, also yellow and blue, with light oak cabinets and a beamed ceiling. The third set of doors off the hallway led to a suite of three bedrooms, each with integral bathroom and built-in wardrobes.

'Look in here,' said Tilly excitedly as she disappeared into the master bedroom. 'A balcony!'

Dominic walked through another bright area to the full-length windows that featured in every room except the kitchen. Outward-opening, double french windows led to

219

a small east-facing, stone balcony that also overlooked the square. Dominic stepped outside and looked back across the square towards Malcolm's house. He saw a glint of sunlight bounce off a camera lens that jutted out of a black Mercedes parked opposite Malcolm's front door. He watched the car pull away, making a note of the licence number: PBX 30. Quickly he stepped back into the room.

'I want to put a small table and two chairs just inside the window then we can have breakfast in here with the doors open. The morning sun will keep our toast warm.'

It seemed the joy of the world was radiating from Tilly's face. Never had Dominic felt more content, more in tune with everything around him, than right now in this empty, yellow room. So what if they were watching him? He could live here with her in perfect harmony despite their snooping. There would be no friction within these walls, just the healing of wounds inflicted by a world beyond this sanctuary. 'You really like it, don't you?'

'I love it,' she said, hugging him. 'We'd be so happy here, Dominic. I just know we would.' She pushed herself to arm's length, her face pert, her lips curling at the edges, her cheeks dimpled. 'As soon as the hall's redecorated.' She laughed as she asked, 'Are you any good at DIY?' Dominic shook his head slowly. 'Good! A professional takes half the time and charges twice as much but they're worth every penny.' She kissed him lightly on the lips. 'Well??'

'It's lovely. Let's put in an offer.'

'Already have.' Her grin took on devilish proportions. 'I put down £1,000 deposit this morning.'

Dominic held her, burying his teeth into the soft flesh of her neck in mock punishment. 'What if I'd hated it?'

'Then I'd have lost £1,000.' She tickled his waist to stop him biting. 'I'll bet that poor little estate agent thinks we're staying the night. Where are *you* taking *me* for dinner?'

'To the club. I thought I had an interview over dinner with the *Sunday Express*.'

'That's been moved to after Christmas,' she said, moving away into the hall. 'They want to do it at the Durrants Hotel. I think it's lunch there on the 27th for publication on New Year's Eve. "Highlights of the past year" feature. They want you to reconstruct your escape.'

'I don't think telling them I walked down the stairs and out into the road without anyone saying a word to me is exactly a riveting story.'

'Then make something up. Tell them how you felt as you walked down the stairs.'

'Scared to death.'

She playfully pushed him through the door, set the alarm and bolted the deadlocks. 'The question remains – where are you taking me for dinner?'

'The Durrants?'

She tucked her arm through his. 'A *very* good answer Mr Bellescu.'

They arrived at the hotel in George Street shortly before eight o'clock. As Dominic stepped from the cab memories of that chilly March evening returned with crystal clarity – the deception of Sergeant Severin, the last meal from room service, the third-floor landing miraculously clear of people, the nervous walk down the final flight of stairs and across the lobby, and the mix of adrenalin and elation he felt as he walked into Manchester Square and out of sight of the hotel. Maybe he could inspire a sympathetic journalist to write an exciting piece about his dash for freedom, although he would always know it was more an agitated stroll than a swashbuckling dash.

Table eight suited them best: there they could sit side by side and hold hands, lock legs and hug shoulders. Heavy petting was not out of the question physically, just out of order, as Tilly forcefully pointed out when Dominic's hand strayed past her knees. She thumped him hard in the ribs and then smiled sweetly at the attending waiter.

They ordered smoked salmon, followed by lamb cutlets with mint and tarragon sauce.

'One thing has always bothered me,' she said, rubbing and comforting the rib she'd nearly broken a few seconds ago. 'Why did the Romanian Embassy choose this hotel? It seems so non-them, so laid-back British. No real security, no TV monitors in reception. I'd have thought they'd go for the Lancaster Gate or Hilton where they could really keep an eye on you.'

'Coach Damchuk told me why before I left Bucharest.' Dominic hoped he could remember the story that had now faded into the back pages of his memory. He took a sip of champagne. 'Apparently a member of our embassy staff was reading a book by Saul Bellow called *The Dean's December*. On a visit to London, Bellow has the Dean stay at the Durrants with his wife and Romanian mother-in-law. He describes the hotel as "less than luxurious" and discourses on the English ability to build cosiness in a meagre setting. Ever mindful of saving money while maintaining standards, the embassy official took the American ambassador here to lunch. The Americans love old-world charm and, according to Coach Damchuk, the ambassador sang the hotel's praises all afternoon. As one victory usually sets policy in our country, from that moment on we were Durrants supporters.'

Tilly curled a piece of salmon provocatively around her fork, her eyes studying Dominic in search of the wind-up or fabrication. 'You should tell that to the *Express*, it's a good ice-breaker,' she said, before popping the fork into her mouth and removing it very slowly minus the sensuous pink strip. 'Tell me more about this afternoon. Did you really "call the play", as Harry put it?'

'When did you talk to him?' Now it was Dominic's turn to search her eyes.

'He called me when you'd left,' she replied. The slight hesitation in her voice suggested a half-truth. Dominic remained silent. 'OK,' she said sheepishly after a moment. 'I called him about five minutes before you got home. I thought you'd stayed on and I wanted you to see the flat in daylight. He said you were on your way and that you'd been the hero of the hour; something about "sussing the moves".'

Dominic told her the story of the divine hunch and how he'd doubted himself when Harry had taken action on his scenario. He told her about the happiness, relief, revenge and satisfaction he'd felt as he'd watched the drama unfold and of the pure elation when Ceausescu was arrested.

'Any news on Nadia?' she asked, knowing full well that was the only part of the story he hadn't mentioned.

He shook his head. 'No.'

The timely arrival of the main course saved Dominic. Although Tilly seemed perfectly relaxed about Nadia, he always felt a tinge of embarrassment whenever her name was mentioned.

'We'll have to skip dessert,' said Tilly, tucking into her cutlets with remarkable aggression. 'You're due at the club in under an hour.'

The Dance Emporium was seething with holidaying, merrymaking, palpitating people. Dominic went on stage just after eleven o'clock ready to try a new number, 'Hey DJ' by Betty Boo. He wanted to dance it alone first with a view to choreographing it for the girls at a later date. As he walked on stage a single chant reverberated from the audience: 'Jive Bunny! Jive Bunny! Jive Bunny!'

So much for well laid plans. Dominic danced 'Swing the Mood' and loved every second. He was dancing through happiness tonight, not as a means of escape, and it felt exquisite.

In between shows Tilly brought a young girl in a wheel-chair backstage. She had spina bifida and looked so bent and twisted that Dominic wondered how one so young could stand the pain she was obviously enduring. He wanted to hold her and tell her it would all be fine, that one day she would dance like him and if she practised hard she could be his partner. But he saw from the look in her mother's eyes that this would never be. He signed her autograph book on the next page to Elton John and her mother took a picture of them both.

'You handle these people very well,' said Tilly when the girl and her mother had left the room.

'It's so sad,' he replied, reaching into the fridge for a bottle of Evian. 'Nature throws enough spanners in the works without us killing each other willy-nilly.'

'This from a man who wants Ceausescu hung by his balls!' She pointed at the bottle of water. 'Yes, please.'

Dominic and the girls did Billy Joel's 'We Didn't Start the Fire' for the second show. It was the first time they'd performed the number and it went down well, but instead of applause the audience chanted 'Jive Bunny' again. There was no difficulty choosing the number for Dominic's last solo spot.

Tilly and Dominic went straight home after the show and watched the late night/early morning news on ITV. The Ceausescu overthrow was the lead story but featured no pictures of him in captivity, in fact no pictures at all, just a stock head and shoulder. Dominic cuddled up next to Tilly on the sofa, stroking the inside of her thighs and contemplating bed. As ever, the ringing phone shattered his fantasy.

'Who *dares* to call Bellescu at this time of night!' he bellowed down the phone in his best sergeant-major voice.

'Commander Harry Cassini!' came the equally curt reply.

He felt an emptiness in the pit of his stomach. 'What's happened?'

Harry's laughter was reassuring. 'They've caught Ceausescu's son Nicu in a roadblock outside Sibiu. Apart from a few cousins the whole family's now under arrest. I thought you like to know.' He gave another chuckle. 'I didn't disturb anything, did I?'

'Not yet, but make this the last call, OK?'

'Goodnight, Dominic. Give my love to Tilly.'

As Dominic replaced the phone he noticed that Tilly was no longer in the room. He turned out the lights and shuffled down the corridor towards the bedroom where a dim light was shining through the crack in the door. As he slowly pushed it open he saw her lying on the bed, her red silk skirt pulled up to reveal the tops of her stockings, the first three buttons of her blouse undone showing the edges of her red lace bra.

'Make love to me with my clothes on,' she whispered. 'I only want to feel the real you inside me.' She straightened her legs to form a perfect A on the satin bedspread, her hands slid between her legs gently rubbing her satin and lace knickers and then, pulling them to one side, she caressed her sex with a perfectly manicured finger.

Dominic's erection was instant. He slid his hands slowly up her legs, across her smooth, white thighs, over her covered breasts and on to her bare shoulders. He moved his pelvis between her legs and put himself at her disposal. She undid his flies, took his penis in both hands and guided it inside her. The outside texture of silk, satin and skin coupled with the inside feeling of warmth and liquid friction excited him immediately to the point of ejaculation. He tried desperately to hold back as Tilly thrust upwards, taking in more of him with every stroke. He heard a gurgling sound deep in her throat as her orgasm spread through her entire body. They shuddered to a premature and overwhelming climax and within a minute of starting crashed exhausted beside each other on the crumpled bed.

'Sex with you is another dimension,' she said, turning towards him and caressing his spongy manhood with a firmness of hand that began to inspire another erection. 'Lust and love together; it's sensational.' They both felt the stiffening. 'Waste not, want not.'

She slid across him, the silk of her stockings touching his thighs, the only exposed part of his body. She guided him inside once more, her expression changing from contentment to anxiousness, hungry for more sexual satisfaction, feeling incomplete; insufficient tantalising him.

Dominic was trapped by his restricting trousers that clamped his ankles like cuffs, and by the weight of Tilly's body. She rode him like a unicorn, gripping his wrists above his head like reins and digging her knees into his sides with every downward movement. The restriction excited him. He watched her breasts heave and crest trying to escape their corseted bounds; the edges of her red skirt contrasted with the whiteness of her thighs and the black of her stockings. She slowed her motion and made long, deliberate strides up and down his length, consuming him completely. She began an almost chantlike moan in the depth of her throat that pushed further to the fore with every completed circle. Slowly her expression turned from desperation to exhilaration to ecstasy as the explosion and then the intoxication of orgasm took her beyond pain and pleasure to the elevation of true release.

She finally flopped on to his chest, motionless. He held her and remained silent, not wishing to spoil her post-coital pleasure. She buried her face in his neck, clung on to his shoulders and let a few contented sighs escape her lips, making no attempt at conversation. Dominic looked past her to the frost-covered garden. He would miss it when they moved; it had so many positive memories of his first, fragile days in England.

'Never before,' she whispered into his ear. She buried her face in his neck and fell silent until the soft purr of her breathing told Dominic she was asleep.

Twenty-eight

Christmas Day 1989

They awoke together at eight in the morning and drifted in and out of sleep for close to half an hour, neither wanting to break the luxurious feeling of touching flesh. The phone rang twice then clicked off as the answer machine in the hall took over. Dominic strained to hear the message as the caller identified himself. He heard Harry's voice say Merry Christmas and a disjointed reference to Ceausescu, trial, help, and call him back urgently.

'Shit!' Dominic spat the word out, annoyed that anyone would dare to interrupt his peace on such a special day.

'Call him and get it over with,' whispered Tilly. 'And tell him you're having a day off. The man is becoming intolerable.' She sat up in bed and handed Dominic the bedside phone. 'I'm not leaving you today, not for a second.'

Dominic punched the Hampstead number into the matrix; the connection was immediate.

'Harry Cassini please, this is Dominic.' He enjoyed a little nibble of Tilly's neck while he waited.

'Dominic! Merry Christmas!' Harry continued talking without giving Dominic time to reply. 'Last night the Securitate attacked the barracks where the Ceausescus are held. Don't panic – they were beaten back by the army but there were quite a few casualties so they're putting him on trial today.'

'Christmas Day?!'

'They can't afford another attack. The Securitate are bringing up tanks and that will lead to mayhem. It's got to be finished today.' He paused. Dominic knew what was coming and remained silent.

'I could use some help with this,' Harry said apologetically. 'We have to rely on Russian coverage for the trial; there's no way I can get a camera inside. I've tapped undetected into Moscow media but without my agents I don't know what I'm looking at. I need you here, Dominic.'

'I'm bringing Tilly. There's no way I'm leaving her alone on Christmas Day.'

The silence from Harry sent a traitor's shiver through Dominic's body. He had broken his promise, betrayed a trust, and he felt ashamed.

'How much does she know?' Harry's voice was clipped, hurt.

Dominic saw no point in compounding the lie. 'Everything. She's going to be my wife, we will have no secrets between us,' he said, hoping his explanation would deflect at least some of Harry's anger.

'And if she's kidnapped and tortured because of what she knows, is that loving somebody?'

'We're not part of your band of thugs,' said Dominic, his temper rising. 'When this is over we're finished with K7. I'm a dancer not a goddamn spy!'

Another moment of silence at Harry's end. 'I'm sorry, Dominic. You're right of course. I care for you both and I don't want to see either of you hurt, that's all.'

Dominic didn't believe him and was sure there would be more repercussions when they met face to face, but at least for now tempers were returning to normal. 'What time should we be there?'

'It doesn't start for another three hours their time. About noon will be fine.'

'And a Merry Christmas to you, Harry,' said Dominic

sarcastically. He put the phone down before Harry could reply.

'How long have we got?' asked Tilly, replacing the phone on the bedside table.

'Till noon.'

The happiness returned to her face. 'That's better than two minutes.' She snuggled up and laid her head on his chest. 'Do you want your present?'

'Do you want yours?' He kissed her forehead.

'Me first,' she said, sliding out of bed and skipping over to the tallboy. She opened the second drawer, removed two brightly wrapped parcels and scurried back under the covers. 'Merry Christmas.'

'Which one should I open first?'

'The choice is yours.'

'Good things come in small packages,' he said, fondling a little square parcel with a big red bow. He opened it slowly, carefully, so as not to damage the wrapping.

'I do that.' She smiled and squeezed his arm.

A green plastic box with a crown emblem mounted in the centre greeted Dominic. He'd never seen this sign before and the mystery added even more excitement. Hurriedly he opened the lid. Inside, mounted neatly on a black velvet board, was a beautiful gold Rolex watch.

The surprise left him speechless. He sat motionless in the bed, his mouth open, and watched the morning sun rays glint off the shiny precious metal and dance a pentagonal ballet on the bedroom wall.

'Do you like it?' asked the soft voice on his right.

'It's beautiful, fantastic, you shouldn't have, I love you, and anything else I should say when I am, in fact, speechless.' He pulled her close and buried his face in her hair.

'Try it on,' she said. Her pleasure at pleasing him exploded from her mouth in the broadest of smiles. 'If it doesn't fit they'll alter it.'

Dominic unclipped the magnificent timepiece from its case and slipped it on to his wrist, studying its simple elegance and craftsmanship. He kissed her slowly and passionately on the lips. 'It's sensational. You're sensational.'

'You like it, then?' she mocked, sliding away from his embrace. 'Open your other one.'

'It's 8.47,' he said, giving his first time check from the first watch he'd ever owned.

Tilly pushed him playfully. 'If you give me a time check every five minutes it'll drive me mad.'

'It's 8.48,' he replied, glancing again at the white and gold face.

'Open the other one,' she repeated.

Her tone made him think the second present was more important to her and his mind whirled at the thought. This parcel was flat and oblong like a book, a picture, or a shirt maybe. Dominic carefully undid the Sellotape from the ends and unfolded the gold wrapping paper to reveal the back of a frame. He turned it over and saw that the narrow black and gold wooden frame surrounded a piece of poetry.

'I wrote this for you,' she whispered almost apologetically, as if afraid her writing was inadequate or that he would somehow take offence.

The Dancer In My Heart

An exchange of words
a sharing of laughter.
Surprise

A growing curiosity
wanting to learn more.
Intrigue.

A finding of common ground
being easy together.
Pleasure

A meeting of eyes
a touching of lips.
Desire

A need to be skin to skin

feelings long forgotten.
Arousal

A fusion of heated bodies
uniting heart and head.
Passion

A joining of two selves
receiving, giving joy.
Tenderness

A soaring of the spirit
a soothing of the soul.
Peace.

He felt emotion swell inside him and run from his eyes in silent tears. No golden watch, no sporty car, no Solomon's mine could start to compare with the value of this gift. Dominic placed it carefully on the bedside table, turned towards her, looked into her eyes and fell in love again. Tilly read his thoughts, as always, with uncanny accuracy. A small twitch of a smile brightened her face.

'I was afraid you'd think it was soppy,' she said, tears of joy appearing in the corners of her eyes.

'I think it's the most beautiful poem ever written.' He reached for her and they fell against each other, the sobs of joy subsiding as they touched.

She wiped her eyes on his cheek and nibbled at his ear. 'Ever since I was a little girl I dreamed that one day I would meet a man who'd cry at poetry, and that I would marry that man regardless of his health, wealth or looks. I never thought it would be one of my poems and I certainly didn't think he'd be a handsome, strong, talented man with the potential to be a millionaire.'

'Sometimes you just get lucky,' he whispered back, prompting the usual dig in the ribs. Only this time she barely touched him, and then she hugged him tightly. This was the best Christmas present of all. He glanced over her shoulder at his new, shiny watch. 'It's 9.10 and 20 seconds. Beep, beep, beeeep.'

'You're going to be impossible with that thing, I can

tell,' she said, pulling away. 'I suppose you're going to say you didn't have time to buy me anything and that we'll go shopping for my present in the January sales.'

'Not exactly.' He reached under his side of the bed where he'd stealthily hidden her present, and handed her a package not dissimilar in shape to her poem. 'This is one I wrote earlier. It's called Slam Bam Thank You Ma'am and it contains a lot of rude words.'

She took the present and played with it, poking, feeling the edges, shaking it to see if it rattled. 'I've no idea,' she said finally.

'Then you'll have to open it to find out,' he said with comic sarcasm.

She teased the Sellotape off the wrapping. Her eyes opened wide as the green Harrods box came into view. Slowly she lifted the lid as if expecting a small furry animal to pop out, or a silly trick snapper to trigger off. When the black leather cover with her name printed in gold on the bottom right corner finally revealed itself she looked at him in amazement.

'What is it?'

'Take it out.' He took the wrapping paper from her and let it float gently to the floor beside the bed.

Lifting the thick volume from the box she placed it across her knees. She ran her hands over the leather binding and traced the golden lettering with her finger. She slowly opened the cover. The first page solved the mystery. 'Harrods Diary 1990'. Not disappointment, more a 'not what I expected' look flashed across her face. This was just the reaction Dominic had hoped for.

'Turn to the second week in February,' he said, before she could speak. She thumbed the pages until she found February the 14th, where he'd Sellotaped the diamond and emerald ring he'd bought from Tiffanys in Bond Street. Under the ring he'd written the words *Wedding Day*.

'If it doesn't fit they can alter it,' he said, mimicking her earlier remark.

Tilly didn't seem to hear. She held the ring in her right hand, not between her fingers where she could twist it to the light and admire it, but in her palm, where she looked at it for only a moment before slowly closing her hand around it and pressing it next to her heart.

'I'll take that as a yes,' he said.

She opened her hand and presented him with the ring. 'Please put it on.'

Dominic slipped the ring on her third finger, left hand. It fitted perfectly. She held her hand outstretched in front of her and admired the jewel at arm's length. 'I can't wait to show Claire,' she said, twisting her hand so the sunlight reflected off the diamonds with brilliance. 'If Christmas dinner's out of the question, let's invite them to breakfast.'

'You call them, I'll cook,' said Dominic, trying his best to hide the true excitement he felt over the Ceausescu trial. He didn't want to tarnish Tilly's morning with thoughts of impending justice for the Romanian people, but his anticipation was bubbling under the surface. Although his happiness here was complete and he felt real optimism for his future, a large part of him wanted to be back in Brasov, to be part of this historic episode in his country's history. He would have to settle for watching it unfold from the detached safety of the Hampstead house. It was the closest he could get to the action.

He slipped out of bed, put on his bathrobe, and went out. 'See you in the kitchen,' he said over his shoulder. 'Breakfast for four in half an hour.'

He set about breaking a dozen eggs and whipping them with milk and chives, slicing strips of smoked salmon, preparing twelve slices of decrusted toast, brewing coffee, grilling twenty rashers of back bacon, and laying four places at the kitchen table complete with glasses of freshly squeezed orange juice. He made little name tags for each setting, folded the Father Christmas napkins in the shape of lilies, and added a log decoration to complete the festive look.

233

Dominic had bought Malcolm a bottle of Remy Martin Louis the Thirteenth brandy, at £160 the most expensive he could find. He placed the brightly wrapped present in the centre of Malcolm's place setting next to his name tag.

Tilly walked into the kitchen as Dominic was approaching the critical point in cooking the scrambled eggs. Not wishing to distract him, she kissed him lightly on the cheek and placed the present she'd bought for Claire beside her place setting. 'What did you get her?' he asked, removing the eggs from the heat and spooning them into a blue, willow pattern serving dish.

'A hair-drier with all the attachments.' She chuckled with satisfaction. 'Now she'll have no excuse to keep borrowing mine.'

'Merry Christmas!' shouted Malcolm from the doorway. Claire clinging on to one arm, two flamboyantly wrapped presents tucked under the other. 'The fab four's first Christmas together. Time for champagne!'

All four exchanged hugs and kisses. Tilly showed off her ring to Claire, who emitted munchkin giggles followed by longer hugs all round.

Malcolm winked at Dominic and placed his presents on the table next to the appropriate names. 'I love the idea of the tags,' he said. 'There's no excuse for forgetting names this morning.' Dominic showed off his Rolex and Malcolm and Claire, with some pride, flashed the matching gold bracelets they'd bought for each other.

Everyone complimented Dominic on his culinary skills, even if it was a very simple dish, and Malcolm opened a bottle of Bollinger to round off the feast. They saved their presents until after they'd eaten. Tilly received a large bottle of her favourite Gucci perfume and Dominic became the proud owner of leather-bound first edition of Tolkien's *Hobbit*.

'What news from Harry?' asked Malcolm, nonchalantly dropping the subject into the festive conversation.

'The trial's today,' replied Dominic in an equally low key. 'I'm going to Hampstead later to interpret for Harry.'

'*We* are going,' corrected Tilly.

Malcolm's dour expression told them she'd said too much. 'How much does she know?' He aimed his question directly at Dominic in a cold, measured voice.

'Enough so she doesn't have to lie blind to the press like in the last nine months,' Dominic replied candidly.

'Hampstead is supposed to be a secure operation,' said Malcolm, his temper flaring instantly. 'Every man and his fucking housekeeper seems to know about it.'

His reference to Tilly was not only obvious but insulting. Malcolm may have been the money behind Hampstead but Harry was in charge, and he was the only person from whom Dominic was prepared to take criticism. On the other hand, he didn't want to spoil this most special of days by starting a slanging match about a subject over which neither of them had control. Tilly, God bless her, came to the rescue.

'I'll bet Claire knows more about it than I do,' she said, a smile fronting her diplomacy.

Over the months Malcolm had obviously told Claire snippets of information and the realisation that he'd breached his own security, if only slightly, immediately calmed him.

'I know you work for British Intelligence and that Harry's SAS. Does that qualify for knowing it all?' Claire's voice was chirpy, irreverent, and touched with sarcasm. 'Will I be shot at dawn?'

Malcolm's anger had nowhere to go. Claire and Tilly had verbally wrapped him in his own guilt and he was forced to adopt the prevailing festive mood. 'What the hell, I'm moving the operation next month so your information's got a lifespan of a couple of weeks, no more. Let's go and watch the finish of Ceausescu and then we'll all go out for Christmas dinner.'

'I'm cooking here,' said Claire, digging Malcolm firmly in the ribs. Dominic looked at both women and wondered if they'd majored in rib-digging at school; they seemed to have a similar style and from Malcolm's pained reaction, Dominic deduced, the same accuracy.

'We were going to cook together,' added Tilly. 'There's enough food upstairs to feed an army.'

'I've got it!' interjected Malcolm. 'I'll help Claire with the cooking while you two are at Hampstead. Bring Harry with you when you come back.'

Malcolm's offer left them speechless. Help? Cooking? These were terms with which he'd never been associated.

'Come on!' he continued. 'It's Christmas. Do you think I can't peel a potato, or what?'

Claire shimmied up beside him, her hand slipped into his open shirt and gently caressed his bulging belly. 'I'll give your willie a kiss for every one you peel properly,' she said.

'How many kisses constitute a blow job?' asked Malcolm, now back on familiar ground. 'I hate things that start but don't finish.'

'Do you *really* want to get into this?' questioned Claire. She had something on him sexually and it was obvious he didn't want to share it, not even with his friends at Christmas time.

'I *really* want to go back to bed,' he said, slapping Claire on the behind.

'In that case I'm sure you'll excuse us,' said Claire, tipping an exaggerated wink and pulling him towards the door. 'When you guys get back, come up to us. The dinner will either be ready, spoiled, or not cooked. If it's the last two we can always get Chinese.' Malcolm opened the door and she pushed him through. 'Come on, big boy. Let me introduce you to Hot Tub Hannah and her horizontal hand movements.'

'I wish you wouldn't be so obvious in front of Dominic and Tilly,' scolded Malcolm, as he closed the bedroom door. 'Why do you do that?'

'Because it embarrasses you,' replied Claire, applying

236

another rib-dig by way of punctuation. 'And I enjoy embarrassing you.' She offered him a warm, generous smile; the kind she only produced when they were alone. 'It's all part of my plan to make you a better man.'

'I like me the way I am,' ventured Malcolm hesitantly.

Claire pushed him hard on the chest and sent him sprawling on to the bed. She jumped after him, straddling his stomach and pinning his arms beside his head. 'As it's Christmas and I think you're basically a nice person despite your surface chauvinism, I'm going to tell you something I've never told anyone. Because I've been, shall we say, overactive in the sexual department since I was fourteen, I was called every unkind name in the book by my peers. Slag, bike, tramp, whore: you think of it, I was called it at some stage. When I met you I could see the same hurt in you. You were the fat boy in school, weren't you?'

Malcolm's face relaxed into repose. 'Yes.'

'I thought so. Well I couldn't help my hormones any more than you could help your weight, but it still hurt like hell. Right?'

'Right.'

'I'm settling down now. I'm much more in charge than I used to be and for the first time I feel content to be with one man, even a man who hasn't even started to reach his own physical potential.' She leaned over him, placing a light kiss on his cheek. 'If you would learn to make love to me instead of trying to fuck me rigid every time we're together I could show you that all your bravado and male ego trumpeting is a total waste of time and energy. People are not black or white, male or female, Jew or gentile – they're just people. Accept what you are and respect others for what they are. You start from that position and you'll begin to feel much better about yourself and I will show you happiness the like of which you've never dreamed of. We're both fat, Jewish kids who've made good. Admit it, at least to yourself. That would be a good start.'

Malcolm's silence was proof she was getting through.

She pushed herself away from him and stood up beside the bed. 'Maybe you think that's shit, but it's the way I feel.'

Malcolm slowly tipped himself off the bed and stood in front of her. 'I lo—'

'Don't say it, Malcolm. I don't think you know the real meaning of the word yet. Just hold me instead of grabbing me. That would be a start.'

The entrance to the Hampstead house was unattended when Tilly and Dominic arrived shortly before noon. Dominic phoned Harry on the mobile. He came down and let them in.

'Everyone's buggered off just because it's Christmas Day,' complained Harry, as all three of them crammed into the small, wood-lined lift. 'And I'm getting fuck-all out of Tirgoviste. Even Moscow's tighter than a frog's ass on a frosty morning.'

Harry offered his code and the lift started its smooth, upward journey. 'It's so bloody frustrating. All I've got are outside shots and guessing commentary, and I know they're filming 'cause I saw the equipment go in.'

'Are they transmitting? Can you tap in?' asked Dominic as the lift stopped.

'Nothing. I've got electronic surveillance gear the CIA would die for and none of it is worth a pony's piss without a bug in that courtroom.'

They walked up narrow wooden stairs and through the steel door that Harry had surprisingly left open. 'Come see for yourself.' He pointed towards the rest area. 'Tilly, coffee,' he said in a most throwaway manner.

Dominic thought Tilly would blow her stack there and then. He winced as he waited for the torrent of verbal abuse. To his complete surprise Tilly said nothing; she just set about gathering the dirty cups and piling them in the round, chrome sink beside the fridge. Dominic focused his attention on the screens above station one. One static exterior shot of the army barracks at Tirgoviste, a map of the area, and Russian Television news, currently showing snow ploughs at work in Ukraine; the rest were blank. Dominic could see why Harry was frustrated. 'How much do you know?' he asked.

'They read the charges out in last hour's Moscow news. They're accused of genocide, corruption, and the destruction of the national economy; also something that sounds like semkin or samkin.'

'Si-emkyin,' said Dominic. 'It means nepotism.'

They monitored Russian, Romanian and Hungarian television for any sign of news: nothing. Tilly cleaned up the room finding dirty cups in the strangest of places, washing them and stacking them neatly.

'Thank you ever so much,' said Harry when she'd finished, giving her a king-size hug and kiss on the cheek. 'I'm sorry I yelled at you earlier, it's so frustrating not being able to follow this.'

'That's all right, Harry,' she replied, smiling at Dominic over his shoulder. 'Consider it your Christmas present.'

Moscow was showing a documentary about Siberia when the 'news flash' caption focused their attention. Dominic's Russian was elementary but decidedly more comprehensive than Harry's. He knew enough to understand what he was hearing. After the bulletin finished Dominic stared blankly at the console, its flashing lights and silver screens blending in his vision like an out of focus carousel. He felt that a marathon had ended and he'd won the race, yet there was no joy, no adrenalin rush of victory; just the tiredness of lengthy competition, the emptiness of completion, and the sadness of remembrance. Tilly gently touched his shoulder and he placed his hand over hers.

'What happened?' questioned Harry irritably.

Tilly was about to sting a cutting remark his way when Dominic snapped back to reality. 'They're dead. Both of them,' he said flatly. 'Found guilty and executed in the barrack courtyard ten minutes ago. It's all over, Harry. The Ceausescus are no more.'

'They shot the wife as well,' Harry quietly confirmed.

'They were as bad as each other,' said Dominic stridently, in case Harry felt any tinge of sorrow for the woman. 'She was his right hand, some say the real nasty one. I've heard she liked a little torture after dinner.' Tilly squeezed his shoulder, stopping further detail. Dominic patched together his memories of the news flash.

'They've appointed Ion Iliescu as interim President, which is good news, Harry; he was a student with Gorbachev at Moscow University and they get on well. Dumitri Mazilu is named Vice-President. He's the former UN representative and was one of the first to denounce Ceausescu's human rights record. The only other name I picked up was Petre Roman. I think he's Prime Minister.'

'Where's he from?'

'Academia. He was the administrator at Bucharest Polytechnic.'

Harry directed his next remark at Tilly. 'Bloody gold mine of information, this boy. Saves me hours of research.'

'Does that mean we're finished here?' replied Tilly, her voice saccharine sweet, playing with him. 'Or will you find another war to ruin our Christmas?'

He leaned over the console and typed CONTROL/RECORD/ALL then SEND DATA TO HQ. His countenance turned instantly from military intelligence officer to jovial Harry Cassini, hard drinker, bon viveur, life of the party. 'My dearest friends. Let me take you to my humble abode and ply you with alcoholic beverages until you both fall over.'

'Let us take you to our place,' replied Tilly. 'Malcolm and Claire are cooking dinner for all of us.'

'Malcolm!?'

'Hard to believe, but true.' Tilly tucked her arm partway around Harry's waist. 'We think he's a reformed man, don't we Dominic?'

'Completely.'

'This I must see,' said Harry, moving towards the door. 'Come on you two, out!'

Twenty-nine

'Have the armoured car out front in five minutes and bring that bitch Nadia to my office *now*!'

General Roman Stenoza was a very worried man. Having failed to rescue Ceausescu at the first attempt, he was planning a second raid when news of the execution was broadcast on state radio and television. His contingency plans for such an event had been in place for weeks and although his priority was for his own short-term safety, he had a second list of objectives that involved the elimination of anyone who could testify against him at a later date. On the top of that list was the name of Dominic Bellescu.

'Ah, the lovely Nadia,' he said sarcastically as she stood before him flanked by two armed guards. 'Tie the bitch to the chair.'

The guards did as instructed. Nadia offered no resistance; it would have been futile. She was bound by her ankles and wrists and a large leather strap pinned her waist to the chairback. Stenoza rounded his desk and delivered the usual hard slap across her face. There was no opium to dull the pain this time. Nadia felt the full sting of his blow and tasted the blood in her mouth.

'I don't know where he is,' she said in a desperate attempt to halt the attack. 'I've heard nothing from him since March.'

Stenoza paid no attention. He picked up a pair of pliers from his desk and stood beside her. 'I'm going to break every one of your fingers unless you tell me what I want to know.'

'I know nothing!' The pliers did their work on the index finger of her left hand. She screamed with agony.

'Silly, stupid whore,' sneered Stenoza, snapping the pliers shut on her second finger. 'To think I used to fuck you. You're too stupid to fuck.'

A single knock, then Stenoza's door opened. Private Popescu stood at attention. 'The car's here, sir. All the files have been shredded.'

Stenoza looked down at Nadia. 'Now why can't you be a good little whore like Popescu. She tells me what I want to know and she does what she's told.' He leaned back against his desk and looked irascibly at the soldier. 'Come here and lick my dick,' he commanded.

As the young blonde walked towards him willing to do as requested, Stenoza pulled his pistol and shot her in the head. Nadia gasped in horror as the force of the bullet slammed Popescu against the wall. She was dead before she reached the floor. He levelled the gun at Nadia. 'Where the fuck is Bellescu?'

'I don't know, repeated Nadia, certain those would be her last words.'

Stenoza stared at her with cold, haddock eyes. He scratched his testicles with his free hand and spat on the floor. Showing not an ounce of remorse, he looked over at Popescu's lifeless body, took careful aim, and fired a bullet into her pubic region. The corpse jumped from the impact. Stenoza laughed. 'If she'd jumped like that when she was alive I would've fucked her instead of shooting her.' He returned the gun and his gaze to Nadia. He stood in front of her and jammed the pistol up her skirt. Nadia flinched as the gun barrel found its mark. She struggled in vain as Stenoza grabbed her breast, squeezing hard, inflicting more pain.

'Ready for the hottest fuck of your life?' Nadia spat at

him defiantly. Malevolently he glared at her and pulled the trigger.

The click surprised them both as the hammer fell on a spent cartridge. Stenoza retrieved the pistol, walked behind his desk, produced a box of shells from the drawer and calmly began reloading. 'Another few seconds to remember where he is,' he snarled.

'I don't fucking *know*!' Nadia was beyond caring. He would kill her anyway, she knew that. She hoped it would be quick – in the head like Popescu. She dreaded the thought of a bullet in the abdomen that could leave her alive for hours, maybe days.

A soldier appeared suddenly at the office door. 'Sir. People are surrounding the car, sir. With respect, we should leave now.'

Stenoza walked from behind his desk as he loaded the last shell. He aimed the pistol at Nadia's head for a second then replaced it in his hip holster. 'Bring her with us,' he instructed the guard. 'She still might serve a purpose.' He walked passed the soldier and into the hall. 'And get me the English newspapers, they're a day fucking late.'

Thirty

Malcolm's decision not to open the club on Boxing Day and give the staff a good break at Christmas was another example of his improving attitude toward his fellow human beings. Claire's influence was certainly changing him for the better.

Tilly and Dominic spent most of Boxing Day lounging around the flat, watching *Star Wars* on television and eating healthy food in a vain attempt to make up for the over-indulgence of Christmas evening. It was a rest day in the true sense of the word, and greatly appreciated; today meant back to business as usual. Tilly had arranged lunch at the Durrants Hotel with Helen Lawrence from the *Sunday Express*. Dominic was to relive his escape in graphic detail and the resulting interview would receive two pages in the New Year's Eve edition. The article had been promoted in last week's paper, so there was no way out.

As usual, Tilly was first up and had scooted out to the shops and returned before Dominic reached full consciousness. She walked into the bedroom clutching the morning's papers and six freshly baked croissants. Sketchy transcripts of the trial featured in all the papers.

The Times devoted five columns to Ceausescu's life under the heading TYRANT WHO SUCCUMBED TO THE WRATH OF HIS LONG-SUFFERING PEOPLE. They chronicled his nepotism, stating that in 1984 no less than eight members of his family sat on the Central Committee; his flirtation with the West, citing the inclusion of the Romanian Olympic team at the Los Angeles games despite the Russian ban; and his one genuine move towards world peace when he was instrumental in promoting President Sadat's visit to the Knesset in 1977. Geoffrey Levy wrote in the *Mail* of the brevity of Ceausescu's trial, saying it was carried out exactly according to law – the law that Ceausescu himself promulgated. He reported that the family had, between them, embezzled over one billion dollars over twenty-five years.

Only one voice spoke against the proceedings, that of the SDP leader David Owen who was quoted in the *Express* as saying it was an utterly disgraceful affair and the West should make it clear that this sort of behaviour, whatever the provocation, is not the proper way of dealing with such matters. Dominic understood his concern but felt his response would be different if he'd lived the last twenty years under this evil regime. Besides, without a fast conclusion there would have been many more deaths as a result of Securitate attempts to rescue their leader. The article also stated that scores of countries, including Britain, America and China, pledged support for Romania's new rulers.

Harry's piece for the *Sun* was well informed and highly accurate, but then it should be, given the information at his disposal. The *Star* had the best pictures, especially the one of Ceausescu's blood pressure being taken by a doctor moments before his execution. Ceausescu looked bewildered, as if it was all a bad dream and he would suddenly awake in his presidential palace still in charge of the country. They reported the arrest of his daughter, Zoia, and the cache of treasure found at her mansion in Bucharest. Millions of dollars in jewellery, gold and money were hidden all over the house and a Romanian spokesman said it could take weeks, maybe months to find all the treasure she'd stashed away over the years. The article

245

also pointed out that while the Romanian people drove 'rust buckets', Ceausescu cruised around in black Mercedes limos equipped with mini-bars. He had nine private jets and three helicopters; each plane boasting a presidential suite, lounge and office plus several bedrooms which he used for sex romps with his mistresses.

The most poignant article appeared in *The Times* under the headline IRAN SACKS ROMANIAN ENVOY. The unfortunate diplomat apparently failed to inform the Iranian government that Ceausescu was a despot and a mass murderer prior to the Romanian leader's three-day visit to Iran on 18 December. They had had twenty years to figure it out for themselves but had conveniently overlooked the atrocities until now. During that visit the Iranian leaders had said the grounds for economic co-operation between the two countries were 'completely fertile', and described Ceausescu's visit as 'totally successful'. The whole episode reminded Dominic of the English expression about the pot calling the kettle black, but it proved, unequivocally, that two weeks can be a lifetime in politics.

'I want you to wear something smart today,' said Tilly, placing a pot of fresh coffee on the bedside table. 'Helen likes men who look neat and tidy.'

'And I like women who look neat and sexy, especially first thing in the morning.' Dominic made an exaggerated grab for her. She stepped smartly out of reach and beamed a smile at him from the safety of the tallboy. She opened a drawer and removed a freshly laundered white shirt, which she deposited on the foot of the bed.

'The rest of the outfit is up to you,' she said, skipping towards the bedroom door. 'Shower and dressed in twenty minutes, please. We leave here in half an hour.'

After much deliberation Dominic finally decided on an old favourite: the dark blue Armani double-breasted suit, black loafers and the bright, floral-pattern tie.

They arrived at the hotel before Ms Lawrence, settled themselves at table eight and ordered a bottle of Perrier to sip while they waited. Helen wafted into the restaurant exactly at the appointed time wearing the most outrageous pink chiffon dress with matching wide-brimmed hat. The outfit belonged to summer by the river not winter in the West End, but she wore it with such authority and panache that the seasons would surely change in order to accommodate her fashion. Slightly plump, she filled the couture creation to the limit of its stitching.

'Tilly Howard! How lovely to see you again,' she said, exchanging polite kisses on both cheeks before turning her attention to Dominic. 'And this is Dominic Dance, the straight Michael Jackson and every woman's dream tango partner.'

'You're too kind.' Dominic stood up, clasping her hand firmly and kissing it gently. 'May I order you a drink?'

'Gin and tonic,' she said, retrieving her hand and sitting down on the chair opposite. 'Good looks, and manners too. You are a lucky one, Tilly Howard.'

Over the past months Dominic had learned to sum up journalists within seconds of meeting them. Most were hardened professionals who would not be fooled by a trumped-up story fabricated by a press officer after a column-inch bonus. This lady looked the hardest of them all. She had a ruthlessness about her that sizzled. He would have to be very careful what he said to Ms. Helen Lawrence. 'Shall we order?' he asked.

'When are you getting married?' she replied, completely ignoring his offer of the menu.

'February 14th,' interjected Tilly. 'Do try the confit of duck with spring onions and port. It's delicious.'

If anyone could prove more stubborn than a journalist after a hot story it was Tilly defending her patch. Dominic decided to confine his tales to the night of the escape and let his beloved handle the hot gossip. 'I'm starting with the timbale of cottage cheese, avocado and prawns on a bed of crispy leaves with balsamic oil, and as a main course I'm going for the marinated loin of lamb rolled in herb crumbs and rosemary jus.'

Helen picked up the large leather-bound menu and

247

started to read. Tilly and Dominic secretly looked at each other. Tilly mouthed the word 'battleaxe'; Dominic nodded agreement.

'What are you two cooking up?' trumpeted Helen across the table.

Tilly placed her menu on the table. 'I was asking him to order the wine,' she lied without a moment's hesitation. 'He's not very well versed on the subject. Maybe you'd like to choose.'

'I love wine.' Helen grabbed the wine list from the waiter and made her decision within a minute. 'We'll start with a bottle of Chablis, number thirty-five, and with the main course a bottle of number six well chilled but not freezing.' Number six had to be champagne; the brand would remain a mystery until the main course.

'Now, about the food,' she continued before the wine waiter could effect his departure. 'I'll start with the duck and then the salmon, the one in chive cream with the caramelised *tartin* of endive.'

It didn't seem to bother her that she'd given her food order to the wine waiter and he was too polite to draw it to her attention. She, however, knew exactly what she was doing. After the waiter left she leaned across the table and said in a low voice, 'I love doing that. Wait till the food bloke comes along, I'll have even more fun.' Dominic hated being embarrassed in public and he had an awful feeling this lunch would turn him five shades of red.

Tilly doubled Dominic's hors-d'oeuvre order and chose sauté of scallops and scampi flavoured with cider as a main course. The waiter then focused his attention on Helen, who stared blankly at him.

'Madam?' he asked

'I've ordered, thank you,' she said, then started talking to Tilly about the weather. It was drivel but the poor man wasn't going to get a word in if he stayed there for half an hour. He finally gave up waiting and walked dis-gruntled into the kitchen. 'Great stuff!' said Helen smugly. 'I love screwing with their heads.'

'I hope you save your head-screwing for the hired help, Helen. Dominic's a little nervous of being misquoted right now, given the recent events in Romania. I'm sure you understand.'

Helen's attitude changed in an instant. 'You know me better than that, Tilly Howard. Games are games but business is business. I won't misquote your precious Dominic. The *Express* want an upbeat, commie-bashing success story. He'll be the hero of the year by the time I'm through with him.'

Things must have been sorted out in the kitchen, as the three hors-d'oeuvres arrived together. They praised the food to each other and the conversation then turned to Helen's new boyfriend who was, according to her, the biggest shit in England because he chose to spend Christmas with his ex-wife and children in Yorkshire instead of bonking Helen silly at her 'luxurious' flat in St John's Wood. Dominic thought the man had made the right choice.

Helen's voice was sharp and very clipped. Luckily, they were the only customers in the restaurant, otherwise everyone would have had the benefit of her dubious wisdom. During the main course, the conversation finally drifted back to Dominic's escape. As Dominic was describing how he felt standing on the third-floor landing looking into an empty stairwell, his eye caught a glimpse of Harry's head rushing past the outside window. Within five seconds Harry stood framed in the restaurant door.

'Get down, Dominic! Hit the fucking floor!!'

Dominic started to duck his head to the right and felt the heat of a bullet as it grazed his cheek and exploded into the leather banquette beside him. He pushed Tilly away from him, sending her spawling on to the floor by the table. From the corner of his eye Dominic saw a flash from the building opposite, heard the sound of breaking glass and a loud thump as another bullet embedded itself in the wooden panel above his head. He grabbed the edge of the table and heaved it on to its edge, sending food, drink and Helen flying. A third and fourth bullet slammed into the oak table top.

Dominic looked towards the door. Harry was gone. 'Tilly. Are you all right?' he shouted, trying desperately to remain calm and decide his next move.

'Yes.'

'Helen?'

'Yes,' came a tiny voice from under the dessert trolley.

'Stay put, both of you!'

Dominic was starting to edge around the table when he heard three more shots outside. He sprinted across the restaurant and into the reception area. The hall was deserted. He ran outside the building and saw Harry standing halfway across George Street, his mobile phone in one hand, a gun in the other. He was pointing the gun at a man lying face down on the opposite side of the street.

'Harry! You all right?!' Dominic shouted.

'Go back inside!' called Harry, his eyes fixed on the fallen man. 'Tell the manager not to phone the police, I've already done it. Do it *now*!!'

Dominic heard the sound of distant sirens as he ran back into the deserted reception. He vaulted the desk and stepped smartly round the partition that separated the office from the check-in; here a tall man in a grey suit was looking out the window and dialling 999. Dominic walked over and placed his finger on the phone button, cutting off the man's call. He had to run a super-bluff to gain the man's confidence and stop the situation getting rapidly out of hand.

'Everything's under control. I'm with Special Services. We've had an attempted assassination here, but it's all over now. My commanding officer is outside and will explain everything to you once the street is secure. The police and ambulance have already been called. Please sit down and stay away from the windows.'

The man seemed to accept the explanation without question. Dominic looked across the street. Harry's gun was now holstered and he was bending over the man, going through his pockets. As he stood up an ambulance drew alongside the kerb. Harry talked to one of the attendants, then headed back across the street. Dominic signalled to the man to stay still and vaulted back over the reception desk.

'Was anybody hit?' said Harry, marching towards the restaurant. 'Tilly? Is Tilly hurt?'

For a second Dominic's heart was in his mouth as he followed Harry into the restaurant. Tilly stood beside Helen, who was sitting at table two looking totally dishevelled and trying unsuccessfully to remove the lamb in rosemary jus that had planted itself firmly on top of her blonde, backcombed hair.

Harry took control. 'I want everyone in the main bar right away. Organise it, Dominic. I mean *everyone*. Waiters, managers, porters, cooks, customers – everyone. Give me five minutes. No one leaves, OK?'

The hotel was running on a skeleton staff because of the holidays, so rounding up everyone was relatively easy. Three kitchen staff, three waiters, two porters, one maid, four reception personnel and five guests were soon assembled in the wood-panelled hotel bar. A blazing coal fire made the gathering look more like a post-Christmas party than an assembly of witnesses to an attempted murder. Tilly stayed close to Helen, the only one who seemed physically affected. She'd cleaned up her hair and rearranged her pink chiffon dress which had been torn across the shoulder. Now she sat huddled in the corner trying to regain her composure.

As they waited for Harry, Dominic thought how lucky he'd been to escape unhurt. If he hadn't ducked at that precise moment the first bullet would have hit him in the forehead. Only now did he feel the shock waves of fear run through his body. Life over death had been determined by half a second. Dominic thanked God and Harry for his deliverance.

Harry appeared, his huge bulk filling the entire

doorway, and addressed the assembly. 'I'm Commander Cassini, Military Intelligence.' He held up his identification card in his right hand and walked slowly into the room. 'The incident that's happened here today involves highly sensitive operatives within our armed forces. Luckily there was no loss of life, and damage is minimal.' He turned as one of the ambulance crew walked in.

'This is Sergeant Copeland, who will pass among you with copies of the Official Secrets Act. I want you to read, then sign it. I'm afraid there's no option on this; anyone refusing to sign will be placed under arrest as a possible suspect in this case.'

A snigger of disbelief could be heard. Harry pounced on the dissension immediately. 'You may think all this is outdated and belongs in a James Bond movie but I assure you it is extremely serious. The reason you never hear about episodes like this is because the damn thing works. As you'll see when you read the paper, it is illegal to talk, write, record, or in any way converse about the events that happened here today under penalty of imprisonment. Anyone breaching the Act will be prosecuted to the full limit of the law.'

Dominic watched the reactions around the room. Everyone seemed shocked and nonplussed by Harry's speech but the message was definitely getting through.

'Please stay here for the next half an hour while we clean up outside,' Harry continued. 'I'm sure the management won't mind if we open the bar; as a matter of fact I could use a stiff drink myself.' The last remark seemed to break the ice. Most of the people relaxed a little, accepting the paper from Sergeant Copeland and talking among themselves.

Harry beckoned to Tilly, Helen and Dominic to follow him out of the room. Outside the bar door stood the tall man in the grey suit. 'This is the manager, Mr Miller,' said Harry as he hurried along the corridor towards reception, ushering the man before him. 'Is there a private room we can use for a few minutes? There's some things you should know.'

The man seemed pleasant enough, especially for somebody who'd just had his hotel shot up. He led them to the first floor and unlocked room 101 with his pass-key. As they'd passed through reception Dominic noticed that three workmen were already carrying out running repairs in the restaurant. He remembered how quickly they'd sorted out Tilly's flat after Sara had been killed and wondered how long it would take them to remove all traces of the frenzied attack that so nearly claimed his life.

Harry made straight for the mini-bar which Mr Miller opened with speed. They extracted miniature bottles of Scotch from the fridge, poured them into two glasses and drank them down in a single gulp.

'I'm glad we think alike,' said Harry, reaching for another bottle. The two men smiled at each other, comrades in crime and whisky.

'Anything available for the victim, his woman and a journalist?' asked Dominic, hoping to refocus Harry's priorities.

'Dominic, Tilly, Helen – please, help yourselves,' he said, leading Mr Miller away from the bar.

To everyone's complete surprise Helen leapt at the bar, flung open the fridge, grabbed two bottles of vodka, opened them and, placing both in her mouth at the same time, downed the lot. 'Now Mr Cassini,' she pronounced, flicking the empty bottles into the small metal basket beside the fridge. 'What's all this shit about the OSA? I've got one monster story here and I don't intend to waste all day sitting on it.'

Harry's smile proved falsely reassuring. 'If one word of this appears in any newspaper you'll be sitting on your shapely butt awaiting Her Majesty's Pleasure. Do I make myself clear?'

'You can't stop freedom of the press. I don't give a shit who you are.' Helen had a serious temper problem and

Harry was about to feel its most severe edge. 'I'm filing this story right now. If you don't like it, talk to my editor.' She took three paces toward the door before Harry blocked her path. 'Let me go!!' she screamed hysterically. 'You have no right to stop me!'

'I have every right and I'll prove it if you'll just sit down.' Harry pointed to the red lounge chair beside the double bed. 'Please.'

Helen looked around the room for support. Finding none and realising she had no physical chance against someone of Harry's size, she reluctantly did as requested.

Harry punched a number into his portable phone and waited for the connection.

'John, good afternoon. It's Harry Cassini. . . . Fine, thank you. I'm sorry to bother you at home but I've a small problem that needs your attention. I've got a code three operation in the West End and one of your reporters has stumbled on to it. She wants to file a story. I wonder, would you have a word with her? Thank you.'

He handed the phone to Helen, who listened carefully to the advice being administered. As the one-sided conversation progressed her expression changed from arrogance through disbelief to obedience.

'Thank you. I understand,' she said finally, and handed the phone back to Harry.

'Thank you, John. A round of golf in the New Year, first fine Saturday, what do you say? . . . . I look forward to it. . . . Happy New Year to you and give my love to Gladys. . . . Goodbye.'

To be involved in a story this sensational and not be able to print is like winning the pools and realising you haven't posted the coupon. Helen sat on the bed, her head bowed, her confidence shattered.

Harry poured her another vodka, this time in a glass, adding ice and lemon. 'Mr Miller is ex-Guards,' he said, 'so he knows what's required. Within an hour you'll never know anything's happened here, and that's the way I want it to remain.' He turned towards the manager. 'Will you take Ms. Lawrence downstairs and ply her with some of your best champagne? I need to talk to Dominic and Tilly. We'll be down in a few minutes.'

Helen perked up at the mention of champagne and as Mr Miller escorted her from the room Dominic had the distinct impression she was showing more than a passing interest in the tall man with the upright military bearing.

'That's the hardest I've worked in years,' said Harry, helping himself to another Scotch.

'How did you know?' asked Tilly, finally finding her voice now they were alone.

Harry drank half the Scotch in one gulp. 'Nadia,' he said almost offhandedly.

'You've found her!' Tilly reassuringly squeezed Dominic's hand.

'She found me.' Harry's voice was quiet and reflective.

'What's the matter?'

Harry sipped at his drink. 'She's hurt, Dominic. She's hurt badly.'

'Tell me all you know.'

'She's been held by Stenoza since Christmas Eve. He thought she knew where you were and he tortured her to get information she didn't have. She contacted my agent yesterday. It was only by chance I went to Hampstead this morning to check the overnight tapes. If I hadn't, my son, you'd be dead meat.'

'How did she know about the hit?'

'The *Express* promoted the article in last week's paper. They said you were going to relive your escape, so Stenoza knew you'd be at the Durrants either today or tomorrow. Once he had a location and a time he didn't need Nadia any more so he shot her in the back and dumped her in a ditch outside Brasov. She's a brave girl. She crawled over two miles to make contact with us. You owe her your life.'

'Why does Stenoza want Dominic dead?' asked Tilly. 'His evidence is obsolete now Ceausescu's gone.'

'Now the borders are open he thinks Dominic will come

after him to avenge the death of his parents or to testify against him – so he decided to strike first. And the situation on the ground has changed since the execution. The Securitate have split into two factions. The new government's given them until tomorrow to surrender or face summary execution. The majority are surrendering on a private judicial promise of light jail terms. Most of them will be back on the street within three years and setting up private security firms. The real bad ones like Stenoza would never make trial and they know it, so they've gone underground. Nadia said he's already moving in on the porn and drugs trade. He's setting himself up as a Godfather and with the firepower at his command it's going to be hard to stop him.'

'Where's Nadia now?' asked Dominic, suddenly uninterested in Stenoza's activities.

'In Brasov hospital. She'll be all right. You can talk to her this afternoon if you want.'

Tilly stroked Dominic's head then cupped his face in her hands and kissed him lightly on the cheek. 'We'll go together,' she said softly.

'Another thing,' said Harry, producing a photograph from his jacket pocket. 'Recognise this?'

Dominic recognised it immediately. It was one of the pictures taken with the Driver family on Hampstead Heath. 'Where did you find this?'

'On the man who was trying to shoot you.'

A connection between the Driver family and the hit man seemed impossible. 'It was taken just before Christmas on the Heath,' said Dominic. 'A family calling themselves the Drivers. They must have been tailing me.'

'Which means Hampstead is blown.' Harry spat the words out, angry at himself for allowing such a blatant breach of security. 'They were watching the house. You were a lucky bonus,' he said, patting Dominic lightly on the shoulder. 'What worries me is we should have spotted them before they got this close.'

He put his drink down and picked up his phone. 'Let's finish up here and get to Hampstead.'

As they walked into the restaurant the last workman was putting his tools away. New strips of red leather had been heat-sealed over the sections of banquette damaged by the bullets, the table was upright and covered with a fresh cloth and the broken window had been glazed. Apart from areas of dampness on the carpet there was no evidence that anything untoward had happened. Helen sat at a table by the window sipping champagne with Mr Miller. She looked relaxed and seemed to be enjoying his company, which removed one niggling worry from Dominic's overburdened mind.

Thirty-one

The Hampstead house looked deserted as they came to a noisy stop outside the front door. Handsome Charlie was polite and silent, as usual. Harry whispered to him and he scurried off in the direction of the unused living area.

They rode the lift to the top floor and walked into the empty communications room. Harry turned on console number one and set about connecting up to his Romanian network. His first try was unsuccessful due to an error in his satellite path and they ended up watching MTV via Intelsat. He left the soundless picture on screen six while he tried again, leaving Tilly and Dominic to guess the song before the caption appeared at the end of the video. They both knew the group was Aerosmith but the song escaped them until Dominic saw two steel doors slam shut. 'Love in an Elevator,' he shouted, rejoicing in his victory.

'Hate in a transponder,' said Harry, failing once more to make his connection. 'This little shit doesn't want to perform.'

His agitation prompted Tilly to change the subject. 'How can you get the pictures through live?' she asked. 'I thought transmitting to a satellite took a great deal of power.'

'Not power, accuracy.' Harry set another path in motion.

He loved talking high-tech and he was especially proud of the Hampstead operation.

'One of Malcolm's boffins invented a sat-finder about a year ago and it's solved all our problems. When a mobile wants to find a transponder – that's the bit of the satellite that collects and transmits the signal – the operator used to do it by trial and error. It sometimes took twenty minutes to find the right satellite. Sat-finder is a microchip that stores information and location details of every tin can – I'm sorry, satellite – we use. When the operator wants to transmit, sat-finder automatically selects the closest can and locks on to it. Unfortunately it doesn't work as well from this end, so it's harder for me to connect with him than vice versa. That's why we have a telephone back-up.' He chuckled to himself. 'Which I'm about to use if this temperamental son of a bitch doesn't work this time.'

The flashing red light on the console signalled another failure. 'He might be switched off,' he said, reaching for the phone. The connection was immediate. 'Hello, Uri. It's Harry. Where are you?'

Gone were the code names and secret locations, now that freedom was raging through the country. Harry switched the phone on to speakers.

'I'm outside the hospital. Do you want Nadia?' Uri's voice filled the room.

'Yes please. How is she?' Harry smiled at Dominic.

'She's better. They've removed the bullet and pumped her full of pain killers. I don't know if she'll make much sense but she wants to speak to Dominic as soon as possible. Give me five minutes to get inside. I'll call you when I'm set.'

'Fair enough, Uri.' Harry disconnected the phone and leaned back in the chair. 'She'll be able to hear you but the visual transmission is only one-way. We can see her; she can't see us.'

'I'll make coffee,' said Tilly, and for the first time a tinge of jealousy was apparent in her voice. She knew how

Dominic once felt about Nadia and loved him enough to understand that some of that feeling would remain. This was the first time even a hint of displeasure had surfaced.

'I'll give you a hand,' said Dominic.

'I can manage, thank you,' she said, turning away from him. Suspicions confirmed. He followed her into the kitchen area and put his arms gently around her waist. She let her head drop back on to his shoulder, her eyes closed. 'It's healthy for a woman like me to show a bit of jealousy for the man I love. Do you mind?'

'As long as you know it's unfounded.' He kissed her neck.

'Go and talk to Nadia. She needs a good friend right now.' Tilly reached for the kettle. 'I'll bring you a coffee as soon as it's ready.'

Dominic sat beside Harry and waited impatiently for Uri's call. He rested his face in his hands and exhaled slowly through his nose until all the air had drained from his lungs. He closed his eyes, feeling safe in the absolute darkness. He started to inhale, slowly savouring the fresh air and the slight hint of Tilly's perfume that remained on his hands. He repeated the breathing exercise for at least three minutes, each breath calming his body, focusing his mind, soothing his spirit.

The coffee and Uri's call arrived together. Tilly stood looking over Dominic's head and gently rubbing his shoulders. As the screens lit up he could see Nadia's face, at first out of focus, and then sharp, full framed.

Her right eye was swollen and nearly closed, a bandage covered her left eye and forehead, leaving tufts of her hair to slip over the bandage and cascade down, partially covering the large bloodstain that had already seeped through. Her neck was also bandaged from just under her chin. Two plastic tubes were taped to her mouth. She looked helpless, broken, near dead.

Dominic tried to remove any thought of guilt, but it loomed large in his mind allowing no respite, no solace for the anger that raged inside him. He wanted Stenoza

260

dead – and looking at poor, fragile Nadia he knew he would have to kill him.

'She's asleep,' said Uri quietly over a crystal-clear line. 'The bullet hit her high and to the right of centre. It missed anything vital but punctured her lung, hence the respirator.' He panned the camera down the bed. Her hands were outside the covers completely wrapped in bandages. 'They've also operated on her hands. Stenoza broke her fingers.' Dominic felt queasy. The camera panned back up; Uri's hand came into picture as he touched the unbandaged side of her face. 'Nadia. I've got Dominic for you.' He removed his headset and placed it gently across Nadia's head. 'You can talk to her now,' he said, his face coming into vision for the first time. He was young and slim with Arian features. He smiled briefly before disappearing again behind the camera.

Dominic pressed the transmit button on the console. 'Nadia. Can you hear me? Nadia. It's Dominic.' She lay motionless, as if in a trance.

'Nadia. It's Dominic.' A flicker of movement from her lips signalled consciousness. 'Nadia. Hello. This is Dominic in London. Can you hear me?'

The flicker became a half-smile. 'Dominic. Thank God you're alive.' Her voice was weak, not even a whisper. She drifted back into sleep.

Uri removed the headset. 'I think we should wait until tomorrow. She's in no state to talk.'

'Thank you, Uri. You did your best.' Harry's voice took over like a welcome friend. 'Has she said anything to you about where Stenoza might be?'

'Either Risnov, Zarnesti or Sacele. He's got places in most of the villages surrounding Brasov; he could be in any one of them. She told me he'd put out a rolling contract on Dominic, so be prepared for another try.'

'Point taken. Can you call me tomorrow 10:00 GMT?'

'No problem.'

'We'll try again then. Take care, Uri.'

'I will.'

Harry disconnected and sat back lazily. We have trouble, my son. We're going to have to deal with this because I can't bail you out again and you most certainly can't appear in public until this is resolved.'

'He must,' Tilly chipped in. 'He's the club. No Dominic, no customers.'

'No Malcolm, no club.' Everyone had been so engrossed in the conversation that nobody had heard Malcolm enter the room.

'We need to talk,' he said, taking a step to the right and revealing Claire. 'I gather we're in a situation where Hampstead has been uncovered, there's a contract on Dominic, the club's in danger from an uninsurable disaster, and you, my good friend Harry, are about to piss off with Boy Wonder and cop a suicide mission – all of which will lead to the Romanian network being exposed for the sake of this asswipe Stenoza. Am I close, gentlemen?'

Good old supportive, surprising, no-nonsense Malcolm. He had the most remarkable ability to say it all in one sentence. 'On the button,' volunteered Dominic before Harry had time to register a protest.

'Then may I suggest we shut down the screens for a while and convene a meeting of the board.'

No one spoke. Harry was about to, then changed his mind and flicked off the monitors one at a time. Dominic looked at Tilly, who was concentrating on her empty coffee cup, then at Claire who stood beside Malcolm; she seemed at ease but a slight unsureness showed her nerves.

'More coffee, anyone?' asked Tilly, snapping from her trance.

'Good idea,' said Malcolm. 'Everyone get tooled up and wee'd out.'

Claire and Tilly both decided the ladies' room was better than making more coffee, which gave the three men a few spare minutes to plan their strategy.

'So predictable,' Malcolm said, slapping Harry on the shoulder as he flicked monitor one back into life. He punched a command into the matrix and the screen
262

revealed a two-shot of Tilly and Claire looking straight into camera. 'Simple and best,' said Malcolm in a self-congratulatory tone. 'Camera behind the mirror gag. Classic stuff, eh Harry?'

'Route One, my son.' Harry offered a three-clap round of applause.

Any thoughts Dominic had about Claire reforming Malcolm's life went directly out of the window. Whatever corners she'd managed to round off didn't come within miles of getting to the man. He was paying her lip service in exchange for great sex and the occasional woman's point of view, which he'd file away and regurgitate when it was politically advantageous. Dominic thought it disgusting that he could spy on his supposed loved one not only guiltlessly but also with relish and a sense of victory. But within ten seconds Dominic was also engrossed in the women's conversation too.

'I don't care what happens,' Tilly was saying angrily. 'I don't want Dominic to go. He'll be killed; I can feel it.'

'Oh Tilly,' replied Claire, embracing her friend and patting her reassuringly on the back. 'You poor love. You mustn't let them get to you. I'm sure Malcolm wouldn't let anything happen to Dominic. You're not to worry so.'

'It's premonition, not worry.' She smiled: a tense, forced smile. 'I'm being silly, I know. I shouldn't let my imagination run away with me. But I just *know* he'll be hurt.'

'What a load of bollocks, eh?' Malcolm flicked off the monitor. 'Pay no attention, Dominic. If women's intuition is so shit-hot how come Claire never knows that I've got a hard on until I put it in her mouth?' He burst into crude raucous laughter. 'We'll get you in and out in one piece if that's what we decide needs doing.' He turned to Harry. 'Does he need to go?'

'This is personal. Stenoza killed his mother and father, mutilated a woman he cares for and has a contract on his life. For life to go on with any semblance of normality Stenoza must be taken out. If we send a task force after him it could end up like Noriega – a battalion of high-profile soldiers chasing him around a country of which he has infinitely better knowledge.'

He paused and looked at Dominic before continuing. 'If, on the other hand, Dominic and I go in with the help of our network and a caseful of American dollars, he's more likely to stay and fight to satisfy his perverted honour and capture a fistful of dollars, and we'll be in and out before you know we've gone. If Dominic can fake an illness on stage tonight we could get him out by ambulance to Northolt. We could be back in two or three days and feed Dominic to the press then, saying he's been recuperating at a health farm.'

'How do you know Stenoza will take you on? How do you know he won't just send his thugs along to do the job for him?'

Malcolm had a point only Dominic could answer. 'As Harry said, it's personal. He expects me to have a go and he'll attend to it himself; that way he gains credibility for his leadership.'

'And you present yourself as a sitting target,' said Tilly, as she and Claire rejoined the conversation completely unaware that they had been observed.

'Would you prefer us to let Stenoza have another go at him here? Would you prefer we invite a bomber into the club to kill God knows how many people to get to him? Is that what you want, Tilly? Do you want that on your conscience?'

Part of Dominic wanted to take her side – tell her about Malcolm's spy camera, retain the truthfulness between them – but the larger part wanted to exact revenge on that evil man who had caused so much appalling misery.

'We'll be all right,' he said reassuringly. 'Harry and I could take on four Stenozas without breaking sweat.'

'Wait a minute!' Tilly's eyes flashed with anger. 'Do you two think this is some macho exercise? Do you think you're going to walk into Stenoza's stronghold, kill him, then walk back out again?! You said yourself, Harry, the man has a psychopath army and an arsenal the size of

Harrods. You'll both be killed before you get within a hundred yards of him.'

'I don't intend to fight; I intend to buy my way in and out,' said Harry, trying unconvincingly to rechannel the conversation. 'There's nothing as mighty as the American dollar when it comes to buying loyalty.'

Tilly's anger intensified. 'Then hire a Romanian to kill him!'

Dominic started to put his arm around Tilly's shoulder. 'Don't patronise me,' she hissed. 'All I hear about is how many agents Harry has in the field and how much of Malcolm's money is needed to shore up this operation. What's so important about having to put *your* head on the block, Dominic? Just spend some more money, hire a few more thugs and get the job done.'

'Because they can't be trusted.' It was as if Malcolm was issuing an order. His voice was clipped and loud, emphasising the word 'trusted'.

A brief lull in Tilly's anger allowed Dominic room to manoeuvre. This time she didn't resist. 'This is stupid and a waste of time. Tilly and I are going home. Call us around eight.'

'We've got to sort this out,' said Tilly, breaking his grip and looking to Claire for support.

'There must be a better way,' tried Claire, her voice unsure, out of place.

'There's nothing to sort out,' snapped Malcolm. 'We either do it my way or we wait for the next attempt on Dominic's life.'

Tilly looked at them all in turn; her expression accusing them of stubbornness, chauvinism, recklessness, weakness. 'Men!' she snapped, and walked from the room with the panache of Bette Davis in full flight.

They rode in silence back to Chester Square. It was the first time Tilly had acted in such a way and Dominic was none too sure how to deal with her. She remained silent once they'd reached the flat, going straight to the bedroom and shutting the door. Dominic brewed some coffee and sat waiting in the kitchen. Finally Tilly emerged ten minutes later: the two-piece business suit had been changed in favour of jeans and a Led Zeppelin T-shirt and her hair was swept back into a ponytail.

'We have to talk.' Dominic said. He poured her a coffee. The distraught look on her face filled him with anguish. This was not a woman having a scornful dig at men flexing their muscles; this was a woman whose intuition warned her of impending disaster. Somehow he had to break through her shield of worry and convince her that he would be not only successful but safe.

'We have no option but to go for him,' he said gently. 'If we do nothing he'll keep on trying until he gets me.'

She accepted the coffee, a tiny, nervous smile escaping the corner of her mouth. 'Why can't you pay someone to do it? Harry's people? The Mafia? There must be hundreds of people capable of murdering for money. Why do *you* have to go?' Her eyes pleaded with him; she was on the edge of breaking down. 'Get sick tonight like Harry suggested, then we'll go off to the country until Stenoza's dealt with. I have a friend in Berkshire we could stay with. No one would know.'

What she said made sense, Dominic knew, but it was her sense, not his. 'If I said I had to deal with this myself in order to find my own peace would you understand?'

'I understand you're willing to risk everything to exact revenge on this man and, to me, that makes no sense at all. You said a few months ago it didn't matter who exposed Ceausescu as long as he fell. Well, that's happened. Why can't you adopt the same attitude towards Stenoza?'

'Because Stenoza pulled the trigger that killed my parents. I must see him dead with my own eyes.' He felt awkward, embarrassed by his inept explanation. 'It's a matter of honour,' he said.

'What about the matter of love?' All trace of anger was gone from her voice, leaving only concern. 'What about you and me? What of our life together? Doesn't that have priority?'

266

'I love you, Tilly. I want to spend my life with you, but I must go back to Romania. I must close this chapter before I can go on with the rest of my life.'

Her expression hardened. She looked suddenly aloof, independent, as she had when they'd first met. 'If you go I shan't be here if you return.'

The second 'if' betrayed her anxiety. 'Tilly. I'll make it back in one piece. I promise.' Dominic smiled at her in desperation.

She put her coffee cup down, slipped off the stool and walked slowly towards the door. She stopped after opening it. 'Goodbye, Dominic,' she said without turning round.

Let's stay talking, don't go, I love you, you win, please turn around, don't be silly, this changes nothing, I need you – all these thoughts flashed through Dominic's mind, yet he remained silent. She walked through the door, closing it quietly behind her.

For ten minutes Dominic stared blankly at the kitchen wall. Nothing made sense to him without Tilly. The Romanian nightmare and the English dream would pale to grey without the woman he loved. The ringing of the telephone interrupted his grief. It was Tilly, he was sure. He would capitulate to her wishes. He *would* pay to have Stenoza killed. A picture of his dead body would be enough. He would organise and observe Stenoza's downfall from the safety of Berkshire just as he had done with Ceausescu from Hampstead. He picked up the phone.

Harry's voice greeted him. 'I've got it sorted,' he said. 'We fly out at two tomorrow morning.' Dominic tried to answer but couldn't. 'Dominic. What's the matter?'

'Tilly's left me,' he blurted out.

'She'll be back,' replied Harry with all the confidence of someone not directly involved. 'Women are like that. They can't stand anything they can't control.' Again Dominic was unable to speak. 'I'll be there in five minutes,' said Harry.

Harry spent twenty minutes telling Dominic all the right things. How Tilly and he were made for each other, how she was being typically female and would change her mind once he was back safe and sound. How it was better for her to be out of the picture until this was over because Stenoza couldn't take a hostage he couldn't find, and how she would have been in constant danger if she'd tried to help, now that Hampstead was no longer safe for anyone, especially well-meaning amateurs. Dominic listened to all he said with the cynicism of the emotionally hurt. 'You've got to get this off your mind,' concluded Harry. 'I need you sharp and on the case, not lovesick and suicidal.'

He was right, of course. Dominic would need all his faculties if he was to survive the next few days. Despite his contacts and military power Harry would be a liability once they were on Romanian soil. His life would be in Dominic's hands. Dominic's duty was clear – and he had to concentrate his mind to the same clarity.

Thirty-two

Dominic arrived at the club shortly before ten o'clock. He'd spent the last two hours trying unsuccessfully to contact Tilly. He'd phoned friends, family, even her ex-boyfriend. Nothing.

Harry had been right about her staying out of the game and therefore out of Stenoza's reach. Dominic felt relieved that she was safe, as well as sad. He also had serious doubts about his own capabilities in a firefight. He'd had no real training in matters of war. The martial arts lessons with Coach Damchuk would help focus him and give a slight edge in close quarters, his fitness ensured endurance, but there was no guarantee he'd have the natural cunning and callousness required. Dominic had spent most of his life avoiding trouble. His championship win had afforded him celebrity status: a smile and a few well-chosen words could calm the most volatile situation. His time in England had also been relatively peaceful. Since the first *Wogan* show people had wanted to help, give congratulations, be friends. This game would be no sporting contest in a Bucharest gymnasium; this was war in the country villages around Brasov. For the first time he would see Romania as a truly hostile place; foreboding and frightening: the killing fields of home.

'All set,' said Harry, storming through the door and

throwing a typewritten page in front of him. 'This is the story I'm putting in tomorrow's *Sun*.'

> Dominic Dance, the Romanian defector who has captured the hearts of the nation with his exceptional talent for freeform modern dancing, collapsed on stage last night at his newly opened club, the Dance Emporium. He was rushed to a private hospital where doctors describe his condition as stable. He is believed to have suffered a mild heart attack while performing the first of his three nightly appearances at the club. A spokeswoman for the dancer said there was a long history of heart disease in his family and although this attack was by no means serious it did mean he might have to cut down on his hectic schedule or face the possibility of open-heart surgery in the near future. His commitments at the club have been suspended until further notice. Mr Malcolm Barrett, Dominic's partner and close friend, said last night that the attack had taken them all by surprise but he was sure Dominic would make a complete recovery.

'It's a *Sun* exclusive. My editor will be chuffed as a chipmunk.' Harry extricated a cold beer from the fridge, opened the ring-pull and took a lengthy swig. 'Better get this down me double quick. I doubt if there's any beer in Brasov, let alone chilled to the right temperature.' He studied Dominic for a moment, looking behind the dancer's eyes, then finished the can. 'If you're going to mope over Tilly you'll get us both killed,' he said, lobbing the empty can into the waste basket. 'Let's get focused on what we're here to do.'

'I've had an awful thought that Tilly's been kidnapped,' said Dominic, feeling foolish for voicing such an unlikely scenario. 'What if they took her from outside the flat?'

'What if Arsenal played attractive football?' Harry put his tree-trunk arm around Dominic. 'If they had her we'd have heard by now. Relax, Dominic. Forget Tilly until this is over.'

Dominic's smile was unconvincing. 'What time do we kick off?'

'Ten minutes,' Harry said, reaching for beer number two.

Dominic walked on stage to thunderous applause from the packed house. No matter how many times this happened it never ceased to fill him with excitement and joy. These people paid money to watch what he'd gladly do for free and their generous praise inspired him in the dance. He felt guilty about cheating them. He danced to 'Street Tuff' by Rebel MC/Double Trouble.

Halfway through the routine he danced towards the back of the stage, slumped to his knees and flopped on to his right side.

The audience's reaction was immediate. 'He's hurt! Call an ambulance! Oh, my God! Dominic, get up!'

Before the nearest worried fan could get within ten feet of him Tor and son of Tor had picked Dominic off the stage like a limp doll and bundled him out of the building into the waiting ambulance.

'All right, Sunbeam. You can open your eyes now,' said one of the ambulancemen. 'No one can see you in here.'

It was the same man who had attended the Durrants Hotel. Dominic smiled at him and sat up on the stretcher. The ambulance stopped on the corner of Exeter Street and the Strand, where Harry jumped in through the passenger door.

'Nice one, lads, Northolt Airport, if you please. No sirens.' He poked his head into the rear compartment. 'Dominic, this is Corporal Davis who you met at the hotel and up front we have Sergeant Copeland.'

Dominic shook Davis's hand and shouted his greetings to the driver. 'What's happening at Northolt?'

'What usually happens at airports? We catch a plane,' said Harry sarcastically, throwing Dominic a brown paper bundle. 'Try those on for size.'

Inside the parcel was a selection of Romanian peasant clothes. A white *camasa* shirt, dark grey *gaci* trousers and a pair of multicoloured *cizme* boots that reminded him of

271

the carefree schooldays when he wore such clothing to perform traditional dances for his teachers, friends and family.

'It's all the rage in Brasov,' said Harry. 'You were easy. I had the devil's own job finding something to fit.'

The thought of Harry attempting traditional dancing lightened Dominic's spirit and he forced a hesitant smile. 'Shall I teach you a few moves in case someone asks you to dance?' he asked.

'Me? Dance!? I'll shoot the bollocks off the first person to suggest it.' Harry took off his jacket and hung it neatly on the peg behind the passenger seat before trying to struggle into his army gear. 'They might have a bigger one at the airport,' he said, discarding the jacket on to the floor. 'I'd just as soon wear army gear than this costume clobber.' He turned his attention to the corporal. 'You got my briefcase?'

Corporal Davis reached behind the side panelling and produced a thin, black leather briefcase with brass combination locks. It looked brand new. He handed it to Harry, who stepped through into the back area and sat next to Dominic on the stretcher.

'Money, money, money, must be funny in a rich man's world.' The tune of the Abba song was barely recognisable. He flipped the locks open and lifted the lid. Inside the case, stacked in neat rows, were bundles of $100 bills. 'Could buy the country with this lot,' he said, slamming it shut again before Dominic could get a good look. 'A hundred thousand dollars, Dominic. And I intend to bring a good deal of it back home with us.'

'Why so much?'

Harry smiled and tweaked his moustache. 'Because I don't want some dickhead offering us freedom for ten bucks when I'm holding nine.'

The ambulance turned off the A40 and into the airforce base at Northolt just before half-past eleven. The guards waved them through after the briefest look at the licence plate. They drove around the grey wooden huts with mani-cured gardens and painted white pathways on to the stealthy blackness of the runway. The headlights illuminated a line of military aircraft that stood neatly spaced along the edge of the Tarmac. They dated from the Spit-fires of World War II to the sleek lines of a visiting F1-11 liveried with the emblems of the United States Airforce. At the far end of the runway the shape of a small civilian jet could be seen, its window lights glowing in a straight line like a row of distant houses.

'Our carriage awaits,' said Harry, gathering together the briefcase and his ill-fitting Romanian clothes. 'Thanks for the lift,' he said to the soldiers, with a quick salute in their direction.

'A pleasure, sir.' Copeland returned his salute. 'And good luck to you, Mr Dance. I hope you're successful.'

'Thank you,' replied Dominic, stepping past Davis into the cold, dry night.

It took ten strides to reach the small door behind the wing of the jet. The whine of the engine increased as they climbed into the interior. Between the hatch and the cockpit four wide, brown leather seats faced each other as if it was a living-room, but without the coffee table. Aft of the hatch various-sized cardboard boxes stood stacked against the fuselage, some unlabelled, one with the trade-mark of Sony emblazoned on its side; the two closest were stencilled with the letters OHMS.

Harry pointed to one of the chairs. 'Have a seat and strap in. I'll just be a minute.' He disappeared through the cockpit door. As the jet was gathering speed, he returned, sat down, and fastened his seatbelt under his girth. 'Game on,' he said with all the excitement of a Boy Scout on his first camping trip. 'Give them ten minutes to clear London airspace then we'll have a proper briefing.'

Dominic sat back into the comfortable seat, closed his eyes and enjoyed the sensation of rapid acceleration as the plane became airborne and banked sharply to the right. From the small round porthole he saw the lights of London twinkling below him like earthbound stars. Suddenly they were in thick cloud; the lights vanished instantly to be replaced moments later by heavenly stars as they emerged from the clouds into a clear, black sky.

The cockpit door snapped opened and into the cabin stepped the most perfect caricature of an airforce pilot: six foot tall, steel-blue eyes, grey hair, sharp features and a handlebar moustache. His uniform was spotless, his trouser creases sharp enough to cut and he wore his polished peak cap at a jaunty angle.

'Fabulous night for a sortie, what say?' His voice was clipped and upper-class, giving the impression of total confidence. 'Have you chaps on the ground in two hours. One slight problem, Commander.' He addressed his remark to Harry. 'Your chappies haven't managed to put Timisoara radar out of action, so I'm afraid we'll have to go in underneath it. Could get a bit bumpy.'

'Bumpy I can deal with. Crashing bothers me,' answered Commander Cassini.

'Wouldn't dare, old chap. The crate's not paid for yet.' The pilot directed his gaze towards Dominic. 'You must be Mr Bellescu. I'm James Holbrook. Pleased to meet you.' He offered his hand, which was gladly accepted. 'Pay no mind to the Commander, I've yet to lose one of these beauties. We'll get you down in one piece.'

'I have every confidence you will,' replied Dominic, retrieving his hand. 'Where, exactly, are we going?'

James Holbrook's jollity suddenly disappeared. 'A small strip between Zarnesti and Brasov. We had a reported sighting of Stenoza about an hour ago in the railway station at Risnov. We can get you to within six miles.' His smile returned. 'Any closer, I'm afraid, and we might land in his lap; and with his firepower that could prove jolly uncomfortable.' He turned once again toward Harry. 'May I take you through the equipment? I don't want to linger on the ground so I'd appreciate you both being armed and briefed before we enter Romanian airspace.' Harry nodded approval.

Showing the manners of his cultured upbringing, Captain Holbrook excused himself as he passed in front of Dominic and pulled one of the OHMS crates from the pile at the rear of the plane. Producing a Swiss Army knife from his jacket pocket he sliced through the gaffer tape and prised open the thick cardboard top. Plastic shavings spilled on to the carpeted floor as he pulled out some sort of rifle wrapped in oilcloth. He carefully unwrapped the weapon and placed it on the floor.

'Gentlemen, what we have here is a Kalashnikov AK47 automatic rifle redesigned by our chaps to a Bullpup configuration. It's twenty-six inches long with a seventeen-inch barrel. Notice the pistol grip, trigger and trigger guard have been moved forward in front of the magazine to give better balance, and we've added a foregrip below the gas port block on the barrel. Our tests proved accuracy better than the full-size AK, with five shot groups staying in about three inches at one hundred yards. The weapon comes with ten fifty-round magazines. Any questions?'

Dominic picked up the rifle. It was considerably lighter than he expected. 'Does it have much of a kick?'

'Hardly any. We've improved the recoil factor by 30 per cent.' The Captain reached into the shavings again and produced two more oilcloth bundles. 'You'll like this, Commander,' he said, unwrapping the weapons with great care. 'The new Beretta 92F 9mm pistol with delayed blow-back double action. Comes with silencer and bioptic night-sight.'

Harry took the pistol and cradled it in his hands like a precious piece of jewellery. He looked at it from several angles, his hands sliding along the barrel and down the handle as if he were caressing a woman. 'Bloody marvellous. Best shooter going,' he said, his voice direct, his judgement absolute.

James Holbrook opened the other OHMS crate, which was divided into sections as if for bottles of beer or wine. He pulled out what looked like a large green oilcan and placed it on the floor between them.

'Smashing tool, this one,' he said with pride. 'The new Alpha mini-mortar. A hundred-yard range, high-velocity impact, easy operation. Set trajectory – so' he tilted the can slightly on its base. 'Press button A – ' he pointed to the red circle near the top. 'And bingo! A six-foot crater. Downside is there's only one bomb per can, they're not reloadable, so use them sparingly. You have six in total. The rest of the weapons are duplicated: one each.'

The armoury on display was impressive, more than enough to eliminate a renegade madman. 'What else are we carrying?' asked Dominic.

'Some clobber to fit Harry, a couple of flak jackets, two medikits, four Marconi two-way communicators, back-packs for the ammunition and – ' he tapped the box marked Sony – 'a new Betacamera for ground crew.' Again he excused himself as he passed in front of Harry. 'I must check the autopilot isn't on a lunch break. Have a rummage around: if there's anything you don't understand give me a shout. And when you've finished be good chaps and lash it down firmly. Don't want cameras flying around the cabin during the bumpy bit.'

Dominic spent the next hour familiarising himself with the new and frightening weaponry at his command. Like most young men he'd had a passing interest in firearms, but guns like the customised Kalashnikov were far beyond his comprehension. He loaded and unloaded it several times, improving speed and getting the feel of this awe-some tool. The killing power of the gun seemed to transfer to his body as he ran his hands over the matt, metal barrel. The smell of the oilcloth that had wrapped the rifle lingered on the weapon, Dominic's hand became moist as it slid down the front handle grip. He held it firmly against his body and flicked the bolt open with his right hand. The clack and slide of machined metal opened the breech and ejected the magazine. He could see straight through the rectangle to the empty magazine lying on its side on the cabin floor. He put his fingers inside the breech and felt the oily wetness of the mechanism, its support flanges and springs precisely tucked away in readiness to receive the next clip of ammunition. Dominic picked up the magazine, jammed it into the bottom of the breech and slammed the bolt shut.

A chuckle emanated from Harry. 'Not bad,' he said, reaching over and placing a glancing slap on Dominic's shoulder. 'One thing, though: safety off after reload. *Always* check your safety is off. This gun is notorious for the safety re-engaging during loading.' The sequence goes: bolt open, check reject, load clip, close bolt, check safety. Do it again.'

His counsel gave confidence to the young Romanian. He repeated the exercise as he'd been tutored, which produced a rare, contented smile from Harry that gave Dominic a sense of achievement.

'And don't stick your fingers in the breech once you've fired it,' said Harry, laughing aloud and nodding. 'It gets a touch hot in there once it's been used.'

Dominic carefully loaded ten magazines following Harry's instructions, making sure, as Harry so delicately put it, that the bullets were all pointing the same way. He placed three mortar shells and the loaded magazines into his backpack before turning to the 9mm pistol. He attached and detached the silencer several times before Harry told him to leave it on as that was the whole point of having it. He showed Dominic the loading procedure, the two-handed firing position, and gave macabre advice regarding placement and grouping: 'Two at the body, one at the head in quick succession.' Dominic felt a chill run through him as he sat pointing the empty gun at the cockpit door and visualising a man standing there. Two shots to the body – he moved the pistol upwards – one to the head. He felt sad, alone, unsure of his ability to kill.

Harry had now dressed in clothes that fitted him properly, painted his face with camouflage make-up and was sitting on the right-hand seat fondling his Beretta when Holbrook appeared from the cockpit. He smiled and nodded his approval at their readiness.

'Lights out, chaps. We're going down,' he said, stepping back up front and slamming the door behind him.

Harry and Dominic strapped themselves firmly into the seats and glanced over at one another. 'Good luck,' said Harry as the cabin went black.

The jet rolled violently to the right and spiralled downwards, picking up speed by the second. Dominic felt his stomach turn over as he fought the nausea. The pressure twisted Harry's face into a grimace; Dominic rolled his head from side to side in an attempt to ease the pressure on his ears. Suddenly the plane levelled out, then pitched and rolled and dropped and lifted as Captain James Holbrook employed every ounce of his skill to fly the jet-propelled coffin at a constant height of fifty feet and a speed in excess of 500 miles an hour.

The ride lasted twenty minutes. It was the longest twenty minutes of Dominic's life. Then, as quickly as it had started, the sound of rubber on Tarmac signalled the end of the rollercoaster from hell. The engines thundered into reverse and the wheel brakes locked as the jet struggled to stop within its allotted space. When it finally came to rest, Dominic made a solemn vow never to fly with anyone named Holbrook again.

Harry was the first to unstrap himself. Dominic remained seated, staying as still as possible, still struggling against nausea to regain his equilibrium. Even Holbrook looked peaked and drawn as he came back to join them. 'Not a time for R&R, gentlemen. I want to be out of here in five minutes.'

He passed in front of Harry, this time without excusing himself, opened the hatch and pushed out the steps that were attached to the door. He turned to face Harry. 'Is the girl ready to be moved?'

'I doubt it,' replied Harry. 'Uri can update you.'

'Did somebody call?' A bright, fresh face peered into the aircraft.

Harry stood up slowly and although still rocky on his feet, clasped the young man's hand and pulled him into the plane. 'We certainly did. Come in. Let me introduce you to Dominic Bellescu and Captain Holbrook.'

Uri shook hands with the Captain and smiled at him briefly before turning his attention to Dominic. 'I'm so glad to meet you. Your defection and success in the West has been an inspiration to us all, and your reading of the Ceausescu flight was absolutely correct.'

'And your courage behind the camera deserves a medal,' said Dominic, returning his compliment. 'Are you Bishop's Pawn?'

'I am.' They embraced spontaneously. 'We beat the bastard, didn't we? Together we beat him.'

'When you two have finished cuddling, can we get unloaded?' Harry ordered from the doorway where he stood, rifle slung over one shoulder, the black briefcase clasped firmly in his right hand.

Uri looked at Harry's blackened face and laughed out loud. 'The camouflage is a bit premature, Commander. We won't get a sniff of Stenoza until tomorrow. Tonight, what's left of it, we'll spend at my girlfriend's place down the road.'

They bundled the equipment into Uri's battered blue Land Cruiser and drove from the airstrip at considerable speed to distance themselves from the noise and lights which could easily attract unwanted visitors. The Land Cruiser's one working headlight reflected brightly off the blanket of freshly fallen snow and illuminated the road ahead.

After about two miles Uri turned on to a dirt track that led to a single house in the corner of four snow-covered fields. As they approached the green wooden building Uri honked the horn. Immediately a light was switched on inside the house. As they drew closer the patchwork, pine-slated roof became clearly visible, then the painted white trim around the windows and the large front door made from wooden planks fastened together by a metal 'Z' bar. Harry jumped from the car and walked straight towards the door.

279

Dominic stood and watched the light from a full moon reflected in the dormant landscape. It was barren, bleak, deathly silent in its winter covering, yet he felt his spirits rise as he stood on home soil. He recalled how beautiful it looked in the summertime when fields of wheat waved in the warm breezes and the violets and wild poppies edged the roads and pathways.

'Come on, Dominic,' shouted Harry from the doorway.

Uri placed his hand on Dominic's shoulder. 'Welcome home,' he said in almost a whisper, not wanting to spoil the moment. 'You'll see it better in the morning.'

The house was spartan inside, plain and uncluttered. A large wooden table dominated the main living area. To its left an old four-ring gas cooker stood rusting against the wall; to the right was a carved dresser with brass handles and brightly painted dishes. This was the family's one status symbol and Dominic immediately commented on its beauty as Uri walked up beside him.

'Thank you,' he said, acknowledging the compliment. 'This is my girlfriend, Shanah.'

Dominic stepped towards Shanah, who sat demurely at the table, her colourfully embroidered, full-length peasant skirt and white linen blouse immaculately cleaned and pressed. Her large, brown, Labrador eyes watched his every move. 'It is an honour to be in your lovely home and to receive such a warm welcome,' Dominic said in Romanian.

'It is your home,' she replied in accented English.

Uri and Harry laughed, Shanah joining in moments later. The ice was broken, the formalities observed.

Even though they all spoke English, Harry remained uncharacteristically quiet as Shanah served them with hot chocolate and unleavened bread. Uri told of Nadia and how he hoped to have her moved to Bucharest in time for the return journey. The new government would be more than pleased if Stenoza could be eliminated, he said, and although they couldn't sanction the raid, proof of his death would guarantee first-class tickets back to London.

Shanah talked of her three brothers who'd died during the revolution. Even though she missed them terribly, she believed their sacrifice had been worthwhile. Harry was moved by her story and took two bundles of money from the briefcase and placed them on the table.

'This won't bring back your brothers,' he said, his voice breaking slightly. 'But it will plant next year's crops and buy some livestock.'

Shanah fell silent with surprise. She handled the dollars disbelievingly, as if they were a mirage. Her eyes filled with tears. She clasped Harry's hands and placed her head on top of them.

'I suppose a beer's out of the question?' asked Harry, embarrassed by his feelings.

Uri left the room, returning moments later with four cold bottles of what passed for beer in this part of the country. Romanian beer comes in litre bottles, tastes more like syrupy wine than ale, and is about three times stronger than the British brew. Six bottles later they all fell soundly asleep around the wood-burning potbelly stove.

Thirty-three

Dominic was first to wake. Beside him Harry was curled up in a grey blanket, his head on the black briefcase, his size ten boots resting on the cold fire-grate. Shanah and Uri lay arm in arm to the right of the stove. Dominic slipped out of his blanket and walked quietly outside.

The sky was grey and held the promise of more snow. Last night's blanket had covered all traces of their drive from the main road. Everything looked so peaceful. In the distance a two-horse cart carried winter feed along the ridge to cattle in an upper field. The faint sound of church bells rang up from the valley and the barks of an unseen dog echoed in the crisp air. Dominic thought how much Tilly would love this tranquil, postcard scene, how she would hold him around the waist from behind and perch her chin gently on his shoulder. It was hard to believe that she'd left because of a moral issue she didn't fully understand. It was also hard for Dominic to believe that he'd come here to deliberately take a human life. Maybe Tilly had been right; maybe this was all very wrong.

'Good morning, Dominic.' Shanah's voice lilted across the yard like birdsong: like Tilly. 'Breakfast in ten minutes,' she said, closing the front door and leaving Dominic to his solitude.

Breakfast was hot chocolate made with water, an apple and a slice of butterless bread. Dominic thought of all the food wasted in London: a sin, really. At least Harry's generosity meant that this household would survive the next year; if nothing else that was a positive and worthwhile result to this otherwise nefarious journey.

After breakfast it was time to prepare. A sharpness infiltrated the atmosphere as flak jackets and clips of ammunition replaced food in the minds of the men. Dominic tied his boots tightly to keep out the snow. Uri gave them sheepskin coats which were very warm and served to hide the Bullpup rifles. Harry checked and loaded the 9mm pistol and tucked it into his belt. Dominic packed half the remaining money, three mortars, ten ammunition clips, the two medikits and two bottles of water into his backpack.

They left the house at two o'clock. Shanah waved them goodbye and watched after them until they were out of sight.

'We'll go to Zarnesti first,' said Uri. 'I have a friend there who's keeping tabs on Stenoza.'

They stopped at the edge of the village. Uri turned off the engine and watched down the main street while Harry and Dominic sat silently in the back. A dozen small wooden houses lined the dirt street, six on each side. Another two dozen or so wooden buildings were scattered up the gently sloping sides of the snow-covered valley and an ice-bound stream wound down the far hillside and formed a small, frozen lake just to the right of where they had stopped. At the far end of the village a twin-steepled church stood imposingly against the grey, wintry sky.

'It's too quiet,' said Uri nervously. 'And my friend should be here to meet us.'

'Get us out of here!' shouted Harry, his mind suddenly alert to danger.

Uri grinded the Cruiser into reverse, backed about a hundred feet up the road then swung left behind a three-walled, roofless shack that was being used to store firewood. 'You two wait here,' he said. 'I'll drive through and see what's up.'

Harry and Dominic crouched down behind a pile of neatly cut logs and watched Uri drive slowly through the village. They lost sight of him momentarily as he drove round the church. The sharp crackle of small-arms fire chased him back. All four tyres on the Cruiser were spinning as he tried to gather speed on the slippery, snow-covered ground. There was the heavy thud of artillery, and a shell exploded just behind the car. Uri fought for control as the blast turned the vehicle sideways on to two wheels. He managed to right the machine but the engine had stopped and was smoking badly. He was a sitting target. He grabbed the Betacam from the passenger seat, jumped from the car and started running along the road, keeping the burning four-wheel-drive between himself and the church. More crackle of gunfire. The dirt flew up each side of Uri as he ducked round the corner of the nearest house.

'I guess we found them.' Uri's voice snapped from Harry's communicator. 'My gun's in the Cruiser. I'm unarmed.'

Harry pushed his transmission switch. 'What made you take the Betacam?'

'It was new.'

'I don't believe Romanians,' Harry sneered at Dominic, his teeth clenched, annoyance flashing in his eyes. 'You can't *stop* anyone with a fucking camera!' he shouted into the communicator. 'Get behind the buildings and see if you can find some transport. Dominic and I will sort this lot.'

As he spoke they heard the thud of more artillery. A shell burst harmlessly into a mound of earth wide of Uri's position. 'We need better cover,' said Harry, tugging at Dominic's arm. 'The first house!'

Panic is a blind driver and how Dominic made it from the woodpile to the first house in the village would forever remain a mystery to him. He started two yards behind Harry and arrived ten yards ahead of him. He dropped his backpack, lay down behind it and rested the barrel of

284

the Kalashnikov on the top, pointing in the general direction of the burning jeep.

'See anything?' Harry flattened his bulk as best he could against the house wall.

'No.'

Harry shimmied along the wall and peered round the corner. 'There'll be at least two sets of them. We've got to find out which houses they're in.' He whipped his head back as he saw the flash from the fourth house along. The bullet smashed into the wall next to him, splintering the wood.

'Let's get the fuck out of here before the artillery has a go.'

They ran to the back of the building and jumped the fence to the house next door, once again hearing the thump of the big gun. The ground shook as the shell destroyed the area where they had just been.

'We've got to get that bastard,' said Harry, tugging at Dominic's arm again. 'Come on, son, follow me.'

They ran along the back of another two houses until they came to an open space. It was unlikely that they could cross it without being seen. An engine started to the left, then a squeaking, clanking, metal sound.

'That's a tank,' whispered Harry. 'Them bastards 'ave got a bloody tank.' He took one of the mini-mortars from his pack and placed it flat on the ground pointing through the gap in the houses towards the main street. 'Let's see if this thing works horizontally. Give me a hand to move this.'

They moved a large rock into position at the base of the tube. Harry found a small broken tree branch near the house and propped it under the front of the mortar to compensate for the rocket's base plate and to give the weapon a slight trajectory. First the tank's gun cleared the edge of the building, then the body of the machine. It stopped in the gap and the gun turret started to swing toward them.

'Work, you bastard,' cursed Harry as he pushed the red

button. There was an instant fizz like a firework rocket leaving a milk bottle; then a resounding thud as the shell exploded against the tank. The force of the explosion knocked both men off their feet.

As Dominic regained his footing, his ears ringing from the pressure, the smell of cordite invading his nostrils, he could see the track had been ripped off but the turret was still swivelling round towards them. Liquid from the belly of the tank arced into the air like a fountain; the shell had ruptured a fuel line.

Harry squeezed off a burst from the AK47. The shells slammed into the steel tank wheels, doing no damage at all. Dominic knew what Harry was trying to do. He fired a burst – not straight at the tank but in an arc across the whole fuselage. His second burst did the trick. A spark flew off the metal body and ignited the fuel. Within a second the tank was engulfed in flames.

'Nice one, son!' said Harry, pulling his pistol from his belt. The tank hatch opened and a man pushed himself through to waist height. Harry fired two silent rounds at the body. Immediately it slumped down, blocking any other escape attempts. A hissing sound from within the tank was followed by a second of silence and then the machine exploded, the gun turret lifting off the main body. The tank lay broken at a grisly angle, smoke and steam seeping from it.

Harry picked up his pack and started running across the open space toward the third house. 'I'm too fuckin' old for this shit,' he cursed.

Dominic hurried along behind him and flopped down next to him at the rear of the house. He no longer felt fear; nor regret for the men he'd just killed. He felt totally alive, alert, aware of everything. Harry was about to speak when Dominic heard voices from inside the house. He placed his hand over Harry's mouth and pointed to the wall. Harry sat on the ground in silence, his eyes scanning the hills behind the village, his AK47 perched and ready across his legs. Dominic strained to make out what the voices were saying. They spoke in Russian. He heard 'English' and 'General'; that was all.

'I think there's two of them in there,' whispered Dominic.

'Let's see if we can get one of them alive,' Harry whispered back. 'You cover me from the window. I'll go in the door.'

Harry crawled along the back of the house and stood up in front of the door. Dominic repositioned his front grip to horizontal on the AK47 so he could lay it flat on the windowsill. All the glass had been blown out by the explosion leaving a broad base from which to fire. Slowly he lifted his head into the window-frame. Two men in black uniforms stood either side of the empty window looking at the carnage before them. Their backs were turned. Dominic could see that both carried a rifle and wore flak jackets loaded with grenades, ammunition clips, knives and small arms. These were Stenoza's elite.

Dominic slid down under the window and looked over at Harry. Drawing an imaginary square in the air, Dominic placed an index finger at each side to indicate number and position. Harry nodded and pointed to himself and then to the left; then to Dominic and right. He positioned himself directly in front of the door. He didn't look fat any more, he looked big. As he started to lift his leg Dominic stood up in the window.

As Harry's boot hit the door Dominic fired a single round into the leg of the man on the right. Before the other man could fully turn a burst from Harry's Bullpup sent him backwards through the window. In six determined strides Harry crossed the room and stood over the slumped man, the barrel of his Kalashnikov planted firmly in the centre of the young mercenary's head. Harry flicked off his backpack, placed it between them and systematically relieved the man of two handguns, three grenades, seven clips of ammunition and a ten-inch knife. He closed and replaced his backpack and took three steps back.

'If he moves, kill him!' he shouted at Dominic before

moving towards the one internal door. As he stepped through, a single pistol shot preceded a burst from Harry's gun.

'Are you OK?' shouted Dominic.

'Bloody marvellous!' came the reply. 'There's one just out the window, Dominic! Coming to you!'

Dominic stood in open space; extremely bad news. A moving shadow reflected on the wall of the house next door. He had seconds only. He ran towards a pile of freshly cut timber about ten metres away. It had been neatly stacked in readiness for building a shed and would give good cover from anyone rounding the building. He was two metres away when he felt a hostile presence to the left. Tucking himself into a forward tumble he attempted to roll into cover.

Dominic heard the snap of a rifle and felt a burning in his upper leg. He landed, back first, against the wood, dislodging the neatly piled planks, and nearly causing the whole lot to rain down on top of him. He saw the door move on a wooden outhouse to his left. He lifted the Kalashnikov and emptied the magazine into the lean-to building. The force of the shells ripped the rotting planking to shreds. Splintered wood flew in all directions. As the building disintegrated he saw snippets of the ballet of death being danced inside as the high-velocity bullets tore into the trapped gunman.

He rejected the empty magazine and was reaching into his pack for another clip when a burst of rifle fire came spitting his way from the corner of the building. Most bounced off, or buried itself in the woodpile, but two shells got through: one missed Dominic's right foot by half an inch, the second thumped into the back of his flak jacket having first been considerably slowed down by the life-saving logs. The force of the impact pushed him forward on to his face, knocking the wind out of him but not penetrating the jacket. He breathed deeply in a frantic effort to regain stability, pulled out the pistol and slithered back to the woodpile on his stomach. He felt a severe pain in his back as he clawed his way up the slippery, splintered planks.

Suddenly he could see right through the pile. About eighteen inches from the top the planks had twisted and rolled in such a way as to form a peep-hole. He looked through the tiny gap and saw a soldier in battledress walking towards him, his rifle swinging left and right like a pendulum. Dominic pointed the pistol through the hole and shot three times. He heard a thud as at least one bullet hit home. Lying flat on the ground, his Beretta gripped in both hands above his head, he rolled five times to the right. As he cleared the logs he stopped on his stomach, looked up and lifted the gun. The soldier's head was no more than three metres away. Dominic shot twice as he saw the soldier's rifle arc in the air. The soldier's head and rifle dropped together.

Dominic rolled back behind the logs, heart pounding, mind clear. Again he felt no remorse about taking a life, just a rush of adrenalin that kept his senses alert. The space around him electrified like a grid on a computer game. He could kill: he had killed and it had been so easy; too easy. His leg and back hurt like hell. He looked down and saw blood seeping from a tear in his trousers.

'Dominic! Are you OK? Answer if you can!' Harry stood in the doorway, the leg-wounded soldier in front of him.

'I'm OK. Clear to your left. One dead to your right, I can't see that area, could be more.'

'I'm coming out. Patrol ahead of you.'

As Harry spoke Dominic saw three figures run between the houses. He reloaded the Kalashnikov within three seconds, gripped it firmly against his body and squeezed off a burst of about a dozen shells. The first two men fell instantly. Harry's gun crackled and the third man fell. Another burst from Harry; the first two bodies jumped as the bullets found their target. 'Come to me,' Harry shouted.

Dominic picked up the Beretta, reloaded it, and stuffed

it into his belt. 'On my way!' he shouted, more to convince himself than pass information. He dragged himself the ten metres to the house, his left leg becoming more useless by the second. He flopped down under the window and smiled at Harry. 'What now?' It was then he saw the trickle of blood on Harry's shirt tail. 'You're hurt?'

'Just a lucky shot that got under the flak jacket,' Harry pushed the prisoner to the ground. 'Let me see your leg,' he said to Dominic.

Dominic levelled his rifle at the Securitate man. The man's face revealed little fear. He was a product of the orphanages, recruited at fourteen, trained to kill, and let out on a leash like a Doberman to serve his master.

Harry produced a sterile bandage from his pack and strapped Dominic's leg. The wound looked clean, a fleshy strike that had missed bones and arteries but had chewed up the quadriceps muscle badly enough to stiffen the leg. 'What now?' repeated Dominic, suddenly fatigued, wanting the madness to stop.

Harry grabbed the prisoner's hair and held his pistol to the man's head. 'Where is Stenoza?' he hissed. 'If you don't tell me I'll shoot you, son of a bitch!'

Whatever the man's understanding of English he got Harry's message. Survival triumphed over loyalty. 'Church,' he replied, visibly shrinking before Harry's intimidation. 'He in church.'

'Thank you.'

Dominic didn't hear the muted crack of Harry's pistol, he just saw the blood explode from the man's head and splatter on the house wall. He looked at his friend and mentor and saw a grotesque face, the eyes evil and predatory, the mouth curled in pain. 'Why?' was all Dominic could manage.

'Because I'm gut-shot,' replied Harry, snapping the words out from a taut mouth. 'I could last ten minutes or ten hours.' Harry placed the Beretta on the ground. 'If I pass out and that bugger shot me, you'd lose. This way it's one on one. That's the best I can do for you.'

Dominic pulled the medikit from his pack and took out a sterile dressing. 'Don't waste time with that,' said Harry, snatching it. 'Just leave me. I can see to myself.'

Dominic looked at him lying hurt and helpless on a mixture of snow, blood and dirt, and seriously doubted his sanity. They were here to cut out a malignant cancer, to right a multitude of wrongs, but what he saw were several dead young men, some killed by his own hand, his friend badly hurt and his own leg getting stiffer by the moment as the muscles tightened.

'Will you stop staring and fuck off!' Harry spat out the sentence like an order. 'And don't say goodbye either, my son. Just get that bastard and make it back here in one piece. I'll help Uri with the transport once I've patched myself up.'

The truth of their mission slammed its message home as Dominic looked down at Harry slumped painfully on the ground. This was a personal vendetta. It had very little to do with saving a country and its people, or with the righteousness of the cause. Dominic was committed to ensuring Stenoza's death. He slapped Harry lightly on the chest and moved past him towards the final confrontation.

Dominic limped behind the third house. Here he had a good view of the village church. He looked across the graveyard. In the church portal lay the body of a man in black robes. Stenoza had killed the priest and dumped him outside the church as a deterrent against resistance from the village population. He was a master of terrorism, able to paralyse people with one heinous act and turn their homes into battlefields and their churches into command centres with no regard for property or sanctity.

Dominic studied the belfry for signs of movement. Either Stenoza was short of men or his arrogance was clouding his judgement: the belfry was empty. Dominic pulled the arm-sling from his medikit and wound it tightly around his leg over the bandage Harry had set which was already seeping blood. He had to keep the leg active: he must overcome the pain and use it. Testing the empty belfry theory would be simple – run across the road between the house and the church wall. If anyone was in the tower they couldn't help but see. He stood at the corner of the house, drew in a large breath and moved his leg to test the pain. Not too bad. Time to go.

He ran across the open space as fast as his limp would allow and ducked behind the low stone wall that separated the church from the main street. He kept looking at the belfry expecting to see movement at any second; nothing. He reached his goal undetected.

The wall which gave Dominic cover extended around the church. Stenoza would expect any attack to come from the village. If Dominic could crawl around the church unnoticed he could still use the element of surprise; that had to be worth at least one guard, if not two. When Harry had said 'one to one' they both knew it was unlikely that Stenoza would be alone.

There had been no firing for at least five minutes; if they were going to get curious it would be now. Every second Dominic delayed shortened his chances. He crawled to the southern corner where the wall became higher, then ran in a stooped position until he reached the back gate. It was a solid, black, wooden structure with a stone arch continuum from the wall.

The door of the church opened. Dominic flattened himself behind the arch-pillar and through the crack between wall and gate watched a man wander among the graves. Nonchalantly he took a cigarette from his jacket pocket and lit it with the second match. Dominic rested the Beretta on the top of the gate, aimed at the base of the man's skull and squeezed off a single, muffled shot. The man's arms shot out sideways as the bullet hit him and he crumpled silently to the ground.

With the Kalashnikov over his left shoulder and the pistol in his right hand Dominic pushed open the gate and ran along the snow-covered path to the church building. He stopped beside the lifeless body and watched the blood seep from its head and form a growing red circle in the crisp, white snow. He stooped and commandeered the man's pistol, viewing the dead eyes with hatred. Dominic was taking his revenge: a cold, calculated revenge of which he hadn't thought himself capable. There was no regret in Dominic's mind for this death; he wanted to kill more, to kill them all.

He slipped inside the church door. He was in a small anteroom, a vestry 'All right, Demetri?' he heard from the other side of the interior door. 'Fine!' he shouted back. 'Demetri?' came the confused reply. He had not been convincing.

The door opened slowly. As soon as half the man came into view Dominic fired twice at the body, once at the head. The impact of the bullets threw the mortally wounded soldier back and the door slammed shut behind him.

Dominic ran back outside, along the back wall and round the corner of the church. He heard automatic rifle fire from inside as the remaining guards peppered the vestry. The windows along this side of the building had been blown out and Dominic could see three men standing with their backs to him reloading guns. He squeezed off two bursts then twisted hard away from the window to avoid fire coming from Stenoza who stood in the nave of the church brandishing an Uzi automatic pistol in one hand and a Smith & Wesson .38 pistol in the other.

Dominic ran to the front corner, hoping to make the main doors before they had chance to regroup inside. As he turned the corner he literally collided with a soldier waiting to cut him off. The soldier kneed Dominic in the groin next to his wound. Dominic dropped both guns and for a few seconds was aware only of the agony of his leg. When he regained his senses he was looking down the barrel of his own Beretta.

'Welcome home, Dominic,' said the gunman triumphantly, his smile twisted and evil.

Dominic was pushed through the main church door. He

stumbled on the stone floor and fell next to the carved marble font.

'Dominic Bellescu. At last we meet.' Stenoza sat astride a wooden bench. His sadistic, close-set, porky eyes looked at Dominic with disdain, almost dismissively. 'I always like to clear up loose ends,' he went on, standing up and cocking the hammer of his Smith & Wesson. 'Now the Bellescus are complete.'

At that moment Dominic resigned himself to death. He was unarmed, wounded and trapped; there was no escape. He thought first of Tilly. He could see her face and smell the fragrance of her hair. He thought of the men he'd just killed, his parents whose spirits had guided him perfectly, only to fail at the last hurdle. Their closeness took away his fear. Dominic looked away and closed his eyes, waiting for the final impact. He heard the crack of a pistol, then another in quick succession.

Dominic snapped his eyes open just as Stenoza dropped to his knees, a large red hole spurting blood from his forehead. The man who'd captured Dominic was also falling, his head almost severed by a bullet that had removed half his neck.

'I just can't leave you alone for a minute, can I?' Harry stood outside the church, his head, shoulders and Kalashnikov filling most of the front window. 'Can we go now? I've got us some transport and my gut's killing me.'

Dominic looked at the lifeless body lying twisted in front of him. All the hatred that had built up for most of his life transferred itself to that bleeding corpse. He felt reborn, liberated, fulfilled. Sweet justice had been served here; retribution for the thousands that had suffered by this man's hand.

Slowly Dominic pushed himself to his feet, testing his leg to make sure it would support him. He limped to the door and stepped outside the battered church into the cold, life-giving winter's afternoon. He had triumphed: he had survived.

Thirty-four

Uri managed to stop most of Harry's bleeding with three dressings from the medikit and a sheet he'd stolen from a village clothes line. The pot-holed roads and the near suspensionless truck Uri had commandeered caused a few anxious moments, especially on the road from Zarnesti to Risnov. Uri had also restrapped Dominic's leg and administered a syringe full of what he called 'Wallop'. He said it would deaden the pain, which it did admirably, especially the sharp, knife-like pain between Dominic's shoulders. The drug also induced a feeling of light-headedness and well-being, so that Dominic found his main worry of getting Harry to hospital turning itself into a song to the tune of 'Here We Go Round The Mulberry Bush':

> Gotta get Harry to hospital,
> hospital, hospital.
> Gotta get Harry to hospital,
> so early in the morning.

Dominic started singing aloud in time with the rhythm of the truck as it rattled along the deserted country roads. Harry's dose of Wallop had rendered him semiconscious but he tried to join in with a steady *boom, boom, b-boom* as a bass line. Uri looked at them both, a fresh, bright smile beaming from his face.

'What's in Wallop?' asked Dominic, laughing because he found the word extremely funny.

'Opium, mainly,' Uri answered casually. 'I put in some speed, a few vitamins; depends really on what's around.'

Dominic had assumed that because the syringes were in sterilised, plastic containers they had come from a hospital.

'The name of the game in this country is survival,' continued Uri, his tone more serious, his smile fading. 'We've got at least twenty thousand wounded people in Romania. We use more opium than milk.' He patted the side of his seat. 'The red box under here contains everything needed for staying alive – bandages, oxygen, penicillin, Wallop, knives to cut you open, needles to sew you up; all gathered by yours truly with the diligence of a ferret and the cunning of a fox.' His smile returned in self-congratulation. 'We have become a nation of blackmarketeers through necessity. I stole this opium from the Securitate so I will give it away. They'll thank me at the hospital.'

ROMANIAN BROADCAST TELEVISION
BUCHAREST

Fax communication

TO: Malcolm Barrett

FROM: Harry Cassini.   DATE: 29.12.89.
_____

Dominic's back needs urgent care. He must return to England
a.s.a.p. My wound is superficial and causing no real
discomfort.

Please advise on possible transport urgently. I want Dominic
in the London Clinic within forty-eight hours.

Five Pounds says the Arsenal get stuffed on New Year's Day.

Harry

Thirty-five

31 December 1989

'Well hello,' came a Leslie Phillips impression just to the right of Dominic's head. 'Let's bring you down and have a look at you.'

Dominic heard an electric motor switch on as his bed started to descend. He saw aircraft windows with their cream, plastic shutters pulled firmly down.

'Where are we?' Dominic's voice was croaky, his mouth dry.

His operator wore a surgical mask that moved slightly at the edges. 'Aboard the Airbus hospital heading for RAF Manston in Kent. Damn lucky, you lot. We were flying back from the Gulf when we got your call. Another hour and we'd have been passed you.' He gently tested Dominic's straps. 'We kept you in the loft while you slept; out of the way, so to speak. But now you're with us I suspect you'll want to see your friends.' A smile was all Dominic could offer. 'I can slide you back level with the other stretcher case but I'm afraid you won't be able to see her. The big man's in a chair, so you'll see him.'

The man looked away. 'Come on through,' he said, gesturing with his hand. 'It's your physiotherapist. I'll leave you two to chat.'

Dominic felt a slight downward movement as the new-comer grabbed the side of his bed. A familiar and wel-come face appeared over the bed rail, a face that raised
298

Dominic's spirits. 'Coach Damchuk. What a wonderful surprise.'

'Hello Dominic.' The coach bent over his pupil and placed the lightest kisses on both cheeks. 'I've missed you, boy,' he said, his voice emotional.

'And I've missed you, Coach. You've never really left me, I still start with the breathing.'

'I'm glad to hear it.' Coach Damchuk stood up, his kind eyes scanning Dominic's face and body, familiarising, memorising. 'Let's get one thing straight: none of this is permanent. You've had some pressure on the spine caused by severe bruising and subsequent clotting. They relieved it best they could at Bucharest and we're now taking you to the London Clinic to do the job properly. It's going to be a long road back to fitness, Dominic, but by no means impossible. That's why Harry Cassini's hired me to look after you. He wants you dancing in six months. He says he can only flog the same story for so long. Does that make sense?'

It made perfect sense to Dominic.

'Make way!' Harry's voice boomed down the plane. Petri Damchuk flattened himself against the side of the bed as the sound clattered by him and stopped. 'Have to redesign this,' he said gruffly. 'Doesn't bloody raise up.'

Dominic strained to see to the bottom right of his vision. He could make out Harry's head, the last few strands of thinning hair, and the gown-covered arm he'd raised in the air. 'I can see your arm,' he told him.

There was a moment of silence, almost embarrassment. Harry would hate to show emotion in front of a relative stranger. They both spoke at once.

'Do you?' 'How's?'

'You first,' said Dominic right away. It was such a nuisance not being able to see Harry.

There was another pause. Dominic relaxed.

'Do you remember *anything* of the last three days?' said Harry, finally.

Dominic took time to mentally focus before Harry

spoke. Three *days*. It had seemed three hours. He tried to calculate but his mind wouldn't lock on to a positive answer. Today was New Year's Eve, or New Year's Day, he wasn't sure. 'What day is it?' he asked at last.

'We're due in Manston at midnight fifteen, a quarter of an hour into the new decade,' said Coach Damchuk, smiling down at Dominic. 'Happy New Year.'

'And the same to you, Coach, and you Harry.' Dominic felt elated, as if he were outside his damaged body, free as in the spirit of the dance. 'I only remember bits. Nothing specific. How's Nadia? How are you?'

'I'm fine. The one advantage of being fat is the cushion of blubber around my middle. They took the bullet out clean. It didn't hit anything important, I just lost a lot of blood that's all. Nadia will be fine too. She's in the back of the plane. We'll slide you along to see her in a while.' Harry waved his hand in the air. 'Can you see that?'

'Yes.'

He gave Dominic a thumbs-up; holding it there and pressing it forward several times as in the football supporters' chant. 'What do you think of this baby?' he asked, his voice ebullient, his arm disappearing.

'I can't see much of it.'

Harry and the coach laughed aloud. It was wonderful to hear, a tonic for Dominic's soul. 'What, exactly, is it?' he ventured as the laughing subsided.

'The one proper use for the European Airbus,' said Harry proudly. 'Malcolm bought it last year and turned it into a mobile stabilising unit capable of transporting a hundred and fifty badly wounded people. The purpose is to hold people steady, life support if needed, rather than operate on board, but we do have a small theatre for real emergencies. We cast breaks, deal with minor bullet and mortar wounds, re-dress bandages, that sort of thing. We have thirty chairs like mine which are stored aft but can move along a sunken monorail, connecting all parts of the plane. And there are a hundred and twenty stretcher-beds that can be mounted, like yours, on to fuselage rails which extend the length of the interior. This mega-ambulance would be useful in a dozen hot spots right now, to say nothing of the customised versions individually designed to fit the needs of your average billionaire. Luckily for us, Malcolm had sent the plane to the Gulf a week ago to scrape a sale out of Sheik Ya Booty, or whatever 'is name is. I spread a few dollars around Brasov yesterday, got landing permission and exit visas, and here we all are.'

Dominic was grateful not to have been part of yesterday's mad scramble. He could imagine Harry's temper fusing with the greedies from the Department of the Interior. It must have cost dearly to get Nadia and Petri out. 'How did you meet Coach Damchuk?'

The grey, sad-faced man gently held Dominic's hand, careful not to exert any pressure. 'Nadia gave them my number, bless her.'

Dominic felt glad and relieved that his coach had escaped. He'd never known Petri Damchuk to bully or harass anyone. He didn't bother with politics, power or control over other human beings. He valued the individual, the artist, achievement through practice and dedication. Petri Damchuk was a teacher; more than that, a guru: mild mannered, polite, encouraging, inspirational. He had also been a good friend in times of trouble and Dominic was overjoyed that he would now spend his declining years in comfort and safety. 'How is Nadia?' asked Dominic, closing his fingers around Petri's strong, leathery hand.

'Let's slide you back and you can talk to her,' said Harry, once again sticking his hand in the air like a school-boy wanting to leave the room. 'You'll have to work it, Damchuk. The release bar's under the head end.'

Petri reached underneath and released the brake. He walked down the aisle at a sprightly pace holding on to the side of the portable stretcher with his right hand. The bed moved easily on the rails; only the slightest push was needed to get it started. Harry followed behind, his chair's motor whining like a lift as he increased speed.

'Don't crash me,' said Dominic, feeling totally helpless.

'You're the only bed on the rail,' reassured the coach.

'Think of it like a tray in a cafeteria,' said Harry. 'You get on at the back, we stick you on a bed and push you along, gathering what you need along the way.'

Petri slowed the bed down and stopped it smoothly about three-quarters of the way along the plane. 'Can we lower Dominic or raise Nadia so they can see each other?'

'Both,' replied Harry confidently. 'Line the bed up with the two blue lines on the rails, push button H and turn that red handle left to go up, right to come down.'

The coach followed Harry's instructions and the stretcher stopped a metre above floor level. Dominic could see Harry's face now; it looked jolly again; relieved and victorious.

'Push Nadia forward to the next notch so Dominic can see her,' ordered Harry gruffly. It was obvious that he didn't enjoy his confinement. Harry was a man of movement, unrestricted movement. He bashed impatiently at the small joystick control and the chair lurched backwards. 'Damn,' he cursed quietly as the sudden movement jarred his wound.

'If you treat that joystick gently your chair will move smoothly,' said Petri reassuringly.

Harry's face hardened. Dominic expected a curt 'bollocks' or 'stupid bloody machine', but was pleasantly surprised when Harry's smile returned. 'You're probably right,' he admitted, removing his hand from the offending stick.

Coach Damchuk had that effect on people. The conviction in his voice inspired confidence in the basic truth of everything he said. He made you believe wholeheartedly. Dominic was sure he and Harry would become firm friends once the question of which English football team to support had been resolved.

As Nadia's bed slid alongside, Dominic saw a bandaged hand and a familiar forearm flop over the rail, then Nadia's half-bandaged face, her chin resting on the top rail. Petri immediately took a pillow from her bed and tucked it between the rail and her bandages. She smiled at him. Two of her teeth were missing. Dominic could imagine Stenoza standing over her and inflicting savage wounds with measured demonic pleasure. Somehow the compensation of his death didn't make up for the damage he'd done.

'They've done a job on you Humpty Dumpty would be proud of,' he said.

'And I love you too, especially looking like a trapped stick insect.' Her voice was strong and mocking. 'Harry tells me you've hooked up with a fancy woman in London.' She added vitriol and sarcasm to the mix. Nadia had never been one for beating around the bush, but the question was direct even by her standards. 'Will you two leave us for a minute,' she said brusquely.

Harry looked at Dominic, shrugged his shoulders and relinquished all responsibility. He stroked his joystick backwards and glided away to the front of the plane. Coach Damchuk gave a knowing smile and followed the humming wheelchair.

'I'm waiting,' said Nadia.

Dominic looked straight ahead at the cabin ceiling. Sadness now mixed with guilt in his feelings for her. He cursed the times he'd come so close to phoning, to making contact. He had to tell her about Tilly and clear the air. The pain this woman had endured demanded the whole truth. Dominic took a deep, cleansing breath. 'Her name is Tilly Howard. I met her the night I defected and I love her very much. We've been living together for the last six months but she left me the night I came to Romania. I doubt I'll see her again.'

Nadia remained silent. What little expression was visible outside the bandages seemed tranquil. The bruising was so severe around her eye it left only a slit. Only her mouth showed any sign of feeling. It quivered at the edge as she tried to smile.

'I'm sorry I didn't try to contact you,' continued Dominic. 'It was a cowardly thing to do.'

'I'm sorry she's left you.' Nadia's threw the statement out, clipped, packaged, postage paid. 'I crawled miles to save your worthless backside,' she said with as much pride as rebuke.

'And it kept you alive,' replied Dominic, not willing to accept all the blame.

'I suppose so.' Her head flopped back on to the bed. 'I have to lie down, my back hurts.'

'You'll be twice as beautiful by the time those London surgeons have finished with you.'

'I'm sure I will.' Her voice had a hint of defiance. 'And when I'm beautiful again I'm not liable to settle for spoiled goods, my amorous little gymnast.'

Dominic recognised the tone of voice she'd sometimes use in foreplay, just before she took control. 'You were a government spy, Nadia. You didn't really love me.'

'I was a whore!'

Dominic looked over, but could see only bandaged fingers curled on the railing.

'Stenoza found me at an orphanage when I was twelve,' she continued, her voice flat, as if deciding on each word before speaking. 'He taught me English, how to listen, how to seduce, how to corrupt, how to fuck. You were my first job.' She paused. Dominic stayed silent, stunned by her confession. 'Only trouble was, I fell in love with the John.' She left another, longer pause. 'I felt you'd try to escape but I didn't tell him. That's why he did this to me. I hoped you'd send for me, find a way to get me out.' Her voice grew fainter, unsure.

'I am so sorry, Nadia. I didn't know.' It sounded inadequate, but she'd never given the slightest hint that she wanted to get out. Dominic felt sure he would have picked up on it, however subtle. They'd monitored her so tightly she'd relied on a telepathy that didn't exist for her salvation – and he'd misread her completely.

'No reason you should,' she said in a throwaway

manner, then chuckled. 'I'll get a fresh start in England anyway. I just wish you'd been more observant.'

'I was always very fond of you,' said Dominic, cursing the fact that he couldn't see her.

'Then maybe I'll let you be the first to take me to dinner once I'm fixed.'

Dominic closed his eyes and drifted in time to the movement of the plane. He felt fuzzy and confused. He wanted to be with Tilly; laughing, loving, hoping, being half of a couple, in love, in harmony. Nadia seemed a blot on the landscape, an intrusion into his life, a hopeless escapade. 'It would be my pleasure,' he said.

'Smooth bastard,' she said, her voice righteous. 'You've fallen in love, that's the truth of it.'

Dominic relaxed. 'I'll take care of you,' he said.

'I wish I could see you,' she said. 'I mean, see you properly.'

The humming sound of Harry's wheelchair invaded the conversation. 'We've picked up a tail wind. We'll be down in ten minutes,' he bellowed from some distance.

'Can we continue this discussion when we're fit and well?' said Dominic, slightly annoyed at Harry, but grateful for Nadia's honesty.

'Got to strap you up for landing,' interrupted Harry before Nadia could answer. 'Coach Damchuk will sort you both out. I'm off to lock myself into the chair rows.' He pushed his joystick forward and hummed past.

'I'll put you two beside each other,' said the coach, working the hydraulics with one hand and sliding Nadia's bed backwards with the other. 'I'm going to the cockpit. I want to see how it's done.' He smiled at Dominic; a warm, reassuring smile that made him feel safe.

Thirty-six

Dominic sat propped in his comfortable bed at the London Clinic and scanned leisurely through the morning papers. There was a threatened strike at Ford, Terry Marsh was being questioned by police about the Frank Warren shooting, five of Scotland's twenty-four High Court judges were under investigation over allegations of homosexuality, and Mrs Thatcher was going on the rampage over the breakdown of the family as the government's social security bill for single parents topped £3 billion.

He had a good laugh at the cover of *Private Eye* which featured a picture of the Ceausescus with the Queen and Prince Philip. 'Does your husband have any hobbies?' asked a bubble above Philip's head. 'He's a mass murderer,' said Elena's bubble. Ceausescu looked straight ahead, grinning. The Queen looked politely away. Her bubble said, 'How very interesting.'

On page six of *The Times* he found the story that made his day. Under the headline TEACHERS APOLOGISE TO CHILDREN FOR MISLEADING THEM UNDER CEAUSESCU, the article quoted a Romanian teacher as saying, 'we realise we did much to lead to the general degeneration of society. Virtually everything we taught was deformed.' According to the article, scores of portraits of Ceausescu had been removed along with the wall posters that dominated every school proclaiming false production figures and other

306

mythical statistics, far removed from Romanian reality. Miss Florescu Mihala, a physics teacher who spent the Christmas vacation replacing the propaganda on her classroom walls with pictures of flowers and quotations from Romanian poets said, 'Every piece of communist thought control has been removed, as has every reminder of the terrible tyrant who some of our children helped to overthrow.'

He read her quote again. Every hardship endured by Romanians both in and outside the country would be worth it if the next generation had at least an even chance of success. He put the paper down and poured a second cup of instant coffee. It was eighteen days since they'd operated to remove the pressure on Dominic's spine. The first week had been very uncomfortable. He'd had to lie on his stomach, awake and asleep, his only respite being Nurse Holman. Twice daily she would expertly massage his entire body. She would start with reflexology on the feet then work up the legs, pummelling and gently digging, soothing dormant muscles with magical hands.

The second week proved much more satisfactory. Dominic was allowed on to his back and Nurse Holman extended her treatment time to an hour, working and loosening unused pectoral and abdominal muscles. Nadia and Dominic spent many happy hours planning her future and exorcising their past. They would not be lovers again, that was mutually agreed. It would be a sibling affection, a caring, born of the need to protect. Both were orphans of war; now they would form the nucleus of a new family in this rich and welcoming land.

Dominic had heard nothing from Tilly – there had been no word, no letter, no contact whatsoever. Harry visited every day and Dominic would ask if he'd heard anything. Every day the answer was the same. She'd moved out of Chester Square the day Dominic had left for Romania and phoned Malcolm on New Year's Day to resign as his press officer. Nobody had seen or heard from her since. Harry had one report from a journalist who'd said she was in New York working for NBC. Dominic phoned that afternoon; they'd never heard of her. She'd dropped out, vanished completely, just as she'd threatened on that last evening at Chester Square.

Dominic still loved her and missed her desperately. With each passing day the realisation that he might never see her again grew stronger. Last night after Nadia had left his room was worst of all.

Today, however, he felt a little better. He was going home this morning and even though the thought of the Chester Square flat without Tilly made him feel somewhat maudlin, he was determined to persevere. Harry had been discharged after four days, on a promise that he wouldn't drink too much and aggravate his healing intestines; a promise he broke within an hour. Nadia was to stay in hospital for another week until her bandages were removed. Dominic promised to visit her daily.

Malcolm had moved the entire Hampstead operation to a secret location. He knew Dominic wanted no part in his spy business so he kept details of the new headquarters to himself, a policy that suited Dominic perfectly. The club was still doing record business, despite Dominic's absence. Malcolm had hit on the bright idea of showing videos of the first week at the club on three big screens at the back of the stage. He'd told the press and the clubbers Dominic was recuperating in the country and wouldn't be back until fully recovered. Everyone accepted the explanations except a diggy little reporter from the *News of the World* who spent each evening badgering everyone at the club to 'give Dominic up'. As nobody other than Malcolm knew the truth the digger got absolutely nowhere and when his free drinks tab was relinquished he stopped coming to the club altogether.

Coach Damchuk had settled into English life with remarkable ease. Harry had found him a little flat off the King's Road, and he'd moved into it last week. Every day he'd tell Dominic stories of the wonderful features he'd discovered – central heating, constant hot water, thick carpets, pulsating shower, entryphone. His landlord was Irish and told him jokes he would repeat each day at the beginning of his visit. He'd also worked out a plan that would return Dominic to peak fitness within two months. It was to start tomorrow morning with a slow, half-mile run and a session on the light weights; the next day, swim and weights.

Dominic looked forward to training for three reasons. He needed to get back into shape, to feel his body hum once more; he looked forward to working with Coach Damchuk again – and training would occupy his mind completely, blanking Tilly's memory from the forefront of his thoughts.

Dominic packed what few clothes he had into his small, black carryall. He peeled and ate one last banana from the mound of fresh fruit Coach Damchuk had brought in and looked around his bright, airy room for the last time. Nurse Holman came into the room clutching a copy of the day's *Mirror*. 'You're a star, Dominic,' she said, placing the tabloid on the bed, open at page five. Below a quarter-page picture taken on opening night the copy read:

> The King of Clubs is set to return to the Dance Emporium within a month. The Mirror can exclusively reveal that Dominic Dance, who suffered a mild heart attack while dancing to a packed house on December 27th, will be back at his club before the end of February. His new coach, Petri Damchuk, recently imported from Romania by Dominic's partner Malcolm Barrett to oversee his training schedule, said last night that Dominic had made a full recovery and that a light exercise programme would commence tomorrow. Nothing has been seen of the dancer since he was rushed to hospital over three weeks ago. Thousands of fans, mainly women, flock daily to the Dance Emporium in the Strand in search of any news about the 24-year-old heartthrob. Miss Jenny McLeod who's travelled every day from her home in Ilford to visit the spot where Dominic collapsed, said last night, 'This is the best news of my life. We're all praying for his recovery.'

'Miss Jenny McLeod must be top of your list for signed photos,' said Nurse Holman, picking up the paper and sending a knowing glance in Dominic's direction. 'It must be nice to have your pick of the entire female population.'

The irony of her statement lowered his spirits, but he was determined not to let his feelings show. 'It has its advantages.'

She kissed Dominic and placed a card in his top pocket. 'My number, in case you want some private treatment. I'm free most weekends.' She turned away and quickly left the room, passing Nadia in the doorway.

'These English girls can't get enough of you, can they?' The jealousy had gone from Nadia's voice. She was teasing, mocking his inability to cope with propositions.

'Come in. Sit down,' said Dominic, not wanting to linger on the subject. 'Will you be all right on your own?'

'Perfectly.' She sat on the bed. 'I hope some of your fans are male and heterosexual. It's not fair if you have all the fun.'

Dominic held her tightly. 'I'm sure we can find you someone suitable. How about Harry if he loses some weight?'

'How about I give you a knee in the nuts?' She hugged his waist. 'Now get out of here.'

Dominic kissed her cheek, picked up his case and walked to the door. 'I'll drop in and see you tomorrow,' he said.

She smiled from the bed. 'I'll look forward to it. Now go.'

A black cab was discharging its fare outside the clinic which saved Dominic from the soaking one can only obtain from English rain. He listened to the swish-clack of the wipers and watched the drenched pedestrians run for cover as the rain intensified and the cab turned left on to Marylebone Road. 'Baker Street's flooded,' said the cabie in a broad cockney accent. 'I'll 'ave to go down Edgware Road to get to Park Lane.' Dominic nodded approval, sat back in the seat and watched the rain sheet down, power-cleaning the streets of London with its ferocity.

They arrived at Chester Square in good time. Dominic paid the fare before leaving the cab and scooted down the stone steps to the basement bolt-hole. The flat smelled musty, damp, unlived in. Dominic switched on the central heating and the kettle. He longed for a good cup of coffee, a quiet bath and a glimpse of his favourite garden. Walking around the flat as he waited for the kettle to boil he saw that it was much as he'd left it. But Tilly's clothes were gone, as was the stack of public relations magazines and the glass cockerel he'd given her to commemorate their first meal at Le Gavroche.

From the patio doors he watched the rain bounce off the shiny paving-stones. He felt good, but not excellent. His leg had healed completely but the odd burst of pain from his back still cut through his body and drained his energy. He wandered through to the bathroom and started to run a reviving tub, adding an extra squirt of Badedas in celebration of his return. The phone rang. He walked into the bedroom and flopped on the bed.

'Dominic Dance,' he said in a businesslike manner.

Silence.

'Go bother someone else,' he shouted angrily, suspecting that a tabloid journalist had somehow obtained the ex-directory number. 'I'm putting the answer machine on.' He was about to slam the phone down when he heard his name faintly in the background. He pressed the phone tightly to his ear.

'Hello.'

'Just promise me you'll never again knowingly take a human life,' said Tilly, her voice soft, almost inaudible.

'I promise,' said Dominic without a moment's hesitation, 'I love you, Tilly.'

The length of the silence seemed eternal. 'I love you too,' she whispered.

The faintest of smiles traced across Dominic's face. Inside, his heart was singing. 'I'm running a bath, if you're interested?'